The Will of the World

M. J. Lindemann

For my husband
Who dragged me kicking and screaming into the world of travel
Who buys me the things I don't buy for myself, and then sends
me the bill
Who has supported me unceasingly through this journey

I love you

Contents

A Moment of Your Time

A short story was written as a companion to this novel. You can claim it by signing up for my newsletter at mjlindemann .com. It stars one of the main characters, Flicker, on her first solo assassination mission. The short is 100% unnecessary to understand the plot of this book, but I've been told it makes some great moments in the novel even better.

Thank you for your time, intrepid reader, and may the will of the world guide your path!

-M. J. Lindemann

Prologue

Death came for Gull Harbor with a thin smile and a practiced bow. Two days ago, the envoy from The Guild of Commerce had arrived to issue a final notice for late payments. After opening their own harbor a half day's ride down the beach, the Guild had stolen nearly seventy percent of Gull Harbor's shipping contracts. No contracts meant no money to pay guild fees, and without the Guild's support, the pylon, the only thing protecting Mayor Sharon Adegast's people from hordes of undead husk, was to be removed in a week.

The town hall meeting room sat cluttered, but clean. Dust motes shone like little stars with sun rays beaming down through various windows, highlighting items in the room like spotlights on a stage. An unlit oil lamp in the corner, a dusty framed copy of the town's original Guild contract hanging on the wall, a cut in the table from Sharon's grandfather when he'd plunged a knife into it out of frustration, and a quill floating across some parchment while Sharon scowled next to it, thinking up desperate plans for a desperate situation.

Presently, Gull Harbor's entire population of wielders shuffled into the room, twenty-three of them all in all. Twenty-three wielders and not a mystic among them. Sharon's son, Ren, had proven himself a good candidate for mystic training, but at eight years of age, his will could barely pick up a rock without shunting it at high speeds in a random direction, let alone charging a pylon or fighting a husk.

Sharon dropped focus on her quill to regard the room, her brown eyes touched on each villager before she spoke, "I have some unfortunate news to give."

"We're right fucked," Shorda Sellens' gravelly voice broke through the murmurs of the crowd.

Sharon winced, but Shorda wasn't wrong. "Yes, we are, but I've spent the better part of the last two days taking stock of our—"

"We'll save you some time there, Sharon. We're leaving with the envoy when he goes. You're the only one's even fought an amalgamation in here. You're great an' all, but you're not exactly Lana Danvers. We're not cut out—" Sharon's hand shot out palm forward, signaling for silence. *Of all the people to act the coward, it hurts the most coming from you.* Sharon let the silence hang for a moment while her childhood friend gave her a blank stare.

"Please. Let me finish."

Shorda opened her mouth to speak again but, noticing the intensity of Sharon's glare, seemed to think better of it.

"I understand you're all scared, and rightfully so. We'll be far more exposed than we were, but we have the focus crystals and the wielders to erect our own barriers while I attempt to call in a favor."

Technically a favor for my grandfather, but it's all I've got.

Shorda frowned. "What is this favor?"

"There's a mystic-level wild wielder and an unregistered engineer that Grandpa Ren told me to call on if we ever had problems with the Guild." *The exact word was 'when' we had problems with the Guild, not 'if', but they don't need to know how preordained this all was.*

Shorda stood in protest. "Fuck that. How long we have to hold out before they get here? Does this engineer have the materials to make a pylon? Is this mystic gonna help us keep recharging the damn thing? Who's gonna do maintenance? And if you think the Guild'll let this stand, you're delusional."

The sudden noise from the shattered oil lamp drew everyone's attention. Sharon's quill stuck in the wall behind where the lamp once stood. Rising from her chair, she pried the quill from the wall with her will and set it lightly beside her on the table. "Shorda. I've known you my whole life. I like to think I've earned some trust, and if not trust, at least enough respect to let me finish explaining myself without you opening your godsdamn mouth every time I pause for breath." *And if you don't shut up, I'll send this quill straight through your hands.* Shorda retreated to her chair, looking meeker than her stocky, muscular frame had any right to be.

"Yes. Both the engineer and the *wild wielder*, not mystic, will stay with us long enough to recruit or train their replacements. You all know Grandpa Ren was a mercenary before he settled down here. The engineer is a fellow merc, and the wild wielder is their daughter. As soon as I discovered the Guild building their shipyard, I sent them a letter. After their current job, they promised to head this way."

Sharon walked with purpose to the contract hanging on the wall.

"Regarding The Guild: my grandfather put a clause in the contract allowing Gull Harbor to maintain its own pylon in the event they decided to pull out," she said and tapped the written clause with her finger a couple of times for emphasis. "So legally they're required to leave us the hells alone once we get up and running again. They can't claim rights on any pylon we construct. Finding the crystals to construct it will take some doing, but after that's taken care of it'll only be a matter of maintaining the highway. That's no small problem, but that's a problem for then, not now."

"I'm sure you've thought this through." Tom Kerrick's voice always took Sharon by surprise. Despite his move to the seaside town over two years ago, she couldn't get used to the high-pitched, unsteady way in which he spoke. Like a singer holding their note at the end of their breath. "And I'm sure the numbers work well on paper, but no matter how well we plan the risk is high. We've had six husk kill themselves on the barrier in just the last week. Now, if that's all that happens between now and when your friends arrive that's well and good, but if a horde comes..." Tom looked around the room. "... well, if that happens, we don't exactly have the power to stop it. There would most likely be... sacrifices."

Sacrifices? What sacrifices have you ever made?

"Tom," Sharon began, an edge slipping into her tone despite herself, "my grandfather and husband died for this town. I know you didn't meet them, but the rest of you are only standing here because of my family's spilled—"

"Stop, Sharon." Shorda stood from her seat again. "Enough. We get it. Cullen and Grandpa Ren gave everything for us, but they weren't the only ones. You're all we have left... and that's not enough. Running ourselves ragged to charge a bunch of focus crystals that can barely put up a barrier strong enough to keep out a single husk is a risk we're not willing to take. I love this town—" *Oh gods, is she crying?* "—but it's not worth my family's life. We're leaving with the envoy and the maintenance team at the end of the week for Prolivgrad. Come with us or don't." With tears in her eyes, Shorda left the room, followed by Tom and the remainder of the wielders.

Pathetic

Alone again, brooding on the loss of the life she loved, the life she'd fought and bled for, Sharon sank into her chair. The people of Prolivgrad hated refugees, and so it was a bit of a surprise the envoy offered housing for a village of their size. How could that possibly work? Usually, relocation after Guild withdrawal was split between several villages agreeing to take people in, but maybe they needed more labor in the capital for some reason. That seemed unlikely. From everything she knew, workers in the capital scrambled and fought to find honest work. Was there some project the people in her small town were earmarked to help with? They were a town of fishers, merchants, craftsmen, and a handful of farmers. What project could accommodate them all?

Even if the Guild didn't have a job in mind, she could find her own, but her talents lie in leadership and combat, not menial labor. She could always try guard work—pain lanced through the tip of her right pointer finger. She brought it to her face and saw the culprit, a splinter, wedged in from absentmindedly rubbing the wound in the table. Brown wood stuck just underneath the dark black of her skin. She plucked it out—probably not guard work, she'd witnessed firsthand how simultaneously dull and dangerous those jobs could be. Unrelenting boredom punctuated by violence. Better to see what the Guild offers and go from there.

And what would life in Prolivgrad look like with little Ren? The silver lining of the move meant he could go to a real mystic academy. Training the boy on her own had proved... difficult. His will reserves already grew beyond her own, and outside of a few precision kinetics exercises, she only had her family's specialized combat forms to help him with his focus. Even then, anything after the first form could spell disaster until he had more will control, the Adegast family's signature technique exacted a toll he was too young to pay just yet. He'd already almost killed himself once with kinetics, shunting a rock at his own head. If she hadn't been there to alter the trajectory the hole would have been through his skull instead of a window.

Stupid boy.

It hurt to remember. A memory of her son growing up in the same home she did. Less than an hour had passed since Shorda and the other wielders left, but a sense of mourning and longing for her hometown already settled in while the sun began to set. Light from the windows angled upward instead of down now, and the dust motes so clearly visible in the bright afternoon seemed faded and smaller. She shook her head and stood, snatched her carefully crafted notes from the table, crumpled them, and tossed them in a corner before she left her little town hall for the last time. No need to worry about cleanliness when the whole place would turn to ruin soon enough.

On her way home there was a flurry of activity. Her towns-folk already preparing for the move. *Word travels fast it seems.* She saw people weighing the pros and cons of bringing this and that item to the capital with them. Some seemed excited about the move, others seemed sad. Walking by Tom's home she noticed he had little to pack. Everything he owned looked to fit in one moderately sized trunk. *The fool never even settled in.* He already had a wagon out front, prepped for the move they wouldn't make for several days. She thought to offer the slight man some help with getting the trunk in his wagon, but her mood was foul, she wouldn't be able to help herself from picking a fight, and then there was the simple matter of the fact that she just didn't want to.

Sharon turned the last corner to her home and rolled her eyes at Ren and Connie, Kord's daughter, rolling around in the mud, both arguing and giggling at the same time, a couple stuffed animals lay abandoned ten or so paces away from them. She could spot bits of mud stuck in Ren's black hair even from this distance, and Connie's sandy hair had a few dirt clods hanging as well. When they noticed her heading their direction they popped up, frantically brushing the dirt and mud from their clothing.

"Sorry Mayor Adegast, but he started it!"

Ren's mouth dropped open, appalled. "Did not! We were playing birthday party with our animals, and you were the one that said you didn't like Flopsy's gift!"

"Jeremy is the one that didn't like Flopsy's gift, and maybe he'd'a liked it if Flopsy ever gave him something besides buttons!"

Sharon approached the two children and looked them over. *They are truly filthy.* She glanced over at the two abandoned stuffed animals and turned back to Connie. "Sounds like Jeremy should appreciate that he got any gift at all."

"Yeah, stuffed animals love buttons," Ren said, a little too emboldened with an adult on his side.

"And where, exactly, did these buttons come from?" She arched an eyebrow.

Ever since Cullen passed away Ren took up stealing. Nothing major. A needle here, some clothing there. Once, he took some of Kord's clothes and wore them around. She shouldn't have found it as funny as she did, but his overconfidence made it impossible not to. A boy drowning in fabric acting like it made him a grown-up. He missed his dad. Perhaps she let her grief color their relationship too much, but she couldn't help it. Cullen and Grandpa Ren died, taking all their support with them, and leaving her to run the town. A mother, a widow, a mayor, a protector, a negotiator... something had to give.

Ren stared at the ground in shame, the spitting image of his father when he got in trouble. "I... found them. Around the beach. People's buttons fall off and I..."

Don't look guilty and then lie about it you dum-dum.

Connie wasn't having it. "Liar! You told me you got them from your mom's drawer!"

Ren glared at her for the betrayal, but then looked back at Sharon. "Ok, fine. I took them, but I was gonna put them back. I just wanted to use them for the game."

"How many times do we have to go through this?"

He reached up to touch her cheek. "What's wrong?"

Sharon touched just below her eyes, and sure enough, her fingers came back wet. *Damnit.* "It was just a hard day." Ren's expression told her he knew there was more to the story, but she didn't have the energy for that right now. He'd ask too many questions she didn't know the answers to.

Connie tilted her head like a curious puppy. "What was so hard about it?"

"Nothing you need to worry about right now." She put on a smile she hoped they'd believe and pulled them into a hug.

"Mom! I'm too big!"

"Oh, shut up and let me have this!"

And with that, she tipped all three of them over and started to roll around, tickling them and giggling in the mud and the dirt.

When they were finished playing, Sharon laid her arms out in the grass. The two children lay on either side, using her arms as pillows. Connie drifted off to sleep and began her infamous snoring. Ren and Sharon exchanged a knowing smile. They looked up into the sky as the first stars started to come out, blinking and twinkling against the ocean of blue and black. The moon and stars took their places in the night sky in the same exact spots they always did.

"I wish I were older," he said.

"Oh? What makes you say that?"

"Because then I could help with whatever is making us leave."

"And who told you we had to leave?"

"I'm not blind. The envoy came. Everyone is packing. You're sad."

He always seemed to catch on to these things faster than he should for a kid his age. Always attentive to everyone else's mood. "Let me worry about that. We'll get through this."

"Is Connie going where we're going?"

The girl's mother died years back, and ever since she'd glommed on to Sharon and Ren. She'd tried to play matchmaker with her widower father and Sharon, but it would never be a good fit. Besides, Sharon didn't have time for a relationship, especially not recently. Especially not now.

"That depends on her dad, but I imagine so."

A grumbling sound came from Ren's belly. Sharon took the cue and began to rouse Connie. "Wake up Con, I'll get some food going for us."

***

The week passed by with little fanfare. Kids still played together in the roads and on the beach while adults and older children continued their packing and preparing for the long journey by drying salted fish and making other durable food, returning borrowed items to neighbors, and most difficult of all, choosing what to leave behind.

Sharon stretched as she walked into what used to be her dining room. The table sat bare. She frowned at how easily the room went from feeling like a home to feeling like any other room in any other house. Buckling a scabbard around her waist, she went through her mental checklist again. Rations? Packed. Clothing? Packed. The horse she'd paid too much for? Fed, hooked up, and ready. Weapon? Sharon drew her will-blade from its sheath. Her mother's blade, forged by an engineer from the capital, had silver circular cross guards with a leather-wrapped grip, comfortably worn from years of use. She put some will into it and felt the edges of the blade extend out with pure, sharpened will. It could slice through a metal beam with little effort.

She relaxed into a starting form and began dancing through the next one, and the one after. She focused hard on her surroundings while her body's muscle memory took over her movements. While in her dance, she only needed to notice a threat and her body would do the rest. She focused in on the table. It made chaotic crashing noises, falling into two pieces, then four, then eight. Settling into her final form, Sharon let out a breath she felt she'd held since the envoy delivered the news a week ago. Sheathing her will-blade, she wiped a bead of sweat from her forehead and smiled.

"Our table!" Ren's eyes were wide as he came running into the room. "You chopped up Grandpa's table? Why?"

"I didn't like the idea of husk using it while we were gone. I granted it a noble death in combat." Sharon put on a rueful grin. The truth was that destroying the family heirloom gave her a sense of finality; it told her there really was no coming back. Gull Harbor was gone. Ren willed a square piece into the air from the middle of the room.

"You can take a piece to remember it by if you—"

It suddenly flew, crashing through one of their windows.

"I don't want any husk using our windows either." They both laughed at that. Once the laughter died down, they grabbed their travel packs, said goodbye to their home, and walked out to their wagon; the horse nickered affectionately as they approached.

Ren jumped up on the seat. "Can I break more things?"

Sharon climbed up to join him. "Given how your training has been going, I suspect you'll break a lot of things whether I like it or not." Then Sharon clicked her tongue, flicked the reins, and headed toward the entrance of town where the envoy would await them. During the short trip, she took in her village one last time. The waves lapping at the beach. Town hall in its constant state of disrepair. *Well, at least I don't have to worry about that anymore.* Ron and Luz's bright yellow corner house. The lighthouse out on the pier. She'd probably never see any of it again, but her people, funneling out and away from the only homes most had ever known, at least they'd be ok.

They pulled up to the town entrance to find a commotion with the envoy standing in the center, smiling that thin smile of his. The shouts made it difficult to discern, but from what she could gather, the Guild's mystic and engineer were delayed. The pylon had little charge left, but would still serve for a while provided nothing too large tried to get in; hardly anything to be worried about. The envoy patted the air and reassured everyone the team would arrive soon. Sharon hopped off her wagon and approached the scrum.

"Good morning, Chuckles."

A crack formed in his smile. "I've asked you, so very many times, not to call me that. Sir will do, or Envoy, or Honorable Representative."

"Yeah, I'm not doing that. Didn't before, and now that you've fucked us, I'm not going to start. Besides, we've known each other long enough. Why not tell me your real name?"

A frown, a rare bit of emotion, flashed across his face. "I'm not allowed to share my name with clients. You know this. Everyone knows this. Why do you insist on antagonizing me?"

"I've earned the right. I saved your ass from a husk."

"And I thanked you for that, profusely—"

"—and my *thanks* was that you axed my village. And we're not your clients anymore now are we, so what's your dumb name so I can curse it before I go to sleep tonight?"

"*I* didn't axe your village. I'm a messenger. Nothing more."

Some members of the crowd pointed down the road leading inland. Someone, a man it looked like, ran toward the village. Fast.

"Oh, that will be the Guild team's messenger letting us know when to expect them. Please. Let me through." Chuckles walked at a deliberate pace toward the running man, and once there, they had a private conversation with the entire village nervously watching. They were far more animated than any Guild employees Sharon had ever seen.

Something is wrong.

After their argument, both men jogged to the town entrance where a flurry of questions greeted them. Chuckles raised his hands out in front of him, quieting the crowd. "I-I must apologize. I don't know how to say this. The maintenance team collected the trade route pylons along the road and was... recalled."

"Recalled?" shouted Shorda. "Ya can't fucking recall them. There isn't enough time to get another mystic to charge the pylon. Who even recalled them?"

Having caught his breath, the runner spoke up, "I did, but the Guild told me to deliver the message to the team and then come to let you all know they had a plan."

"Listen here you shit-for-brains. We need more than a plan. We need action, and we need it now." Shorda advanced on him as she spoke, and the runner backed away at almost the same speed.

Sharon put on her mayor voice, commanding respect. "You, Chuckles, your wielding is almost at the level of a mystic. Put what you can into the pylon. We'll have to drag it along as best we can to Vicksbough. Shorda's right. We can't stay here overlong with a weakened barrier."

Turning back to address Shorda her eyes went wide with horror. It wasn't the size of the amalgamation that surprised her. It wasn't the speed. It wasn't even the way in which it effortlessly bisected both Shorda and the runner, their gore painting the ground beneath them. It was how quiet it was. Sharon's eyes took in the eight-foot, heaving, bipedal monstrosity with its fetid flesh and wicked claws, but other than bodies and organs hitting the ground, all she could hear were gasps from her fellow townsfolk. *Is this real? Is this happening? It's breathing, it's moving, why can't I hear it?* The amalgamation's skin sizzled from withstanding the barrier, but even that didn't make a sound. Sharon blinked and five more people just in front of her were gone. Reduced to red paste. *Fuck it's fast.* Sharon drew her will-blade as everyone else ran for their lives. Taking a breath, she focused all her attention on the amalgamation and fell into her first form. It may have speed, but she wouldn't give up without a fight. Not when she could still save her people. Not when she could still save her son.

The amalgamation shifted its weight to leap toward Chuckles who had already started running to the pylon. Sharon bolted to intercept, cutting off its claw just before it would have segmented him. The rotting hand fell to the ground with a thud, and it screamed in agony. At least it appeared to scream, but all she could hear was her breath and Chuckle's footfalls as he ran.

Now that she had its attention, she'd have to be cautious. The monstrosity swung its remaining claw, she dodged back, but it was a feint. *Too clever for a normal amalgamation.* She barely had enough time to put her body in a blocking position before its massive, decayed foot connected, launching her into the air. Her focus sharpened as she tried to predict where the next blow would come from. *There.* She twisted her body in mid-air and thrust her sword out, piercing its palm. The beast recoiled from the stabbing wound, and Sharon hit the ground, hard. Screams from her friends and neighbors echoed around her. She forced herself to stand up. Now, the creature rushed around devouring or killing everyone in proximity, it had decided on easier prey.

Sharon took in her surroundings. Chuckles made it to the pylon, thrust his hand out toward the massive focus crystal hovering above its base, and began charging it. *Where's Ren?* Sharon ran toward the cart, but he was gone. "Ren!" her voice failed her. Still recovering from the kick that threw her in the air. Frantically looking around, she spotted him. *Koth's bloody asshole. You brave, stupid boy.* Ren stood over Connie's body, facing off against the amalgamation with a rock floating in front of him. Ren let his rock fly, piercing straight through its chest. It staggered backward, Sharon took the opening and leapt suicidally for its neck. Everything went white.

"...om!"

What happened?

"Mom!"

Ren? Is that you? Oh, Kohru's light, get out of here.

"Yes, it's me! Get up! Mr. Chuckles says the beast broke the pylon."

Coming to, Sharon sat up amidst a nightmarish scene. The ground was strewn with gore, and the sounds of violence from a silent killer rang through the town. A piece of her she'd held together since Cullen died suddenly broke apart. The dam holding back a flood of rage, and grief, and hate, and anger burst, and the fury she'd barely held at bay with her love and her obligations let loose.

I need to get Ren out of here. Now.

"Chuckles!"

The envoy was already running to her side. "I tried. I tried to give the pylon enough to repel that thing, but it—"

"Shut the hells up and listen." A quill and a piece of paper flew out of Sharon's pocket and started scribbling down an address. "Take Ren. Go to Vicksbough. Send a letter to this address for Tender Bolin. They're an Engineer. They'll take care of Ren. I'll cover you."

"What? No!" Ren stood in objection. "I'm not leaving!"

"Honey, I'm sorry but you don't have that choice. I can't be worried about protecting you right now, and this thing will kill all of us if I don't stop it. There's something about this one that's different from anything I've ever seen." Sharon pulled Ren into a tight hug. She pulled back and cradled his face, it looked so much like Cullen's except for his sharp jawline and skin tone, only a few shades lighter than her own. *I can't say goodbye to that face again.* "Chuckles, take him."

Tears streamed down the envoy's face. *That's new.* Grabbing Ren, he said, "Tolkar"

Really?

"Your name is the least of my worries right now. Just please, do what I said, and tell whoever gave the order to withdraw the Guild team that if I make it out of this, they're as good as dead."

"I'm not going to do that, but I will see your son to safety." Tolkar, pulling Ren along with him, sprinted toward the entrance of town. Sharon watched her son dragged away by one of her least favorite people in the world. She turned around with will-blade in hand and focused, listening for the sounds of violence. A scream. She ran toward it. *Sorry, Shorda. Sorry, Connie. It's been years. Kohru help me, I hope I don't tear myself apart.* As she sprinted toward the amalgamation, she centered her focus on her forms, willing her body to move faster. The world blurred as if everything she saw was obscured behind frosted glass. Save for one thing. With crystal clarity, Sharon made out the amalgamation standing in the middle of the road holding Tom up by the neck. *Sorry, Tom.* Popping his head off with the casual violence of a child stepping on an ant, the amalgamation turned to regard Sharon.

If I'm dying, you're going down with me.

Ten years later...

Ren

Ren sighed watching Professor Dunreedy go over a simple controlled will maneuver. A highly glossed cube of metal floated in front of the professor, slowly spinning in place, causing the light from the sun to reflect off it, coruscating around the room. An effect that gave Ren a headache.

These were the last months of the last year of Ren's time at the academy, and Dunreedy's insistence on beginning each lesson with basic warmup techniques stood as a testament both to Danvers Academy's dedication to structure and Ren's visceral need to get the hells out of there. The overwhelming heat and humidity in the classroom only worsened his already foul mood.

Danvers Academy had been like a second home to Ren when he first arrived at the capital. Countless classrooms, libraries filled with tomes upon tomes of will techniques, and well-stocked practice rooms gave the impression that anything was possible if you only worked hard enough. A comforting lie that took only a few years to dispel once the weaker children started to get expelled. Danvers wasn't for everyone, and without large will reserves, proper control, or rich parents, your days were numbered. Furthermore, the older Ren grew the clearer the academy's real purpose became: recruitment for the Guild of Commerce. The Guild held a monopoly on focus crystal trade throughout the world and held onto it viciously. Ren had no intention of working for them, but he would gladly use their facilities, learn their techniques, and take his mystic license at the graduation ceremony before trotting off to the Lodge to become a merc.

Dunreedy nodded, and all the students dutifully raised their cubes to begin spinning them, practice tools designed for easy manipulation with will. Skipping ahead in the warmup, Ren spun his cube while orbiting it around a fixed point in front of him. With increasing speed, he finished his orbitals and jumped into elemental infusion. The ball of fire he turned his cube into is what finally got a reaction from the professor.

"We're not there yet, Mr. Bolin, and if I recall correctly, you were told not to let your flames extend out that far."

"I'll fix it."

The flames dissipated in the blink of an eye, and ice crystalized on the tool. Extending from the corners, down the edges, and finally into the middle of the flat surfaces where the ice started to bulge out to form a spherical ball. Rolling his eyes, the professor began leading the rest of the class in the next steps of warmup.

Ren dropped focus on his ball of ice, caught it in his hands, and cooled his forehead and neck with it while the rest of the class worked through their exercises. He didn't need warmup anyway. Warmups trained control, and he could run circles around everyone else in the room in that department, even Dunreedy. Some needed the practice though, Seffin in particular. His will reserves exploded a few years back, and from what Ren could tell, he still didn't have a handle on them. He tended to avoid practicing with him for that exact reason. The last time he did he spent the entire session helping Seffin contain his fire elementalism rather than working through his own techniques.

Dunreedy tapped his podium with a knuckle. "Right, so today is a practical showcase on the basics of elementalism. Your goal is to create balled fire and ice without the assistance of our practice cubes. Seffin, please, to the front of the class. And Ren, if you would be so kind as to come up here as well."

Ren, could you babysit Seffin? The thought crossed his mind as he stood up from his desk and made his way to the front of the class. He could only be so annoyed, though. Just a handful of students could exert enough will to keep Seffin in check if he lost control. Not to mention he'd been goofing off, so choosing him over the other students should have been... expected.

Seffin met Ren's eyes with the constant intensity he was known for. "Fire or ice first?"

"Fire. Let's get the harder one out of the way."

Nodding, Seffin raised both his hands up as if gripping an invisible ball, furrowed his brow, and began to focus. A red bead of fire formed between them. Ren took a step back and leaned up against Dunreedy's podium. He wasn't afraid of Seffin losing control. They'd both improved since their last practice session with each other, and it would surprise him if he needed any more than a gentle nudge to keep the flames from shooting out somewhere.

With a swift motion, Seffin threw his hands outward. The bead of fire exploded out to a one-meter diameter flaming sphere. A drop of sweat dripped down Seffin's face as he strained against the will fire's natural tendency to expand. Ren poked at the sphere with his will to check its stability. Seffin took a couple steps back and brought his hands out toward the fireball again, catching both Dunreedy and Ren's attention. They flashed each other a look that said, '*What the hells is he doing?*' just as he made another outward motion and the ball doubled in diameter. Ren threw his hand out instinctively, wrapping his will around the ball to stabilize it, but it proved unnecessary. The sphere hovered between them, stable but putting off enough heat to make the room unbearable.

"Enough, drop it," barked Dunreedy.

The flames winked out of existence.

"That was good, but next time you want to try something like that, you might warn your partner... or me for that matter. Ice now."

Thrusting one palm out, Seffin made a marble of ice that he grew, violently, into a two-foot spiked ball. *Well, at least the humidity in the room is good for something.* Without warning,

Ren raised his hand out, palm up, and enveloped the ball of ice in his own will. Seffin noticed the gesture and dropped his focus on it. In seconds, Ren melted the ball of ice back into water, separated it into two orbs, refroze them, assembled two equally sized balls of fire, and began orbiting all four of the spheres around a fixed point.

"You're much better than last time," Seffin said.

Ren's face went hot, but he knew after four years in the same class that Seffin didn't intend it as a compliment. He didn't make compliments. He only stated facts as he saw them, which was honestly more flattering in its own way. Regardless, his straight-talking demeanor didn't make him any friends. Factual or not, Seffin's remarks were often unasked for and frequently impolite.

On top of that, Seffin's family, the Rashees, came from old money. He wore his family's colors every day—red, same as the National Party—a reminder of their former nobility. But wearing family colors was a practice that made little sense in today's day and age. Nobility in Prolivgrad had long since become outmoded, wealth was the primary indicator of status now. It was good fortune, then, that the Rashees had strong ties to the wealthiest organization in the world, The Guild of Commerce. Seffin's father led the research and development division. Between his background and his behavior, everything about Seffin was off-putting at best, and intimidating at worst.

Dunreedy clapped his hands twice. "Ok, Ok. You can stop showing off now. Take your seats."

The professor called on the next two students. Class dragged on as Ren watched everyone afterward struggle to create a simple, stable sphere. Earlier in his education, he learned the rate of mystics who could control elements well enough for practical use was one in ten, and in their class that stat bore out almost exactly. No one else had the deep will reserves or control Ren and Seffin did, Kaylee Sorenson came closest, but her spheres only grew to a one-foot diameter, maximum.

Even within the category of elementalists, both Seffin and Ren stood out as anomalies. Ren's control and power were rare, but if Seffin were let off the leash he could probably level the whole building before running out of reserves. His flat affect, floppy brown hair, and unassuming physique belied a rather terrifying level of power. The faculty at Danvers didn't know what to do with him other than drill control exercises and hope he didn't blow up another practice room.

Dunreedy clapped his hands once to signal the end of class.

"Seffin and Ren, would you stay for a minute? The rest of you may go."

Gods, this again.

As the rest of the students shuffled out of class Ren lagged behind with Seffin.

"I can't help but notice that neither of you has registered to a division in the Guild."

Ren's mouth dropped open. *Wait, what? Seffin hasn't registered either?*

Dunreedy pressed, "Can I help with making the decision?"

Seffin looked down at the floor. Possibly weighing his words carefully, though Ren had never seen him do that before. It seemed wrong somehow, like a hoarwolf eating a salad. Usually, words tumbled from his mouth the moment someone else stopped speaking. Like he'd been waiting to answer your question if only you'd just stop asking it. Not rude per se, but not normal either. "I don't think I'm required to tell you my decision," he said, matter-of-factly.

"I still took the liberty of letting your father know I'm here to help—"

"Why? Does he have to approve my application?"

"No. I just thought I'd let him know that I'm here to help if needed."

"Ok, but why does my father need to know you're here to help if it's my decision?"

There he is. That's the Seffin I know.

Dunreedy appeared nonplussed. "Because you haven't made a decision yet, so... I thought I'd—"

"That doesn't seem helpful." Seffin's gaze drifted toward the door. "Is there anything else?"

Ren watched in amusement as Dunreedy squirmed. His attempt at manipulation had backfired. Seffin didn't normally assert himself; he may be direct, but he usually respected authority. Dunreedy must have thought bringing Seffin's father into the conversation would snap him back in line. He miscalculated.

"No, that's all. You can go."

Seffin left the classroom, but Ren couldn't wipe the smile from his face. "You going to try talking to my guardian too, or is that a strategy reserved for legacy students?"

"Shut it. You're as much a legacy student as he is, but we both know Tender has no interest in helping the Guild out with recruitment."

Tender was Ren's guardian, though Ren never called them that. Their children called them Poppy.

"Listen. Tell whomever it is that's pressuring you to sign me up to the Guild that you did your best. I'll even pretend I considered it for a bit if that gets them off your back, but I'm just here to get my mystic license."

"That's not really what I asked you to stay after for."

"Oh?"

***

The city of Prolivgrad was tiered and built on Mount Brinidor with the capitol building at its peak, the seat of power for the country of Egal. The mountain itself inclined gradually which made it easy to build upon, but the truly impressive part was how every building sparkled when the light hit it. Brinidor's focus crystal deposits were the only ones like it in the world, and they shaped every facet of life in Prolivgrad. Even down to the structures, most of which were infused with the crystalline byproduct of the mining process causing the city to glitter. A design chosen not just for its beauty, but also for function. The entire city acted as one giant pylon charged passively by the many mystics that resided there. Ren let his excess will flow out and into the surrounding structures as he strolled past. Helping to charge the city whose protective barrier kept even the most terrifying amalgamations from coming within a mile of its border.

An aroma of coffee and pastries wafted passed Ren as he went by JoJo's Café on his route home. Grabbing a croissant would be nice, but a beggar sitting at the entrance pestering customers steered him away. With little coin left, he could choose between a pastry or a donation to the homeless man. He decided on neither and passed by the shop. The right decision. A National Party member, easily identified by the splashes of red many of them wore, came out of the shop and started yelling at the beggar. Telling him to get a job. A conflict Ren wanted no part of.

As the smells of the café faded behind, a wave of energy rushed through him. It wouldn't be long now before he could start work as a mercenary. His final project was the only hurdle left. A project, Dunreedy had just informed him, to be completed in cooperation with Seffin.

Babysitting again.

Students pushed themselves for the final, using the most advanced techniques they knew. For most that meant kinetics and control, but for Seffin and Ren that meant elementalism. After he'd destroyed two practice rooms in the last year, Seffin earned himself some notoriety among the faculty. They assigned Ren to keep him in check, wanting to ensure the building still stood at semester's end. What did a final project look like as a team though? How was he supposed to showcase his talents while making sure Seffin didn't immolate them both?

Coming up on his home, Ren decided to worry about the project later. He had weeks to work on it, and a solution likely wouldn't be found on his walk home only minutes after finding out. The Bolin residence was a variation on the tan brick rowhouses all over the city. Poppy's status in the Lodge system afforded a bigger footprint than most, but what extra space they had was taken up by the engineer's various machines and tools they needed for their work. After leaping up all four steps at once, he pushed open the heavy wooden door, entering the comforting, cluttered mess he called home.

"Why were you in my room?"

Ren turned to see Kulelika, Ka for short, her straight black hair spilling down over her face, sitting at the kitchen table reading a book. "I was, uh..."

"Lie to me. I dare you," she said without looking up.

"I was just borrowing some—"

"Stealing you mean." Ka raised her head, her brown eyes piercing into his own. "You stole my money. You also looked over some of my merc contracts."

"How do you even know that?"

"Unlike you and Poppy, I keep my room clean for this exact reason. I like to know when people go through my things, especially people prone to *borrowing* without asking."

Shit.

Ren used the money to buy new boots for his upcoming final and graduation. Did he need them? No, but he loved the way a fresh pair looked and felt. A new pair for a new chapter in his life he thought.

"I'll pay you back."

"Oh, you already did. Poppy bought you a pair of boots from Sven's for graduation and left them on your bed. I took the liberty of selling them back."

"You what?"

Ka went back to her book. "I took back enough of the money to cover what you stole and left the rest on your bedside table. It's quite a bit. They were expensive."

"You absolute—"

"Absolute what?"

Ren paused a moment to consider the relative danger he was in. She wouldn't harm him permanently, but his older sister had no qualms about cementing her point with a well-placed punch or a carefully aimed household item like, say, the heavy tome resting in front of her. "I'm... going upstairs to think on what I've done."

She smiled. "Sounds good." He began trudging upstairs. "Oh, and Ren."

He paused.

"If you steal from me again, I'll do more than get even. You want to buy twenty pairs of shoes that's on you, but I'm not fueling your weird foot fetish."

It's not a fetish.

Ren climbed up to the second level, retreating to his room. Money rested on the table next to his bed. A lot of money. She hadn't exaggerated. The only cordwainer in the city that charged this much was Sven, and he could charge those prices because his footwear lasted years longer than his competitors and were comfortable to boot. He pouched the money from the table, picturing Poppy's disappointment at losing the gift so quickly. He'd have to try to get them back somehow. A knock at the front door echoed up to his room. Another solicitor?

A second knock came.

Descending the stairs, Ren glanced over at Ka on his way to the front door. "Don't get up or anything."

Without looking up from her book, Ka slowly raised her hand and gave him a thumbs up. Shaking his head, Ren opened the front door. *Shit.* A tall man wearing a "Want a winner? Vote for Winnow!" badge on his vest stood on the threshold.

"Good afternoon, Mr. Bolin. I'm a volunteer with the Winnow campaign. Have you given any thought to whom you'll vote for in the upcoming election?"

This would be Ren's first election he could vote in. Saunders, Winnow's opponent, had some crackpot plan to work with all the other countries to put a stop to the husk hordes coming out of Gogallo, and Winnow's pet issue was improving Egal's economy by forcing an increase on the price of focus crystal distribution. The idea being the Guild could pay their workers more if they had more profits. But Ren had experienced firsthand what it looked like when a town didn't have the protection of a pylon, and he wouldn't wish it on his worst enemy.

"I was planning to vote for Saunders, actually."

"Oh, I'm sorry to hear that. Can I ask a question? Do you believe that Egallans should utilize our gods-given crystals that we work so hard to mine to better our own country, or do you believe that we should continue to provide handouts to the likes of Estabans and Garvellians?"

"No."

"Oh good, so you don't believe we should keep bailing out the—"

"No, I mean you can't ask me any more questions."

Ren shut the door on his face and started back up to his room. Before he did, he paused and turned to Ka. "Did you know who it was at the door?"

Peeling her eyes from her book. "I suspected. It was your turn though; I took the Saunders one earlier."

"And how'd that go?"

"Same fervor, less cultish dogma." She closed her book and stood from the table. "Stay down here and help me with dinner."

She pulled out some carrots, a cabbage, and some other vegetables while Ren went into the cupboard and grabbed the cooking pot before getting the fire going. She started chopping vegetables and he boiled some water to begin making the broth. Before long, the familiar smells of thyme, rosemary, and sage permeated their home. Ren tossed in all the ingredients Ka had finished chopping and dropped the lid on the pot just as Poppy ducked through the door holding a package.

Abnormally tall with broad shoulders and thick arms, Poppy had to duck through most doorways, and with the war hammer on their hip, they'd strike an imposing figure if it weren't for their gentle, seemingly bumbling demeanor and calming voice. Apparently, they'd been quite the war hero during The Sol War, but Ren had a hard time seeing it. His greying guardian rarely ever raised their voice. How could someone like that fight in a war?

"Ka. Ren." Looking at each of their children in turn. "Stew tonight I see."

"We threw all the food in the house in a pot and boiled it. Just for you," Ka said, smirking.

"Well, it smells good anyway. Let me get my boots off and get washed. Heads up!" Poppy tossed the package they were carrying to Ren, who snatched it out of the air.

"What's this?"

"It's a belt to match your boots, it'll hold the will-blade I'm picking up for you tomorrow."

"A will-blade?" He could barely contain his excitement.

"A new kit for your new profession. How do the boots fit?"

Ka and Ren exchanged a look. Her eyebrows rose; an audience member excited to see what'll happen next. Ren's heart sank as he saw the excitement on Poppy's face. It's not like the Bolins were poor, but these gifts weren't exactly cheap either.

Poppy took Ren in when his mother died without a second thought, and if he was honest with himself, he'd caused no shortage of trouble. Suspended twice for fighting early on, he managed to grow out of that particular behavior, but one-upped himself by stealing almost anything he wanted that wasn't nailed down. A habit he obviously had yet to break, but Poppy didn't need to know about his most recent relapse. Not yet anyway. For whatever reason, the older he got the harder resisting the impulse became. A desire would start it off, then an itch would form in his fingers, and before he knew it the deed was done. Something about the process satisfied him, just like getting an unexpected gift. He started weaving a web of lies he told himself was for Poppy's benefit. "They fit great! I can't wait to try everything on together."

"Excellent! Old Sven is particular about his sizings, but I didn't want to bring you in for it and spoil the surprise." They walked into the kitchen and began setting the table. "And how's school going?"

"Dunreedy wants me to do my final project with Seffin."

Poppy paused to look at Ren with a raised eyebrow.

Ren chuckled nervously. "Yeah, he said Seffin learned a lot the last time I helped him, and that it's a way to make up for... the incident."

They frowned. "You snuck in after hours to practice. They should be rewarding your dedication not threatening suspension." Finishing the last setting at the table they put their hands on their hips. "Welp, whatever it takes to get your license. On the bright side, you should be registered for merc work before long, and you'll never have to worry about jumping through these types of hoops again."

"No," Ka added. "Just different types of hoops for needy clients."

"Well, at least those hoops pay money," Poppy said.

Ren wanted to become a merc ever since coming to Prolivgrad. Poppy told him tales of merc contracts they and Great Grandpa Ren took on before the Lodge system was even set up, like heroes out of a story. Escorting caravans on unregistered trade routes, taking down rogue mystics, protecting people from criminals. Even jobs as small as carrying packages to and from unregistered towns had their own form of excitement. Ren wanted to see more of the world. To see if the rumors of stifling conformity in the Garvelle Empire, the massive, continent-lint-spanning nation to the east, were true. To see if the Nashowans to the south and west were as gruff and rude as they say. To journey to the edge of the Nari'ko wilds and its endless forest on the north-western portion of the continent of Sol, the continent he lived on.

With any luck he could find a contract that would take him back up north, to Vicksbough, so he could detour to the ruins of Gull Harbor and pay respects to his mother and all the others lost in the massacre. The thought of it made his finger itch and gave him a sinking feeling in his chest. There had been so many bodies. So many people. They would have all turned to husk without the pylon to prevent it. An image came to him of a young girl, cold and perfectly still, her body crushed into the ground by a monster, slowly rising again, unsticking herself from the mud she was pressed into. He shook his head and snapped himself back to reality.

They all sat down to dinner. Ka retreated into her book as she shoveled the stew into her mouth while Poppy fiddled with a round metal ball they called a grenade. They popped it open to reveal a mass of gear wheels and springs. Hairs stood up on the back of Ren's neck. "What's that for?"

Poppy twisted the screwdriver a few final times before answering, "If you hit this button, it'll start a timer. Once the timer stops it blows up." They tapped a small piece on the ball twice. Ren flinched with each tap.

Ka looked up. "And you're working on it at the dinner table?"

"Oh, it's not armed. I'm going to try it tomorrow on a group of husk we spotted out by the barrier's edge."

Ren's eyes widened. "Husk by the barrier? Can I come?"

He hadn't seen a husk in years—the reanimated corpses which relegated most of the world of Kohru's population to living underneath a pylon barrier—Poppy's leniency as a guardian had only one exception, the edge of the barrier was off-limits. The only time Ren ever saw them genuinely angry happened six years ago when he went out to the barrier alone, wanting to see a husk. He had no idea how Poppy found out, but the punishment stuck with him. Grounded for three months, only allowed out for school and training, and he had to handle all chores in the home the entire time. It may not have stopped him from making trouble in other ways but, going forward, Ren dutifully kept his distance from the city's edge.

A husk wouldn't prove much risk to him now though, and he wouldn't mind a change in scenery either. The glittering city lost a bit of its luster after the first thousand days or so of squinting every time a person walked out their door.

"No," said Poppy

"But you'd be there! I just want to see, and like you said, I'll be taking on my own contracts soon enough."

"And when that happens, we can go to the barrier. I'll show you some husk. We'll kill them. Grab an ale afterward."

Ka stood up from the table to put away her dishes. She remarked over her shoulder, "He's not in danger from a few husk anymore. It wouldn't be a bad idea. Then he'd get to try out all his new equipment. Break in those boots, right Ren?"

Ren's eyes narrowed at his sister. *What game are you playing?* Just as the thought occurred to him, Poppy gave a pensive look, and after a moment... "Ok."

"Yes!" Ren's fist pumped the air.

"But you need to do exactly as I say."

"Of course."

"And don't engage with any husk unless I tell you to."

"Absolutely."

"The last thing I need is to worry about protecting someone else while I complete my tests."

Ren excitedly cleared the table. "Yes, yes. I won't be a problem. I promise." He grabbed Poppy's empty bowl and brought it to the washbasin where Ka, a mischievous smile on her face, stood in the process of cleaning the cooking pot. She lowered her voice so Poppy wouldn't hear. "Forgetting something?"

His stomach dropped. The boots. Ka touched his shoulder, reassuring him. "I sold them back to Sven and told him to reserve them for you. If you have the money, he said he'd sell them back to you at cost." Ren dropped the dishes he worked on and hugged his sister. "What did we learn?" she asked.

"Don't steal from you."

"Right." She returned the hug. "And if I ever catch you again, I'll kill you." Then she kissed him on the forehead.

Poppy looked over at their two children suspiciously. "Is there something going on I need to be aware of?"

"No," they said in unison.

Flicker

"Alright Connie, this is where you'll be spending most of your time." The receptionist gestured at a sad desk in a sad corner of a small, windowless room. "Senator Washburne wants you here Monday through Friday, but keep in mind that on Wednesday—"

"He's at the Guild's offices for meetings. I reviewed the schedule before I came." She flashed her best people-pleasing smile. "I'll get started on addressing these constituent letters, respond to the easy ones, and elevate the more... prickly... ones as needed." Gesturing to the stack of letters Dale, the receptionist, so kindly prepared for her first day. "If there's anything else you'd like me to get to today don't hesitate to drop it on my desk."

He nodded in approval. "I see the letter of recommendation from Coral Crowley's office wasn't lying. You'll fit in splendidly. Welcome to the Washburne family!" And with that, he left.

She sat down and flipped through a multitude of letters from Washburne's constituency; several regarded the closure of a local pub, Blackbill's Brews, due to repeated public disturbances, another about a café that stopped serving the coffee someone liked, more about the pub, a few regarding some husk that came too near the barrier, a noise complaint, a beautifully worded letter about the gridlock in the senate affecting miner jobs, and finally a letter from someone named Cara Soledar regarding funding for a Guild project. *Wow, that's lucky.* She stacked the pub letters and the miner letter aside, pocketed the letter from Cara, and threw the rest in the trash. She spent the remainder of the morning responding to the patrons of Blackbill's Brews with a form letter and drawing up a tentative response to the miner.

She finished and brought her stack out to the main office to have the letters signed by Senator Washburne. Dale was dealing with a particularly aggressive constituent. Trying his best to calm them down, he paused his coddling to address her, "You can walk those into the office and set them on his desk if you like. He should be back in a while to take care of them."

Dutifully, she made her way into the Senator's office, closed and quietly locked the door behind her, then began to count out a full minute. *One, two, three.* The first thing to catch her eye was a giant portrait of Washburne himself sitting on a gaudy red chair wearing judicial robes. To the left of the portrait, a green and blue Egallan flag. Directly below the flag a giant, oversized desk with a small bust of the judge himself resting in a corner. *He doesn't want for ego. Twenty-nine, thirty, thirty-one.* To either side of the room stood shelves filled with books. On a table near the desk sat a whiskey decanter and some glasses. Dropping the stack of letters on the former judge's desk she began rifling through drawers. *Fifty-nine, sixty.* She strolled to the door and shook the handle, waited a few seconds, and shook the handle again.

Nashow. The Guild. He's gotta have something in here.

"Hello?" She called out.

"Hello!" Dale called back. "I think you accidentally locked the door. Turn the lock."

She grabbed the door handle and tugged and pushed as if she were trying to get the door open. "I'm trying, but it seems to be stuck. The lock won't budge."

An audible sigh came through the door. "Ok, Washburne should be back in an hour, he's the only one with a key besides his wife. Do you think you can just wait in there until he comes back?"

Putting an apologetic tone in her voice, she said, "I'm so, so sorry. I'll be fine. I'll wait."

Perfect.

She resumed shuffling through the drawers in the desk. There were papers on the logging industry, some data on the washout from the mining activity in lower Brinidor Mountain, and some funding requests addressed to the Chair of the Energy and Natural Resources Committee. Nothing that piqued her interest overmuch. Sitting down in the same gaudy, red chair featured in the Senator's portrait she considered the room. Nothing under the drawers. Nothing on the shelves.

Nothing in plain sight. The bust caught her eye again. Delicately, she lifted it to reveal a key. She snatched it. *Now, what are you a key to?* Looking up at the portrait on the wall, she rolled her eyes. *Really? How are the idiots the ones that always get elected?* She strode over to the portrait and pulled on the edge; the portrait was on a hinge and behind it sat a safe with a keyhole. *Stupid.*

Inside the safe was a goldmine; funding for an off-the-books project for the Guild, a lot of communications with Cara Soledar, and several letters from Coral Crowley discussing the tariffs between Egal and Nashow. Her heart started racing. After years of searching, she'd caught one of the higher-ups in the organization with a direct line to The Guild. She stole some paper and a pen and took some hurried notes. The documents went back in the safe, the key back under the bust, then she plopped herself in a chair to wait for the senator.

While waiting, she mentally reviewed the research she completed in preparation for this day: prior to his election, Roger Washburne had been a district judge handling mostly cases regarding land ownership, property rights, and mineral rights. Almost all cases involving The Guild of Commerce came down in their favor, especially any involving focus crystal mining. A boring way of saying a lot of people lost their homes because mining companies claimed mineral rights on their land.

Once Washburne got his senate seat his antics only increased. Appointed to the Energy and Natural Resources

Committee he set up tax incentives for the sole benefit of The Guild. Bills deregulating the mining industry started coming out of committee with 'do pass' recommendations which resulted in fatalities at mining sites spiking up drastically. A secret discretionary fund controlled by the committee was created. The records of which were classified, but suspiciously, Washburne's personal wealth rose drastically. Within two years of being elected, he and his family moved to a mansion near the Senate building. He opened several businesses in Prolivgrad that were strangely successful. One of which was a pub whose competition, Blackbill's Brews, was just forced to close their doors.

Most elected officials she investigated had a few crooked dealings, but nothing on the level of Washburne. He made a full-time job out of fleecing his fellow countrymen, and he did most of it in plain sight. Anybody could find the information she had. Nobody seemed to want to put in the effort to fight him, or they were afraid. After all, Washburne's political opponents never lasted long. Of his three elections two of his opponents died during their campaign, and the last was caught in a murder investigation a week before the vote.

How many people have you killed? How many lives ruined?

The lock made a loud clicking sound, and the door swung open. She stood to welcome the senator. For all the man's ego, he wasn't much to look at. He stood only slightly taller than her and had an average build with a head of hair that was far more gray than brown. Doing her best to sound as subservient as possible, she said, "I'm so sorry sir. This will never happen again."

Washburne gave a wide smile, accenting all the extra skin and wrinkles on his face. "No apologies necessary. Dale told me you've been hard at work already this morning." He walked over to her and extended his hand. "I'd expect no less from someone so highly recommended. How is that old crow, Crowley?"

Grasping his hand, she noted how hard he squeezed and tried to match it. A stupid pissing contest for stupid people. "Last I checked she was up to her neck in it, but the situation in Nashow right now is precarious at best. I'm sure you're aware. Though it seems the assassin that was tearing through the nobles and their administrators has taken a break of late."

He squeezed her hand harder as he shook it. "Oh, yes. I'm aware. Next time you talk to Crowley please let her know I wish I could have done more."

One of these fuckers. She put some muscle into her hand. Washburne's eyes went wide, and he pulled his hand back, ending the inane game. "That's quite some grip you got there."

She laughed, intentionally projecting nervousness. "Yeah, sometimes I don't know my own strength."

He clapped his hands together. "Well, we're happy you're a part of the family now. I have a tradition where I share a whiskey with each new hire. Could you join me at the end of the day for a glass?"

She bowed her head. "Certainly."

He's gift-wrapping himself.

She left the senator's office to find Dale grinning at her. "Don't worry about doing something like that. Loyalty is the only thing he cares about. He's pretty relaxed otherwise."

After accepting Dale's reassurances, she retreated to her office and reviewed an upcoming bill Washburne planned to propose. A bill increasing the funding allocation to his committee's budget. She studied it, line by line, to see if she could glean any more details about the project the funds were going to. Her last job had been easier. Nashow, the nation to the south and west of Egal, was a monarchy and had far less bureaucracy than a democratic country like Egal. Threads were a lot easier to follow when they didn't tangle into knots with committees and bill drafts and political parties.

At the end of the day, she made her way to the senator's office. Stopping for a minute at Dale's desk, she told him he could go home for the day. Washburne was about to have his whiskey-talk with her, and she could manage anything that came up during that time. She thanked Kohru that he left without questioning it. Dale seemed nice. It would be a shame if he were here for this.

She walked in and Washburne rose from his desk. "That time already? Pour us both a glass if you would." He leaned over to sign a few more documents, placed them in an envelope, and tossed the envelope in an organizer on his desk.

She strolled over to the decanter to pour their drinks. *Two drops of sunback venom would handle him, but he needs to talk first.* Handing him a glass of whiskey she took a sip of her own and started in, "Who is Cara Soledar?"

With his glass halfway to his mouth, he paused, and gave her a puzzled expression. "Cara? She works for The Guild. She has a project we work on together. How do you know about her?"

She produced Cara's letter from earlier and set it on his desk. "What's the project?"

"That's... classified. Was that sent to the office? Why didn't you put that on my desk with the rest?"

"Well, depending on how this conversation goes I'll need it to copy her handwriting."

The realization seemed to hit him like a waterfall as the blood drained from his face. "Coral..."

"Is dead. I drowned that snake myself. Wasn't easy. She's quite the capable wielder." She drained her glass of whiskey and willed it into the air in front of her. "She was the last person on my list in Nashow, and in a way, it's not a complete lie that she recommended me to you. Your name *was* one of the last things she said."

His eyes narrowed. "That cowardly—"

The sound of glass shattering cut him off. Shards floated in the air between them. Making eye contact, she put some edge into her voice. "I wouldn't speak ill of the dead. She lasted longer than all the others. I doubt you'll last so long."

"What do you want?"

"If you had asked me years ago that would have been a simple enough answer, but every time I cut one head off three more pop up. I'm trying to find the heart, so I can stab it and bury this once and for all. Who's Cara? Really."

"She's…" He paused. "Just a Guild emp—ah!" He yelped in pain as a shard of glass plunged into his right eye.

"Roger. I know you're aware of my handiwork in Nashow because I'm the one that wrote you those letters on behalf of Coral. Stop lying to me. Now. Or things are going to get a lot worse."

Clutching his eye, the senator took a few steps back. "She's a liaison for a project lead for The Guild. It's something to do with crystals and husk. That's all I know."

That's every project the Guild has ever done, you idiot. Gonna have to do better than that.

As if teleporting to the spot, she was suddenly behind him, leaning into his ear. "I know you know more than that."

Shards of glass sped toward his left eye, but he got a hand up just in time. He yelped in pain again as the shards plunged into the meat of his palm. With his lip quivering and tears forming in his eyes he said, "Ok, they're preparing for something. They're making weapons. That's all I could piece together. They haven't told me any more than that. Please, believe me."

"Well, I guess Cara is up next then."

"Thank you."

"You think I'd let you go after all you've done?"

"Wh-What do you—"

"The bills that got all those miners killed. The people you've displaced with your crooked rulings. You've been on the Guild's payroll for the last twenty years. The shit you've pulled has killed more people than I have. Which, honestly, that's quite impressive at this point."

"Please, I have a family. We'll leave. You'll never hear from me again."

She let out a malicious laugh. "Oh, I spoke with Jenny and Camden. You should have left your family out of your shady dealings, Roger."

His remaining eye opened wide in an expression of terror. "Y-you monster! Who are you? Why are you doing this?"

"Why? Your son runs the mining company with the highest fatality rate in the country and has, surprisingly, never even been fined, and your wife runs a charity for the sole reason of making money off the displacement you caused with your rulings. I'm shutting down your family business. That's all. I'm almost glad you're all so awful. With all three of you gone, there'll be fewer questions. I've already sent the letters explaining you'll be taking a family vacation, just the three of you. As far as who I am? I used to go by the name Flicker." A wicked smile spread across her face. "Can you guess why?"

Roger fell to his knees next to his chair, openly weeping. The blood and tears mixing and spilling onto the floor. "Please. I'm begging you."

She looked down at him. A judge begging for clemency. She'd give him justice instead. "Fine. I'll answer it for you."

She let out a breath and settled into the technique she named herself after. Flickering. Her boot sped through the air, connecting with enough force to launch him upward. He made a hacking sound from the blow. In the blink of an eye, another kick shattered the senator's gaudy chair he seemed to love so much to pieces. Now, below his airborne form, she jumped and slammed her fist into his stomach, pushing him up, further into the air. She spun her whole body and kicked him, sending him careening toward his painting in the back of the room. His arms and legs flailed like a rag doll. Then with sudden, deadly force, she willed the splinters of his chair through the air, pinning him to his own portrait. His blood flowed down the portrait.

Exhausted from the effort, Flicker picked up an empty glass and filled it with whiskey. As she took a sip, she looked up at the Senator, dazed and gasping his last breaths. "I'm not much of an artist, but this is quite the improvement if I do say so myself."

Ren

Just outside the city but still within the barrier, Ren sat on a boulder next to some crumbling ruins, marveling at his new pair of boots while waiting for Poppy. Without enough money, Sven had been kind enough to take some of his older boots in trade. An extremely lucky break. A cordwainer with the reputation Sven had didn't need to stoop to buying used boots for spare leather. Anyway, they fit perfectly, Poppy had gone the extra mile in making sure the measurements were right. Ren hopped down off the boulder, rubbing his backside after sitting on its hard, lumpy surface for so long. He started pacing around, wiggling his toes and stretching the leather of the boots to conform to his feet.

The morning was sunny and pleasant, though a slight breeze brought a bit of the city smell out to hang in the air around him. He stretched and yawned, as the heat of the day ramped up it always seemed to make him sleepy.

How long are they going to make me wait?

Poppy said they'd bring his new will-blade out to try on the husk today, but his excitement turned to impatience the longer the morning dragged on. This would be his first time using a real will-blade. The practice blades he used at Danver's Academy were attuned to blunt instead of sharpen. Real will-blades projected a cutting edge so sharp they could slice through anything save for another willed weapon, and the edge could extend out as far as the wielder wanted, provided they had the control to keep it stable. Most didn't have enough control to keep even a small edge stable in the middle of a fight though, which is why skilled will-blade wielders were both rare and sought after. Ren sat against a nearby tree, leaning his head back against its bark, he fought the impulse to nap under its shade with the pleasant, if somewhat smelly, breeze cooling him.

A jolt in his foot snapped his eyes open. Poppy stood looking down at him and dropped a sheathed blade in his lap. Apparently, he'd lost his battle with drowsiness. They hobbled over to the boulder he'd been sitting on earlier and set a few of their grenades on it, pulling out some tools to start making adjustments. Tender, the name everyone who wasn't their children called them, had injured their leg a long time ago. They'd said something about a curse, but all Ren knew for certain is the injury couldn't be healed. Not even Ka, the most skilled healer in the city, could mend it.

"Not enough sleep last night?" Poppy said over their shoulder

Ren jumped up to a standing position in answer and unsheathed his new weapon. Glittering silver with a simple cross guard and a grip with freshly wrapped leather. He put some will into it and a semi-translucent edge of focused will extended out around the blade. He made a downward slash, cutting into the tree he'd been resting on.

"Careful, maybe save that for the husk."

"I'm being careful," he said with probably a little too much attitude in his voice, but it wasn't like he'd never swung a blade before. Poppy always worried after him like this, though he had to admit he had a knack for destroying things. Windows while he learned kinetics, and a chair that one time, and then that time he broke his door off its hinges when he slammed it with will after he got grounded for going out to the barrier. Then there was the blanket he started on fire when he was practicing elementalism. Yeah, Poppy had a point, actually.

As if on cue, they turned to look at him. "I mean it. Will-blade users are rare because they get themselves killed with the things more often than not."

Ren brushed aside the nagging and kept experimenting with the blade. He changed how much will he put into it and felt the edges expanding and contracting. Willing the blade out of his hands and into the air he kept the edges extended, a technique he read about and trained on practice swords. An easy thing to do when standing still, but in the middle of a fight maintaining focus on both the blade and its edges took skill. Either the edges could retract, or worse, they could extend out and kill someone you didn't intend to. Not a move he'd want to use in combat anytime soon.

Ren dropped focus and sheathed his sword. Poppy stood over their grenades, tinkering with each of them in turn and holstering them into a belt they'd prepared especially for the new tools. For someone so focused on helping people they certainly did love their deadly inventions. Hopefully, they'd stop tinkering soon. Ren came out here to see husk, and so far all he'd seen were trees and rocks.

A stench wafted past Ren's nose.

Poppy looked up from their toys and glanced at Ren. This wasn't the stench of Prolivgrad, of refuse and too many people gathering in one location overlong, but one of rot and decay. Of husk. Closer to the city proper than he expected, but with a barrier this size and projected in such a unique way—charged through crystal dust embedded in most of Prolivgrad's build-ings—the edge constantly moved. Poppy didn't seem worried though, instead, they had a smile on their face.

"Oh, good. We won't have to walk far; I can feel the edge just over there."

"Really? I thought the smell is what gave it away."

In smaller towns, the edge was a faint shimmer in the air, but large barriers were almost impossible to detect for anyone without training as an engineer. Poppy described it as a note humming just beneath their awareness, whatever that meant.

"How do you have such an easy time spotting the edge?" Ren asked.

Poppy stopped, considering their answer for a moment. "It's not something I see so much as something I feel. Once you learn how to tune into it, it's actually kind of annoying. Like someone singing the same song... forever. That's why if something were to happen to a barrier any engineer in the area would know immediately. To us, it would be like if the sun suddenly went out."

"Do all barriers have the same... erm, song?"

Poppy holstered their last grenade and regarded Ren directly. "The short answer is no. We have nine pylons in Prolivgrad, each with their own frequency."

Ren raised his eyebrows in surprise. He'd never heard they had nine pylons. Why didn't they go over that in school? He was on the mystic track, sure, and pylons were engineer business, but this seemed like basic knowledge.

"The crystal dust embedded in the buildings isn't tuned the way a normal pylon is, so they needed eight slave pylons to take in all possible frequencies, and one master pylon to take the energy and project the barrier. Prolivgrad is like striking a chord whereas the barriers everywhere else are like a single sustained note. Make sense?"

"No." Ren scratched his head. "I thought it was the single sustained frequency that kept husk out."

"Not entirely wrong." Poppy chuckled. "Really, the important thing to know is that husk don't harmonize with any frequency that a pylon can put out while everything else in the world can. Something about what animates them makes it impossible."

It still didn't make sense to him, husk are dead bodies and dead bodies existed just fine under barriers, but he nodded understanding anyway. He wasn't an engineer, and as long as barriers kept husk away that's all he cared about. And anyway, his impatience to see a husk overtook his curiosity for pylon harmonics.

Ren gestured away from the city. "Shall we?"

Poppy nodded and they made their way out, away from Prolivgrad and the mountain it rested upon. The land around Mount Brinidor rolled with hills and forests punctuated by ponds, rivers, and freshwater lakes. A lush carpet of green in the summer that turned orange and gold in the fall. Unfortunately, it also made for a perfect hiding spot for husk. The thick trees and numerous hills made great cover for roamers and hordes alike, not to mention the bears, wolves, and few species of colossi—large variants of animals—native to the area as well. Stench usually heralded the husk provided the wind didn't mask their odor, but a stalking hoarwolf could pounce from almost any direction here without alerting its prey. While the canopy of the forest would help predators hide, it also provided an abundance of shade for which Ren was grateful. Trekking up and down hills with the sun beating down on them sounded terrible.

The stench soon became overwhelming as they crested a hill to find the horde ambling among the trees. The hairs on Ren's arm stood up. He'd never seen so many husk in one place, bumping and shuffling past each other, they seemed to move together, as a unit. Poppy leaned in to whisper in Ren's ear, "They're on the verge of amalgamating."

Amalgamations happened when husk gathered and combined. Merging their bodies with one another. The worst amalgamations were when they found a colossus corpse and merged with it. The silent werewiller that had destroyed Ren's village had been one of those. A husk amalgamated with a colossus, though the one from his village was from a normal amalgamated colossus, the process didn't usually grant completely soundless movement. These were just run-of-the-mill husk though. Not something to worry about. Ren certainly wasn't scared. Not at all. The tight grip he had on his sword was standard practice to make ready for a fight, certainly not because the writhing they did unsettled him, and certainly not because their groans and raspy breaths reminded him just how sad and pathetic and final death was.

"Hey!" Poppy yelled in the direction of the horde.

Ren looked over at Poppy, his palms were sweating and his finger itched. "What are you doing?"

"I want them chasing us. I need to figure out the ideal arming time for the grenades."

"That sounds dangerous."

"Ahhh you'll be fine. If I can do it with this leg of mine, then so can you." Poppy smiled. "Hey you! Koth's shit smells better than you lot! Come get your fresh meal. My boy here's got lots of will for you to chow down on!"

"Really Poppy? What the fuck?"

"Language."

The horde began shambling in their direction, faster than Ren anticipated. He had an idea in his head of decaying bodies with rotting muscles that didn't move well, but these sprang forward with fervor. Tripping over each other to race toward him. Poppy's voice came from behind, "I'd run if I were you."

A small metal ball sailed past his head landing in front of him and rolling down the hill. Ren turned and bolted toward Poppy. "Did you seriously throw one of those things right past my head?" The explosion left a ringing in his ears. Too close for comfort. Far too close. *I'm going to die. I'm going to get blown up and then eaten.* Poppy loped with an heir of nonchalance. Ren pumped his legs to try and catch up while they looked behind to eye the horde. "Hmm, I'll need a shorter arm time then."

As they continued their running, another grenade arced past his head. "Stop doing—" The explosion cut him off, but it sounded different this time, wetter and more muffled. When he turned to look, all that was left of the horde were a few husk. A couple still shambling at them, and one, nothing but a torso, dragged itself across the gore-ridden ground.

Poppy turned to him. "Clean those up for me, would you?" They sat down and began to fiddle with their remaining grenades.

Ren narrowed his eyes. *Excuse me, son. I almost blew you up just now, but could you "clean up" the things trying to eat us? I have some screws to tighten on my new toys.*

Regardless, this *is* what he came for, so he unsheathed his blade and threw some will into it. He fell into a fighting stance he learned at the academy, balanced and meant for flexibility with his strikes, but before he could think the first husk was on him. *Ok, so they're even faster than I thought.* Dodging to the left he swung his blade into its neck, but it only went halfway through. He'd lost focus on the edge and the blade wedged into the meat of its neck. With his blade stuck, he tugged, trying to pull it out, but he only succeeded in pulling the now-dead husk closer. The limp body landed on top of him as he fell backward. *This is not going how I expected.* A few more explosions rang out as he struggled to get the corpse off. Apparently, Poppy had finished adjusting their grenades. A decayed arm landed a few feet from where he lay.

Adding insult to his growing pile of insults, a growl came from his right. He turned to see a husk running straight for him. Letting go of his sword, he barely got his hands up as it fell on him, snarling and biting at his neck. Ren pushed it off just as Poppy's hammer came crashing down on its head, smashing it like an egg and splattering him with rotten brain, bone, and coagulated blood.

"Your control with that blade could use some work." Reaching down with their hand, Poppy had a smug smile on their face.

Sweaty, covered in husk, and thoroughly demoralized, he grabbed Poppy's hand and stood. "You don't say?" A final straggler ran their way. Poppy hefted their hammer up, but

Ren had already made a sharp lance of ice and flung it at the husk which pierced its chest. It flopped to the ground. He had had enough husk for one day. He busied himself tugging his new blade out of the husk's neck he'd left it in.

"I'm glad I brought you out here," Poppy said.

"Really?" Ren grunted as he finally got his blade loose. "I figured losing my weapon and almost dying would qualify as a bad day."

"Nah, it's an important lesson to know how dangerous normal husk are, and now you know why I was so adamant you stay away from the border."

Clotted blood and bits of bone clung to his sword. He wiped it off and sheathed it. "I didn't expect them to be that fast."

"No one ever does. They're not overly dangerous if you know what to expect though." Poppy sat on a fallen log, massaging their injured leg. "It's gotta be getting to noon. Don't you have to meet Seffin?"

Ren slapped his forehead and squeezed his eyes shut dramatically. "Yeah. I forgot."

"I've got a couple more tweaks I need to make with these grenades. Better get going. I'll see you at home tonight."

Ren gave them a quick hug. "Thanks for the blade, and for almost blowing me up."

"Love you too," Poppy said.

Ren turned and ran back toward Prolivgrad, the gentle breeze of the day cooling him as he did.

***

Danvers Academy was an imposing building. The two large, wooden doors that led into the main entryway were framed by decorative depictions of Lana's last stand. A time in Kohru's history when the husk ran even more rampant than now, and almost overtook the entirety of the known world. On either side of the entry to the main campus were two towers, scraping at the sky. One for each field of study within the academy, mysticism and engineering. Stained glass windows depicting important events in Prolivgradian history hung all over the outside of the building, but a keen eye could discern the windows were made of focus crystals. The most sought-after material in existence. Truly one of the most expensive structures ever made, and Ren couldn't wait to be done with the place.

Seffin waited next to the door, his eyes following Ren with their usual intensity as he walked up the steps. Like he knew something about Ren that he didn't even know himself. He didn't dislike Seffin, but he didn't exactly like how uneasy he made him feel.

"Why are you so dirty?" Seffin asked. "Did you get in a fight?"

"Something like that."

A moment passed where Seffin glanced behind him, and then back at him directly again. "Ok. I signed out a practice room."

The halls felt wide and lonely without any kids bustling around. Few people came here on the weekends save for some faculty and seniors practicing for their final. Seffin and Ren made their way to the far back of the building where all the practice rooms were. He'd signed up for the largest one, a wise choice.

The room sat empty save for a wooden dummy sitting in the corner, burns and gashes peppering its body, and a large basin filled with water resting in the opposite corner. A wooden sign above the basin stated in clear, block lettering "Please refill basin before leaving." They set their things down and rolled up their sleeves.

Ren started, "What are you thinking for the final?"

"I didn't know you had a will-blade." Seffin reached for the scabbard.

Ren willed the blade away from Seffin and into his own hands. "I just got it. Have you ever held one before?"

"No. Do you think we can use it in the presentation?"

Ren drew the blade and put some will into it. "Here. Look." Holding it out in front of him he tilted it to make it easy for Seffin to see. "Don't touch it though. They're real dangerous. That edge will cut you and you won't even feel it." Ren drew some water up and turned it into a ball of ice. "The nice thing about them is they don't take a lot of will to use. Just a lot of control." With a swift motion, he cut the ball of ice in half. "Probably not a good idea for you to try it. At least not right now. You'd probably cut the room in half."

"My control has improved since last time."

"Are you willing to bet our lives on it?"

Seffin paused, Ren could swear he saw cogs spinning behind his eyes. "No."

"Me either," he said, sheathing his blade. "I've thought about using it, but we should figure out your part of the presentation first. Obviously, you'll need to do that fireball again. Back in class... is that the largest stable fireball you've made?"

"No, but I can't move anything larger than that without losing control."

"Ok, well let's start there."

Seffin put both hands out with his palms spread apart, facing each other. A bead of fire appeared in between his hands, he threw them outward, and the full-sized version of the fireball exploded into existence. Ren walked all the way to the other side of the room and yelled, "Ok. Toss it to me."

Seffin cocked his head. "Are you sure? I've never actually thrown one this size without intending for it to hit the target."

"I'm sure. Just take it slow. You're not shunting it. You're tossing it. Just make sure to drop focus on the movement once you get the momentum right or we're going to be fighting over where it goes."

Seffin closed his eyes.

"Don't do that!" Ren yelled. "You need to see where you're going."

"I apologize." He dripped with sweat, the red of his coat jacket darkening from the moisture.

"Look at me," Ren said. "Look at me and just imagine where you want it to go. Then just put in enough momentum to set it on its path and release control of the movement. I'll take care of the rest." Their eyes met, and the orb started moving. Seffin furrowed his brow as it gained momentum. "Ok, you need to let go now." The orb stopped accelerating but continued to float gently toward him. Like a toy boat let loose on a stream. He felt the heat of the fireball as it came closer. Wrapping his will around it, he slowed it to a stop, reversed the direction, put enough energy behind it to get it going again, and dropped focus. All the while maintaining eye contact with Seffin. "Ok, now wrap your will around it when... yeah. Like that. Now drop it completely."

The fireball winked out of existence, and Seffin doubled over taking in gulps of air and sweating through his clothes. Ren jogged over. "Are you ok?"

"Not really," Seffin said. "I thought I was going to kill you."

"Aww, worried about me?"

"Of course I was. Just a couple weeks ago I destroyed a room like this with a fireball half that size."

This was new. Seffin never expressed worry or fear, or joy or sadness or frustration, or much of anything really. An aura of intensity is the only thing Ren sensed in all the years they'd gone to school together. Tightly wound, sure, but never any-thing so human as emotions. He was practically as stoic as a Guild envoy.

Come to think of it, he'd never even tried to get to know Seffin before this year, or anyone in his class for that matter. Bound for merc work, he didn't see the usefulness in bonding with a bunch of future Guild workers. That felt short-sighted now, but he set that feeling aside to focus on Seffin. Hesitantly, he leaned over and put a hand on his shoulder, there was a lot more muscle there than he thought. "Hey, it's fine. There's a reason Dunreedy paired us. I can handle this." Ren consid-ered how best to help. "Here. I'll prove it to you. Let's try something." He gripped Seffin's hand and pulled him up to standing. "Ok, make a fireball. Doesn't matter the size as long as it's stable."

"Just a second."

He pulled off his red jacket and tossed it next to the wall. Then pulled off his linen shirt, balling it up and throwing it next to his jacket. Sweat still streamed down his body in rivulets, starting from his hairline and snaking down his neck, chest, and past a scar on his belly, a raised arc slightly lighter than the deep tan of the rest of him. *Blessed Kohru.* He took both hands, wiped his face, and shook out his hair. When he finished, his wet hair lay in delicate spikes bouncing with the movement of his—the fireball exploded into existence in front of him.

Oh, right.

Ren wrapped his will around it. "Ok. Now try to expand it." He shook his head. *Focus on the fireball.* Seffin threw his hands out. Ren could feel the orb of fire struggle to expand against his will. "So, I'm keeping it from expanding. If you put too much fuel into it, all that'll happen is the fire will go out. Stop trying to contain it and we'll see if I can hold it by myself."

He felt Seffin drop focus on containment, and the effort it took to manage it surprised him. *He does this by himself while fueling it and throwing it?*

"Ok, that's harder than I thought, but I can handle it. Just focus on putting enough fuel in to keep it going."

Without the effort needed to contain the fireball, Seffin's shoulders relaxed. "Ok, so now you have control over a fireball that I'm maintaining. What are we supposed to do with this?"

"You can stop fueling it now." The fireball winked away. "I have an idea. Do you think you can make two of them while I contain them?"

"I can try."

"Ok, if we can get that to work, I'm thinking we can use that to show your power and my control." Ren willed some of the water from the basin into an orb and positioned it above his outstretched palm, trying his best not to be distracted by Seffin glistening with sweat only a few yards away from him. "Anyway, we can't show off our kinetics with those fireballs since they might explode, but we can do something with ice."

"Oh!" Seffin grabbed the globe of liquid from Ren with his will and brought the entire rest of the water from the basin over to join it, forming a large sphere hovering above both of them. *Gods, he holds that much water so casually.* He raised one hand toward the orb and extended the other toward Ren, beckoning him over. *Is that a smile?*

"Come here," he said.

Ren walked over. Seffin grabbed him with his free hand, spun him around, and put their backs up against each other. The contact gave him goose flesh, and he felt his heart beat faster. *Godsdamnit focus.* He could feel Seffin's breathing against his body. "Brace yourself," Seffin warned. *What's that mean?* The entire globe of water collapsed onto the two of them. The pressure would have knocked him to the ground had they not been leaning up against each other. Just as soon as the water drenched them, however, they were suddenly dry again as it spread across the room into a thin pool covering most of the floor except where they stood. Ren felt him let out his breath as the water began to freeze, he then made a rapid movement and, with a crash, millions of needle-thin icicle stalagmites shot from the ground hitting the ceiling and the walls in all different directions. The only safe place in the chaos that Ren could find was the small circle where he and Seffin stood. Ren couldn't see the walls of the practice room any longer, only seemingly infinite icicles piercing the air, locking the two of them in a small zone of safety. *Amazing.* He reached out to touch a strand of ice, but Seffin grabbed his hand before he could make contact. "They're sharper than they look, and if it breaks it could fall on us."

"Ok yes, we're using this. Somehow."

They continued workshopping their presentation. When they finally wound down, they began to pack up their belongings.

"I was surprised to hear you hadn't picked a division in the Guild yet," Ren said.

Seffin looked up from packing his notes in his bag. "My father wants me in research and development with him, but... yeah, I'm not certain yet."

"But what? Does working with your father make you nervous?"

"No." He paused, thinking. Yesterday and today is the most he'd ever seen Seffin think before speaking. Then he nodded, to Ren or himself he couldn't tell. "My hesitation is with the Guild itself."

Excuse me, what?

It was rare to hear someone else in Prolivgrad criticize The Guild. Especially a legacy student whose father ran one of the divisions. They provided a huge portion of the jobs in the city, and Egal's economy was tied to focus crystal trade which the Guild controlled exclusively.

"You have a problem with The Guild?" Ren asked.

"Don't you? It seemed clear you had no interest in joining."

"I have my reasons, but mostly I just think merc work is more exciting. I can get out of the city and see the different countries. Plus, as a merc, there's plenty of chances to improve my will techniques."

"It's dangerous though, and unless you only plan on taking low-level contracts, the likelihood you'll have to kill people is high."

Ren knew mercs were often hired to stop rogue mystics or wild wielders, but he hated the idea of killing someone. As a wielder himself, and soon to be a registered mystic, he knew people like him were almost impossible to properly jail. Few things could cause more destruction and death than a strong wielder, so stopping a wielder of any kind almost always meant killing them.

Killing a husk this morning didn't feel like anything. They were monsters without their own agency, hungering for and attracted to anything with will—the power every human possessed to varying degrees of strength. Putting them down felt right and proper. A person though? He thought back to Gull Harbor, bodies peppering the ground, of running past Shorda Sellens' body lying in pieces while Tolkar dragged him along. The idea of killing someone made him nauseous, and for some reason, angry. *What did Poppy and Ka do? I can't imagine Ka killing someone. Let alone Poppy, but... they must have. Poppy was in the war.*

"I think I'd be fine," he lied, trying to mask the hesitance in his voice.

"Interesting," Seffin said, before strolling over to his shirt to put it back on. Ren watched and felt... fine about that. Actually, he didn't feel anything about it. Totally not concerned about it at all. In fact, he should be dressed. Not that he cared.

Seffin put his pack on before making his way to the door. He waved. "I'll talk to you later." Ren had known Seffin long enough not to be surprised at his graceless exits, but he got the sense Seffin withheld something from him.

"You never said what your problem was with The Guild."

"I know. Neither did you." He walked out of the room. Closing the door behind him.

Jessica

Jessica was a child again, standing in the middle of the road, crying. Five minutes ago, her mother's screams came to an abrupt stop as a husk sank its teeth into her throat, and in about three minutes her father would come to grab her hand in an attempt to bring her to safety. The only reprieve from the terror was the brief, fleeting hope she felt at her father's touch.

A little over a minute after her father grabbed her, a husk would flank them. Her father, not seeing the danger, would fall to the ground with the creature's teeth clacking as it kept trying for his neck. While he fought for his life, she would throw her hands out and begin to draw in the air around her, squeezing and shaping it, something she'd learned from a wild wielder who came through the village.

Always, a man would interrupt her, trying to pull her back and away from her father still struggling against the smelly creature on top of him, and always this man would himself be interrupted by another husk that would bite at his arm and strike at his head. She never saw what became of him, her eyes never left the thing tearing away pieces of her father. Pieces he needed. Bringing her hands to her chest with one palm up and one palm down, facing each other, she flattened the air as much as she could, before throwing her hands forward, shunting it toward the creature. The clawing stopped immediately, and it fell apart as if it were a doll she'd decided to destroy.

Too late again.

Always too late. Her father's eyes stared blankly up into the sky. *What are you looking at?* She thought, as her gaze shifted to the puffy clouds floating lazily in the air. A hand, soft and strong, would grab her wrist and drag her into the woods at the edge of town. Into the shadows the nightmares came out of. The wild wielder from before, the one that taught her how to shape the air. At some point, her arm would become sore, and she would tug out of the woman's grip. Falling to the ground, her blonde hair would fall in a mess in front of her face, obscuring her vision. Or were those tears?

This is usually where she woke up, but this time, it went further. Days and weeks further. A flash of the hut next to a waterfall, of learning to move air and earth with her will, of the unsettling feeling at the top of her spine—where her neck connected to her skull—when the woman made her control small squirrels and skunks and bats, of cooking and laughing and bathing in the cold river. Of the woman's dead eyes peering through bloodied blonde hair, darkened by the relentless monsters who know nothing but hunger, and of the birth of her hatred. No less painful and no less beautiful than delivering a child. An exquisite ember born of her confinement that would grow into a magnificent inferno if only she nurtured it properly.

***

Jessica woke with a start when her carriage hit a bump in the road. Tia stared at her with that disappointed look she had started to think was a permanent fixture of her campaign manager's face. She kept her hair pulled back in a tight, strawberry-blonde bun and had eyes that seemed to cast judgment on anything they rested upon. Even objects. The way she looked at a pencil you'd think it insulted her family. The carriage jostled its way to Jessica's debate with Paul Winnow, the National Party's candidate for president.

"Good of you to join us. Can we continue with debate preparations or does Princess need another nap?"

Jessica yawned. "Queen. Not princess." She blinked the sleep out of her eyes and picked up her notes. "Go ahead."

Tia rolled her eyes. "Ok, he's going to try to hit you on unemployment. That's when you talk about working with his own party on deregulating the mining industry to create jobs. He'll counter that a lot of the jobs created from the mining deregulation was offset by immigrants taking jobs from Egallan citizens—"

"Yes, yes. Then I admit that unemployment is still far higher than it should be and counter with referencing how the majority of his own workers at his many construction businesses are underpaid, unregistered immigrants, and how the Gogallo Initiative will open up work opportunities for everyone. Then, because he can't help himself, he'll dive into talking about how foolish the initiative is, which is *exactly* the topic I want to be talking about anyway."

The carriage began to slow. Jessica peered out the window as the Koka Theater came into view. A large, stone open-air theater named after Immanuel Koka, the first President of Egal. The focus crystals embedded in the construction materials made it glitter in the evening light. Tradition dictated her final debate with Winnow would take place here, and she wanted to make it count. The man wasn't just detrimental to her plans, he was dangerous. His Egal First policies would kill a lot of people—in other nations, mostly—by increasing the cost of focus crystals. Nations that they already had a tenuous relationship with due to The Guild of Commerce's iron grip on the valuable resource.

If that wasn't bad enough, his supporters made life hell for workers from outside Prolivgrad. Harassing and even killing them in some cases, despite the fact there were precious few of them to begin with. Traveling wasn't exactly easy. It's not like there were frequent influxes of immigrants to Prolivgrad. Reducing worker protections had ensured business owners loved his plan, though, and a fairly vocal contingent of workers bought his scapegoating of immigrants for the lack of jobs. Fools. Most times the people they thought of as immigrants were their own countrymen after a town's Guild registration had been pulled, but because the displaced citizens weren't born and raised in Prolivgrad they were called leeches. Simple-minded people looking for simple explanations for a complex problem. Winnow had just decided to offer them the simple explanation they were looking for.

A crowd of reporters waited at the curb for Jessica to step out. She never cared for reporters. She respected their hustle, but it never felt good talking with people fishing for a reason to knock you down. Vultures waiting to pick her clean at the first misstep.

Jessica adjusted the collar of her green suit jacket and checked to make sure her blonde ponytail didn't have a hair out of place. The jacket meant to say *take me seriously,* and the ponytail meant to say *I'm just like one of the workers.* She stepped out of the carriage to a flurry of questions: How are you feeling about tonight's debate? What do you say to the National Party's claims that you weren't born in Egal? You're up by six points, what do you credit your strong lead with?

Jessica issued the usual stock, insubstantial responses signaling she's not willing to talk right now but she doesn't want to go on record stating that fact. Navigating through the viper's nest of reporters to make her way into the theater, she spotted Paul. Brown hair with streaks of gray lying limply across his balding head, and suits that never seemed to fit right. *Best get this over with.* Without hesitating, she strolled toward him for the required, amicable greeting to show everyone they could behave themselves. She stopped a few paces from him when he put his hand out for a shake. A trap she never fell for and never would. The men in the National Party repulsed her with their little game of grip strength. A game for people with small dicks and even smaller brains.

She spoke loudly so both he and the reporters could hear, "Always nice to see you, Paul. I hope you're ready for tonight."

He made a display of looking at his hand and then at her before he put it down. "You better believe I am. Do you not like shaking hands? Or is it just my hand you don't like shaking?"

Every time I think he couldn't be dumber.

"Oh, you mean that children's game Nationals play? No. I have no interest in seeing who can squeeze each other's hand the hardest."

His face went red. "I'm not the child. You're the child."

Jessica chuckled along with a few reporters. "Save your iron-clad arguments for the debate stage, Paul." She turned to head for her dressing room. Away from reporters and away from Paul. Tia caught up with her while she walked.

"That could have gone better."

"How? He looked like a fool. Like he always does."

"Yeah, well his base eats that macho stuff up. Beating him at his own game could help you."

"Ok, well next time I'll break his hand in front of reporters, because from what I've heard that's what it takes to get the man to stop."

Tia's smile seemed genuine. If the thought of breaking his hand could make even her smile it might not be a bad idea. Approaching the dressing room, Tia opened the door for Jessica, and they both walked into the spacious lounge.

"Please tell me you remembered it."

"Of course."

Tia pulled out a pipe, put some leaf in it, and handed it to Jessica. She lit the pipe, and pulled out a flask filled with her favorite, cheap vodka. As rituals went before stressful events it wasn't the most scandalous affair, but she still didn't want reporters seeing. Even if keeping this a secret was only for the benefit of a few voters. That's a few voters she'd rather have than not. As the pleasant buzz of alcohol and leaf hit, she sat in a wooden chair and closed her eyes. *Stay on message. Answer his attacks and pivot back to what I want to talk about. Hammer his hypocrisy.*

After a few minutes, Tia spoke up, "It's time."

She took a final drag on her pipe before blowing the smoke out slowly. "I'm going to destroy him."

***

Jessica sat in her office reading the morning newspaper and reveling in her victory. The stupid man put his foot in his mouth so much she thought he must have liked the taste. After admitting to hiring illegal workers he then promised he'd fire all of them. The boos from the audience seemed to shock him. If his base didn't revere him like a god, he'd be a joke. Nothing but a bunch of animals. This morning's *Egal Gazette,* more propaganda than paper, managed to downplay his blunders, but not enough. According to Tia, the talk of the city right now was how unhinged he sounded.

A knock came from the door.

Who in the hells could that be?

"Come in."

A tall, muscular man in his thirties entered the room. He had the same blue eyes as Jessica and the same blonde hair. The strong chin came from his father, but she couldn't say where he got those big ears. Troy was the youngest head of The Guild of Commerce in history, and also her son. She'd had him installed as a quid pro quo for the mining deregulation which greatly benefited the Guild. Unfortunately, his time as the Guild's president proved only moderately useful to her. He had a hard time playing loose with the rules when she needed him to and tended to lean too heavily on his division leads, preferring to spend his time in pleasure houses instead. Lazy but principled. An odd combination she hadn't expected from someone she gave birth to.

"Good morning, Mother. I do believe congratulations are in order after last night." Troy gave a genuine smile, but his smiles were always genuine. That's one of the things she disliked about him. His earnestness. He also didn't know how to lie properly, and for that reason, she couldn't really trust him.

"Thanks. I appreciate that." She flashed a thin smile. "You didn't come all the way to the senate just to congratulate me I hope?"

The look of disappointment on his face was telling. *Yes, son, believe it or not, these are my working hours and Mommy is busy.* His gaze fell downward and he put his hands in his pockets, another habit he had that Jessica hated.

"One of my division heads, Pulpin Rashee. I saw that he takes regular meetings with you, but when I asked what about he told me it was classified. He said something about national security? I did some digging, and there are funds earmarked to the Guild that I wasn't aware of." He looked up to make eye contact with her. "I'm just wondering what my employee is getting up to is all."

This is going to be a problem.

Jessica stood up from her desk, walked around it, and sat on the edge closest to Troy. "Hey, I'm sorry for not warning you, but I honestly thought it'd be best if you didn't know because Pulpin is right. It's classified and I can't speak with you about it."

Troy set his jaw and looked up at her. "All government funds that go toward a private enterprise are supposed to be record-ed, and as the president of the Guild I'm supposed to sign off. What could be so secret that you'd break the law?"

"Honey, I assure you we've broken no laws. The spending was voted on and set aside specifically for this project. I can't say any more than that, though. As much as I want to." She reached out and grabbed his shoulder, giving it a little squeeze like she used to when he was a child. Because he had a childlike understanding of how the world worked, and because it usually seemed to disarm him.

"So it *is* for a specific project."

Jessica dropped her hand to her side and stood up, frustrated. "Of course it's for a specific project. What? You think we just give money to the Guild for fun?"

"No, of course I don't, but between a good chunk of my Nashowan contacts going dark, the miners threatening to strike, and my head of R&D going behind my back to do a project with my own mother I'm beginning to wonder if there's fire behind all of this smoke."

The fucking miners are threatening to strike? I'll have Clem's balls on a platter.

"I'd heard something was going on in Nashow," she said, feigning sympathy. "I just heard about Coral. That must hurt, but I don't see what it has to do with my project. And what's this about the miners striking?"

Troy gave a lost look. "Probably nothing. I'm sure it's coincidence this is all happening at the same time. On top of it, all our recruitment is down. We're having to hire mercs for almost fifty percent of our trade escorts now."

Aww, poor thing. Are you having to do your job for once?

Jessica tried to give a look of pity that didn't come off condescending even though every impulse she had said to lay into him. "I'm sorry honey but this is the job. This is what you're paid to handle. All I can say is that I'm not at liberty to discuss this project with you. At least not right now." She paused to let that sink in. "But... I *could* see what I can do about the miner's striking. It's a bad look for us if a strike happens during the election."

An extreme understatement. The Miners Union was easily the largest and most reliable voting bloc for Labor in the country. If they broke ranks now, just before an election, it could be disastrous. Jessica's son was the president of The Guild, and a fight between her constituents and her blood is all *The Gazette* would need to start crying corruption. It would make the race too close for comfort. Far too close.

Troy stepped back and put his hands up. "That's not what I meant, and besides, what would that look like to the public? President of the Guild meets with his mommy and she squashes a labor movement? No. It's best if I meet with Clem and the mining companies myself to see what we can work out."

Jessica made her way back around her desk and placed both hands on it, leaning forward. A power position. "I wasn't asking for your permission. This is a political matter for me now, and I'm going to handle it. As far as what it might look like for you? That's another part of your job. You'll need to manage that on your own." She put on a polite smile. "Now, with that news, my schedule for the day has suddenly filled up. Could you please send Tia in when you leave?"

The hurt on Troy's face was plain as he left the room. Gods, his sensitivity could get old. It made him easy to manipulate when he was pining for her approval, but in the last few years, he'd started to gain a backbone. Jessica had never fully grasped what people were talking about when they gushed about the irreplaceable bond between a parent and their child. Troy was her son. She gave birth to him. He grew up. It wasn't some magical, life-altering process. There was a certain amount of affection she had for him, but she had long suspected that could be chalked up to simple familiarity. Like a pair of shoes you'd worn for so long they seemed to become a part of you, but this pair of shoes was starting to wear holes. She continued with her polite smile and gave a wave as he left.

When the door closed behind him, she breathed a sigh of relief. He was starting to get close now. She'd hoped his blind trust would last long enough she could finish her work, but if he kept going down this road something would have to be done. Hopefully, when the time came, he would back down. If he didn't... she set aside the dark thoughts. Better to familiarize herself with the file she had on Clem than go through hypotheticals about what it would take to keep her son in check.

Barely a minute went by before Tia came bursting through the door. "When were you going to tell me your son was coming to visit? Last night went great, but there's no time to celebrate. We have donor meetings this morning, and another speaking event with the—"

"We'll have to clear out my morning. Clem and the Miner's Union are planning a strike."

Tia, bless her heart, took only a moment to process the information. "I'll see if the donors can do some sort of group luncheon this weekend, and I'll get this afternoon's speaking event rescheduled."

"I should be able to make this afternoon work. Clem won't take long." Jessica clenched her fist into a ball and then relaxed it to stretch her fingers. It helped her release some of her frustration. "It'll burn a bridge, but it's not a bridge I was planning to use again anyway."

"Very good." Tia handed Jessica some papers. "This is a rough draft for this afternoon's speech. I'll fetch the carriage and meet you out front in... five minutes?"

Jessica nodded as she flipped through Clem's file. This should be easy.

***

Clem's office was a mess. Papers were strewn across a desk with a pickaxe hanging off the side, other tools lay about in a haphazard manner, and a hard hat sat precariously on top of a cupboard which had a dirty, rusted shovel leaning up against it. A layer of sparkling, crystalline dust covered everything. As Jessica entered, Clem stood from his desk with obviously feigned surprise that shifted far too seamlessly into a warm smile. "If it isn't my favorite candidate for president. I was hoping you'd stop by."

Jessica gave a terse smile. "For being your favored candidate you certainly aren't doing me any favors. I heard you're planning a strike?"

Clem looked scandalized. "I would never intentionally harm your chances. Labor has done a lot for our little union."

Jessica scoffed. "Clem, let's stop with this little dance you've prepared. You're attempting to capitalize on an opportunity here. You're betting that I'll win the presidency handily, and you're pulling this stunt in the hopes it dips my approval just low enough to scare me into caving to whatever it is you want. The truth is that this could swing the vote to Winnow, and we both know how horrible that would be for your little organization. Imagine the legislation that would come out of a Winnow presidency. You're making a risky bet. One you wouldn't make unless there was something valuable you wanted. What is it?"

"I want a promise that you'll reverse the mining deregulation, and I want it made public *before* the election. I've had five deaths in the last two weeks alone. Mining is dangerous work, especially in Brinidor. We understand that, but management is forcing fifteen-hour workdays. They're foregoing safety protocols left and right. We've held out as long as we can, but it's time for the Labor Party, *our* party, to have our backs."

Jessica looked at some dust she'd gotten on her hands from touching the doorknob and wiped it off. "Is that all? You just want me to undo the most important piece of legislation of my career? Do you think I'd be winning right now on union support alone? Tell me you're not that naïve."

"Our people are *dying*."

"People are always dying! Small towns in every country get overtaken by hordes monthly. Garvelle fights off near-constant waves of husk from Gogallo on their eastern border. Husk kill people by the thousands every year, and that number would be even higher if not for the protection granted by the focus crystals *your people* mine. I'm trying to stop thousands of lives from being snuffed out every year, and you're telling me you want to make that number *bigger* because a few miners died."

Clem shook his head. "I'm sorry Jessica. I know people rely on the crystal trade, but we can't keep going on like this."

Jessica gave a rare, genuine smile, this is a part of the job she liked. "Here's what's going to happen. You're going to call off this strike. Then you're going to make a statement of full support for my campaign."

"Excuse me?"

"Then you're going to go back to work, and you're going to thank whatever god you pray to that this meeting didn't go some other way."

"Why would I do any of that?"

"That is an excellent question." Jessica willed a pickaxe into the air and set it to spinning. "Because your union only exists because we let it. Because I can have you replaced within the week. Because the only reason you can sit behind that desk and call yourself president of the Miner's Union is due to your predecessor, Ms. Ballard, refusing to play ball with us."

She saw Clem take a moment to do the mental math. "Are you saying you set her up?"

"Oh me? No. I thought you did. At least that's what I've been led to believe by your vice president and secretary."

"They wouldn't..."

The hiss of air elementalism filled the room and the pickaxe she was spinning came apart. Like a carrot under a chef's knife, the wood of the handle and the iron of the head both cut into countless, even pieces while floating in air.

"You're an elemantalist!" He said, stupidly.

She orbited the pieces around him menacingly. "Clem, I appreciate that you've found a spine since we first met. Seriously, great job on self-improvement there, but your brain needs to catch up. Now, it took time and effort to manage getting rid of your predecessor. Effort I'm not willing to put in this time. If you catch my meaning."

Clem watched the bits of his pickaxe float around him with nervous eyes. Sweat began to drip down his brow. "I think I know what you mean."

"Good." She dropped focus on what was left of Clem's pickaxe, the pieces clattered to the floor. "I'm going to be crystal clear here. Because you apparently need this spelled out. I. Will. Kill. You. Unless. You. Do. As. I. Say. And I won't pay someone to do it. I'll cut you to ribbons myself if you get in my way again."

"I understand. I'll call it off today."

Clem's eyes watered and his face turned red. Whether from anger or fear she didn't care. Jessica turned to leave the room. Just as she opened the door she turned around. "Oh, and Clem?"

He trembled.

Fear then. Good.

"Yes, Senator Saunders?"

"Thank you for your support."

She slammed the door behind her as she left.

Seffin

The foyer of the Rashee home in the afternoon glowed brilliantly with sunlight cascading through eastern windows and reflecting off marble floors. In the evening however, without the light brightening it, the room took on an oppressive, lonely feeling. Isolating in its spacious, dim sterility. Back home after his practice session with Ren, Seffin closed the door behind him and hung both his pack and his red jacket in the closet next to the entrance. He stood there for a moment and let out a contented breath. He had an affinity for the space in the late afternoon, the emptiness calmed him. It expected nothing of him.

Down a darkened hallway, light spilled from the open kitchen door. His mother, Carula, must be eating already. She usually waited for his father, but lately, his work kept him well into the night. Practically starving after all the exertion of the day's practice session with Ren, he reluctantly made for the kitchen, already frustrated at the conversation his mother would inflict upon him.

Carula sat on a stool pushed up against the wooden island munching on a salad with a steaming piece of meat pie resting next to her while she read over a file from work. He could tell she was unhappy. Her brow furrowed as her eyes scanned the page and, setting down her fork after a bite of her greens, she pinched the bridge of her nose and squinted.

Guild jobs varied widely, but Seffin knew for quite some time now the position his mother kept at the Guild never satisfied her. When she was younger, she worked as a Guild mystic traveling around to aid in charging pylons and keeping the routes clear. She sounded like an entirely different woman in her youth. She would go on about how they had the best tea in Nakonipol to the east, the amazing fried fish from Lanneshire in Northern Nashow, and how the people of Lighton far to the west were friendly but preferred to keep to themselves. He could tell when she spoke, by the tone and tenor of her voice, that she missed the freedom she used to have. A freedom she hadn't had since he was born.

On the other hand, his father had barely ever left Prolivgrad. Dedicated to his work and obsessed with his legacy, Pulpin did nothing except talk about his projects. One of which happened to be ensuring Seffin joined a division at The Guild. A job Seffin had finally decided, as of today, he wouldn't take. Which meant an uncomfortable and consequential conversation in the very near future.

Carula looked up from reading and her face lit up as Seffin entered the kitchen. She opened her arms wide as a request for a hug. He humored her, allowing the embrace which always seemed to last a little too long. She released him with reluctance as he pulled away. Something about her affection seemed off-putting of late, desperate and clingy, or maybe she'd always been this way and he only recently noticed it. The possibility went through his mind that his reticence to apply for the Guild made him feel differently about his family. Maybe it was him, not her.

"How was practice?" She asked.

He went for the meat pie on the counter. Kent, their butler, knew it was his favorite meal, and said he'd make it tonight for Seffin to have something to look forward to after practice. Grabbing a slice, he nabbed a scoop of seasoned, mashed peas as well. "Good..." He thought about Ren's excited expression when he'd done his icicle trick, the wide, toothy smile he had on his face the rest of the session, and how his brown eyes always seemed bright when something caught his attention, especially set next to the dark of his skin, and how those eyes lingered on him after he took his shirt off. It made his mouth dry out to think about it. A feeling of excitement so jarring he almost mistook it for fear. "Fun actually. The final will be ambitious, but I think it'll turn out well."

"I'm sure your father will be glad to hear that."

He ignored the comment and took a bite of his peas instead. The buttery garlic and pepper flavor almost hurt at how rich it tasted after spending all day with nothing in his belly but water and a piece of toast.

"I hate to be a nag, but have you, perchance, decided on which division you want to apply for?"

This one he couldn't ignore. He swallowed his peas. "I'm focused on my final right now."

The pressure they were putting on needled at him. He did as he was told his whole life. They wanted him at Danvers Academy, so he went. His mother wanted him at the Church of Kohru's mass with her every week, so he went. Pulpin gave him a dog when he was younger to teach him responsibility and socialization, and despite never wanting one, he dutifully cared for it until it passed away three months ago. Hopefully, the poor thing couldn't sense how much Seffin thought of him as a burden, but it's not like he could do anything about it now. Regardless, he felt at peace with it all, genuinely. Making his parents proud was important to them, and life was better, or at least easier, when his parents were happy. The decision to join the Guild or not, though, rested with him and him alone, and he wouldn't be browbeaten into joining solely because it's what his parents wanted.

"I know your father would love to have you in research and development with him."

She'd said this same statement in the same voice using the exact same words so many times in the last few months. The desire to ask her if she was happy with the job his father chose for her tickled at the back of his mind, but he stopped short of asking it. Ever since he decided to make this decision his own, he found himself censoring his statements more... well, censoring his statements at all really. Before this, he never worried what he said or how it was perceived. Even big things, like when his father got him a dog, he told him right away that he didn't want one, but his father insisted so he complied. He could tell a majority of people tended to watch what they say most of the time, at least a little bit. How though? How do people walk around all day never actually saying what they mean? What little effort he had started putting into it already tired him.

Hiding behind vague statements had been working so far, at least with his mother, so he gave it another shot. "I just want to make sure I choose what's right for me."

He shoveled a bite of meat pie into his mouth and hoped she would drop the subject. Physically exhausted from practicing with Ren, he didn't want to add mental exhaustion on top of it.

"No matter what division you choose we'll be proud of you. Pulpin may not like it, but he'll get over it. Will you be joining me for service tomorrow?"

"Yes," he said simply. The nice thing about services at the Church of Kohru was that he didn't have to do anything to make his mother happy. He could just sit and think about something else. Not a lot of people attended Kohru services either, which he enjoyed. Outside of atheism, Svoboda was the most popular god in Egal. A religion that valued freedom and self-interest above everything else and a perfect match for a city with the same values. Svobodan services always looked packed with people spilling out their church doors. It seemed contradictory that a faith dedicated to freedom held services on a regular schedule, but who was he to judge other people's religion when he allowed his mother to drag him to services he couldn't care less about?

Carula went back to reading her forms. She probably sensed he didn't want to talk. He finished his slice of meat pie and excused himself. Using the back staircase he plodded to his room, the soreness of the day's exercise and the empty feeling in his chest from using so much will made climbing the stairs feel far more like exercise than usual. His will reserves would recover within the next couple hours, but the soreness would only get worse. Adding a workout routine before prepping for his final might have been prudent. The hallway leading to his room contained his father's study and the second-floor service closet. Creaky wooden floors, red-painted walls, and pictures of Rashee ancestors escorted him to his doorway.

He pushed into his room and stripped off his clothes before putting on some green linen pants and a blue, loose cotton shirt. A book on his desk titled *Variant Methods of Control* sat closed with a bookmark sticking out. Grabbing it, he flopped onto his bed and started reading. The techniques he'd gleaned from the book were effective. Visualizing his influence on the pieces it took for elementalism rather than just grasping and sorting through all the particles had helped, but committing the shape, weight, and speed of the pieces he needed to memory is what made all the difference.

There was a knock at his door. Seffin rolled out of bed with difficulty. Fatigue from practice this afternoon was starting to set in. He opened the door to exactly who he thought it would be, his mother. "Hello?"

She scratched at her palms and fidgeted like she did when she was nervous about something. "I know I already said so, but I just really want you to know we'll love you no matter what. We just want what's best for you."

There was a time a few years back when Seffin would have heard this and felt relief. Relief that she would accept him and that she wanted to comfort him. That time had passed, though, and he knew better now. She wasn't trying to make him feel better. She was trying to make *her* feel better. Seffin forced a smile onto his face. "Thanks, Mom."

That seemed to work.

"Well, good night. Your father said he wanted to talk to you in the morning."

Seffin let out a rare sigh. "I don't need to ask what about, do I?"

Carula began fidgeting again. "No," she said with apprehension. "I imagine you know exactly what it's going to be about. Just... he's got this project he's working on that has been stressing him out. He thinks... he knows you're brilliant. He wants his son working with him."

And that was it. He suddenly knew exactly what he was going to do. Seffin wondered if his mother knew what she was doing, how she accelerated everything with such a short conversation. He liked to think she was smarter than she let on, so he chose to believe she knew how thin the ice was that they stood upon. It didn't help her case.

Seffin felt his smile straining. This whole business of lying and hiding behind vague statements was starting to take its toll. "I'll sleep on it," he said.

***

Seffin allowed himself to sleep in a little after all the hours of exercise he put in yesterday. His muscles protested when he sat up. Their soreness had crescendoed overnight, but he had laid in bed too long already. Time to get up, grab some food, and head out for more practice. As if in protest to this thought, his calf started cramping, and as he scrambled to stretch and release the tension, he could hear footsteps approaching down the hall. The footsteps stopped at his door and were followed by two rapid knocks. Which meant it was Kent, their butler.

"Come in," Seffin said, still stretching out his calf.

Kent opened the door. Tall and with arms that looked like they belonged on a gorilla, his presence in a room was always felt whether he intended it or not. "Is there something wrong with your leg there, Sef?"

"Just a cramp." Seffin sucked his teeth. "Doesn't seem to be letting up."

Kent walked over to the bed. "May I?"

Seffin nodded. He sat on the side of the bed and took Seffin's calf into his hands, massaging the contracted muscle. It hurt at first, but as he pushed his thumbs along the calf and directly into the muscle it began to release. He collapsed backward in relief while Kent continued to massage out the tension. He'd been the Rashee family butler for as long as Seffin could remember, and a pillar of support for him as he grew up, filling the considerable gaps his parents left. Only Kent ever asked how Seffin actually felt. Only Kent ever truly listened, and his attention never came with expectations. He was the first to know Seffin's will reserves expanded to the size they are now, and the first to know he had problems controlling said will reserves. Seffin already relied on the man far more than was probably appropriate, which made this next question difficult to ask.

Kent set his leg down. "You haven't been stretching like I taught you."

Seffin didn't hear him, too busy worrying what the day would bring. "Can I ask you a favor?"

"Sure."

"I think I'm going to get kicked out today. Can I stay at your place?" And then he quickly added, "Feel free to say no."

Kent gave an indiscernible look. "I'm..." he started, "I'm not... Why is it you think you'll get kicked out?"

"I'm telling my parents that I'm not joining The Guild."

Kent's mouth dropped open in surprise. He closed it before saying, "Oh. Yeah. That'll do it."

Seffin reached out and grabbed Kent's hand, a kitten wrapping its paws around a lion's. "Please, I know it's a lot, but you're the only person I can ask. I just need to graduate, get a couple of jobs done at the Lodge, and I'll be out of your hair."

"Coruscare burn me! You're going to be a merc? Buddy, you'll be more than kicked out. You're going to get disowned."

Pulpin hated mercenaries, for what reason Seffin never found out. He simply made a disgusted face every time they were mentioned. Kent looked down at Seffin's hands wrapped around his own with puzzlement. Seffin pulled back and took a shaky breath. Frowning, Kent set an enormous hand on his head and tousled his hair before chuckling and standing up. He walked over to the wardrobe and started pulling out Seffin's clothing.

"What are you doing?"

"Well, if we're gonna be roommates you'll need your clothes. When are you gonna tell your parents?"

Seffin leapt out of bed with tears in his eyes and gave the big man a hug. Kent grinned down at him. "Did you know you're leaking?"

He backed away. "You're making fun of me."

"I am." Kent smiled. "Get used to it. I'm gonna be your roommate now, not your servant."

***

The final three members of the Rashee clan—the Sol War took the rest of them—sat at the breakfast table enjoying eggs, toast, and sausage served by Missy, one of the maids. A woman of very few words who swept in and out of rooms so fast you could hardly tell she was there. Pulpin sat reading the paper while Carula read her *Book of Kohru* like she always did before Sunday service. Seffin entered the brightly lit dining room and sat in his usual spot, opposite his mother and adjacent to his father, before digging into a few links of sausage and a fried egg.

Pulpin wasted no time in setting his paper down. "Say, Dunreedy got a hold of me the other day, and I've been meaning to talk to you about—"

"Yes, the divisions. I heard. I told him I hadn't decided yet."

Clearly unhappy with the interruption, a stern expression flashed across Pulpin's face. "That's ok. I've already drawn up an application for research and development for you."

Seffin's mother, who had been happily enjoying her breakfast and readings, set down her *Book of Kohru*. "Honey, don't you think you're overstepping a little."

Seffin swallowed what he expected to be the last link of sausage he would ever eat under this roof. "It's ok." He turned to look directly at his father. "Can I ask what you plan to do with an application I haven't signed?"

"I was planning on having you sign it today. I need your help on one of my projects."

"What was your plan if I refused?"

Sternness shifted quickly to anger before his brow softened and his jaw relaxed back into his typical dispassionate, stoic demeanor. Pulpin cleared his throat like he did when he was about to make a demand. "I'm delivering an application to one of the divisions tomorrow whether you like it or not. All your classmates have already applied and accepted offers from the divisions they wanted."

Seffin met his father's eyes with a blank expression. "I'm not signing anything. It's my decision—"

"You will do as you are told." He didn't recognize the voice that came out of his father. More of a growl than a yell.

Silence overtook the room as both his mother and father waited in anticipation of his response. Considering his words and the consequences they would have one final time, he started. "I'm not joining The Guild—"

"Excuse me—"

"Let me speak!" Seffin yelled. It was the first time he'd ever yelled at his parents, and probably the last. "I'm *not* joining the Guild. I hate the Guild, and I hate that you think you can dictate what I do with my life."

His mother and father both looked stunned. Seffin had always echoed his father's dispassionate way of carrying himself like the good little puppet they groomed him to be.

He continued, "I don't care what threat you have prepared. Kick me out, cut me off, remove me from my inheritance. I've done what you say when you say it my whole life. I attended the school you wanted. I go to mass when you ask. I've gotten the grades you asked me to get. I dress in our family's colors because you demand it. I took care of that dog because you thought me too unsociable." Seffin's voice started to break into anger. "And what does a dog have to do with socializing anyway? Don't you think a dog would have a better life with someone who wanted it over someone burdened with it? What a stupid, cruel thing to do. You've never even asked me if I have any hobbies. You don't even know if I have a friend. All you care about are my grades, how my wielding is going, and what division I'll be applying to. The Rashee legacy."

Carula pleaded, "Please reconsider—"

"—And I've never complained." He bowled over her. It was his turn to say his piece and he wouldn't be deterred. "It doesn't bother me to make you two happy, but I can't live my life based on that. So, no. I don't care about your legacy. I don't care about my last name. My skills are mine to use how I like. The decision of what I do with my life is mine. You won't be making it for me."

Pulpin's skin was a dark tan, same as his son, but his face looked redder than red right now and the veins in his neck wanted to pop out of his body. "Pack your things and go, you little ingrate."

An expected reaction. Seffin only nodded before walking out of the room, but halfway to the foyer, he could hear his mother's church heels clicking after him.

"Please, everything we've worked for, and you're just going to throw it away? What do you have against the Guild anyway?"

"What do I have against the Guild? The Guild holds more power than most countries, and they use that power to play god to decide which towns survive. Why do they get to decide which settlements live and die? Why would I want to help an organization that ruins that many people's lives?"

She stood there, brow furrowed, eyes wide, mouth partly open with a disbelieving smile working its way into the corners of her lips, a look of betrayal. "What did I do to—"

"Yes, what *did* you do, Mom?" Seffin pointed behind her, back toward the dining room. "You let that man walk all over you, you let him force you into a job you hate, and then when you saw him doing the same to me you supported it." Seffin put his hands on his hips and looked up to the ceiling. A frustration so intense he couldn't contain it. "You know, for the longest time I thought there was something wrong with me? Do you have any idea how much I felt like a failure because I couldn't get my control to match my will reserves? And all Dad could say is that a real Rashee wouldn't have problems with control. A real Rashee wouldn't make excuses." He lowered his head and looked her in the eyes. "Well, I'm done being a Rashee."

Seffin walked the final few steps to the foyer where his luggage lay waiting for him, the morning light reflected off the marble floor and flooded the room, giving everything a glow.

He picked up his two suitcases and donned his pack before turning to his mother, still standing there, aghast at what was happening.

"Goodbye. May Kohru's light allow you to process this change with the grace and understanding you never gave me."

Flicker

With Washburne on an indefinite, unplanned family trip, Dale became overwhelmed. It was lucky, then, that the senator had left such perfect instructions for what to do in his absence. With Washburne out of the way, Flicker spent that evening and the following weekend forging a great many documents and instructions for what to do during his sudden hiatus. A bit odd when Dale didn't question any of this, but he *had* said Washburne cared for nothing in his subordinates besides loyalty. So maybe this was just that; the yes-man fulfilling his role of blind obedience. Either way, it was useful to her for the senator's office to have the appearance of functioning normally.

Sitting down and reviewing the notes at her small desk in her windowless room, she began to realize her next target, Cara, could prove difficult to isolate. The back-and-forth communication between her and Washburne indicated she worked at the Guild, used to be an envoy, and now worked as a liaison for... someone.

Flicker scouted out the office Cara's letter came from, but the place was a fortress. High gates, guards posted at the front, and only two avenues of ingress, the front door and a strange, large service entrance in the back that led into a basement which piqued her interest. There are few things on Kohru she could think of large enough to require that. Some large beasts, like a werewiller or an elephant maybe, but bringing a werewiller into the city would be disastrous, the giant, furry creatures walked on two legs, had huge claws, and she knew firsthand how dangerous they were when cornered. Plenty of amalgamations were large enough to require a door that big, but, within the barrier, an amalgamation didn't seem like a possibility.

Flicker had pondered over how to get in for a few days now, and the simplest solution still seemed like the best: delivering a return letter from Washburne's office, personally. That wouldn't do anything about the guards though, and she couldn't isolate Cara for questioning if things got loud. Still, she'd be able to locate her office and do some reconnaissance, maybe find out what that huge door was for. She set her course and drew up a response to Cara's last letter.

***

Other than a sign clearly stating the building belonged to the Guild, it had no label or posting indicating its purpose. It was simply a large, stone building in the middle of a commercial district only ten minute's walk from Danvers Academy, with a stone wall surrounding it. When Flicker came here earlier the only thing she thought strange, besides the massive door in the back, was the number of guards posted out front. Three. She'd surveyed plenty of Guild buildings before, and almost all had one guard at most. After all, the Guild should appear like any normal organization. What would be the reason to have three armed guards posted at the entrance? Something important, surely.

The Guild's guards were usually martial combatants. Either retired mercenaries or wielders strong enough to fight but too weak to go through formal mystic training. They wore standard mail armor with swords on their hips. The one in the front seemed smaller than the others. She imagined if any of them could wield well enough to be lethal it would be the less physically imposing of the three. She approached him. "I have a letter to deliver to Cara Soledar personally from the office of Senator Washburne." She held the letter out for inspection.

As he moved to look at it, she noticed his sword wasn't just any other weapon. It was a will-blade. A rare weapon to see. *Best to avoid this one if things go wrong.*

"Washburne sent a courier?"

"Y-Yes." Flicker intentionally fidgeted and acted nervous to appear meek. "Washburne is on vacation, and he told me to..."

He shook his head. "It's not a problem. Her office is second floor, south side. Have you ever been here before?"

"No"

"Rules are you can go on the first and second floors. If you're caught anywhere else…" He gripped the handle of his blade. "Well, just don't get caught anywhere else."

Flicker nodded, the guards parted, and she passed through. Entering the building, there was no indication of the basement she knew it had, only a stairway going up to the second floor. No secretary and no desk, simply a hallway going either right or left with clearly labeled doors on either side, but nothing that went deeper into the building. Which meant the offices on the north side were either exceptionally large, or they hid something. Flicker made her way to Cara's office on the second floor and knocked. A man with a weak chin and sunken eyes answered the door.

"Ms. Soledar's office, can I help you?"

"I'm here to deliver a letter from Senator Washburne. I'm supposed to hand it to Cara, personally."

He looked her over and then nodded. "I'll fetch her."

Flicker surveyed the hallway as she waited. A guard patrolling turned down the stairs. *So many of you here.* She needed to get into the north side of the building somehow, but with no idea what to expect she'd have to be careful about it.

The door opened and a slight woman with blonde hair and piercing green eyes wearing a wool sweater appeared. Immediately, Flicker knew she was in danger. For starters, Cara hesitated a moment before fully opening the door, and almost imperceptibly, her eyes darted at both of Flickers' hands, a habit assassins like Flicker had to start assessing a potential threat. *What's an eye doing here?* The worst-case scenario was for Cara to notice that she saw the tells of her assassin training. Flicker gave as bored an expression as she could muster to mask her realization.

"Washburne sent you?" Cara asked.

With hairs on end, she waived the letter casually, still trying to project as much nonchalance as she could. "Are you Cara Soledar?"

Cara snatched the letter and opened it. If she truly was an eye—an assassin from the Eyes of Koth—she'd notice even the smallest errors in the forged letter. *Stupid, stupid, stupid. I let my excitement get in the way of taking precautions.* Cara scanned the letter in front of her. Attacking first might cause an unnecessary fight, but letting Cara get the drop on her made for an even worse outcome.

Time to make a choice, or at least it would have been had Cara not chosen for her. Flicker barely dodged the ice lance that came bursting through the doorway she stood in. *Wielding without using her hands to focus? Impressive.* With the element of surprise safely lost, Flicker brought her will to bear and slammed a fist into Cara's chest, but it was like hitting rock. Her hand ached with pain as Cara stumbled backward into the office, gasping for breath she still managed to ask. "Why the fuck is an unregistered assassin here?"

Why the fuck is an eye stationed here like some common guard?

Flicker rushed into the room to take stock of the situation. Her target was an elementalist, clearly trained as an eye, and wore something protective under her sweater. The room was a simple office, and the man with sunken eyes hid in the corner. Noise from the fight would draw in the guard from the hallway, and soon the guards from the front would be here as well.

This couldn't possibly have gone worse.

She needed to neutralize Cara first. In a flash, her whole world turned to fire. Flicker got her hand up to divert the flame with her will fast enough to prevent permanent damage, but Cara's palm was out, and fire rushed forth like water bursting out a broken dam. She couldn't keep this up for long, her will reserves were far below mystic level.

The whole room started to catch flame. Flicker dodged around her, but Cara followed with her violent stream of fire. Caught up in the wave of flames, her officemate began to scream as his whole body became engulfed. Flicker retreated out of the room. From the corner of her eye, she saw the hallway guard rushing for her. Grabbing the ice lance Cara had thrown at her with her will, she launched it at the guard but didn't have time to make sure it connected before ducking out of the way of several more lances hurtling out of Cara's office. *Enough of this.* Flicker centered herself, her world blurred as if behind frosted glass, and she was suddenly behind Cara. Bringing her elbow up and putting as much will and strength behind it as she could, she brought it down on her neck. A snapping sound pierced the air as her neck broke. She crumpled to the ground with a thud. Screaming continued from inside the inferno as Cara's poor officemate burned alive.

After grabbing as many documents from Cara's desk as she could, Flicker bolted from the room. A glance down the hallway confirmed she had indeed downed the patrol from earlier, but the one from the front door with the will-blade stood over him, scanning for the culprit. Catching sight of her, he began running in her direction. With no way out besides the doors on the opposite side of the hall, Flicker slammed through the closest one into the north side of the building.

Upon entering, she had multiple realizations. The first was the lack of a barrier. She'd studied enough engineering to feel the ambient hum that barriers projected, but either someone figured out how to make a dead space or the barrier for the entire city of Prolivgrad conveniently went down just as she passed through the doorway. Knowing the latter was far less likely, she assumed the former. Next, there were no offices. The northern side was all one large lab filled with cages upon cages of husk and animals, mostly colossi. *Of course.* Her final realization came from the layout of the room which offered no escape from line of sight. Whoever followed her in here would find her instantly. She needed an exit, but the large door was on the back side of the building on the basement floor. A stairwell caught her eye, and she sprinted toward it.

While she made her way, she saw nightmares. Husk in the middle of combining into amalgamations. Amalgamations absorbing different animals; gorillas, horses, and werewillers. A young laranee lay dying in one of the cages with an amalgamation slowly enveloping the cub. *Koth's asshole, what kind of monsters would do this?* The husk made the building smell like a fetid swamp. While she sprinted by the laranee pen, one of the guards caught up to her. He came swinging from her left. She dodged low, but his boot was already on its way to her head. *Smart.* Flicker caught his foot with one hand and snapped his shin with the other. He yelped and fell, his sword clattering to the ground. With barely a thought, she snatched the blade up, plunged it through his neck, and left it there as she rushed away. She made it to the descending stairway and leapt down, taking five steps at a time.

Grotesqueries awaited her on the basement level. Massive, rotted creatures with extra limbs and eyes rattled against their cages when she entered the room. An amalgamation of a gorilla with four huge, muscular arms screamed and pounded at its confinement. In one cage sat a mound of rotting flesh with waves of fire and ice emanating off it. In yet another cage a fully grown, amalgamated laranee—a tawny cat the size of a rhinoceros—moved in what seemed like bursts of extreme speed. Just like flickering. Its cage seemed to be made of some special type of metal. *What could possibly be the point of all of this?* She heard the second guard coming around the corner, but she broke his skull against the laranee cage before he even realized he'd caught up with her. The cat hissed at the sudden sound.

It's time to go.

From where Flicker stood, the exit should have been just to the east of her, but as she turned to head that direction she came face-to-face with the last guard. The one with the will-blade.

"I'm going to be very disappointed if we fight and you don't actually know how to use that thing." She goaded him and it worked. He ran straight for her. The willed edges on his blade kept extending and retracting which meant he had poor control; he couldn't rely on them. He would have to swing with the intent to hit her with the metal blade itself. *Not a master, then.* She could play this defensively, and if she waited long enough, she'd get her opening.

She hadn't expected him to be so stupid as to throw the blade with his will.

A will-blade's edges are limited only by the amount of will placed in the blade against the amount of control of the wielder. A thrown blade held by will could lose control easily with the wielder trying to split their focus between controlling the blade itself and controlling the edges. A thrown blade would turn into a massive, uncontrolled cutting edge if the wielder couldn't keep the edges contracted. In some battles that could be useful, but in a building filled with experimental monsters inside cages, the wisdom of using this technique seemed... questionable. Flicker knew she had to be on either side of the blade's cutting edge or risk being split in half. She dodged behind the laranee cage just as the blade activated. A cacophony of screams and growls came from all the husk he'd clipped with his attack, but the most alarming sound came from the metal door on the laranee cage clattering to the ground.

Laranee were cats as tall as a full grown man and native to the Nari'ko Wilds with long, black-tipped tales and fangs that jutted downward out of their mouths. Flicker had seen one once, but it had already been killed. Taken down by some hunters she met on the road. They lost three of their group of fifteen, and that was considered a successful hunt. It would be suicide to fight one that moved in the way this one did, or at least not a fight she wanted to have. She stood perfectly still. Every hair on her body stood on end. She held her breath and tried her best not to provoke its attention. The guard started to use his will to recall his blade. Its scrapes across the ground echoed around the room.

Did he not notice the cage?

The laranee took a step out of its confines and turned in the direction of the guard. He froze. Rotted, and with pieces of flesh sloughing off, it stalked toward him. Quietly, Flicker rose to her feet and began to creep closer to the exit. The guard, still frozen, caught sight of her as the laranee closed in on him. Was he hoping it would become bored? He made eye contact with her and gave a helpless look as the beast went in for a sniff, and then the top half of his body wasn't there. The lower half fell to the ground and made a wet, thudding sound. The laranee's flickering had liquified the guard's upper half.

Flicker continued to creep toward the exit, hoping the creature wouldn't notice her. Upon reaching the door, she noticed the track it was on; it would have to be lifted. No matter what she did, the noise of the door would alert the laranee. A commotion from above meant more guards had come to investigate. With no time to find another way out she grabbed the handle and threw the door up. A deep, angry yowl came echoing behind her, but she sprinted from the building with as much speed as she could. Stealing a glance, she saw the cat bounding toward her. Using a bit of will, she leapt the stone wall that encircled the building and landed, pumping her legs as hard as she could down the street.

As she ran, the sounds of death and destruction echoed behind her. It was loose in the city.

Ren

Poppy sifted through a mess of people just ahead of Ren. They'd brought him to the Lodge—the base of operations for mercs—to introduce him to Jacinda Khan and Cal Severin, the merc board manager and head of the bounty office, respectively. Prolivgrad's Lodge was a massive building by anyone's standards. The giant wooden structure stood out in the city's sea of brick and clay. Its wooden support pillars towered up to the roof, and from the entrance, Ren could see into the second of four levels where people swarmed to pick up contracts off a merc board. Next to the entrance on the first floor was Mallory's, a full pub set up inside the Lodge where throngs of people, mostly mercs, pushed in and out. Everywhere he looked, people were moving past each other in a rush. Four floors of the nation's finest warriors and wielders all choosing their next job, networking with other mercs and mercenary bands, or for some, finally taking a needed break.

Poppy needed to stop at Mallory's, but every other merc they passed wanted to bend their ear about Lodge business, any new inventions they'd created, or politics. Everyone here seemed to be voting Labor. Unsurprising, considering how many mercs chose this profession specifically to get out from under the thumb of the Guild. Everyone *knew* the Guild was in bed with the Nationals despite the Guild president himself being the son of the Labor candidate. As they spoke, everyone seemed to weigh Poppy's words heavily. It was a weird feeling knowing the person who raised him was one of the most influential people currently living. Ren ate dinner every night with the hero that helped end The Sol War and created the Lodge system, he'd been grounded and had a screaming match with them too. Odd to think a person with so many accomplishments still managed to have such a mundane life.

After wading through the sea of people, they made it to Mallory's and sat down next to the reason they came, Sent'o. Poppy's client and old friend sat drinking some wine and people-watching while he waited. Sent'o had a youthful appearance with long brown hair, blue eyes, and fair skin. He was almost as tall as Poppy and dressed in animal hides, wore a crown of twigs, and looked different than anyone else Ren had ever met. He'd been introduced to Sent'o before, briefly, though he went by a different name then. Whenever Ren met someone who underwent the change it always surprised him both how much and how little the difference was. For the most part, Sent'o was just how he remembered him, uncomfortably friendly and staggeringly attractive, but also different, more at ease than he used to be.

When he spoke, his voice sounded calm and soothing, "Aye Tender, thanks for meeting me before I left the city."

Poppy smiled and went in for a hug that Ren thought seemed to last a little too long. *You old dog.*

"And Ren, you're bigger than last I saw."

Ren went to shake hands, but Sent'o pulled him into an embrace. The level of intimacy seemed inappropriate, but he didn't want to offend by pulling away. His heart beat faster and faster the longer it went on. "It's good to see you," he said with his face pressed against Sent'o's chest.

Sent'o leaned down and kissed him on the forehead. "May the will of the world guide the will of your body into the Sea of Intention gracefully."

Ren felt his face get hot and his mouth began to dry out. "Y-you, too," he stammered. Sent'o squeezed his shoulder before releasing him.

Poppy held Sent'o's hand as they spoke, "It'll be months before we can start the contract, we're still missing a piece of the puzzle, and anyway, I have my hands full dealing with some more thorny goings-on here in Prolivgrad for now. Are you sure you can't give me more details?"

"Shaia knew you would be held up and planned for the delay. I only needed to give you this." Sent'o slid a crystal over to Poppy. It had the appearance of a focus crystal, but with a black hue instead of the normal semi-translucent, milky appearance that most others had.

"What is it?"

"I wish I knew. It came all the way from Karm, which is strange enough on its own, but Karm's council was tightlipped both on how it was procured and what its purpose is. They walked it directly from another ship over to mine and bid me take my leave immediately. I tried putting will into it like a focus crystal, but nothing happens. It's just a bottomless pit." Sent'o shrugged and took a sip of his wine. "Caretaker Shaia said to protect it with your life, and that it wasn't going to be an easy task."

"That's a delivery. What's supposed to be so difficult about that?" Ren asked.

When Sent'o turned to speak to him, Ren's heart beat faster again. "Egal is so caught up with this election, it's no surprise you haven't heard. A horde of husk has amassed outside of Nari'ko. It's the largest in memory with the notable exception of the hordes outside the Gogallo border."

"Gods," said Ren.

Sent'o smiled. "Not to worry. We are quite skilled at keeping them at bay but getting to Nari'ko will be difficult for now. Braving the husk horde or taking a ship through Kelsig are the only ways, and, at least for now, Kelsig will not offer passage to anyone other than Nari'ko Wilders. I imagine that's why Shaia wanted Tender, the Hammer of Garvelle, to handle it, but I cannot say for certain. It is not for me to question the motivations of The Caretaker."

Shaia Tekk, The Caretaker, was the leader of the Nari'ko Wilds. They were supposed to be the Vessel for Kohru, the goddess the world was named after, and were said to have a direct line of communication with her. Ren didn't know if he believed that, but whomever they were they had an interesting title for Poppy. "The Hammer of Garvelle? I hadn't heard that one."

Poppy rolled their eyes as if it were a childhood nickname they were embarrassed of. "Kelsig is a dead end, but I've got a plan for the horde. Are you sure Shaia is ok waiting?"

Sent'o touched Poppy's cheek. "You know the importance of what is asked. The Caretaker trusts you."

Poppy took Sent'o's hand away from their cheek and kissed it. "I'll see to it that trust isn't misplaced. Are you planning to be in Prolivgrad long?"

"I'm leaving for Nashow in the morning, and then off to Estaba."

"Very well. I'm afraid we can't linger. I'm introducing Ren to Jacinda and Cal." Poppy stood from their chair. "May the will of the world guide your own."

"Just so."

Leaving Sent'o to his people watching, Poppy and Ren made their way up to the second level of the Lodge where Jacinda's office sat next to the merc boards. Safely away from earshot of Sent'o, Ren said, "So, he was even *friendlier* than last time."

Poppy chuckled. "Nari'ko Wilders are a very..." They paused like they were trying to think of the right word, and said, "... intimate culture. I lived in Nari'ko for years. It was probably the most peaceful time of my life. Especially after Garvelle."

"When you say intimate..."

"I mean just that. They value close connection. Even with people they've just met."

Ren squinted at them in accusation

"... and yes, that means physically intimate as well. They view their people as one large unit. They don't have too many bonded pairs. Almost everything is communal there other than people's homes."

"They're horny. Got it."

Poppy made a frown, clearly uncomfortable. "It's more than that. They view sex differently, and uhh—oh hey look, it's Jacinda's office. We can talk about this some other time."

Poppy banged on Jacinda's door. A woman with a stocky, muscular build and tan skin answered it. On her back was a great sword, and judging by the size of her arms, she knew exactly how to use it.

"Tender! You piece of shit how are ya?"

"Not too bad. Say, I don't suppose your better half is in there with you? We have to speak to him too."

"He is indeed. Though I may have to fight you on the part about him being my better half."

A voice came from inside the office, "No, Tender is just as right about that as they are about most things. What can we do ya for?"

Poppy gave Ren a pat on the shoulder, "This one will be looking for work. I wanted to give him the official introduction and help him pick out a few starting contracts."

A man with beige skin and a mess of white hair on his head, Ren presumed this was Cal, peaked his head through the door. "Oh? Fresh meat?" Cal waved some papers in their direction. "We did just get an escort contract from the Guild that seemed like it wouldn't be so bad."

Poppy frowned, but there was something more to the expression that Ren couldn't put his finger on. "Those ones always seem easier than they end up."

Ren grabbed the contract and looked through it. An escort for an envoy to Oleksandra's Harbor that paid—he read the payout one more time to make sure. It paid extraordinarily well. "I'm not a huge fan of my first contract being with the Guild, but if it pays this much and gets me out of the city I'm not going to complain."

Jacinda snatched the contract out of Ren's hands. "With a payout like this it'll get claimed the second it's posted. On that note, maybe don't tell anyone we gave this to you before it hit the merc board."

Poppy's frown softened. "As a member of the board of administration, I'll pretend I didn't hear that. How many mercs is it requesting?"

Jacinda flipped to the front of the contract and pointed at the top of the page. "Two fives are the minimum, but you're a special and Ka just made five so Ren here will just be gravy."

They scratched at their chin and looked down at the floor before grunting a begrudging affirmation. "I guess I'm fine with it if Ren is."

Jacinda, Cal, and Poppy all looked to Ren. Smiling, he asked, "How much was the payout again?"

***

After spending his morning at the Lodge, Ren rushed across town to Danvers Academy for practice. He climbed the front steps two at a time hoping Seffin hadn't waited long. Surprisingly, the practice room sat empty when he walked in. Sticky with sweat after running across town, he popped his shirt off to change into a fresh one for practice when the door opened and Seffin walked through, similarly drenched.

"You running late too?" Seffin said, dropping his pack on the floor next to the door. Ren nodded at him. A strange feeling set in while he stood there in silence with Seffin's eyes on him, scanning. Ren couldn't figure out if it was just Seffin's usual intense stare or something more. No. His eyes moved up and down his body and lingered in spots. Suddenly feeling more exposed than he liked, Ren scrambled to get his shirt on. When he pulled it over his head, he noticed Seffin's face had flushed, and he averted his gaze. Now he felt bad. A moment passed where he thought about taking his shirt off again, but no... that would be stupid. Too strong a signal at this point in their relationship, and too weird besides. *Relationship? What relationship? Gods, what am I thinking?* Ren's finger started itching and his face went hot. He'd thought about Seffin often since they started their project, but every time he did some reflex told him to stop, like a red-hot coal warning him off from touching it.

Focus, Ren.

He picked up his will-blade and started some exercises extending and retracting the edges while Seffin started changing into a dry shirt. *Were Seffin's arms always that big?* The focused edges on his blade dropped away. *He's lost some weight, too.* Indeed, the practice sessions had affected both of them, but Seffin's transformation was more pronounced.

Seffin finished pulling on his shirt. "Something wrong?"

He realized he'd been staring. "N-No. Sorry. Let's run through what we have."

Seffin took his position on the opposite end of the room and began throwing ice lances in Ren's direction as Ren cut them out of the air with his blade, up until the last one which Ren caught with his will. Breaking the ice lance into smaller pieces he threw them back at Seffin who created a firewall to melt them away. Now the taxing part, Seffin created a fireball and threw it in Ren's direction. Ren wrapped his will around it and raised it above his head as if he would throw it back, but another already headed right for him. Ren caught it with his free arm and seamlessly hurled both back at Seffin who willed the entire basin of water over, wrapped them with ice and detonated them. The whole room shook, and steam billowed everywhere.

"Should we reduce the fireballs a bit? We don't want to bring the building down on us," Ren said.

"That wasn't the fireballs."

The room shook again.

Ren looked toward the door of the room. "What the hells was that?"

An inhuman roar echoed around them followed by crashing and screaming. Exchanging a look, they both rushed for the door.

"We need to find out who's screaming and get them out of here," Seffin said.

"Agreed."

Ren's heart pounded against his chest as he pumped his arms and legs, running toward the noise. It sounded like nothing he'd ever heard. As if whatever made the sound was being strangled while it roared. Then it hit him. A husk. Not just a husk, but an amalgamation. *How? How did it get inside the city's barrier, and what the hells am I doing running toward it?* They turned the final corner to the central training courtyard. This is where they'd do their showcase, but it looked nothing like he remembered. The water basins leaked out of broken sides, bricks and wood lay everywhere, and a haze of sparkling dust hung in the air.

In the middle of the destruction stood Dunreedy, holding off the largest cat Ren had ever seen by lighting pieces of wood on fire with his will and shunting them. The giant was an amalgamation of a laranee. He'd only seen one in a book before, and they were terrifying enough to look at without being amalgamated. Massive fangs thrust down out of its mouth. It moved in bursts of speed so fast his eyes could barely follow. A memory of the silent amalgamation from his childhood flashed through his head. *Connie.* The cat held its ground against the spikes of flame Dunreedy plunged into it. Seffin created a fireball between himself and the creature, and Ren pulled out his blade. Dunreedy saw them out of the corner of his eye and yelled, "Get the hells out of here!"

"You need help," Seffin said, still in that matter-of-fact tone of his. A colossus amalgamation destroying their school wasn't enough to warrant displaying emotion.

Ren rushed forward to stand next to Dunreedy. "Your fire sticks aren't going to kill this. I know we're students, but—"

"You go to the right. I'll distract it to the left. Seffin will hit its flank."

Dunreedy gathered a bunch of detritus, lit it on fire, and slammed it into the creature's face. As he ran the creature turned to follow him. Ren sprinted to the right and slashed at the creature's hind leg. The hind kick barely registered in his perception. Reflexively, he brought his blade up to block with the flat side, but it wasn't fast enough. The next thing he saw was the sky as he lay amongst the rubble, brilliant blue behind peaceful cotton clouds floating slowly across his vision. *No, not again. It can't be happening again.* An explosion rang out and a wave of heat washed over him. He tried to prop himself up to see what happened, but his left arm didn't work. Putting all his weight on his right instead, he sat up and took in the scene.

The creature was missing a good chunk of its right side. On the opposite end of the room, Dunreedy lay on the ground. *Gods, is he unconscious or dead?* The laranee stalked toward Seffin, a low raspy yowl escaping its throat.

"Hey! Over here!" Ren grabbed his will-blade with his good arm, took careful stock of both Dunreedy's and Seffin's locations, and sent it spinning in a horizontal arc, throwing as much will into it as he could, hoping to sheer its head off. The blade's edges exploded outward, and the laranee roared in pain, but he'd missed his target. Minus one ear and a sizable chunk of its skull the cat turned its attention toward him. Seffin slammed a massive ball of ice down on its head, distracting it long enough for Ren to retreat back, joining his position. It lurched forward, but Seffin threw both palms out, sending out a stream of will-fire hotter and with more force than Ren had ever seen. The smell of fetid flesh cooking nauseated him, but the laranee didn't stop advancing.

Seffin struggled to focus the stream. *He's putting so much power into it he can't focus enough.* Ren moved up next to Seffin and put his good hand on Seffin's forearm, grasping around and letting his will flow into the technique, combining their efforts. Together, and using all the focus he could muster to condense the stream of fire, the cone of red flames turned to blue and then white as it became a tight beam of pure heat and light. The laranee collapsed dead. A hole that started the size of an apple pierced straight through both the laranee and the structure behind it, growing in circumference the further it bored.

Silence settled on the courtyard save for some rubble shifting and falling, the heavy breaths of both Seffin and Ren, and the laranee's limp form beginning to sizzle and ash the way husk normally did within a barrier. A groan came from across the room. *Unconscious then. Thank the gods.* They ran over to Dunreedy who had already started sitting up. The aging professor held the creature off alone for a long while before they showed up. It surprised him. He'd always viewed Dunreedy as just another fragile, old teacher.

Seffin helped the professor to his feet. "How could an amalgamation make it into the city?"

"As far as I know, what we just experienced is impossible." Dunreedy's eyes seemed to stare off into the distance. He reached up to touch an open wound on his head. "Whatever that amalgamation was, it's something new."

Ren knew better, though. Different than the monstrosity that destroyed his village, sure, but an amalgamation with strange, lethal traits that could withstand a barrier wasn't new to him. A soundless horror destroyed Gull Harbor, and now Danvers Academy had almost turned completely to rubble by a warping cat.

The three of them made their way through the debris, toward the entrance. Ren noticed the first body. The creature must have chased whomever he was into the school.

"That's Paul. He was in my kinetics lecture... or was his name Peter?" Dunreedy gave an exhausted sigh and touched the wound on his head again. "Awful."

Continuing, they walked over splinters that used to be the front door and broken shards that used to be windows. The scene outside was made worse by how familiar it all felt. A community reduced to a sea of gore and debris. Bodies were everywhere. Some torn to shreds by fang and claw, and others simply missed huge portions of their anatomy. A man kneeled with a crying baby in his arms next to a woman with no left side. It pulled Ren back to the day Gull Harbor fell. Death and confusion and fear and panic. Connie, lying dead on the gravel road only a hundred or so feet from her home. Tolkar tearing him away from his mother. Ren could almost see her stand, turn, and run into town, back toward the creature, her form shimmering through a veil of tears.

Seffin sat on the top step, looking around with a blank expression. Ren sat next to him, careful not to lean on his broken arm, and Dunreedy collapsed into a seated position on the other side of Seffin.

A few minutes of silence passed before Seffin spoke, "The courtyard is gone."

"It is," said Dunreedy.

"How are we going to do our final?"

Ren spun his head to look at Seffin.

Really? Dead people everywhere and you're worried about the final?

Dunreedy gave a joyless laugh and looked up at the sky. "Oh, I don't think the showcase is necessary at this point. Why don't you two just consider yourselves graduated."

Seffin nodded and turned to continue gazing out into the street. His vision panned back and forth over the tragedy. An indiscernible look on his face.

Jessica

The outgoing president of Egal was a small, severe woman by the name of Janie Karikit. She rose to power as a senator from a coastal district and brought the sensibilities of a rugged, hard-working dock worker to her office. At least, that's what the public knew of her. In reality, she ruthlessly chewed up and spat out anyone who got in her way. There were few people Jessica both admired and feared more.

Janie sat at the large, oak desk in the office of the president as Jessica took a seat in front. "Seventy-eight people dead. Two hundred and fifteen casualties. My assistants are saying the creature originated from an off-the-books, government-funded, Guild-owned warehouse. Care to tell me what the fuck your son thinks he's doing at the Guild?"

Troy doesn't even know it exists.

Jessica hadn't planned on Janie figuring out the funding source this quickly. The woman was a force to be reckoned with. "It's a research facility for aberrant amalgamations found in the wild. If you recall Gull Harbor from ten years ago."

A small lie. Best if she doesn't know everything.

"How the hell could I forget? The news broke the week I got elected."

"Well, Troy wouldn't know about the facility. It's funded with government money and the research is top-level classification."

"I'm stepping down in a month, so I'll skip the obvious question of why the *fuck* I wasn't briefed on this and get straight to asking how you want to handle it?"

"We'll tell everyone the threat from amalgamations is growing, and to curb their progression Senator Washburne earmarked funding to study them. The creature appeared to be dead when it was brought in for study, but it woke up and broke out. The National Party takes the hit for endangering the lives of citizens and putting a bit of fear into everyone about the husk blends well with my Gogallo Initiative."

"I like it. Who's on the chopping block for this?"

"Washburne will have to."

Janie frowned at Jessica in disappointment. "What do you mean? He was assassinated. I thought you knew."

"But... he's on vacation."

Janie chuckled. "He's dead. My people found him pinned to his own portrait in his office. His staff seem none the wiser though, the room was sealed so the stench couldn't get out. Anyway, it's one less legislator to get in my way for now so I just left it. That'll be your problem if you win."

For the second time since sitting down Jessica was stunned by Janie's information network. Since when was Washburne assassinated? How long ago? His wife and kid were on vacation as well. Were they also dead? What was the assassin after? Washburne was her guy on the inside of the National Party. He's the one she had fund the lab in the first place. The pieces started to fall into place. "You're saying whoever killed Washburne let out the amalgamation?"

"Aww, it's kinda fun watching the cogs move in your head as you catch up." She laid it on thick. "I'll save you some time though. The rogue assassin running loose in Nashow has come to Prolivgrad. They killed Washburne, and somehow managed to kill the eye you hired to standby at the lab." She pulled out a roll of tobacco and lit it. "Not a bad plan, by the way." She puffed at the cigarette and blew the smoke out the side of her mouth. "Anyway, since assassins don't just go around killing each other I checked with the Eyes of Koth. Sure enough, they don't know who this is either. Now you have to decide what to do about a rogue assassin working their way through your network."

Jessica thought for a moment. A sitting senator's murder should have made enough of a vibration on her web to pick up. *How could I miss that? Am I too distracted by the election?*

"How is it that Washburne's death hasn't gotten out yet, and how did you even know to look into that?"

"When the head of the largest mining company in the country goes on vacation with his powerful senator father during an election season it raised a few alarms." *Stupid. I should have caught that.* "I personally sent someone to look into it. Their houses were clean, but I imagine whoever killed him had quite the grudge to leave his body rotting there." Janie chuckled. "It's a good thing we're under a barrier or we'd have a husk version of Washburne to worry about. Can you imagine that prick as a husk? Running around even more slack-jawed than usual. Good riddance."

She drew another puff. "My suggestion is that you figure out whomever this assassin is targeting and serve their head on a platter as a peace offering. And if it's you they're after? I would run." She exhaled the smoke she'd been holding in her lungs.

Jessica was rattled. Not since she was a child screaming in the street as the world collapsed around her had she been taken so flat-footed. Years upon years of planning. Contingencies upon contingencies upon fucking contingencies, and now some asshole threatened to bring it all down around her. How long had Janie known about the lab? How long had she known about Washburne?

"There's far too much at stake to run."

Janie nodded in mock solemnity. "Yes. Far too much at stake." She rolled her eyes. "Seventy-eight people, a colleague, his family, and an eye all dead. Whatever the stakes are, they're costing an awful lot."

"The world?"

Janie gave her a blank stare. "Excuse me?"

"The world is at stake. The Gogallo Initiative isn't just some political ploy. The husk are getting out of hand. There are more and worse amalgamations every month. There were more towns wiped out by amalgamations this year than in the last three years combined. Garvelle has been forced to cede territory to the Gogallo hordes on their eastern border. We need to take any and all actions necessary to—"

"I didn't ask for your stump speech," Janie cut in forcefully. "I'm aware of the husk problem. I'm not convinced your solution of uniting the world's armies into a massive force and smashing everyone's best fighters to smithereens against a wall of meat and bone is a sound plan, but I'll admit it's got an air of grandiosity to it. You seem to have done a good job convincing the public of it anyway." Janie set her cigarette down, walked over to the door, opened it, and extended an arm out the threshold telling Jessica it was time to leave. "Regardless, you have a campaign to get back to, and I've some statements to issue about your pet problem."

Jessica walked out of the room embarrassed. She'd just shown her ass to one the most powerful women in the world. Still, better Janie tell her about the assassin now than wake up with a knife in her back.

***

Jessica had found Pulpin just starting his his career with the Guild. He'd been sniffing around looking for government support for some experimental research on controlling amalgamations using intentioned will—a type of will wielding used to control small animals among... other things. The ethical considerations alone were reason enough to refuse him, but she had counted herself lucky. In all her planning to finally confront whatever festered at the Heart of Gogallo she still hadn't found a military solution, and here, dropped in her lap, stood the type of person she'd need to start making progress. Breaking through the amount of husk concentrated in Gogallo would require an imaginative solution and having her own army of controlled amalgamations seemed just imaginative enough.

Despite working with Pulpin for over twenty years, she never liked the man. His arrogance annoyed her even if it wasn't unfounded. He was a certified genius when it came to husk experimentation, and his work on intentioned will was groundbreaking as well. Though she wasn't a stranger to the darker side of will techniques herself, she'd even had a hand in advancing his research. Regardless, he let someone infiltrate his lab, kill her eye, and let loose one of their experiments. He was on her shit list. Which is why she'd summoned him for a meeting.

"Good afternoon," Pulpin said, walking into her office.

She didn't respond. He could wait a couple minutes while she finished drafting her speech on *his* fuckup. To his credit, he simply stood there silently. Maybe he'd finally learned when to check his ego. Writing down the closing line of her first draft she dropped her pen and addressed him, "Do you know why I helped fund your experiments?"

"I imagine it was because my research directly helps your long-term plans."

Ignoring the insolence, she said, "When I found you, I dug deep into your history, and what I found was a meticulous, thorough researcher that, above all, understood the value of discretion. I've tried my best not to micromanage you since we started working together. I've granted you all the rope I could possibly give you, confident that you would pull my plans to fruition with it. Instead, you've fashioned two nooses and thrown them around our necks."

Pulpin took a seat in front of Jessica's desk. "I fail to see how an assailant from Nashow is within the scope of my responsibilities."

Still too proud to know when to eat shit.

"The security and confidentiality of the facility are under your scope. The fact I hired an eye to standby should have been overkill. You stationed three guards outside and had three patrolling inside and you thought that would be sufficient?"

"Again, an assassin was never discussed as a possibility. My strategy was to maximize security while maintaining a low profile. Painting a target on the building by staffing it with forty security guards per shift would have attracted attention."

Guild facilities never have many guards to begin with. Forty in the building would have given it away just as much as the three at the front door.

"Regardless, the amalgamations are supposed to respond to commands. How was this one allowed to rampage down a street and into a school?"

Pulpin pinched the bridge of his nose. *Is he really acting exhausted with me?*

"The commands only work for one person, and if you remember, we used your blood and tied it to you. You were the only person that could have stopped it without killing it."

But she knew that already. She only checked to make sure everything was done that needed to be. With the assassin infiltrating the lab it was only a matter of time until they found Pulpin and paid him a visit. One of the contingencies she put in place when she hired Cara was to plant documents to make it appear as if Pulpin headed the project, and with Washburne already dead, taking care of Pulpin should close the case as far as anybody on the outside would know.

Unless they're after something other than the project.

"Did they take anything?"

"Not that I know of. The only room they had access to was Cara and Todd's. After that, all evidence suggests they made a mad dash for the back exit."

Jessica stood from her desk, walked to her window, and looked out onto the city below. "What are you after?" she wondered out loud.

"I assumed it was our research, but if that's what they wanted they got precious little of it. I utilized Cara for clerical needs. After all, she was an assassin. Not a researcher."

What would a Nashowan assassin want with research from a Guild facility? She thought back to Washburne's death.

"Maybe this is personal," she said. "Do you have any enemies I'm unaware of?"

Pulpin looked surprised. "N-no. Not that I can think of."

"Well, if I were you, I'd think hard about who might want to kill you, and I'd make sure to hire some protection."

Putting him on alert was the most she would help him. Twenty years working together, and he couldn't even muster the respect necessary to apologize when his own facility blew up in their faces. Her gratitude for his research wasn't boundless. He'd have to settle for being hailed a hero posthumously. Jessica knew Pulpin didn't have anything in his past bad enough that a rogue assassin would be after him. No, it had to be something to do with the project. She just had to figure out what. That would narrow down the who, and once she knew that it was just a matter of finding out what they cared about.

"Do you still want me to get production up and running?"

"Of course. We'll need demonstrations in time for the summit with the other nations, and I won't have some rogue asshole getting in the way of my life's work. Gogallo will fall and the husk with it."

Pulpin gave that slimy smile he always did when he was genuinely happy. "Very good. The lab is already being set up at another site outside the city wall, and the production facilities are prepped and ready for subjects. Am I correct in assuming you still want to be tied to the entirety of the first wave?"

"Nothing's changed, Pulpin. I want the same amounts, same creatures, everything. I want all options available for the demonstration. If I'm to convince the likes of Garvelle's Empress or Estaba's Prime Minister to pledge their forces, I'll need an impressive display. Once we have them on board, we'll worry about spreading out whom we tie them to."

"I'll get started."

Once he was gone, Jessica racked her brain. There had to be some loose end she missed. Throughout her tenure as senator, she'd made no shortage of enemies, but she dealt with them meticulously. Washburne is dead, she just put Clem back in line, Winnow didn't have the balls to send an assassin after her, and then there was the unfortunate situation with Ada, the reporter from the *Egal Gazette*. But she took care of Ada herself. The reporter had targeted Jessica after her senatorial election and wrote lies. It's one thing to expose truths, but lying she couldn't abide. Ada didn't have any family though, and she certainly didn't have any friends.

Thinking of colleagues, a few senators from the noble districts had no love for her, but no one with the resources to afford an assassin willing and able to take on an eye and come out the other side with their life. None of those senators had any connection to the project, nor did Clem. No, whomever this assassin happened to be they were a result of something unexpected. Something she didn't know about or something she thought she'd taken care of. Regardless, she couldn't waste time thumbing through all her old memories hoping to find a clue. Too much had to be done. She sighed and looked down at her desk, a career-defining speech lay in front of her, waiting for review.

Seffin

K ent's home seemed cramped compared to the mansion Seffin came from. The low ceiling and smaller rooms were claustrophobic at first, but with time came familiarity, and with familiarity came comfort, and a room that felt suffocating before now felt cozy and secure. It didn't help Seffin's acclimation that Kent preoccupied himself with collecting garbage. An odd habit for someone who spent his life cleaning another person's home. Kent insisted on the value of each item, but he didn't seem to complain when Seffin cleaned up the clutter either. Cleaning after his own butler, the irony was not lost on him.

Menial chores notwithstanding, Seffin loved living with Kent. He no longer had to wear his family's colors in public, or attend his mother's church, or go to school, or worry about The Guild, or explain where he'd been. The feeling of liberation was overwhelming at times. Like his world had suddenly tripled in size with no path to follow or map to orient himself by. Like he'd been walking down a hallway his whole life and suddenly the walls fell away and revealed a wide, beautiful, terrifying world of possibility and doubt.

At least, that was the feeling he had for the first couple weeks, before the incident with the laranee. Before Ren was injured, and the school was destroyed, and before the impromptu graduation thrusting him into adulthood. Dunreedy meant to do him a favor by letting him skip his last month of school, but Kent agreeing to take him in had one caveat. Once he graduated, he'd have to start paying half the rent. Which seemed fair at the time, but that was when he had a month to figure out how to become a merc. Having never been to the Lodge before, nor even formally meeting a merc, he worried if he'd be able to do it. The best course of action would be to visit the Lodge and figure it out from there. Maybe they had some sort of tutor or a class he could take.

From Kent's home, the way to the Lodge was straightforward, just up the road a ways. Even this close to the Lodge though, homeless people peppered the sidewalk, and the streets were strewn with garbage and waste—the stink of Prolivgrad. In the noble district, where he used to live, the stench would waft in from time to time, but it was nothing compared to the feeling of being bathed in it like it was here. Still, the closer to the Lodge the nicer the surroundings became. Shit-stained gutters gave way to clean streets and the smell of unwashed bodies to the pleasant aroma of bakeries, cafés, and taverns with happy customers piling into and out of their doors. Before long, the huge wooden structure known as a Lodge came into view with its doors always open and welcoming. With some hesitance, he joined a throng of people crowding into the building.

Everywhere he looked, people were on a mission. Lined up in a queue at the registration counter, sitting at the bar or visiting by the fire in a pub just inside called Mallory's, or reading the contracts on the boards. As he stood there gawping in the entrance, the crowd managed to sweep him up, landing him in line at the registration counter, uncertain if he should be there or not. The line wasn't long though, so he figured once he got to the front, he could ask the clerk what to do. He contented himself people-watching while he waited.

"New here, little buddy?" a tall man with kind eyes, beige skin, a flail, and a shield addressed him.

"Yes."

"Need some help?"

"Yes."

He stood there for a moment, waiting. The silence grew awkward. "Help with?"

"Oh! With everything. I need help with everything." Seffin stuck out his hand because that is what you do in these situations.

The man shook it. "Well, you're in the right line. What are you looking to do... uh... what was your name?"

"Seffin. I'm looking for work."

"Seffin, eh? I'm Don." He pointed at a sign above the counter that read from left to right; bounty, delivery, escort, trades, and specialty. "What type of work are you looking for?"

"Oh, I'm..." Seffin scratched his head, and said, "not exactly sure. All of them maybe?"

Don chuckled. "No. You can't really..." He shifted from one foot to the other. "I'll start over. Do you have a rank?"

"Rank?"

"Yes." Don gave a puzzled look. "Do you live under a rock, kid? Everyone knows mercs have ranks." He held up a piece of paper that said *evaluation* on the top. "I just made three. You'll start out at one. They go up to five and then there is a specialist rank."

"And ranks matter because..."

"Contracts are rated on difficulty. Sometimes they'll ask for a total ranking, and sometimes they'll request a certain number of people with specific rankings."

Rankings, contracts, registration. This all seemed important, but Seffin only had one goal in mind. "I really just need to pay rent."

Don looked Seffin up and down and squinted his eyes. "You're wearing a silk shirt and boots that look brand new. I wouldn't figure someone dressed like that would have problems making rent."

He looked down at his clothing and considered the fact that he never thought about how he dressed before now but, judging himself against everyone here, he had to admit Don had a point, he did look like someone from money.

"I didn't want to join the Guild, so my dad kicked me out and now I'm living with my butler." The words seemed to fly out of his mouth.

Don's eyebrows went up in surprise. "Oh, uhh..." He looked at a second piece of paper in his hand. "Hey, so I'm just here to update my rank, but my band has a delivery contract we were going to do this afternoon. They're not the most exciting, but this one pays pretty good." He gestured to the piece of paper in his hand. "I'll let you tag along if you're willing to take a half share. Unless you're living in a palace that should get you enough to survive on for the week, and then I can show you the ropes."

Seffin looked around at the Lodge. All the merc boards, all the lines, all the people. All of it was chaos to him. Don was offering some order.

"Deal."

***

Seffin came to on the floor next to Kent's kitchen table. A pile of sick dripped off the edge onto the back of his head as he lay there. In the threshold to the kitchen stood Kent, still in his work clothes, looking down at him. "Rough day?"

Seffin groaned. His head felt full of cotton with a dull ache creeping in, his mouth tasted like acid, his throat was dry, and he couldn't focus his eyes. "No." He sat up and grabbed his head. "Money."

"It's ok, I'll give you some time to get things in order—"

Seffin waved his hands. "I mean, no, it wasn't a rough day. I have some money." With great effort, he stood up. Steadying himself on a chair he pointed to the portion of the table without vomit on it, at a small pile of coins.

"For me? You shouldn't have." Kent made his way over to the table and began counting. "There's enough here to cover you for the month, but where'd you get it?" Kent paused his counting to gesture at the vomit dripping off the table's edge. "And what happened?"

Seffin stood as straight as he could and puffed his chest out. "I'm a *murr*—" He retched. Righting himself he tried to get the words out. "I'm a *murr*—" He retched again. This time almost losing his balance.

Kent pocketed some coins and went to put his hand on Seffin's shoulder, steadying him. "You're a murr?"

"I'm a merc now." The effort of the words exhausted him.

Kent whistled. "Well, Mr. Merc, did your contract also tell you to get drunk and throw up on my kitchen table instead of in the street like a civilized person?"

"I'll clean it up!" Seffin began walking to the shelf with the towels, but without the chair to steady him he lost his balance.

Kent caught him before he fell but stood as far as he could with arms outstretched like he was holding a soiled diaper.

"Sit," Kent commanded, shifting a chair with his foot, and pushing Seffin into it. "I'm going to get some water warming for a bath. Once you're in it you can explain why you got pickled on a Tuesday evening." Kent motioned to Seffin's vomit-covered shirt. Like a toddler, Seffin dutifully raised his arms. Kent pulled the shirt off him, wiping the vomit from the back of his head with the unsoiled portion he then tossed it into the washbasin before busying himself with starting the fire.

"I can help with that." Seffin put his palm out and began to focus.

"No!" Kent rushed over and slapped Seffin's hand down. "I know I told you no rules, but I lied. There is one rule. No elementalism in the house when you're drunk"

"I'm not drunk. I'm hungover."

"*Or* hungover."

Kent warmed the water, pulled out his wooden bathtub, and set it in the kitchen by the fire. Seffin's head began pounding in earnest as he wobbled back and forth at the kitchen table like a child's toy.

"Alright, let's get to it." Pulling Seffin up from his chair, he helped him out of the rest of his clothes and eased him into the wooden tub. Without the brain fog, Seffin might have had the decency to feel embarrassed, but in his current state, he only felt gratitude. For the kindness of strangers, for his new life, but mostly for Kent. He leaned back into the water and relaxed into the bath while his former butler started cleaning up the table and floor.

"I feel like I owe you for cleaning up after me."

Kent frowned at him, but there was some cheek in it. "Oh, you already paid me a little extra for that." He pointed at what was left of Seffin's money and winked at him.

He chuckled and then winced at the pounding in his head it caused. "Why are you helping me so much?"

Kent dropped the washrag he'd been using into the washbasin, grabbed his bath brush and a bar of soap, and tossed it into the tub, splashing Seffin in the face. "The simple answer is because you need it."

"Ok, but what's the not simple answer."

His smile faded a bit. "Your situation reminds me a lot of my own, and I wish I had someone to help me when I needed it."

"You were kicked out?"

"No, I wish I'd been that brave." He sighed and sat in a chair. "I come from a military family. My grandfather and father were both guard officers. My older brother signed up as soon as he could, but it just—" He shifted in his seat before saying, "—never appealed to me. When Grandpa died in the Garvellian invasion my dad didn't seem to care. He was almost happy. I guess it was pride, but it still felt awful. He died in a war fought over money and crystals. Two things this country already had plenty of. Why take pride in that?"

"So you did or didn't join the guard?"

"I did. My father made it clear he'd disown me if I didn't enlist. A friend of mine enlisted with me so I'd have someone to lean on." His voice broke, and he looked up at the ceiling.

Seffin realized where this story was going. "How'd it happen?"

"We were on patrol around the edge of the city and a husk got him. The barrier's fluctuations were bad that day and a horde slipped onto our patrol route." Kent's gaze lowered back to meet Seffin's. "He never would have been there if I'd done what I wanted in the first place. After his funeral I quit the military, my dad made good on his promise to disown me, and the next month I got hired by your father. I just think... he'd still be here if I had left my family. Done my own thing."

Seffin felt a warmth growing in his chest. Like an ember catching tinder, the warmth bloomed outward, pushing up against a barrier by his heart. "I don't know how to thank you." A tear slipped from his eye.

A smile spread across Kent's face. "You're leaking again."

"I'm serious," Seffin said more forcefully than he'd meant to. He wiped the tear away from his cheek. "My father was cold my whole life. My mother didn't even want a child. She'd rather be off exploring the world."

"Seffin—"

"—I thought there was something wrong with me. For not being able to control my will. For how I talk. But not with you. You've always made me feel... normal. Safe."

Something shifted inside of him. A wall he built around his heart, around who he was, started to crack and falter. His parents couldn't hurt him if they couldn't know him. Their expectations were for someone who didn't exist, and their disappointments for someone they'd never met. He hid from himself, though, behind the wall, and now all he wanted was to break it down. To meet himself. To see and feel and think without obstruction. All it took was this one genuine connection and it started to break apart. Flimsy as far as walls go, but strong enough to serve its purpose all these years. He looked up at Kent and felt a surge of embarrassment.

The big man slapped his knees. "Alright, your turn for storytime. What the hells happened to you today?"

Thankful for the abrupt change in topic, Seffin said, "I went to the Lodge to see about getting work. I met someone there, Don. He helped me."

"By getting you drunk?"

"No, we had a drink after the contract."

Kent gave Seffin a pointed look. "Several drinks you mean."

He ignored the comment. "It was just a delivery to a small town outside the barrier, but we still ended up running into some husk—I didn't expect them to be so fast. Anyway,when I burned them up, he asked if I'd ever fought husk before, and when I told him about the laranee at the academy he said he had to buy me a drink."

"Several drinks."

Seffin gave a blank look. "Yes. Several drinks. We've established it was several drinks."

"So, he got you plastered and helped you earn some money. Sounds like a nice guy."

"He asked me to join his band."

Kent stood from the floor and began the finishing touches on cleaning the kitchen. "Did you take him up on his offer? There's safety in numbers. The few mercs I know are paired up or in a band."

"I told him I'd think about it."

Seffin hadn't considered teaming up with somebody else until today. His parents' hatred of the Lodge prevented him from knowing even common information regarding merc work. He'd always pictured mercenaries as rugged loners, but the Lodge felt welcoming. Like a fellowship. His ignorance and inexperience would be a major risk if he were to break out on his own. At least in a band he could ask questions and learn from people that do the job every day. Even with a head full of fog, the decision was clear. "Yeah, I think I'll join a band."

Kent set down the brush he'd been using to scrub the table and wiped his hands on a towel. "I think that's smart, but I wouldn't just join the first person that asked you. At least not without getting to know them more."

"I think I have a good idea who I'm going to join."

"Oh?" Kent yawned and made to leave the kitchen. "That's good. I'm going to knock off. I'll see you in the morning. Make sure to dump the water out before you go to bed." He paused to look back. "And no elementalism. I don't want to come down here in the morning to a soaked kitchen."

***

Seffin made his way up the steps and knocked on the door. The home surprised him with its size, and with the various gadgets sitting on the roof, their gears spinning and axles turning. After a full minute had passed, he repeated the knock, stronger this time. On the third attempt, the door opened halfway through Seffin's pounding.

"—was YOUR turn to answer the—oh, hey Sef, what's up?" Ren stood in the doorway, slightly taller than Seffin himself, with a dimply smile and eyes that always seemed sad until they focused on something. They were focusing on Seffin right now.

"I'm joining your band."

Ren's face contorted. "My what?" He scratched his head. "I don't have a band."

"Well, we can just pair up then."

Ren looked inside the house and back at Seffin. He stepped out and closed the door behind him. "Don't you mean, 'Can I pair up with you?'"

Seffin furrowed his brow. "No. I said what I meant."

"Well…" Ren looked down at the ground and then back up again at Seffin. "I guess that's fine, but we need to work on your manners."

"My manners?"

"Yeah. Usually, people ask to be a part of a group instead of telling."

Seffin cocked his head. "I've found if I state my intentions instead of asking, I usually have more success."

"Right, but that's just because people feel pressured to go along with you."

"Exactly."

Ren chuckled. "Good point. Still rude."

"What's the difference?"

Ren sucked in his teeth. "Well, would you rather work with someone you pressured into working with you, or would you rather work with someone who *wants* to work with you?"

Seffin began to worry. "Are you saying you don't want to work with me?"

"No, we can work together. Just… never mind. Won't your parents kill you for being a merc?"

"I'm living with my butler," he said simply.

Ren's mouth dropped open. "Ok, well now I'm curious." He opened the door and began to usher Seffin through.

Halfway through the door, Seffin paused. "So, we're teaming up?"

"For the third time, yes. Now get in here and tell me what the hells happened that you're living with your butler."

Jessica

The fall of Jessica's hometown, Stockton, was hardly a headline when it happened. One hundred and fifty-six people dead, and no one seemed to care. It was hard to stomach, but the reality is they were just one tragic town in a sea of tragic towns. When one is wiped out it's a disaster, but when one is wiped out every other week it becomes routine. There's a maximum amount of tragedy people can pay attention to, and it just so happened people reached that limit around the time the husk burned Stockton from the map.

The problem only worsened as time passed. Towns lost to the husk were spoken of in the abstract, and deaths were relegated to data points and graphs. Easier to ignore the actual suffering when it's referenced as a trend. Even the word *trend* made it seem like an unsolvable, unreachable problem. Like things are going that way whether you like it or not. Add in the Nationals' hatred of refugees and it made the problem seem not just unsolvable, but unpalatable. Helping people from destroyed communities became "handouts" and trying to explain the horror of what went on outside of Prolivgrad became "propaganda". In some ways, she could never forgive herself for becoming a part of the system that dehumanized so many people, and in other ways, she knew she could only forgive herself if she completed her mission. It helped that she loved the fight. There truly was nothing sweeter than watching the light leave the eyes of an opponent as they realized they'd been beaten. All for a greater purpose.

The end of the husk.

When she pitched the idea, everyone thought she was crazy. The husk were a part of nature. It was like telling people you planned to end all thunderstorms. Except thunderstorms weren't made from the bodies of the dead, and they didn't try to consume or fuse with every creature in their vicinity. The fact they'd always been a part of the fabric of reality didn't mean she had to accept it. Gogallo was the epicenter of husk activity. If a key to getting rid of the husk existed, it would be there. Everyone knew it. She was just the first person willing to make the hard decisions necessary to attempt to eradicate them.

After dedicating the better part of her life to making a single attempt on Gogallo, Jessica had to admit the effort had taken a toll on her. The election was sapping her energy, too. At the same time, she had to maintain her existing position as senator and keep Pulpin's secret lab under wraps. Beyond that, Troy finally taking initiative with his position came too little too late. She knew installing him as president of the Guild came with risks. Including him in her conspiracy without his knowledge exposed him to danger unwittingly, and unless he went along with her plans it would create a vulnerability. His tenure as president of the Guild became a continuous balancing act between his principles and his laziness.

Now, he'd chosen the wrong moment to assert himself and, stretched so thin, she didn't have the attention span to protect him. It took all her effort just to keep her own plans afloat let alone her lazy son. The pressure was mounting, and Janie's humbling meeting had snapped her back to reality. She had to make the hard decisions now so no one else had to later.

Jessica scheduled her meeting with Troy for one. A last chance for him to show her he could be trusted. At half past noon, he barged through her office door with Tia on his heels repeatedly asking him to sit in the waiting room. She waved Tia away.

"I assume this is urgent?" She made the impatience in her voice obvious.

"Do you know how insulting it is that I have to wait in line to speak to my own mother?"

Not a good start.

"I thought I'd raised you well enough to appreciate the situation I'm in, but at thirty-four years you're still using tantrums to get your way." Troy's face turned red. His power move had failed. *Whether he's embarrassed or mad I don't fucking care at this point.* "Now, honey, I called you for a meeting at one. What's so urgent that it couldn't wait one half hour?"

He gathered himself. "I asked you about the project Pulpin was involved in, and you refused to tell me. Now my name is being dragged through the mud by the press, and your colleagues in the Senate are trying to make me responsible for funds *they* voted to keep secret from me. I'm trying to get any answers I can at this point, but every thread I pull on either blows up in my face or starts unraveling another atrocity I wasn't aware of."

Atrocity? You mean like the abhorrent concessions I had to make with the Nationals because you wouldn't play ball?

"It's not my problem you don't know what's going on at your own—"

"Oh, stop it, Mother. You know what's happening. I'm asking nicely. Tell me what these experiments are actually for, and please, the truth."

There was a silent *or else* at the end of that sentence, and Jessica bristled at the idea of being threatened by her insolent, ignorant, indolent... and impudent son. "So you didn't read the press release?"

The look of disappointment and frustration on his face was visceral. He wanted real answers, not the public spin she released. She felt for him, truly. It didn't matter that he deserved it. That he'd practically asked for it by ignoring her guidance for years. He was still her son and it never felt *good* to dismiss him so callously. *He had his chances. It's his own damn fault he's in the dark on this.* She couldn't look at him as her son anymore, too much on the line to allow something as small as blood to get in the way.

"Mom. It's me. I'm asking for help. I know you pulled strings at the Guild for my position. I know I disappointed you. I'm sorry. I took what you gave, and I never paid you back. But I can't fix this unless I know what's going on, and the more I figure out, the more I realize you're at the center of it."

You spoiled brat. You're not sorry. You're just mad you're facing consequences.

When she helped to install Troy at the Guild, she hoped he would be grateful. Instead, he decided to play with the power he'd been given. Whoring, gambling, drinking, partying... the list went on. She needed someone to provide cover for Pulpin, to help her with the mining legislation, to work with her. Instead, he left Pulpin to handle his division unaided, he opposed the mining legislation, and he ignored her council at his whim. He was her greatest failure. He took and he took and he never gave, and here he was again reaching his hand out for help. The answer was no. She'd given him too many chances already and the idea of bringing him into her inner circle, when he'd only ever betrayed her trust, made her ill. He was a question mark where she needed a period, and there were far too many lives riding on this for her to make the same mistake twice. She took what was left of the affection and love she had for her son and did her best to lock it away.

"Everything I have to say about the Iaranee incident was said in the press release."

There it was. That dejected, pouty look he got on his face whenever he was about to shut down. Except he didn't shut down. Instead, he set his jaw and met her eyes. "Gull Harbor."

Motherfucker.

He had said he was pulling at threads, but she assumed it was with the same level of laziness he did everything else. He was right about one thing. This thread would blow up in his face. He moved his piece on the board from a passive participant to an active threat. She did her best to mask her emotions. "What of it?"

"I've made some mistakes pulling Guild support for so many villages. I'll admit that, but Gull Harbor wasn't one of them. A team was scheduled to pick up the pylon and escort the population. I was setting up jobs for when they arrived in Prolivgrad. The original contract for the town was a nightmare to get out of. I personally made sure everything was set up properly, but something happened, separate from my authority. The mystic team got orders to pull back and the only survivor was the envoy who said he had no idea what happened. Only that the amalgamation present had traits *never before seen in husk.* That sound familiar to you?"

Jessica hardened her heart as best she could. Her son was committing suicide and she was being made to tie the noose. She looked into his beautiful blue eyes staring daggers back at her. "Troy." She approached him. "I'm sorry, but I don't know what you're talking about."

He backed away from her. "I'm sorry too."

And then he left. He didn't walk out angrily. He didn't sulk. He simply stood up, turned, and left the room. She called Tia into the office before she lost her nerve, but Pulpin walked in instead.

Great. Why even have a schedule?

"Was that Troy I just saw leaving?" The worry in Pulpin's voice scared her. Even though she didn't care overmuch for the man, seeing his concern rattled her. His stoicism was only matched by his ego, and for either of them to break meant nothing good.

"He made a mess I need to clean up," she said simply. Trying to hold onto her nerve.

"We have a problem."

"Gods, what now?"

"He's been doing some digging on the labs."

Jessica squeezed her eyes shut and dug her fingers into her desk. "Well he's certainly not discreet. I'm handling it."

"That's what I'm here about. I was just at his office to talk him down, but he already prepped his staff to run things for the next couple months."

Impressive. She'd made this meeting as a last-ditch effort for him to prove himself, but for him, it had been a last chance for her to come clean. This amount of forethought and planning on his part would have been an asset a few years ago. Now, it only aggravated. Odd timing though. He'd miss the election. If he didn't plan to work against her presidency, then what was his goal?

She moved to the window and watched the bustling city sprawling out in tiers beneath her. Thousands of small tragedies and miracles happened every day outside her nine-by-ten pane of glass. This is what she wanted to protect. There was a beauty to the mundanity of everyday life. People working, eating their food, raising their children, fighting over meaningless disagreements. Living and dying amidst the struggle of making ends meet in a world that didn't care about you.

That was the goal.

She didn't fight for a world that cared for people—though that would be nice—she fought for a world that wasn't so openly hostile. That didn't leave its people to die at the rotted hands of the husk, perishing to their gnashing teeth. Failing in a world that hunted you wasn't failure. It was inevitable. By comparison, a world where a person could live and die by their own gumption sounded like paradise. The people of Prolivgrad almost had the paradise she wanted, but at the rate the husk were multiplying, even Prolivgrad would fall. Whether people admitted it or not, they were all heading toward oblivion unless they could stop the husk, or at least slow them. She had a thought and turned to Pulpin. "He can't be that stupid."

"About what?'"

"He's heading to Oleksandra's Harbor."

The envoy assigned to Gull Harbor, Tolkar, had been the only survivor of the massacre. He surprised everyone when he reported back. The poor man suffered a lot of trauma, and while the cleaner solution would have been to eliminate him, both Jessica and Pulpin agreed on an alternative. They stationed him in Oleksandra's Harbor, the shipyard co-sponsored by Nashow and Egal that went in down the coast from Gull Harbor. He knew the area and it would be a good fit. It didn't seem fair for the man to escape death only to be executed. Jessica didn't have any qualms about tying up loose ends to serve her greater goal, but Gull Harbor was her and Pulpin's mistake, the deaths served no purpose, and her conscience got the better of her.

"That envoy didn't know enough to matter," Pulpin said.

"Troy's not planning to stop my election. He's going to try and stop my assault on Gogallo. By proving Gull Harbor was caused by one of our amalgamations he'll try to convince the other nations not to back me. Tolkar knew more than what was written in his report. Any detailed description of the amalgamation will lead Troy straight back to the labs, especially after the laranee incident."

"Even if he makes it public that some of our experiments got loose, we have control of them now. It's been our goal from the start."

"You're right, and I'm sure that would be enough to convince some of them. Maybe even most of them, but all it takes is for Empress Zollinger to withhold her support and our plans fall apart. We can't take that risk."

Pulpin shifted back and forth. Probably reluctant to speak the implication out loud. Jessica did it for him. "We should have another hunter ready by now, yes?

"Three actually and not quite. The imprinting process is two weeks out, but the commands only work until they are fulfilled. After it's done, they'll revert to the instincts of a normal amalgamation. Killing anyone in the area."

"It's worth it."

Pulpin looked taken aback. "I just want to make sure I'm understanding you. Your son. He will most likely die."

Jessica pinched the bridge of her nose. "And I will grieve when I have time to, but he put himself in our way. Our chances of success are suffering enough already. Just..." It seemed like an eternity. The split second it took her to finalize the execution. The wrongness of it made her stomach lurch and every instinct she had told her not to. Better off jumping out her window and falling to her death than finishing the sentence she started, but she ignored what her heart said. She ignored what her stomach and her bones said. "...do it."

She waved Pulpin away. A dismissive gesture he would normally balk at but, whether out of respect or fear or pity, he obediently left the room, closing the door behind him. She turned back to look out her window, down onto the city with its pain and suffering and joy and beauty.

And she wept.

Ren

Fall colors painted the rolling hills and thick forests of the Egallan countryside with golds and oranges and reds. Hordes found easy hiding spots within the trees, but as long as a person stuck to the Guild-maintained highway the danger was minimal this close to the capital. The further north a person went the leafy trees, with their warm colors, would give way to their needly evergreen cousins that thrust upward, lancing toward the sky. North is where they were headed, escorting a taciturn envoy and his mule to Oleksandra's Harbor on the Sea of Corince whose waters Ren hadn't seen for over ten years.

The road was a well-maintained, Guild-sponsored trade route. Even without an escort, the path was mostly safe for people to navigate. Patrols regularly cleared the route of basic husk, and amalgamations in the areas closer to settlements were reported on and put down before they had the chance to cause too much trouble. Ren couldn't imagine an easier first contract. Four mercs for one Guild envoy to an established trading hub seemed excessive, a recipe for boredom really, but Ren wasn't about to complain about easy money.

Week one of the two-month assignment went by awkwardly. Seffin hadn't been told envoys were prohibited from giving out details of their personal lives, and his incessant questions were poorly received. After several tense incidents with the envoy, Poppy finally took Seffin aside and told him to leave the envoy alone. A poultice on a wound that needed surgery, but it worked for now. If the envoy was grateful for the effort, he didn't show it. Preferring to brood behind the group as they marched north. Ren wondered if all envoys were secretly sad and lonely or if it was just the two he'd met.

During the trek north they encountered other travelers. Guild teams returning from charging the pylons of smaller villages, and merchants or families on their way to and from Prolivgrad escorted by mercs. Once, on the second week of their trip, they saw a young woman traveling alone on her way to Vicksbough. She matched pace with them for a few miles and chatted about the election. Her wife had died in a mining accident a few years back and she blamed the Nationals for weakening the miner's union. After the accident, she moved away. The danger of living in a small town was preferable to the stench and struggle of living in the capital. It was obvious to Ren that she just needed a change after her wife died. Forward momentum probably helped to distract from her loss. He kept the thought to himself, but Seffin had the same thought and decided he'd voice it. Shortly afterward the woman picked her pace back up and shrunk into the horizon before them.

Another victim of Seffin's inability to read the room.

It wasn't until the second week that they even saw a husk. A single shambler who must have wandered from a horde on its way west. The creature wouldn't have noticed the group if it weren't for the envoy letting out a yelp. Ka cut it down with less fanfare than turning a page in one of her books. A flick of her wrist and a hiss from a wind blade sent its head flying and its body crumpling to the ground. A maneuver that could be mistaken for kinetics, but Ren knew it to be air elementalism. He'd considered learning air and earth now that he no longer attended a mystic academy, but the training for any element took years. That would be a project for later, if at all.

Following the husk sighting, they decided to take a break. Setting down their packs, they fed the mule an apple and grabbed some rations. Ren wished they'd packed more than salted fish and bread. The pungent meals had started to affect his mood. Every few days Ka would hunt down some rabbit or pheasant for supper to break up the monotony, but it hardly helped. He spent his time eating rabbit dreading the next time he'd have to eat salted fish again. The fishy taste always seemed to stick to his tongue.

As they munched on their fish, Seffin broke the silence, "Are you the same Tender Bolin that ended the Sol War?"

Sitting apart from the group, the envoy stopped eating his food to look toward them. The most engagement they'd gotten from him in days. Poppy seemed surprised by the sudden question. "I did fight in the war, yes. But I don't know if I can claim to have ended it. Empress Kiko had a lot more to do with that than I did."

"I just don't remember hearing about you injuring your leg is all."

"Oh, this isn't from the war." They pulled up their pant leg to display the injury. Ren had seen it countless times, but the gnarled scar tissue wrapping around Poppy's shin always made him a little uncomfortable. "It's a curse from a wild wielder."

Seffin and the envoy both looked confused.

Ren spoke up, "A curse is a type of intentioned will. You know how wild wielders can sometimes control small animals? Rats and rabbits and stuff like that?"

Seffin nodded. The envoy simply stared.

Ren continued, "There's two ways to use intentioned will. One is to control simple-minded creatures, and the other is curses. They're unfixable unless the original wielder releases the curse."

"They also need to have massive will reserves. Even then, it takes a lot of time and effort to perform a curse. No amount of healing can help it. Believe me, I've tried," Ka said.

The envoy stood and walked over to Poppy. He examined their scar. "When you say curses, what does that even mean exactly? This just looks like a bad scar."

"I've only ever seen it with wounds like this," Poppy said, "but there are stories of curses having a more general effect.

I met a merc in Lighton that said he'd been cursed with bad luck."

"That sounds made up," the envoy said.

Poppy shrugged their shoulders. "He was killed by a lightning strike four days later. Could have just been coincidence, but if I've learned anything in my old age it's that wielding is far more complex than academically trained mystics would have you believe. Elementalism, for example. They can't even properly train healers at the academies because they refuse to work with air or earth. On top of that, healing isn't easy to teach, it's different for each person."

"It's a feeling," Ka said, "and you need to have familiarity with all four elements. Guild healers are only half as effective as a wild healer because they can't get their heads out of their asses and realize it's all just wielding."

Ka's opinions on the academies were well known to Ren. An old wound she kept open for reasons he couldn't comprehend. She trained with a wild wielder from a young age which disqualified her from all the mystic academies. She could use fire and water as well as Ren could though, and her wind and earth wielding were top-notch. Not only that, but her healing kept her in constant demand at the Lodge. She was practically drowning in coin, which is why he didn't feel too guilty about stealing some from time to time.

"What happened to the person that cursed you?" Seffin asked

Poppy swallowed another bite of fish. "I'm not sure. The contract wasn't to bring them in, just to drive them out of the area. Of course, I looked, but Ka had just been born and I didn't want to be away from her too long."

"You're welcome," Ka said, smiling. An old joke between the two.

The envoy started putting away what was left of his rations. "So if this person was found you could be cured?"

Poppy made a waving gesture. "Bah! It's been too long. I wouldn't know the first place to look and convincing them to remove it would be... challenging. To say the least."

"Couldn't someone use this intentioned will you're talking about and make them?"

Poppy, Ka, and Ren all gave the envoy a disgusted look while Seffin simply cocked his head. It was Ka that said something, "No. I mean technically it's possible, but no one's ever had will reserves big enough to do that. Even controlling something as simple-minded as a squirrel takes a lot of will. More importantly, taking away the agency of another creature is... monstrous."

"But if this wielder cursed you, why do you care what happens to him?"

"It's not about him," She said. "If you're willing to play at being a god for something as simple as revenge then what's next? You could force people to do whatever you want."

"I don't see the difference between making someone do exactly what you want and killing them. I mean if I had a choice between having my mind controlled for a bit and dying, I'd choose mind control," Seffin said, taking the last bite of his salted fish.

Poppy shook their head. "You wouldn't be saying that if you were forced to kill people at someone else's whim."

Seffin swallowed. "You mean like being in the guard?"

Ren clapped his hands. "Ok, no offense, but Seffin Rashee isn't who I'm going to for advice on ethics. Maybe we should start getting a move on—"

"—and Ren the pickpocket wouldn't be high on the list either," Ka said. Always good at getting a jab in right at the end of a conversation.

The envoy turned to look at Ren. "Did you say Rashee?"

"Erm, yes."

"As in, Pulpin Rashee's son?"

"I doubt he'd call me that right now," Seffin said.

"Sorry, I'm just surprised the son of a division head would be taking merc work."

Seffin shrugged. "I live with my butler now."

The envoy gave a confused look at that response and shook his head. "Yes. Let's get a move on."

After lunch, they spent the remainder of the day in relative quiet. Seffin entertained himself with control training using a practice cube Ren nicked from the academy. Ka broke away from the group at dusk to find some game for supper, another meal of grilled rabbit. It would be their last one like it for a while. Husk became more numerous the further away from the capital a person traveled, and they were far enough north now that venturing off into the woods for fresh meat became less and less worth the trouble. The remainder of the group set up camp just off the path next to some old ruins.

Ruins were common to find along the main roadways, and if the professors at the academy were to be believed they were common deeper into the wilds as well. Most of history before Lana's sacrifice was lost, but you didn't need to be a historian to figure out many of the structures were from completely different time periods. Some had domes, some had peaks, some were dug into the ground. The only thing they had in common is that the people who once lived there were dead and gone. Or turned husk and still ambled around. The idea of aimlessly wandering for thousands of years sent a shiver up Ren's spine.

Seffin began charging their traveling focus crystal to set up a safe zone, Poppy busied themselves with the fire, and Ren began pitching tents with the envoy. "How much would that focus crystal stop if we were actually attacked?" The envoy asked.

Ren finished pounding a stake into the ground to anchor his tent. "Poppy says it'll stop any normal husk, and it would deter any amalgamation that showed up." Ren thought for a moment. "I figured you would have used a focus crystal for traveling before."

"I've only been on assignments with traveling pylons."

"How fancy. How'd you go from having the safest assignments to one where you're outside a barrier for most of it?"

The envoy took a while to answer. "I can't talk about Guild business, but I requested this one."

Ren took notice of the envoy's belongings as they traveled. Silk sheets, an exquisitely crafted sword, a fat coin purse that Ren ensured was imperceptibly lighter than he found it, even his mule was in pristine condition at the beginning of the trip. He lived a high-class lifestyle. It didn't surprise Ren that he acted skittish around husk, but it was surprising that an envoy this important would use mercs to travel instead of a Guild escort. He decided not to ask about it. The envoy wouldn't answer anyway, and if it didn't affect the job, it was none of his business. Ren focused instead on getting the man to open up a bit. He'd only spoken twice today. More than the last three combined, but it still made him an awkward traveling companion.

"I haven't seen you practice with your sword at all since we left. If you need a sparring partner let me know. Poppy says we'll probably find more husk in the next week, so there might be need of it."

"I thought that's what we hired you for."

"There's no harm in brushing up, and it could be fun."

"We'll see how fun you think it is after a couple rounds."

Ren grinned. "So does that mean I should fetch the practice swords?"

The envoy nodded. Ren went to find the mule to grab the blunted swords out of its saddlebags. It stood near Seffin, nipping and nudging at his shoulders, as he worked on the focus crystal. At some point during the trip, the mule had decided Seffin was his favorite, and now it rarely left his side. Ren approached the camp supplies that were set aside and pulled out the practice blades. Ka, who had since returned with a selection of cute-but-dead woodland creatures to eat, cocked her head as he pulled them out. "Are you sparring with yourself?"

"I asked the envoy."

That seemed to pique her interest. "And he said yes?"

He nodded. She dropped the squirrel she was skinning and wiped her hands off. "Yeah, I'm coming to watch and make sure you don't kill him."

Returning with the practice swords, he tossed one to the envoy. Ka found a tree and sat up against it.

"An audience?" The envoy asked.

"Ignore me," Ka said. "I'm just curious how you fight."

He shrugged, set his sword down momentarily, and slipped his Guild robes off. Ren took notice of the envoy's features back when they started the contract. Blonde hair, blue eyes, and a face that seemed too pretty to be real, but he'd always worn his Guild robes. Now, without the fabric swallowing his form, it was clear to see the envoy kept a strict workout regimen, at least when he wasn't traveling. His arms looked bigger than Ren's thighs, and his thighs looked like the trunk of a tree. Ren looked over at Ka who looked back at him. They said nothing, but in a way that only siblings can, they had an entire conversation. *How is this the same man that yelped at a single husk?* The envoy picked up his practice sword and turned to regard Ren. *Why does he somehow seem taller now?* He struck a pose Ren hadn't seen before.

"What style is that?" He asked.

"Estaban. My teacher was a sword master from Estaba."

Ren readied his practice sword and fell into form. "Ready?"

"When you are."

Ren rushed him, trying for a low attack. The envoy hopped backward and swatted him on the side of the head with the wooden sword. Wasting no time Ren lunged forward. The envoy knocked his sword aside, closed in, and slapped him across the face before dancing back. Ren's head buzzed. He'd been slapped plenty of times before, Ka practically made a sport out of it, but the envoy's slap felt more like being hit by a brick than being slapped.

"Ow!" Ren yelled. "What the hells?"

"If this were a real duel that'd be a knife in your head."

Ka snickered off to the side. He was right. If they'd been fighting for real, he'd be dead twice already. Of course, he wasn't wielding any will and that could change everything. Ren prided himself on holding his own in a sword fight even without wielding, but losing the exchange so easily made him question himself. The envoy fell back into that stance of his. Ren decided to try a different tactic and stood there, waiting for the envoy to attack first. He could have sworn he saw the man crack a smile before coming at him. He closed the gap fast, but Ren still managed to parry the high attack. He noticed one of the envoy's knees coming up in time to dodge to the side.

Ren squatted low and spun around. Using the momentum to bring his sword into the back of the envoy's other knee, or he would have had the envoy's leg still been there. He'd leapt into the air, and as Ren noticed the move, a wooden practice sword smashed into his face.

"Oof!" Ka said from off to the side. "That looked painful."

Ren collapsed back onto the ground and grabbed his face where the envoy struck him.

"We can be done if it's too much," the envoy said.

Ren couldn't tell if he was mocking him or being genuine. He spat blood on the ground and stood up, noticing blood dripping from his nose as well. "No," he said, "Ka can stop the bleeding and we can keep going."

After some first aid, they resumed their match. Ren waited for him to attack again, but this time he rushed forward to parry his sword, getting inside his space. The move made him nervous. Intentionally putting himself in range of all that muscle felt unwise, but he committed to the rush and head-butted him. The envoy reeled back from the assault, and Ren used the opening to strike his knees which gave out, bringing him down to a kneeling position where Ren wasted no time in putting his sword to his neck. Out of breath and panting, Ren noticed that even kneeling he still came up to his chest.

The envoy sat back and laughed. "You got me. I would have bet all the money I brought that you wouldn't have moved in that close."

"Do most duels end with bloody noses? Seriously, what would you two have done if you didn't have a healer with you?" Ka said.

"I imagine we'd have learned a lot less of each other," Ren said. "You can tell a lot from how someone fights, but one thing I don't understand is why you're so scared of husk when you can fight like that."

Ka was already helping with the envoy's nose when he said, "I use a dueling style. It's not exactly designed for hordes or large targets."

Ren had an idea. "You show me some of these duelist moves, and I'll show you what I know of fighting husk and amalgamations."

"Says the guy who's only fought one amalgamation," Ka interjected.

Ren smiled. "It was one hell of an amalgamation, though." He turned to the envoy. "But to be honest, Poppy or Ka would know a lot more than I do."

The envoy had an easy smile on his face. The first since the beginning of the trip. "No that's fine. The sword practice will help me get my mind off things."

"Oh? What things?"

Ka finished closing the wound on the envoy's face. He stood up. The smile and laughter gone from his expression and replaced with grim seriousness. "Just some Guild business."

The envoy tossed the practice sword back to Ren and started to leave.

"Ya know," Ka started, "we're under contract. If you tell us to keep quiet about something, we kind of have to, and I'd prefer if you worked out whatever you're going through, because the moping is getting annoying."

He stopped his gait and turned around. "I'll try and mope less."

"Thanks," she said and walked away. Back to the fire to finish skinning and cooking their supper.

"That was pretty blunt," he remarked once Ka was out of earshot.

"It's one of her more annoying traits, but she's not wrong," Ren said.

"So, you think I'm annoying too?"

"I think we have a lot of weeks left in this trip and it would suck if you spent the entire time brooding."

The envoy let out an exasperated sigh. "Noted."

Ren finished setting up camp while the envoy returned to his tent. He put the practice swords away and met Seffin, Ka, and Poppy by the fire. Ka and Poppy were busy skewering a couple rabbits and some squirrels, and Seffin had just finished charging the focus crystal. Ren could see it resting next to the fire, giving off the pale white glow indicating the barrier was active. He sat next to Seffin and gave him a friendly nudge. "Wanna hear a secret?"

Seffin turned to look at him and then cocked his head before nodding enthusiastically.

"Ka has a crush on the envoy."

A raw, skinned rabbit struck Ren in the face. Ka yelled from across the fire. "There's your dinner, asshole."

"Ow!" Ren said

"How do you know?" Seffin asked.

"Well, she's not denying it."

Ka glared. "There's a difference between a crush and finding someone attractive. I don't have a crush on him."

"So, you just want to have sex with him?" Seffin asked.

Ka looked up in thought, and then back down at Seffin. "It sounds worse when you say it like that."

Ren made kissing sounds to continue teasing her.

Poppy interjected, "Ok, this is a weird conversation to be having with your parent present, right? I can't be the only one that thinks that."

"You are not the only one that thinks that," the envoy said. He had been standing over by the mule, petting it.

Ren could see Ka's face blush deeply even in the firelight. Ka was always so organized and serious. He rarely had the chance to embarrass her, and he enjoyed every second of it.

"S-sorry," she stammered. "I'm uh..."

"It's ok." The envoy sat down by the fire. "I thought a bit about what you said, and you're right. We're going to be traveling for a while, and it doesn't help any of us if I'm constantly bringing the mood down."

"Oh. G-Good." She set one of the skewers into the fire and started working on another rabbit, "And like I said, if you need to talk about anything at all. I'm here."

"I know," he said, their eyes meeting for only a moment before they each found something else to focus on.

Ugh, now they're flirting. Gross.

For the first time since the contract began, they all ate dinner together by the fire. The evening light faded, the stars came out, and the moon started peeking out from behind a hill that overlooked them, coming to rest in the same exact place it did every night. Conversation continued late into the evening until the last logs of the fire were nothing but cinders and ash, and the chill of the night wind turned uncomfortable. Poppy peeled off first. Then the envoy. When Ka rose to her feet, Ren gave her a sly smirk and a wink. She flipped him off before heading toward the tents. Ren and Seffin sat in silence for a while before Seffin pulled some moisture out of the air and doused the embers.

As they both stood up Seffin turned to Ren. "Thank you for letting me come."

Ren chuckled. "I don't know if there is any *letting* you do anything."

"No, I mean." Seffin shifted his feet a bit. "It's nice to be around you guys."

Ren's breath caught in his throat. He tried his best to ignore his feelings. Not just because it was difficult to gauge Seffin's interest, but also because he wanted to focus on his goals. Becoming a merc. Seeing the world. He'd imagined, after a couple years with Ka and Poppy, he'd go it alone. It was a simple plan, but now every time he thought about it, his feelings for

Seffin kept bubbling up. Complicating everything, the more he thought about it, the more complicated they got, and the more complicated they got the faster his heart raced, and the faster his heart raced the more he felt like he wanted to run. Not to run away or anything, but like he had no choice but to run, to make his body match the energy that his heart was putting out. A simple plan complicated so simply.

"We're happy you're here too," he said.

Seffin smiled. "You have first watch, right?"

"Yeah."

"Do you mind if I sit up with you for a while?"

A feeling of innervation washed down the back of Ren's neck and continued out and over his body. "Sure, I'd like that."

They sat down and settled into a comfortable silence. Listening to the crickets and the frogs as they looked out into the night, watching for anything that might threaten their peace.

Seffin

After waiting in line to get into town for several hours, Seffin and the others finally walked through the main gate a little after noon. For a settlement that hadn't existed more than twelve years ago, Oleksandra's Harbor already approached the size of a small city. Roads paved with cobblestones laid out in a grid-like pattern connected the town's wood-framed buildings to one another, and a main street packed with stalls and shops snaked from the entrance all the way to the beach. Few paved roadways existed outside of major cities. A testament to the amount of money the Guild had funneled into it.

The streets were alive with fishers calling out their day's catch, captains and merchants haggling over transport prices, and food stalls crying out their daily menu to the crowd. It all mixed to make a cacophonous background ambiance while they all searched for the harbormaster's office. A baker, whose attitude visibly soured once she learned Seffin only wanted information instead of bread, directed them to a green building on the shore to find the harbormaster, but when they arrived, every building there had been painted green. Not a very helpful baker. Tender suggested they split up to look and meet back up in an hour. The envoy walked off with Ka while Tender hobbled away by themself, leaving Seffin and Ren to pair up for the search.

Peckish after waiting in line all morning, Seffin grabbed some fried fish as they walked the shore, watching for any building that might house the harbormaster. Ren commented on the fishy smell of his food, but Seffin didn't care. He hadn't eaten anything fried in oil since Prolivgrad, and he was beginning to learn from the Bolins' family dynamics that Ren just liked to whine in a way that invited mockery. Almost as if that was the intent. He would whine, Ka would say something critical, and Poppy would close the loop with a quip targeted at one or both of their children. It took a while to realize what was going on. That it was a practiced exchange. Bantering. Seffin yearned for that level of closeness with someone else, but he didn't have it. Not even with Kent, and he didn't really know how or where to start, just that it seemed cozy and comfortable.

They strolled along the shore until Ren spotted a shoemaker and insisted they stop in. He'd known Ren for years, but it wasn't until the time he spent with him on their final project that he realized his obsession with footwear. He'd packed three different pairs: one for walking around towns, one for the road, and one for combat. Seffin felt like teasing him on how unlikely it was a fight would break out with enough warning to change into the pair for combat, but he hesitated. Ren's attitude had cooled over the last week, after the night by the fire. He talked less, and when he did talk, he mostly complained about food. Probably just the amount of time they spent on the road, or at least Seffin hoped that was the reason he was grumpy. Maybe his complaints about all the salted fish weren't just idle whining?

That would be disappointing.

Dating someone whose mood shifted so drastically over a few meals sounded tiresome. Not that they were dating... yet. He considered simply asking Ren if something was wrong, but he found himself hesitating with that, too. A fear of saying the wrong thing niggled at him. A fear of being cast aside like his parents had done. Of misinterpreting words or misreading a situation. Of not being accepted. Regardless, despite only a minor interest in looking at footwear he agreed to stop by the shoemaker's shop, hoping it would brighten Ren's spirits.

A bell rang above the door as they entered, and a grey-haired old woman with thick glasses and a weathered voice popped up from behind the counter. "Welcome!" she said with a practiced earnestness bordering on fakery. "Have a look around, and let me know if you need anything." She disappeared behind the counter again, going back to whatever it is a shoemaker did behind their counters. Seffin didn't know. He'd never even bought shoes before. They'd always just appeared as if by magic whenever his current pair started to wear.

Ren perused the different shelves and displays with a look of concentration. Trying not to look out of place, Seffin meandered around the shop and feigned interest. He picked up a purple shoe that had a three-inch platform.

"Those are for people that wear dresses or robes. That way you can look taller than you actually are," Ren said, suddenly standing beside him.

"They look uncomfortable."

"They are. Extremely," he said, smiling.

Seffin set it down and walked over to the boots. He didn't *need* boots, but his current pair were the only ones he owned, it couldn't hurt to have a backup. He picked one up with a high top and buckles, turning it over in his hands. Ren sidled up to him again. "I had my eye on those, but she doesn't have my size. They should fit you though."

Ignoring that Ren somehow knew his shoe size, he shrugged his shoulders. "I could use a backup pair."

"Well, buy them then." Ren nodded toward the counter with a strange, intense look in his eye, like anticipation or hunger.

Seffin brought the pair of boots up to the counter and the old woman popped up. "Find what you're looking for?" The thin veneer of earnestness in her weathered voice had some boredom creeping in.

He nodded and pushed the boots toward her. When she told him the price, he thought he'd misheard, and when she told him the price again, he felt sick. The boots cost more than two months' rent living with Kent. "Oh, I think I'll just keep looking."

Seeing his reaction, her face soured. "If you can't afford to purchase anything, what are you doing in my shop?"

Embarrassment washed over him.

Ren came up to the counter and waved a finger at her. "You can't talk to your customers that way!"

Seffin put his hand on Ren's shoulder. He wanted this stop to help Ren's mood, and here he was getting in an argument over boots he didn't even really want or need. "It's ok. I don't need another pair. I'll meet you outside after you're done looking."

He exited the store before the clerk could say anything more and entertained himself watching the townsfolk go about their business. A skinny, pale man with thinning blonde hair in blue robes across the street flirted with a fishmonger. She frowned and furrowed her brow, looking thoroughly unimpressed. Seffin watched the man's face sink when she rebuffed him, but he finished his purchase, gave her a thin smile, and walked down the street into the town's Guild offices. It dawned on him that the harbormaster's office in a harbor owned by the Guild would probably reside within their building. Obvious, now that he'd thought of it. The shoe shop's bell rang, and Ren walked out with a smile on his face.

"Pick up something nice?" Seffin asked.

"Yes, actually," he said. "Sorry it took so long."

Seffin pointed over to the Guild offices. Ren slapped his forehead with his palm. "Of course."

They crossed the street, dodging people and wagons and a cute little stray dog scanning for scraps—Seffin gave him the last bite of his fried fish. The entrance to the building was open. It didn't have a receptionist, so they wandered around, stopping at a door labeled Harbormaster Tolkar's office. Ren's eyes got big. "Coruscare burn me." He pounded on the door.

"Aren't we supposed to meet with Tender first?" Seffin asked.

The door opened and an overwhelming smell of fish wafted out. Ren immediately covered his nose. Standing before them was the thin man in blue robes.

Ren spoke in a nasal tone while he covered his nose. "Are you serious right now?"

The blood drained from the man's face.

Ren seemed furious, but the nasal tone dulled the emotion in his voice. "You seriously took a position in the harbor responsible for bankrupting my town?"

"What's going on?" Seffin asked.

The man craned his head outside his office door to see several people looking at the commotion. He motioned them inside and closed the door behind them.

"It's not like I had much of a choice," he hissed. "What in hells are you doing here anyway?"

"We're the escorts for your envoy. How could you keep working for them after what happened?" Ren asked.

The man, Seffin presumed this was Tolkar, took a deep breath and massaged his temples. He produced a flask from his desk, took a long pull, and offered some to Ren.

Ren kept his nose plugged with one hand and waved the offer off with the other. "I'm good."

Tolkar took another pull and began, "I didn't have a choice. I've worked for the Guild my whole life. I don't know anything else. Besides, I got the feeling I wouldn't be alive right now if I didn't take their offer."

Seffin cleared his throat. "How do you two know each other?"

Tolkar gave Ren a questioning look.

"We can tell him." Ren recounted the tale of Gull Harbor to Seffin, and how Tolkar dragged him away on his mother's orders.

Seffin knew Ren looked nothing like the rest of his family. Ka had long straight hair with light beige skin, and Tender was much taller than both their children with pale white skin. Ren's skin was a deep brown, bordering on black, he considered the possibility they weren't all directly related, but even with that consideration he wouldn't have guessed Ren was an orphan from a destroyed town. Especially one famous for having no survivors.

"So, how'd you end up living with Tender?" Seffin asked

Tolkar looked stunned. "Wait, are they here?"

Seffin nodded. Tolkar took another pull from his flask.

"I don't know who it is you're escorting, but they're not an envoy. The Guild wouldn't pay for a specialist to fulfill a simple escort contract," Tolkar said.

Ren rolled his eyes. "Obviously."

"Wait, how is that obvious?" Seffin asked. He was beginning to feel more and more out of his depth.

"Whomever that envoy is he's barely ever been outside the city. He was terrified of a single husk, but somehow knows how to fight better than any of the instructors at Danver's Academy. He carries more money in his pouch than most envoys make in a year. And, on top of that, envoys usually can't fight—if they could they'd work as an escort—their whole job is delivering messages to and from Prolivgrad, and their pay is notoriously terrible because it's hardly work. They're a glorified letter carrier."

"Don't be rude," Tolkar said.

"And you didn't think to tell me? Do Tender and Ka know?" Seffin asked, the frustration becoming more evident in his tone.

"I genuinely thought you knew, but it doesn't change much. We're still getting paid by the Guild to escort someone they're claiming is an envoy."

Seffin thought about how much he didn't know about Ren, and then how much he didn't know about... a lot of things. How everyone around him possessed a depth of knowledge and understanding about the way the world worked that seemed both natural and beyond him in ways he couldn't fathom. Frustration and doubt had built within him for some time. His parents didn't raise him; they groomed him. Ren didn't respect him; he tolerated him. Kent didn't care about him; he pitied him. He felt a flash of anger. Not at Ren, but at himself. He'd been playing catch-up since he walked out from under his parents' wings, and the thought occurred to him that he might never actually catch up. He felt ill-equipped and hated himself for it. Regardless, he'd traveled all this way to do a job, and more than anything, he didn't want to be a burden.

"Let's go tell Tender and Ka," he said.

"Wait, they're *both* here?" Tolkar asked.

Ren sounded annoyed. "Yes, can we meet somewhere else? Maybe somewhere that doesn't reek of fish?"

"There's an inn a few blocks from here named Crowley's," Tolkar said. "I know the owner; he can get us a private room if we ask."

"Great." Ren nodded at Seffin and the two left the office.

On their way back to the meeting spot they passed by the fishmonger Tolkar had flirted with. She had a line of customers with annoyed faces while she spent all her time on a short man in the front who made eyes at her. They continued ambling through crowds that were becoming more and more over-whelming as the day wore on. The harbor's size hadn't kept up with its popularity. Ren kept looking over at Seffin. After a while, he turned to him. "You seemed kinda lost for a minute back there."

"It's fine," Seffin said. It wasn't, really, but he didn't want to bother Ren with his insecurities. Now wouldn't be the time to explain how completely out of his depth he felt. Especially given how moody Ren had been lately, and the meeting with this Tolkar fellow didn't seem to help things.

As they walked, Ren fished something out of his pack. The boots Seffin had looked at earlier. He tossed them over and Seffin caught them.

"Why?" He asked.

"I figured you could use them. The boots you're wearing are hardly fit for travel at this point."

That simply wasn't true, but the surprise gift helped him forget how lost he felt. They paused on the side of the walkway, Seffin pulled his boots off and replaced them with the fresh pair. They felt stiff and smelled new. He'd have to break them in before they'd feel comfortable. "I'll pay you back."

"Don't worry about it. Seriously," Ren said.

When they made it back to the meeting spot, Tender already sat waiting for them, and both Ka and the envoy joined soon after. Seffin explained the situation; that they had found the harbormaster, and they were to meet him at Crowley's this evening. The group decided to Lodge there for the night. Tender met with the bartender in the common room and arranged for three rooms. Seffin and Ren in one, Ka and Tender in another, and the envoy in a third. The inn had a nice-sized tub room, and everyone took turns washing up after their weeks of travel. Seffin hadn't realized how good a tub of warm water could feel until he lowered himself in. Using some kinetics to heat it up, the room soon filled with steam. Twenty straight days of walking had made his muscles sore; muscles he didn't even know he had. He laid his head back against the wooden rim of the tub while he soaked and let his mind drift.

Less than a year ago, he would have sworn to anyone who asked he'd end up working at the Guild with his father. Now, he lay floating in a tub in Oleksandra's Harbor on a merc contract, disowned by his family and desperately trying to learn enough just to keep up. He learned his friend was never who he said he was, the envoy they escorted wasn't who he said he was either, and somehow that was obvious to everyone else. Staring up at the wooden ceiling, his eyes followed the grain, twisting around the knots and winding to the end of a board before picking another board and doing the same. He took a deep breath of steam in, held it, then exhaled, warming his core and making his lungs tingle pleasantly.

He closed his eyes and tried to organize his thoughts. A lot of people were helping him. Ren, Tender, Ka... and Kent. The last thing he wanted in the world was to disappoint Kent. The man took him in when he had nowhere to go. He had to make this work, and to do that he'd have to listen and learn, and he wasn't going to do that by wallowing in a tub of water. No matter how comfortable and relaxing.

Exhausted from overheating, Seffin dressed and trudged downstairs. An evening wind blew through the open windows of the inn as he made his way through the common area, sending a chill up his spine after his hot soak.

A small, stuffy side room was set up for their meeting. He sat down next to Ren. Soon after, Tolkar entered and did a poor job hiding his shock at the sight of the envoy.

"What brings you out to my humble harbor?" Tolkar asked with a thin smile.

"Gull Harbor," the envoy said. "I need a full report. I want to know exactly what happened."

Everyone turned to look at him with varying levels of surprise.

Tolkar glanced at Ren and then at Tender. "I believe my report included everything. There isn't much to say. An amalgamation attacked. I ran."

The envoy's face hardened. "We both know it was more than that."

"Are you sure this is the right—" Tolkar looked at the mercenaries. "—setting, to be discussing this?"

The envoy gaze panned down as if lost in thought. Nodding to himself, he addressed the group, "There's no point in hiding my identity anymore, and it's probably safer if you know who I am and what to expect. My name is Troy Saunders. I'm the President of The Guild of Commerce. I told you I was an envoy because I'm hiding from the people who I believe are responsible for what happened at Gull Harbor. They're likely trying to kill me. Despite that, I'm here to find out exactly what happened." He turned his gaze back toward Tolkar. "Now. A *full* report. If you would."

Tender and Ren exchanged a look with Tolkar while Seffin tried to wrap his head around all he was hearing. It was plain to see Ren was pissed.

Tolkar started, "I delivered the news to Mayor Adegast that Gull Harbor would lose trade route status with the Guild. Per my orders, we planned for a Guild mystic and engineer to escort the pylon back to Prolivgrad. The villagers decided to take the Guild up on their relocation offer. On the day the mystic and engineer were supposed to arrive, we all gathered at the entrance to wait. Instead, another envoy came to tell us the team had been pulled back. That's when the amalgamation showed up and started killing everyone." Tolkar's complexion paled considerably while he spoke, which was impressive considering how fair his skin was already.

Troy nodded. "Yes. I knew that much, but how did the amalgamation withstand the barrier? I checked before I came. According to the records, there should have been enough charge left to deter even something as big as an amalgamation for at least another few days."

"That's true. I'm no engineer, but when I ran to charge the pylon, even I could tell it had enough charge to repel a normal amalgamation."

Troy arched his eyebrow. "I thought you ran immediately."

"I... I did. After I attempted to charge the pylon."

"So, an amalgamation attacked. It was killing everyone. Then you ran further into the town to charge the pylon. That's lucky it didn't catch you."

Tolkar shook his head. "Well, it would have. Mayor Adegast distracted it."

Troy nodded like he knew what Tolkar was going to say. "That's one of the details that bothered me. The Adegasts were warriors, and Sharon was no exception. Your report said nothing about a fight. Odd, considering Gull Harbor housed one of the best sword masters in the world."

"The best," Tender corrected. "She was the best." Seffin could have sworn he saw Tender glance at Ren when he said it, but Ren only stared daggers at Troy. "The only person I know who could match her is Kiko Zollinger, the Empress of Garvelle."

Troy turned to Tolkar. "Tell me what happened to Sharon."

"She died," Ren said, "protecting me."

The shock in Troy's eyes matched the shock Seffin felt. Not just an orphan then, but the son of the greatest sword master in the world according to Tender. For a simple escort contract, this had turned into a meeting of some of the most important people in recent history. Tender, Troy, and now Ren... next they'll say Ka is a princess.

Troy continued, "I didn't know she had a child."

"It would be odd if you did," Tender said. "She settled down when she had Ren, and she was cagey about that information.

Her history painted a large target on her back. That's part of the reason we've kept his last name a secret."

"I'm sorry to have to ask this, but did you see her die?" Troy looked to Ren.

"No," Ren said through gritted teeth, "she had Tolkar take me away before that."

"Tell me about the amalgamation. If it withstood a barrier and was a match for Sharon, it must have been bad."

Ren's hands gripped the side of the table. "Nothing it did made a sound. I watched it slice people up, but all I could hear was bodies hitting the ground... and screams."

Troy's gaze fell downward. He shook his head. "That's confirmation as far as I'm concerned."

"Of what?" Ka asked

"I'm sure that amalgamation escaped from a Guild facility. That's how they knew to pull the team back."

Ka looked disgusted. "Why would they pull a team that could have helped protect the village?"

"Because they knew how dangerous it was. The amalgamation that rampaged through Danvers' Academy was from the same program. To be frank, we're lucky the thing didn't kill far more people. Which is to say your mother must have succeeded in killing it."

Ren perked up. "You think she could be alive?"

"I didn't say that. I'm saying if that amalgamation had gotten away it would have gone for more people. Mercs would have been recruited to kill it and we would have heard about it. They were lucky she took care of it."

"Stop saying *they* as if you're not the president of The Guild." Ren's eyes were wet. "You're one of them."

Troy shook his head. "I didn't know. My mother and his father—" He pointed at Seffin. "—set up a project off the books. It's true that it was my decision to break the contract with your town, but I had no idea about the mutated amalgamations. And it wasn't me that recalled the Guild team."

"My father is responsible for Gull Harbor?" Seffin's face went hot with anger and disbelief. "And Danver's Academy?"

He knew his father cared more about his job than anything else. More than his mother and more than Seffin for sure, but he didn't expect this. That his father would be willing to let people die. No. That his father would be willing to kill people.

"Both of them, yes," Troy said it matter-of-factly.

Seffin felt like a metal pin had stuck through his brain. His ears rang.

"What's the plan then?" Tender asked. "Let's say we expose Jessica and Pulpin. They'd end up in jail, but that leaves the presidency in a runoff. We all know who wins if that happens."

"Paul Winnow," Ren said, but he had an edge of barely contained rage in his voice that Seffin hadn't heard before. He'd seen Ren mad. He'd seen Ren frustrated. This was different, almost murderous.

Ka looked like she wanted to throw up.

"That'll likely start a war," Tender said. "Garvelle, Lighton, and Estaba are all rightfully livid at the stranglehold Egal has on crystal distribution. Winnow's Egal First strategy would make that scarcity several times worse. As much as everyone thinks your mother's Gogallo Initiative is a joke, it involves cooperating with the other nations instead of sentencing their smaller towns to death."

Troy threw his hands up, frustrated. "What would you have me do then?"

"She belongs in jail. She belongs in The Pit." Ren's words came out slowly, venom dripping off each one.

Ka looked like she had a realization. "So the people you think are trying to kill you—"

"My mother," Troy said with a practiced, dispassionate tone. "And his father." He pointed at Seffin again.

"The Pit is too kind for someone willing to kill their own son," Ka said.

The Pit was rarely talked about. A dungeon for murderers and rapists, nobody came out alive. Not unless it was for an execution.

Tender frowned. "You're all too young to remember just how bad the Sol Wars were, but whichever path avoids a war between the nations is the one I recommend. The world will have enough problems with husk numbers spiraling out of control."

Seffin startled as Ren slammed his fist on the table. "She killed my whole town, Poppy. She killed my mom."

Tender put a hand on their son. "I know, but if Winnow wins, he'd force the hand of the other nations. A war with mystics on both sides and Prolivgrad at the center? Think of how much damage you can do just by yourself, Ren. Think of how many more people would die with mystics on either side icing and blowing each other up."

"I don't think I can stomach just letting her get away with it," Troy said.

Tender gave a sympathetic smile. "This is why, other than sitting on the board at the Lodge, I turned down leadership positions after the war. I've made enough of these choices already. This one's yours to make." They gestured to the room. "I'll go along with whatever you all decide. All I offer is my council."

A heavy silence overtook the room. Ka seemed lost in thought, Ren had his eyes in his lap and a grim look on his face, Troy sat frowning like he'd just been made to swallow nails, and Tolkar's eyes kept flitting to the door like a scared animal searching for an escape route.

Seffin's head started spinning. "I'm sorry, I think I need to go get some air." He stood up to a table full of concerned looks.

"Are you feeling ok?" Ka asked.

"I'll be fine. I just need a second." He left the stuffy meeting room and made it out into the common area. The breeze blowing through the open windows cooled him down, but the din of patrons drinking and eating made it difficult to focus. Pulpin, his father, was responsible for killing Ren's mom? For the massacre at Danver's Academy? He shook his head and decided to go outside for a walk. Halfway to the door, a familiar, weathered voice shouted from across the room, "There you are you thief!"

Seffin saw the greying older shoemaker from earlier stomping toward him. "Me?" he asked, pointing to himself stupidly, as if me could mean anyone else.

When she reached him, she shoved him to the ground, hard.

"Take those boots off before I call the guards."

Seffin looked around at everyone staring. "They were a gift."

"I'm sorry. Did I gift wrap those for you and forget about it?" The woman feigned a thinking pose. "Oh, no I think I'd remember that. Take them off, now."

Tolkar must have heard the commotion from the other room because he was suddenly standing over Seffin, getting between him and the old shoemaker. "What's going on here?"

"This little monster stole from me."

"Is that true?" Tolkar looked down at Seffin.

"No!" Seffin said. "They were a gift. Ren got them for me."

Tolkar frowned knowingly and turned to Ren, standing in the doorway of the meeting room. The guilt on Ren's face was obvious, he avoided eye contact and looked at the ground. He'd stolen them. Seffin couldn't catch his breath, like someone just knocked the wind out of him. He felt violated and betrayed. He removed the boots and handed them over. "I didn't know."

"You stay the hells away from my shop." The older woman stormed off, shoving her way through the common room.

Ren rushed over to Seffin. "I'm sorry—"

Seffin shoved him away. "What the fuck is wrong with you?"

"It's just that... they were the perfect size, and I wanted you to have something nice." He reached out to put a hand on Seffin's shoulder. "And she was so godsdamned rude—"

Seffin shoved Ren off him again and this time he stumbled back, tripping over an empty chair and falling to the ground. "Stay the hells away from me."

He turned and ran through the common room. Dodging around chairs and pushing through people until he made it out the door, out into the night. Catching his breath, he picked a direction and started walking, trying to get as far away from Ren as possible. His doubts from earlier rushed back into the forefront of his mind. What was he thinking? No one respected him, especially not Ren. No one wanted him here or liked him. He was just the naïve kid they had to babysit because he demanded to come along. A burden. The thoughts buzzed in his head as he wandered the streets teary-eyed, bare-footed, and alone.

Ren

The morning sun in Oleksandra's Harbor shone through the window at a perfect angle to catch Ren's eyes. Morning after morning he woke up squinting, hating the sun for daring to disturb him. He glanced at Seffin's bed to see if he'd already left for the day like every other morning this week. Seffin had been avoiding him. Ren hoped today would be different, the day they'd start the journey back to Prolivgrad, but Seffin had already packed and left. Ren sat on the edge of his bed, alone in an empty room.

After dressing for the day, he went downstairs where breakfast was already underway. Ka and Troy sat across from each other at a bench in the dining room of the inn, eating some toast and laughing about something. Ka tore off a piece and threw it at Troy's head, which only brought on more laughter. They were flirting. *Gross.* Ren grabbed a seat next to them and craned his head, searching for a server. He'd grown attached to his morning coffee, and he wanted one last cup before they hit the road.

Ka looked around. "Still no Seffin?"

Ren shook his head. "I don't know how he's still so mad after five days?"

"How are you so dumb?"

"What do you mean? I didn't steal *from* him. I stole *for* him."

When the words left his mouth Troy winced, and Ka pinched the bridge of her nose the way she did when she was frustrated.

"How many times do we have to go over this, Ren? Stop stealing things. It's not hard. It's not complicated. You'd think after being caught so many times you'd get it by now, stealing makes you an asshole. You're an asshole!" Her voice crescendoed until she was shouting at him in the middle of the dining area. Some people turned to see what the problem was, but they all went back to their meals in short order.

Ren couldn't explain why he stole. He knew it was wrong, and he knew it hurt people, but in the moment, the excitement and desire overtook his inhibitions, his thoughts would darken, and suddenly it was done. Like he was dying of thirst and whatever object he wanted was a drink of water, and when he drank, the feeling—the euphoria—of being alive would energize him from his head to his toes. Even thinking about it now, he could feel his skin tingling. His fingers itching.

"You betrayed him," Troy added.

That didn't seem fair. He wanted to do something nice for Seffin, and he wanted that shop owner to pay for being so rude. "How is it a betrayal if I did it for him?"

"You made him a part of something he didn't want or know about, and it blew up in his face. Like if I gave you a poisoned apple and watched you bite into it. That's hard to forgive."

Putting it that way *did* sound bad, even if getting advice from a man who moped half the way here didn't sit well with him. A man who lied about who he was and whose actions bankrupted his hometown. But Troy didn't recall the Guild mystic, his mother did. Just like Seffin didn't help create the amalgamation that killed everyone, his father did. None of that mattered anymore anyway. They'd ultimately decided *not* to expose Jessica. Troy was going to blackmail her into behaving herself going forward, and that would have to be good enough. None of them wanted a war on their conscience. Though, seeing Jessica and Pulpin disappear into The Pit, never to be seen again, would have felt amazing.

Ren's coffee arrived, but he ignored it. He stood to leave and find Seffin to... do something. He hadn't thought that far ahead, but as he started to move away from the table Ka grabbed his arm.

"I want to give you a warning," she said. "I talked with Poppy, and this stealing business is over. If we catch you again, you're done working with us. Our next contract is a big one. We can't take anyone that's going to be a liability. This is the first settlement you've been to since moving to Prolivgrad and you stole something on our first day here. It's juvenile and thoughtless and stupid and not to mention illegal and—"

"—Ok I get it!"

"—and selfish. If you weren't family, we'd have removed you from the contract and left you to fend for yourself."

Ka had been angry at him many times in his life. He'd been punched in the face, slapped, had his ear pulled, and his mouth washed out with soap when he'd called her names, but this wasn't anger. And it was far from the begrudging forgiveness she usually extended after the dust settled on whatever wrong he'd committed. Something had shifted.

"I understand," he said.

"Good." She let go of his arm. "You're an adult now. Time to act like it."

When she released him, he practically ran from the building. The smell of the salt air and fish assaulted his nose. Even growing up by the sea, he'd forgotten—or glossed over—the offensive smells of living on the coast, which were somehow worse than the warmed-over-trash odor prevalent in Prolivgrad. He'd be happy to be rid of the place.

Seffin would be practicing his control in a clearing on the edge of town about a half mile from the shoreline, the same place he'd spent the last four mornings in a row. Ren passed by the Guild offices on his way there and, out by the shimmering edge of the barrier, found him barely containing a fireball that looked like it could level half a city block. It winked away when Seffin noticed him watching. Shirtless, he glistened with sweat in the morning sun from the heat of the fireball he'd been holding.

"Is it time to go already?" he asked.

Ren approached. "No." He paused, trying to think of how to say what he wanted to say. "I—"

"I'm not interested in another apology."

Godsdamn, he's making this hard.

"I'm not here to apologize again. Just... let me say something, and then I'll leave you alone."

Ren felt a chill as Seffin froze the sweat on his body to cool down. The technique was a simple one that Ren had taught him, but it required a good amount of control—for Seffin at least—to perform without getting frostbite. He'd been making progress, but there were still some red spots and sores on his skin from cooling it down too much. A raised line by his waste that led down—

"Looking at something?" Seffin asked

Peeling his eyes away he said, "I..." He took a deep breath to calm himself. "I'm sorry—"

"—I just said—"

"—Please just let me finish." Ren caught Seffin's eyes. On his way here he'd thought about what he wanted to say. About all the times he treated Seffin unfairly. "I'm sorry for before. For treating you like you were a burden in the academy. I'm sorry for talking down to you while we prepared for our final. I'm sorry I didn't help you more on this contract. I got so caught up in doing my first big job that I didn't think about how completely new everything about this is to you. And I'm sorry about the boots. I should have known better. I *do* know better. I just... I'll never betray your trust again. Whether we're friends again or not. Whether you come along on our next contract or not. Whether you never speak to me again or not."

Seffin's face was unreadable. The moment stretched on uncomfortably while they stared at each other. He walked over to his shirt and put it on, then turned back to Ren and said simply, "Ok."

"Ok?"

Seffin walked past him on his way back to the harbor. "Yeah. Ok, but for not being another apology there were a lot of sorries in there. Also, for the record, I didn't think you talked down to me during the final." He looked at Ren. "Are you coming?"

Ren ran to catch up. "So we're ok?"

"I don't know, but my control needs work, and it would be stupid to ignore your help."

Better than nothing. Ren counted himself lucky. The last week had been relentlessly boring. He'd spent every day by himself or with Poppy who only ever talked about tinkering and pylons... when they weren't lecturing him.

They headed toward the harbor area and started on the way back to Crowley's Inn which led them past both the shoe shop and the Guild's offices. Food stands had opened since he came through earlier and people milled about now where earlier the road was almost empty. The smell of cooked meat and melted butter cut the briny fish smell a little, but not enough. It could never be enough. Tolkar stood next to an empty fish stand looking dour. He waved at them. "This is your final day here, yes?"

"No progress?" Seffin asked. Ren didn't know what he meant.

Tolkar looked down at the ground and shifted his feet before saying. "She might have taken the day off."

"I think you should leave her alone," Seffin said.

"Excuse me?" Tolkar's face turned a deep crimson.

"I've seen her flirting with other people. She's a lot younger than you too, and you're the harbormaster and she's a fishmonger... it's not like she can ignore you or tell you to go away. It just seems like you're not—"

"—Ok you don't know what you're talking about."

"Are you harassing young women?" Ren decided to pile on even though he hadn't a clue to whom they were referring.

"I'm not. It's not like that." He shook his head. "Anyway, I thought you two were leaving."

"We are. We're just heading over to meet with Poppy and the others."

"Good," he said. "No offense, but you're quite a lot of trouble."

"I could say the same thing," Ren said.

Tolkar flashed a strained smile. "Say bye to Tender and Ka for me." Then he turned and left, disappearing into the crowd in the direction of his office.

Ren didn't think he'd ever like Tolkar. He'd only ever seen him think of himself, other than saving his life in Gull Harbor, and even with that, he only escorted Ren to Prolivgrad because his own life was on the line. Ren remembered the trip all those years ago vividly. Tolkar couldn't wait to get rid of him. Sure, he wasn't the easiest child to escort. He tried to run back to Gull Harbor several times, and when they stopped in Vicksbough, he kept stealing money from people until they were kicked out of town. But he'd just lost his mother and everyone he'd ever known, and it's not like Tolkar offered any compassion. At one point, they met up with a caravan heading to Prolivgrad, and he practically disappeared, leaving Ren to walk alone or bother the other caravanners. When they finally made it, he brought him straight to Poppy's doorstep, where he waited only long enough for the door to open before he started backing away. Not even a goodbye. He deserved his loneliness as far as Ren was concerned.

Back at the inn, where the rest of the group had already packed and readied for the trip, he walked past Ka loading the mule up for the road. She pulled him aside. "How'd that go?"

"Coulda gone better. Coulda gone worse."

She slapped him on his back. "Atta boy. Just remember. If you fuck up again, he'll probably never forgive you. I wouldn't."

"You always know just what to say."

She winked and went back to packing the mule.

The rest of the morning went by without fanfare. The group was on the road before midday and blessedly left the salty sea air and the pungent smell of fish behind them as they went.

The incline coming out of Oleksandra's Harbor stretched on for miles and miles, and to Ren, after a week of sitting around, it felt like walking upstairs the whole time. Throughout the day, Ka and Troy's affectionate back and forth turned into open flirtation. Obnoxious, but at least Troy's mood would fare better on the way back than on the way here.

They stopped for the day as the sun set, and before long the night birds began their hooting and cawing. Falling back into the routine they had grown accustomed to, Troy and Ren began setting up the tents, Seffin started charging the traveling crystal while Poppy set up the fire, and Ka, responding to Ren's preliminary whining about the rations of fish they'd brought, disappeared into the forest to gather some rabbits and squirrels. The woods held less danger this close to the harbor, but tomorrow and for the next couple weeks, it would be back to salted fish. If Ren never saw a fish again after this trip it would be too soon.

The first howl came while Ren worked on one of the tents. Deep and menacing, it echoed around him, sending a chill up his spine. Hoarwolves sometimes ranged near Prolivgrad and howled during the night, but this one sounded wrong, warped. Amalgamated. Dropping the unfinished tent on the ground he jogged over to where Poppy sat by the fire.

"You heard that too?" Poppy asked.

A rhetorical question, a deaf person could have felt the vibrations in the air. "Where's Ka?" Ren asked.

"Still in the forest." Poppy continued stoking the fire. Readying it for rabbits or some other unlucky rodent.

"Wait, she's still out there?"

Poppy finally looked up at him. "Your sister is more than capable of taking care of herself. In the woods especially."

Ka learned wild wielding from the Nari'ko Wilders during the years she and Poppy spent there before Ren moved in. Poppy was right, between her earth slipping and her wind blades he couldn't imagine an amalgamation that would be able to catch her. Another howl pierced the night, closer this time.

"It's coming here," Ren said, worry slipping into his voice.

Poppy sighed in exasperation as they rose to their feet. "I was hoping we'd make this whole trip without anything big like this happening, but these Guild contracts always end up with complications. Where's Seffin and Troy?"

Troy, who had been relieving himself in the forest, approached the campfire. "Here." He stopped to stand next to Ren. "I saw Seffin on the way. He went to grab your blade."

The ground vibrated to the rhythm of footfalls. The creatures were closing in quickly.

"Troy, your job is to stay alive," Poppy said. "We'll handle putting it down."

Seffin popped out of the darkness between the trees, tossed Ren his blade, and took a spot next to Poppy who already had several grenades in their hand. *Do they just carry those around?*

"What are those?" Troy asked, looking at the grenades.

Poppy held one aloft. "They explode."

"They what?"

The sound of the night birds stopped, and everyone fell silent. For a moment, they heard nothing but the crackling of the fire and felt nothing but the rumbling in the ground. Ren squinted his eyes trying to see deeper into the forest. Hoping to give himself any forewarning of when the attack would come. The sound of a hundred branches snapping at once blasted out of the trees as an amalgamated hoarwolf as tall as a full grown man leapt out of the darkness, landing directly on top of where Troy would have been had he not tumbled out of the way.

Ren met its lifeless eyes and felt a moment of pity for the creature. Hoarwolves were dangerous, but they usually left people alone. This abomination with its rotting flesh, blood-soaked fur, and frothing mouth barely resembled the noble creatures he used to daydream about in class. Bones snapping sounded around the campfire as Poppy slammed their hammer into one of its hind legs. The creature barely seemed to notice. Ren made an ice lance and hurled it but missed the mark when it used its remaining legs to leap at Troy again, catching his arm in its mouth. Troy screamed as he stabbed at its face with his sword. Running forward with his will-blade, a lance of ice pierced through the beast's side. The creature flinched, releasing Troy but causing Ren's sword thrust to miss its neck.

Could you stay still for even a second?

Poppy swung their hammer at the creature's hindquarters again, but the wolf leapt away into the woods before the hit could land. The smell of rotting flesh permeated the camp. Troy lay on the ground cradling his arm. Poppy willed several of their grenades into the air. "Seffin, some light please."

Seffin summoned a fireball above the camp as bright as a small sun. He increased the amount of fuel and allowed the ball to burn through it to intensify the illumination. *When did he learn how to do that?* It was unstable, though. He was biting off more than he could chew. Ren wrapped some of his will around the fireball. Their eyes met in the red-orange light.

The wolf hobbled around, circling the camp. Poppy positioned grenades between themselves and the amalgamation. Out of the corner of his eye, Ren spotted a second wolf, and then a third.

"Poppy..."

"I see them."

"I can take care of the injured one if you'll let me drop the light," Seffin said. The three wolves continued to circle. Grotesque puppets performing a dance resembling the lives they should have led. Stalking prey and running as a pack.

"Do it," Poppy said

The fireball dissipated in an instant. Seffin pulled water from the air with one hand and raised his other up, creating a wall of fire behind the injured wolf. *Smart, two techniques that don't require a lot of control.* Cornered, it launched itself toward the group. His ice lance bloomed out the back of its head, and it landed with a thunderous crash that shook the ground. In the ruckus, the remaining two wolves took the opening. One had its mouth around Seffin before he could jump out of the way. Still in its jaws, he screamed and thrust a hand down the wolf's throat. Thousands of needle-sharp icicles burst out its body. The wolf went limp and fell with Seffin still in its jaws. The other ran face-first into one of Poppy's grenades. They activated it, and the wolf barely danced back fast enough to avoid the blast.

Just then the wind picked up, snuffing out the campfire. *Finally.* Thick dust and ash filled the air. "Cover your mouth!" Poppy yelled over the sound of the howling gale. Ren did as he was told. He squinted to see in the moonlight, through the haze of dust and ash whipping around them, Ka strolled through camp. Her dark hair thrashed around while she raised her hand out in front of her, fingers spread wide. Her face looked... terrifying. She was more a force of nature than anything resembling his sister. She closed her hand into a tight fist and the howling wind pulled in the direction she held her arm. A muffled shockwave slammed past his head which left his vision blurry and his ears ringing.

It was done.

The air still swirled with dust and smelled of rot and ash. Seffin stood up from inside the mouth of the hoarwolf that tried to eat him and dusted his clothing off. The wolf couldn't have truly bitten down given how little blood was on him. Troy groaned from where he lay and Ka rushed to his side while

Poppy started limping toward the last hoarwolf, dead twenty or so paces into the forest. Ren caught up with them and Seffin followed suit.

The scene was gruesome. Its jaw was broken with dirt, sticks, and debris propping it open. The body was barely recognizable. Every part of it from the throat down had holes with dirt spilling out of them, a trail of organs and entrails fanning out behind it.

Seeing Seffin, Poppy grabbed him by the shoulders and looked him over up and down. "No puncture wounds. That's lucky." They patted him on the back. "You did well back there. Really well."

A flash of jealousy jolted through Ren. Thinking back on the battle, he might as well have not been there, whereas Seffin saved Troy and killed two of the hoarwolves almost completely on his own, and the laranee was mostly him as well. Ren looked over at Seffin who blankly returned his gaze. *Who would have guessed?* Only a few months ago he was bound for work at the Guild, another cog in their machine. What a waste that would have been.

Poppy sighed and looked at the wolf. "We'll have to move camp if we want to escape this smell." They turned back. "How's Troy?"

"Ka's tending to him," Ren said.

Poppy nodded and hobbled off. Seffin stared down at the wolf. "Do you think..." He started to say and then looked up into the canopy of the trees. Ren's heart skipped a beat seeing the moonbeams illuminate his face. Even covered in dirt and sweat he was handsome. Worry gripped his insides thinking how they all could have died. Hells, Seffin almost *did* die in the mouth of a hoarwolf.

"Do you think my dad knew I was here?" Seffin finished.

The realization hit him like a hammer. He'd forgotten about Seffin's dad with everything that happened after their meeting in the harbor. "I... don't know." He went to put a comforting hand on his arm, but Seffin pulled away.

"It's fine, Ren." His eyes shimmered with tears. "I just need some rest." He made his way toward camp.

Instinct said to let him go, but that didn't make it hurt any less. Whatever reassurances Seffin needed couldn't come from him. Not right now.

How could I forget about his dad?

He knew the answer, but he didn't like it. It's because he only ever thought about himself. He hadn't stolen the boots for Seffin. Not really. He'd stolen them so he could impress him, and when that backfired, he spent the week worried only about seeking forgiveness. Not one thought crossed his mind of how the meeting's revelations might have affected Seffin. Not one thought about anyone other than himself. Ka was right. He was both thoughtless and selfish.

They packed up the tents and moved a mile down the road where the smell of rot couldn't reach. The mule took some encouragement after all the excitement, but some coaxing from Seffin and an apple got him moving again. Ka worked on

Troy's arm by the fire while Seffin charged their crystal and Poppy made progress on the rabbits and squirrels Ka brought back with her. The relative peace of the moment felt jarring after the violence from only an hour ago, and Ren found he couldn't sit still. Maybe it was jitters after the attack, maybe it was that he hadn't done his nightly sparring session with Troy, or maybe it was that he couldn't keep his mind off Seffin, but he found himself in the woods alone, practicing his forms with his will-blade at a frantic pace.

He flowed between the five base forms from the academy and danced between different augmentations and then back into the five base forms and then through the form his mother taught him before he lost her. His biceps and shoulders ached from the effort, and he loved it. His thighs and calves screamed for him to stop, but he refused. Denying himself felt empowering. He'd been taught to listen to his body when he practiced, but listening to himself never got him what he really wanted. He listened to himself when he stole. He listened to himself when he begged forgiveness instead of earning it. He only ever listened to himself.

No more.

The itch started in his finger like it always did, but this time it didn't stop. Spreading up his forearm, over his shoulder, down his back, and all the way to his feet. He swung harder and faster. Dipped lower and leapt higher. The itch overtook him and made itself his whole world, but he didn't care. He let it wash over him like a shower of needles. He danced and swung and danced and swung and he found that it wasn't an itch at all. It was the world. It was reality. He felt every bead of sweat on his brow, every pine needle on the ground, he could smell the rot from a mile away, he could see the air flowing around him and his blade. The night blurred as if behind frosted glass and was replaced with a truer, more complete version of itself.

He vomited.

His skin burned like fire. His sweat turned to steam, and the salt within it left a stinging film on his body. The air he sucked into his lungs wasn't enough. It could never be, but the thought of exhaling felt like suicide. His vision went fuzzy, and he fell to his hands and knees, dropping his sword on the way. With all the strength he could muster he held himself up off the ground, but it didn't last. He collapsed onto the bed of the forest.

***

Ren awoke in a tent. His tent, probably, but he didn't remember coming back so he couldn't be sure. When he made to sit up his body responded with pain. Groaning, he tried again with similar results. Ka poked her head in with a disapproving look on her face as he collapsed back onto his pillow.

"Morning, idiot."

"Ouch," he said.

She sighed and sat next to him before laying her hands on his bare chest and closing her eyes. He realized he was completely naked underneath the blanket. *Where are all my clothes?* He felt her will bump up against his own. Exhaling, he let it flow through him.

"You didn't think my hands were full enough with Troy's broken arm and Seffin's bite? What the hells happened?"

Ren thought about what happened and he couldn't rightly say. All he knew is one moment he flowed through his forms and the next the world collapsed on him.

"Where are my clothes?" He asked.

Ka pointed to a pile of sweat-soaked clothing in the corner of the tent. "Seffin found you burning up. He brought you in here and did that cooling down trick you two do."

Ren's eyes went wide. "S-Seffin brought me back?"

Ka gave a wicked grin and waggled her eyebrows. "Oh yeah, he certainly did." She pressed on his chest and a soothing ripple spread out from her palm and over his body. "You just seem sore, but your skin is warm and swollen. Like a sunburn."

"Doubtful, it's pretty hard for me to sunburn."

She smacked his chest. "I know, dummy. That's why I asked what the hells happened last night. Practicing some elementalism?"

"I was practicing my forms and suddenly everything went..." He fought for the words to articulate what happened, but he didn't know if he'd make any sense. "Blurry? I remember puking."

"Yeah, we found that," she said, and pivoted her palms. Raising her hands, Ren could feel her pulling her will out. The pain and the burning faded away until only an echo remained. Ka explained that to him once. Something about how bodies weren't meant to heal this fast, so the feeling can stick around until it realizes it's better.

"Try moving," she said.

Ren told his arms to move, and they obeyed.

"Now try standing."

"I'm naked."

"Oh right, well if you find you can't stand, just yell or something."

She patted him on the head and left. Standing up, he dressed quickly, still a little sore despite Ka's healing. The sweat salt and oil on his skin felt gross, too. *Three weeks until I can get a proper bath.* He packed his tent and made ready as fast as he could, not wanting to hold the group up any longer than he already had.

Back on the road, Poppy matched his pace, a worried expression on their face. "Ka says your vision went blurry?"

He shook his head. "Everything went blurry. All my senses felt fuzzy."

Poppy nodded. "Practicing your forms?"

"Yes."

"Interesting. Feel ok now?"

"I feel like I need a bath, but other than that I'm good."

Poppy looked back at Seffin, walking next to the mule, and then over at Ren again and chuckled. Ren scoffed. "Would you two stop? Gods, it's embarrassing enough without you rubbing it in."

"Aww, but think of how fun it is for us. Let me know if you need a break." They smiled and fell back to walk next to Ka and Troy.

Ren kept himself in the front of the group. If he looked forward at the empty road, he could convince himself he was alone, and if he was alone, he didn't need to worry about feeling embarrassed. That worked for the five minutes before Seffin caught up with him. Ren rubbed the back of his neck. "Oh, morning Sef."

"I had to take your clothes off because they were soaked, and I didn't want them to frostbite you while I cooled you down."

Straight to the point no matter how mortifying.

"Oh, that's fine." It wasn't. "I'm... uh, glad it was you, actually." He wasn't. "It would have been much more embarrassing if Ka was the one that had to do it." He would have preferred Poppy.

"Oh? Good then," Seffin said. "I just wanted to make sure you didn't think I was *trying* to take a look at your pe—"

"Nope! Didn't assume that! We're good." He chuckled afterward to try and keep things light. Not anxious laughter at all. Not in the least.

"I mean—" Seffin's eyes gazed into the middle distance, "—it was... it's quite... it's not like you have anything to be ashamed of."

Ren silently wondered if it was actually possible to die of embarrassment. Seffin gave him that blank look he did when he tried to process a conversation, then blinked a couple times, shook his head, and asked, "Soooo, what happened?"

"Not sure. I was practicing my forms. Things went fuzzy and I collapsed."

"That can't be all," Seffin said, stating the obvious. Again. Like he always did.

Ren thought back. He'd been taking his frustrations out in his practice, intentionally trying to burn himself out. He remembered pushing well beyond exhaustion, and then for a moment everything changed, or at least his perception of everything.

"All I know is that I was practicing hard. Everything went fuzzy and felt—" He scratched his head. "—more? Somehow. Then I puked, my skin felt like it was on fire, and that's the last I remember."

Seffin looked lost in thought for a moment. "Do you think Ka would teach me air and earth elementalism?"

Finally, a topic that wasn't about him. For once, Ren didn't mind the whiplash-inducing conversational shift. "One of her favorite things in the world is acting superior, so if she's not busy with something else—" Ren nodded toward Troy, who gave a confused look and nodded back. "—I bet you could convince her. Why? Are you getting bored of fire and water?"

"After last night they seem far more useful than what I was led to believe."

"The academies downplay how useful the wild elements are. Ka told me they don't like wind and earth because they're harder to teach and take longer to master."

"The academy said it's because they're *uncivilized* elements."

"The only thing uncivilized about them is that a bunch of crotchety old professors don't like to admit they're bad at something. That's what I think anyway. There was a split in the teachings way, way back in the day, but to me it just seems like old people doing what old people do."

Seffin cocked his head. "What old people do?"

"Refusing to change. Pretending their way is the only way. Even Dunreedy thought the whole thing was stupid, but as far as professors go, he's young."

Seffin nodded. "So they're harder to master?"

Ren tried out some air elementalism with Ka a year back and he still couldn't produce more than a strong gust, let alone the wind blades and gale-force winds Ka made. Fire was easy to make, but hard to control. Making sure it had enough fuel and containing it until you wanted to release was the only hard part. Water was easy to control, but harder to make. You either needed a source of water or you had to be proficient enough to pull it out of the air or plants or something. At least water liked to stay together though; air was like trying to move a mountain of sand with a fishing net. When he practiced with her, Ka said his net had too big of holes. Either way, he set it aside, and he never even tried earth after that.

"I don't know if it's a matter of difficulty so much as they're just different. A lot different. It's like having to re-learn how to walk."

Seffin seemed to accept that answer. Without saying anything he fell back to where Ka and Troy were walking. No doubt trying to immediately set up a time for her to teach him.

Ren found himself alone at the front of the group again. Which was just fine. Despite the disappointments of the last week, he smiled at the thought of completing his first big contract. The first thing he'd do is buy Seffin some boots, and the second thing he'd do is stock up on jerky. Never again would he spend weeks on end eating salted fish every day.

Flicker

On a cool night sitting in the dingy corner of a grimy pub on a run-down street in the seediest part of Prolivgrad, Flicker could practically taste the finish line. She'd climbed the ladder of underlings for years, and when she found herself missing a rung, she piled up enough bodies to climb up anyway. Nothing would bar her path. The next mark should be her last, and then... what? She drained her tankard of ale and slammed it down on the table, when the barmaid glanced over at the noise Flicker already had her finger raised, asking for another round. She knew what came after, and it terrified her. Hence, all the ale. She had a day before her window opened on her target anyway, so she could afford to indulge herself.

That's what Noah was for.

He sat across from her with his shaved head and dopey brown eyes looking impressed. Impressed at what? She didn't know. She didn't really care, either. She'd found him at a different grimy pub on a separate rundown street a few days ago looking sad and lonely. Philandering had lost him his wife and, instead of coping with the consequences, he decided to drown them instead. Flicker needed a distraction so she planted a seed of interest and trotted off to make sure her new plaything wasn't caught up in any business that would bite her in the ass. Running into another Cara would spell the end of her mission, and she'd come too far and sacrificed too much not to close the book on this. After some digging, the cheater turned out to be just a cheater, so across from her he sat until on top of him she would be.

She flipped a coin to the barmaid as she dropped another tankard off and took a few gulps of ale, rubbing her foot up against Noah's calf as she did it. The man startled, but a smile crept across his face.

"I've never known a seamstress to put back ale the way you do," he said it in the teasing way a man does. To let you know you're not acting feminine, but that he's ok with it. That he finds it amusing. She hated him for it, but that's what she wanted. Something pretty she could toss in the trash after she was finished without a second thought. And he *was* pretty. Mining had given him strong arms and big shoulders, and his kind smile and sad, dumb eyes had been a gift from his parents. She took another drink.

"I've never known a man to sit with a woman and let her drink alone." She stopped rubbing his calf and brought her foot back to rest underneath her. A not-so-subtle way of telling him to get with the program.

He dutifully drained his cup and ordered another. *That's better. Next time I'll have to look for one with a bigger beer gut.* The night went on and the conversation turned to the election. He'd voted for Saunders. Right choice. Flicker had had her fill of politics and tried her best to avoid the topic, but even a fool could see Winnow was a nutjob. He'd rather start a war than make even the slightest dent in Egal's crystal economy. In fairness, Saunders was also a nutjob, but at least her malfunction was all about holding hands with the other nations. Holding hands while marching into the gaping maw of Gogallo, but at least soldiers would die to husk instead of other people.

Noah's words began to slur, his eyes glassed over, and he kept trying to hold her hand. Time to play. They went back to his place. The apartment looked like a herd of porcine colossi ran through it, the walls needed repairing, the ceiling above the bed had a pronounced dip in it, and the whole place smelled of rock dust and body odor. Not exactly an intoxicating scent to most people, but Flicker welcomed it. After nothing but Nashow sailors and their fishy odors for the last eight years a miner was like a freshly bloomed rose.

They barely made it through the door before she was on him. She kissed up his neck and nibbled at his ear while she gripped his arms, massaging his shoulders. He wrapped his hands around her and pulled her in close.

"I could get used to this," he said.

"You and me both," she lied and went in to kiss him. He stopped her and looked her in the eyes.

"You mean that?" he said. "I just..."

"I'm not going anywhere." She drunkenly cradled his dumb face between her hands and forced the kiss before he could say anything else stupid. They stumbled to the bedroom leaving a trail of clothing along the way. Moonlight illuminated their bodies, and she took him all in. The shoulders, the arms, the hair on his chest, the shaven head, and the sad eyes. Eyes that reminded her of him. *Cullen, it's been too long.* She shoved him down on the bed the way he liked, and they made love.

It wasn't until the second time that the veil between reality and fiction lifted. That her mind refused to let Noah be Cullen. They went another time after that because Noah was good. Real good. A rare find in the pools she'd been fishing in for the past years, but she'd sobered, she was sleepy, and tomorrow would be a big day. Time to move on.

She waited until he was asleep, snoring like one does after a night of drinking before she dressed and watched him splayed out on the bed nude. His chest rose and fell with his breath. She found herself sitting back down on the side of the bed with her palm on his greasy belly. Felt the warmth of his body against her hand. Desire bubbled back up in her throat. Threatening to overtake her again. She gave him one last squeeze and left.

After the coziness of a lover's bed, the chilly, early morning air out on the streets of Prolivgrad gave her goose flesh. She kept a hurried, not frantic, gait at this time of night. Trying her best to project a don't-fuck-with-me facade rather than an I'm-lost-and-helpless beacon. It generally worked. When it didn't, she knew a good place to put the bodies.

More than a few people had lost their lives by mistaking Flicker's smallish frame for helplessness. The decade she'd spent in Nashow, pulling on the threads of Coral Crowley's shady dealings, she'd practically had a part time job cleaning up the streets of Port Kimberly. The streets came alive at night once word got around that a vigilante was killing thieves and belligerent drunks. Flicker was no vigilante, but thieves and bullies were cowards by nature, and the presence of even one person willing to stand up to them sent them back into hiding. Hopefully, Port Kimberly hadn't reverted back to its cutthroat nature after she left.

Flicker's apartment rested on the top of a four-story building. A shit location for someone that worried deeply about egress options, but there couldn't be any complaining of the view from her balcony. Everyone always said Prolivgrad shone like a jewel during the day, but Flicker found it blinding. The true beauty of the city revealed itself on a clear night like tonight, when the Brinidor mountainside twinkled from the light of the moon. A blanket of glint underneath an ocean of stars. If you squinted just right, it felt like you were in that ocean. Floating amongst shimmering points of light.

With effort, she broke her gaze over the city. The hour was late, and while she could go days without rest it didn't mean she enjoyed it. She secured the door and the balcony then checked and rechecked her kit before collapsing into bed, satisfied.

The sun blinded her into consciousness as it always did, as she intended it to by positioning her bed to line up with the window. After performing her morning security checks, she threw on some clothes and left. The window wouldn't open until tonight, but there were still preparations to handle.

She expected Pulpin would be the target after finding all the experiments in that Guild warehouse. He was the division lead after all, and that kind of operation couldn't exist without someone higher up leading it. The papers she took from Cara's desk made it clear Pulpin didn't just know about the facility. He was the principal decision-maker, which meant she'd done it. This would be over soon. She could go back to her life, or what little was left of it anyway.

The Rashee residence kicked up their security after the laranee incident. Just another sign indicating their guilt, but it made it that much more difficult to get Pulpin alone with enough time to confirm he was the leader of this cabal. He'd hired some brute by the name of Nessa who fancied herself a will-blade wielder. Flicker had spent a week shadowing her, and unlike the guard at the warehouse, she carried herself like someone who knew how to use the thing. A terrifying prospect. Few things in the world were more dangerous than a competent will-blade wielder. It's not like she'd never killed one before, but they tended to make things messy. The nice thing about being this close to the top of the food chain is she could afford to make more of a splash. The only person that could care about getting wet would be dead soon anyway.

After weeks of staking out the residence, she found a gap in their security. A half-hour window opened on Wednesdays, when the shift change occurred, where the only one home was the butler. Enough time to slip in and find someplace to wait in ambush.

Flicker took up position on a rooftop a block down from the Rashee's. She'd chosen the location due to the concentration of crystals in the building materials. The sun reflecting off the building would blind anyone that looked directly at her location. The city's reflective nature made for a veritable buffet of hiding options for any trained assassin. A city designed by idealists.

The changeover happened on schedule. Descending the outer staircase of the building and crossing the street, she strolled up to the front door and picked the lock, slipping into the foyer with twenty minutes to spare. The sun beamed in through the windows as she crept around looking for a spot to wait in ambush. She heard the butler's footsteps in the distance. Far enough away she'd be safe to move about provided she kept tabs on his location.

On the second floor, Pulpin's study was exactly where she expected based on her scouting. Another locked door, but she made short work of it. As she opened it, though, the hinge screamed out her location. With haste and as much subtlety as she could muster, she closed and locked the door behind her. A large desk, a wardrobe, a family portrait, and only a few chairs occupied the office. *Shit.* No good place to hide.

This could get messy.

She willed a quill from the desk over and took up position in the space behind the door as footsteps approached.

"Hello?"

Walk away.

Metal on metal sounded in the room as the key entered the lock. It clicked open, and the hinge screamed again as the door swung inward. The butler was a large man. She'd seen as much during her stakeouts, but he struck a more imposing figure when she saw him through the crack in the door. Flicker didn't know if he doubled as a bodyguard or not, but she couldn't take the chance now that he'd all but discovered her.

"Hello?" he said as he walked into the room.

Sorry man. Wrong place and all that.

He turned around and saw her. He opened his mouth to say something, but the quill flew from her hands and straight into his neck. She leapt up and straddled his chest as she clamped her hands around his mouth. His eyes were a combination of confusion and fear. The first punch caught her off guard, but she held firm onto his mouth. *It's almost over. You're almost done.* He swung wildly with his other arm, but she was able to shift her body around to mitigate the damage. He collapsed backward to the ground with her on top of him. The inevitability of what was happening must have hit him because he stopped struggling. His eyes moved to the portrait on the wall and rested there. Sitting on top of him she could feel his breathing slow. Each inhalation took more effort than the next until, finally, his last breath escaped him and the light behind his eyes went out.

Flicker took her hands off his mouth and felt them trembling. A shiver jolted through her body, and she found her breath catching in her throat. *What in the hells is this?* She followed the butler's sight line to the Rashee family portrait hanging on the wall and then looked back down to the man whose life she just stole. His blood pooled beneath him. She shook her head to snap out of whatever this feeling was. She could analyze it later, after she finished.

Ten minutes remained before Pulpin would arrive home. She had to move the body, clean up the blood, and find a hiding space. Just down the hall, a linen closet held some sheets she used to wrap up the butler who she then hid in the son's bedroom closet. Not a great long-term solution, but the son no longer lived with the family so there was little chance of it being discovered before she finished her task. After that, it wouldn't matter. While cleaning the blood up off the floor she heard the faint sound of the front door opening. Voices echoed through the house.

Gods, this is messy.

The wardrobe would have to do. Nothing else provided the access she needed to Pulpin. She wiped up the final specks of blood, locked the door, and hid in the corner of the wardrobe clutching the bloody linen she'd been using to clean with. Trying to make herself as small as possible.

"Kent!" Pulpin's voice echoed through the house. "Where are you? Dinner boiled over in the kitchen."

Flicker clenched her jaw; disappointed in herself. She'd had jobs go bad before, but this would be a contender for the top spot. Luckily, she'd be retiring soon. A few moments passed, and the sound of two pairs of footsteps approached the office door. The click of the lock sounded in the room followed by the now familiar screeching of the hinge.

There was some time between when Flicker realized she was made, and when her body would be able to react to that realization. She had spent years making that window of time as small as possible. Honing her reflexes and improving her re-actions through mind-numbingly repetitious exercises taught to her by The Eyes of Koth.

It might as well have been for nothing.

The wardrobe exploded in flame with her inside of it. The linen she was clutching caught fire, burning her hands and face as the inferno sucked all the air out of her lungs.

She closed her eyes and dreaded what came next.

The world dissolved behind frosted glass and the feeling of burning alive amplified beyond what she thought comprehensible. It was as if she could feel every inch of her body separately and simultaneously. As if she wasn't just her, but thousands of people burning at once. All of them together, scorching their lungs while gasping for air.

Flicker burst from the wardrobe covered in flames like a demon escaping one of the six hells. Jessa stood next to Pulpin who was willing a torrent of fire at her. As she circled the two at a speed most people couldn't follow, she caught Nessa's eyes on her, only confirming her fear that the monstrous woman would be a major problem.

Still engulfed in flames, Flicker went for Pulpin first. Nessa wouldn't go down easy, but she wouldn't go down at all with someone like Pulpin helping her. She closed in on his flank, planted her foot, and put some will into her fist before punching the arm he wielded with. The audible snap came followed by Nessa's will-blade cutting between the assassin and her target. A close call.

Pulpin yelped in pain from the broken bone as Flicker danced back and willed three flaming splinters of the wardrobe into the air before flinging two at Nessa's head and one at Pulpin's remaining arm. Without waiting to see the result of her volley she rushed forward. She had to end this fight quickly or the flames would end it for her. Nessa deflected all three projectiles with lightning speed, but the final splinter caused her to overreach. Flicker's leg connected with Pulpin's remaining hand during the split-second opening. A play with a small degree of necessary risk. There are elementalists in the world that don't require their hands to focus. They could freeze a small pond with a thought. Pulpin couldn't though, she'd confirmed as much before she walked into the Guild building months ago. The crunching sound of the bones in his hand shattering confirmed she could now focus her full efforts on Nessa.

The bodyguard struck a defensive pose as her charge cried out in agony. The woman would try and stall to let the fire do its work. It was the smart, pragmatic play. It's what she would have done in the same situation, but she anticipated that. Flicker dashed around the corners of the room launching objects at Pulpin. Nessa continued to block everything she threw, but it kept her planted next to him. Which is exactly what Flicker wanted. Like waving a match around to put it out, she flitted around the room until all that remained of the flames on her body was charred, bubbling skin and tendrils of smoke wafting off her.

She stopped near the still-burning wardrobe and met Nessa's eyes; behind them, she saw fear. Flicker knew exactly what she was thinking.

"You want out," Flicker said.

Nessa's face hardened and she let out a joyless laugh. "I thought you were dead. If I'd known it was you who'd be coming, I never would've taken this job."

That surprised her. She hadn't figured her reputation would've survived this long.

"What in hells are you chatting for? Kill her!" Pulpin yelled from behind the bodyguard. Nessa elbowed him in the mouth and brought her blade up to his throat.

Flicker arched an eyebrow. "Bad girl. I thought you were here for his protection."

"That was before Sharon fucking Adegast burst out of her coffin."

Pulpin's eyes went wide. "Adegast? The mayor from Gull Harbor?" Nessa clipped him again with her elbow.

"Keep your fucking mouth shut."

"So, either I let you go, or he dies before I can interrogate him?" Sharon asked.

"That's about it."

A pounding of footsteps came from down the hall. The guards for the evening shift must have arrived. Nessa met Sharon's eyes. This would be her chance. Either Nessa would kill Pulpin, leaving Sharon in her burnt state to face off against a will-blade wielder and two more guards, or Sharon could let Nessa go and dispatch the two guards without issue. With her will reserves tapped after so much flickering, half her body in excruciating pain from the burns, and some whisper of regret over killing the butler she decided to leave the loose end hanging.

Fuck it.

"Leave the blade. Take the window out. Don't make me regret this."

Nessa chucked the blade at Sharon. She caught it in her hand at the same time the window shattered, and she was gone. Sharon extended her will out the tip of the blade and made a casual horizontal slash toward the hallway. Disbelief spread across Pulpin's face when two surprised screams and the thump of bodies hitting the floor sounded through the room.

"That's a shame," she said, walking toward Pulpin. "I was almost tapped. She probably could have got me had she played her cards right."

"You have no idea what you're doing."

"Oh, I have *some* idea of what I'm doing," she said. "Your wife will be home in the next few minutes. It'll be your decision whether I'm still here or not." She pushed him to the ground, stepped on his forearm, and hacked his broken hand off. Without putting any will into the blade, it took several swings. He screamed and she backhanded him. "Unless I tell you to speak you keep your mouth shut."

His eyes darted around the room. She slapped him again. "Pulpin, I don't know what you're thinking, but you're not getting out of this one. Carula is probably turning the corner on your street right now. The information in Cara's desk. It indicated you ran this whole operation. Is that true?"

Something like anger contorted his face before he turned his head toward the family portrait. *There we go. Think of your family.* He closed his eyes, tears streamed down his cheek as he turned back to her. He mumbled something.

"What was that?"

"You don't understand! Everything will have been for nothing. All the deaths will have been for nothing—" She slapped him again.

"Answer the question or I will kill your wife in front of you. Slowly."

"Pulpin!" A woman's voice echoed through the house.

Sharon gave a look of mock surprise. "Look at that. She's home early."

Pulpin's gaze fell to the portrait again. "Saunders," he said.

Godsdamnit, really? I thought the president was some idiot playboy.

Sharon sighed. "Thank you."

"Please. It's not what you—"

She put some will into her blade and slit his throat. She didn't have time to listen to him beg for his life. Not with the wife coming to interrupt. A scream rang out from the hallway and Sharon dashed out the window, rolling as she hit the ground. The pain from the burns lanced through her body. Looking down she finally took in the extent of the damage. All that remained of her clothing was her left pant leg, her smallclothes, and some scraps of her shirt. A red cloak drying on a clothesline flapped in the wind a few feet from her. Carula's wailing cries rang out from the office window above as she snatched it and threw it around herself. She could still hear the wailing from halfway down the block.

What a fucking mess that turned out to be.

Seffin

The apartment Kent owned didn't have a couch, so Seffin sat at the table next to some wilting yellow and white flowers left over from the funeral. Clutching the urn in his hands he could almost lose sight of his fingers in the tan of the jar. His gaze drifted upward into the spotless kitchen. Kent had finally listened to him and cleaned out most of the clutter. Only an ashtray and a newspaper escaped whatever purge he committed on his myriad possessions while Seffin was gone. The paper had this year's academy graduates listed. Seffin had told him to just throw the paper away, but Kent only smiled and smacked him on the head with it before tossing it back on the counter. It hadn't moved since.

He brought the urn close to his chest, hoping to feel something of his friend other than a softness deep behind his eyes, in the center of his head, pulsing slowly. A heartbeat in his thoughts. A rhythmic whisper in and around everything he did or saw or heard. The unceasing reminder of loss threatened to crush him if he focused on it too long.

A knock at the door startled him, and he hugged the urn tighter for a split second as if every act outside his own movements threatened it. He shook his head, placed the urn next to the flowers, padded over to the door, and opened it. Ren stood holding some groceries with the same expression of pity on his face he'd kept since they learned of the murders.

"Hi," Ren said, giving a meager wave and an unsure smile.

Seffin only sighed and waved him in. Outside, the sun shone brightly through a cloudless sky which made him want to vomit. Ren followed inside, closed the door behind him, and took off his shoes. The murder happened days before they got back into town, and in the week since, Ren had taken it upon himself to make a daily visit with food and quiet company. A gesture Seffin appreciated but didn't have the energy to show it. His limbs felt heavy, and his words felt heavier; too heavy to speak them for fear of breaking halfway through. He sat back down at the table, resting his hand on the base of the urn. He could feel Ren's eyes on him for a moment before he took up his position in the kitchen, chopping vegetables and heating a pot.

"You talk to your mother yet?"

He hadn't. Not since the day he returned. He remembered the feeling of guilt when he told her he wouldn't be attending his father's funeral, and anger when she admonished him for attending "the butler's" funeral in its stead. Accusations of betrayal rang hollow coming from a woman who sat idly by while his father disowned him for the crime of choosing his own career. Still, he couldn't hate her for it. That would require him to think about her. Which he didn't. Not unless someone else brought her up.

"No," he said, "probably not for a while."

Ren threw all his ingredients in the pot, gave it a stir, tapped the spoon on the edge, and covered it. "You need to get out of the house."

Seffin heard him but it took a few seconds to register the absurd statement. "Why?" he asked, meeting Ren's eyes, genuinely curious what he could possibly say that would coax him out into the sickening sunshine.

"You need to move around," he said. "Trust me, you need a break from sitting here. Come with me after we're done eating."

"I don't think—"

"It wasn't really a question. Unless you plan to burn me to death, I'm taking you out."

Seffin's anger flashed but he couldn't maintain it. Too big an emotion to hold right now, but he had no idea how he'd manage leaving the apartment. "I've been out," he lied.

"All the same. I have something to show you."

He grimaced. "Koth take me."

He almost meant that statement. The god of death and undeath could do whatever he wanted to him as long it filled the void in his body. Any of the gods could. Coruscare could burn him to ash, Kohru could bring him into her embrace, Gaku could overwhelm his mind in transcendence, and Svoboda and Torthuil could do… whatever it is they did to bring nonbelievers into their respective hells. He didn't care. He just wanted this to stop. Or have his friend back, but the only god who claimed they could do that was Koth, and not in a way that mattered.

Ren's skills in the kitchen were impressive. An observation not based on experience. Seffin had a hard time tasting anything since the murders, but it had a pleasant smell. Ren served them and he dutifully finished his bowl of soup, trying his best to think up an excuse not to leave the house. An impossible task with the thing in his head pulsing away. Before he knew it, Ren ushered him to the door where his boots should have been but weren't. Only two pairs; Ren's, and a pair he'd never seen before.

"Have you seen my boots?"

"I put your old ones away and bought you these four days ago," he said with another grin. "I thought you'd been out of the house."

He rolled his eyes so that Ren could see and said, "Yeah. I lied."

"Well, you're bad at it."

Seffin donned the boots and stood up. They were frustratingly comfortable. "How expensive were these?"

Ren gave a wry smile. "As if I'd tell you." He opened the door and sunshine flooded the entryway. "Out with you."

Seffin groaned and gave him a withering look before stepping out onto the front step. Fresh air invaded his lungs as the sun warmed his skin. He hadn't realized how stagnant the apartment had become. He made a mental note to, at the very least, crack the windows when he returned. His last time outside was Kent's funeral. If a person could call it that. Save for their little band of mercenaries, no mourners attended. Seffin called on Kent's parents, but his father had been as cold and callous as he'd made him out to be. The man almost seemed amused. Like his son's death proved a point in an argument Seffin wasn't privy to.

The streets bustled with an annoying amount of people. Ren led them away from the city center, toward the business district by the route Seffin used to take to school. Blue streamers and blue flags for the Labor Party still hung off many of the buildings for President Saunders' win, so much celebrating for a woman with so much blood on her hands. After a few blocks, he spotted their destination. The Lodge peaked out from behind the roofline. "What are we doing at the Lodge?"

"You'll see."

The thought of being around even more people set Seffin's teeth on edge, but turning around would be an argument and the benefits of getting up and moving around proved annoyingly accurate. His legs loosened up and moving forced him to focus on things other than death. He made another mental note to get some exercise. They rounded the last corner, and the Lodge came into full view. The size of it still struck him with awe every time. A giant log cabin in the middle of a sparkling city of brick. The building couldn't look more out of place.

Inside the walls of the Lodge, countless people milled about. Ren seemed to be on a mission and led them straight through the crowd to a window he vaguely remembered. Ren set a piece of paper down on the windowsill and nudged Seffin in the ribs. "You forget about getting paid?"

He had.

The attendant took the contract and looked it over. A sigh loud enough to be heard over the din of the crowd came from the window. "In the future, please make appointments for payouts this large." They handed the piece of paper over to another worker. "Come back in a couple hours."

"Perfect," Ren said.

"Not perfect," Seffin said. "How long are we—"

"Seffiiiin!" A jovial voice came from behind him. "If it isn't my little angel of death!"

A man with beige skin, a shield, and a flail dropped his arm around Seffin's shoulders before he had any time to react. It was Don, the merc band leader who helped him out the first time he came to the Lodge. He bristled at the touch, and his thoughts started racing. Coming out was a mistake. The tall man's kind eyes had mischief behind them, or maybe they were just glassy. Given their last interaction it wouldn't surprise him if he'd already started drinking for the day.

"The last time I saw you, you were so drunk you could barely speak!" He smacked Seffin on his back and laughed. "And who's your friend here?"

Ren extended his hand and smiled. "I'm Ren. How do you know Seffin?"

Instead of shaking his hand, Don put his other arm around Ren and turned the two toward Mallory's, the pub just inside the entrance of the Lodge. "That's a fun story, but it's best told over a few drinks!"

A pleasant buzz to sand off the edges of his discomfort didn't sound like a bad idea, actually.

"Don this is Ren. Ren this is Don. Yes. Drinks. Now."

They found a table in the corner by one of several fireplaces that peppered the immense dining room. As soon as they sat down Seffin ordered two ales straight away, Don regaled Ren about the courier contract turned husk massacre. His accounting of the contract may have been exaggerated for effect, but Seffin had neither the energy nor the inclination to dispute it. Instead, he sat there and listened while the friendly waiter kept plying him with ale. Occasionally, Don would look to him to confirm some outlandish thing he said, and Seffin would provide him a "You got it" or "exactly". Enough to get the attention off him and back to the story.

Ren shifted to sit closer and whispered into his ear, "Did he really ask you to join his band?"

"Yeah," he tried to whisper back, but between the booze and trying to make sure Ren could hear him over the noise of the pub it came out more as a hushed yell, "he did, but I like you more." Then he patted Ren on his head and leaned back in his seat. Don laughed hard at that.

"I don't blame ya for saying no anyway. You saved the lot of us from regular husk. Not exactly an impressive display on our part, but hopefully I can still count you as a friend. I did buy you all that ale afterward."

"You did and you can, but I think I earned that ale after the small cut of the reward you gave me," Seffin said.

"Heyyy," Don said as he gave an exaggerated shrug, "you agreed to the cut before the contract. What? Was I supposed to cut out my band?"

Seffin wanted to say yes. Yes, he could have given more of the cut, but even drunk he had to admit that running across Don was a stroke of luck given how helpless he was when he first walked into the Lodge. "I'll just have to negotiate better up front next time."

"I like that!" Don said. "So you're saying there'll be a next time."

"Oh please," Seffin said, smiling, "you can't afford me anymore."

That brought all three of them to laughter.

They passed the time trading stories and making promises to connect again. Ren clunked his mug down on the table with purpose. Time to go pick up the pay for their contract. It took Seffin a second to find his balance, but once he did, he went over to Don and gave him a hug before patting him on the head and walking away. He heard Ren say goodbye behind him before he caught up. Seffin put his arm on his shoulder for balance. "I like Don," he said, and then lowered his voice, "but his band are terrible fighters. There were only ten husk. The only reason I couldn't take them all out at once is because they kept getting in the way. Not like you." He gave his shoulder a squeeze. "You keep things away from me *and* stay out of my way. Things just go smoover..." Seffin stopped for a second. "Smoover?"

"Smoother?" Ren offered

"Yes, that." Seffin nodded. "They go like that with you."

Arriving back at the window, they collected their money and Ren gave Seffin his cut. He knew the amount of money the contract was worth but seeing the number and holding the coin were two completely different feelings. He had a full year's rent resting in his hands. "This is so much."

Ren chuckled. "We were gone for almost two months. If jobs that big didn't cover people for months at a time no one would take them." Ren looked down at his own pile of money. "Though, this one did pay a lot more than most other escort contracts. I'd say taking down three hoarwolf amalgamations and almost dying means we earned it though."

Seffin pouched the coin and the two made for the Lodge's exit. The crowd in the streets from earlier had thinned out, and between the booze, the sun going down, and all the money he'd just made Seffin let out a contented sigh. He felt better than he had in over a week. The fog in his head still enveloped everything, but it seemed lesser now, more manageable, or at least less unmanageable. He owed Ren for pushing him out. He could be a selfish idiot, but at least where Seffin was involved, his intentions had always been good, if a little misguided and more than a little criminal.

As they walked back to Kent's apartment they passed by several cafes and restaurants with patrons in the middle of telling each other stories or complaining about their work. The smell of home cooked meals permeated the air as children were called home for supper in this area of the city. The streets around the Lodge were always more relaxed than the area Kent lived in. A mixture of ease and unwinding replaced the frantic energy from earlier. The air cooled to a more comfortable temperature, and a breeze kicked up intermittently as if gently pushing them toward home.

They reached Kent's door, and Seffin felt a sinking feeling in his gut. Despite his protestations the day had been nice, and he didn't want it to end. The idea of sobering up alone in an apartment with nothing but the ashes of a murdered friend for company felt like backsliding. He turned to face Ren who stood slightly taller than him. Broad, muscular shoulders and brown eyes that always looked sad until something caught his attention. Despite everything they'd been through in the last few months he didn't actually study him too often. Ren's presence always had less to do with his physicality and more to do with his attitude. "Stay for a bit?" he asked.

Ren flashed a dimply smile and shrugged. "Sure."

Crossing into the apartment, Seffin was forced to fully come to grips with how suffocating and stagnant the air in here was. It felt like walking into a musty changing room. He ran around to open some windows while Ren found the whiskey and poured them both a night cap. They sat at the table, Kent's urn holding sentinel over them.

"Can I ask you a question?" Ren started.

Seffin's heart thumped in his chest. "Sure." He hoped he sounded calm.

"What does it feel like to have so much will?" he asked.

Seffin couldn't help but feel a little disappointed. This is not the question he thought was coming, but outside of preparing for their final he'd never really talked shop with Ren. He had control, Seffin had power, and as far as strategy was concerned that's all that mattered.

"Sometimes it feels like I'm walking through water," he answered. "You know how you can feel your will? Dunreedy said to think of it like appendages reaching out?"

Ren nodded. "Yeah, sorta. It definitely feels like I'm reaching out whenever I use it."

"For me it's not like that at all." Seffin made a gesture with his hands like he was holding a ball. "For me, it's like I'm inside an orb. I don't have to reach for anything unless I'm trying to will something from a long way away."

Ren cocked his head. "I don't know how that can be. The first law of wielding is that you can't control any part of another person's will, and I've made plenty of ice and fire around you."

Seffin took a sip of his whiskey. Ren was confused, which seemed to happen a lot for someone with such pristine control of their will. He was wondering how he could perform elementalism while in the middle of Seffin's bubble of will. The thought occurred that this conversation may be far too technical given how deep they were in their cups, but putting his mental effort into something besides wallowing and dread felt good so far so he continued anyway, "Right, I'm not *controlling* an orb around myself at all times. I just don't have to reach. When you use will around me it just displaces mine. Like putting an object in a full cup of water." He thought for a moment. "For a fireball it takes effort to put fuel into it, right? You find the fuel in the air, start the flame, and then feed it?"

"Sure."

"Well, I don't need to find the fuel. I feel it around me all the time. Same with water. Most people have to reach out and grab it, then pull it where they want. I don't have to reach. I just pull everything where I want it to be."

Ren shook his head. "I can't even imagine what that's like. Have you ever actually run out?"

"The laranee is the closest I've come since my reserves got so big. At the end I threw everything I had at it, but even that didn't do it. Back when we first learned fire elementalism I went to a practice room and shot fire into the air until I couldn't anymore just to see. It took me over an hour. That was years ago. I'm not sure how long it would take me now."

Seffin hadn't thought too much about his will reserves. He focused on his shortcomings. His control. If he couldn't properly control his wielding his strength didn't matter. The size of an explosion was meaningless if it didn't explode where he needed it to, and oftentimes his strength seemed to get in the way of his control. Harder to adjust the flow of an ocean than divert a river.

"So, last year when we did testing at the academy to make sure we all fell within the parameters of becoming a mystic, they gave us a ranking—"

"I'm number one," Seffin said. "They said my will reserves are the highest they've ever recorded. Of course, that's just within the academy system. Wild wielders aren't recorded, and both Karm and Kelsig would never share that information."

The island nations of Karm and Kelsig kept to themselves for the most part. Karm's location to the east, off the shore of the continent of Griela, necessitated a certain amount of cooperation with the Garvelle Empire to keep the husk hordes in check, but they kept to themselves beyond that. Kelsig on the other hand might as well not exist. Other than the name of the country and its location in the northern ocean little was known about them other than how they helped during the time of Lana Danver's campaign on Gogallo, but that was over a thousand years ago.

"Number one," Ren said in disbelief. "I knew you must be up there, but number one?"

"Yeah." Seffin yawned. "it's pretty meaningless when you think about it though."

"Meaningless? How? You're the most powerful mystic on record."

"Power is meaningless without control," he cited a lecture from Dunreedy

"Ok, hold on." Ren set his drink down and shifted his chair to directly face him. "Your control gets better every day, and you practice constantly. I only had to help a little bit during our fight with the hoarwolves, and honestly, that's the only thing I did in that fight. You, Ka, and Poppy did the rest. At least you can work on control. I'm stuck with the will reserves I was born with."

Seffin usually hated compliments. Nothing felt more awkward than someone telling him how impressed they were with him. Especially at his will reserves, something completely out of his control. Having his hard work recognized felt good though, or at least it felt more genuine. But Ren overlooked that his own will reserves weren't far down the list in rankings, and his control was unmatched by any mystic Seffin had met. Even Ka begrudgingly admitted that. The fact he used a will-blade when he was such a powerful mystic was beyond strange.

"Thanks," he said, "but I still wish I had the control you do."

Ren put an exaggerated, smug smile on his face. "Yeah, well that'll be hard to do." He dusted his shoulder off. "I'm ranked number one in the world for control."

"Oh, really?"

"No!" He chuckled. "No. I don't think there are even rankings for that. My mom started me out young with control exercises, and Ka kept them up when I moved in. Control needs to be almost perfect to effectively use a will-blade, and that's been my goal since I was a kid."

"Like your mother?"

"Yeah." He looked down at his glass. "Wish she coulda taught me, but nothing I can do about that." He downed the rest of his whiskey in one gulp. "Can I ask you something else?"

Seffin hesitated before saying, "Yes."

"What was Kent to you?"

He suddenly became aware of the softness in the middle of his head again, but it no longer pulsed as if knocking up against his thoughts. It simply sat there, a presence in his mind. Not intruding. Not taking over. Just resting in the background. His face went hot, and his eyes reflexively went to the urn in the center of the table. "A friend."

Ren raised his eyebrows. "Just a friend? That's a really nice friend to let you move in without a job or any way to pay rent."

Seffin sighed. "We weren't lovers if that's what you're asking."

"It's not."

"Good." Seffin took his turn downing the rest of his whiskey in one gulp. "He was like an older brother, I guess. When I lived with my parents, I remember he would always ask me questions that seemed odd at the time." Seffin absentmindedly started thumbing the glass in his hand. "They seem pretty normal now. Especially after hanging out with you all."

"What kind of questions?"

"Simple questions like 'What do you think about your teacher?' or 'What do you want to do after you're done at the academy?' or 'How was your weekend?'." Seffin set his glass down, reached over, and touched the base of the urn again with his fingertips. "He treated me normal when I didn't realize what normal was. He probably thought I was weird at first." He chuckled. "I *know* he thought I was weird at first, but it didn't change how he acted around me. After I moved in with him, he said how much he hated the way my parents treated me, but he didn't want to say anything that might get him fired."

"That's fair," Ren said.

"Very," Seffin agreed, "but it would have been nice to have that realization years ago. That the way my parents treated me wasn't normal, or good. He said he had a friend that was there for him when he needed him, and he wanted to be that friend for me."

"Sounds like he was," Ren said.

"Yeah." Seffin looked down at the floor while his hand continued to hold the base of the urn. The closest he could get now to a physical connection with Kent. He'd been there for him and, looking around at the apartment, continued to be there for him. Seffin's feelings got the better of him and his eyes began to water. The truth was he planned to rely on Kent. He hoped he could lean on him. At least for now, or until he could pay him back for all his kindness. A tear dropped from his eye. He wiped it away and looked up at Ren who returned the gaze with a kind smile.

Picking up the urn, he walked over to a shelf, the lone surface in the living room, and set it there. As if throwing wide a flood gate, the softness in his head spread throughout his whole body. A warm, comforting feeling that no longer intruded on his thoughts and actions but were simply a part of them. It didn't change the fact a part of his heart felt empty, but the space took the form of a man whose silhouette still provided some level of comfort. Still had value.

Feeling impulsive, he strode over to Ren, leaned down, and kissed him. Ren's hands reached up and cradled Seffin's face, gently separating them. "Are you sure about this?"

"No," Seffin said, "but I don't want you to leave tonight."

Ren looked taken aback. "You don't need to kiss me for me to stay. I'm not here hoping for a date."

"I know," Seffin said, "but if I'm being honest with myself, it's tiring being angry at you. I like you Ren. A lot. But I couldn't trust you." He met his eyes. "But right now I don't care. I just don't want to be alone right now."

Ren stood from his chair and wrapped his arms around him. He was so warm. "You're not alone," he said. "As far as Poppy is concerned, you're a Bolin now." Ren squeezed him tighter. "And whether you trust me or not I care about you. I meant it when I said you can count on me now."

"Will you stay?"

"I... don't know if we should—"

Seffin's face went hot. "No, not for that. I mean..."

"Oh," Ren said. He looked down at the floor, smiled, and then brought his eyes back up to meet his own. They seemed to look through him. "Sure, I'll stay."

Jessica

A large, circular wooden table rested in the middle of the room with five chairs sitting equidistant from each other. Flags from each nation stood by their respective, assigned seats, and pitchers of water sat off to the left of each placement, with glasses turned face down on cloth napkins, and a stack of papers piled neatly in front of each spot. Jessica had the staff paint the room a deep blue—Labor's color—for the occasion, and the curtains thrown open to provide light which had the unfortunate effect of reflecting off the polished wood of the table, blinding anyone that looked at it. She ordered the curtains drawn. Light would have to come from the wall sconces and the chandelier above. She chose this room for the meeting due to the impressive chandelier anyway, though the disappointment of losing the view of the city for the first half of the day still bothered her. She wanted to make an impression.

Duncan Mitchell arrived first. The president of Lighton had a reputation for ostentation, and he did not disappoint. Bright green robes swept around him, and a crown of flowers bounced on his head as he practically danced over to Jessica. "It is an honor to finally meet you, my dear."

You look like a clown... or a bard in a back-alley pub.

Jessica gave only a slight, cordial bow. Duncan's ostentatious personality was only half his reputation, the other half was his complete lack of respect and conniving nature. The breadbasket of the west held the second-best economy on the continent of Sol, and he used his position as gatekeeper of grain to brow beat his fellow statesmen at his whim. It didn't seem to matter to him that the only reason he held so much power was because every other country contributed to Lighton's defense against the husk. Almost half the focus crystals that came out of Brinidor went to Lighton.

"President Saunders," Jessica corrected. "Or Jessica if you like, and I assure you the pleasure is mine. Thank you for traveling all this—"

"You've been telling us about this Gogallo Initiative for years. What is this secret weapon you've been hiding away?" He smiled wide and toothy.

Gods, you will be tiring.

Even his letters dripped with condescension, and those were written with time and forethought. "You will learn of that along with the others. Please have a seat, and if you require anything don't hesitate to ask."

Duncan made no effort to hide his annoyance, but he acquiesced and took his seat all the same. Prime Minister Bruhier Rahal from Estaba slipped in without so much as a word.

Unsurprising, considering he refused to respond to her letters until her election. He would be a hard one to impress. Duncan wasted no time in assaulting him with conversation, and Jessica forced herself not to smile at that.

Edward Kimberly, King of Nashow, and Knight Aisha Bahati, consort to Empress Kiko Zollinger, entered together. Kimberly and Bahati chatted like old friends, but Jessica knew neither harbored much affection for the other. A relationship formed out of necessity. Nashow's coastal geography necessitated a specialty in nautical travel, and they handled the bulk of transportation and trade between Garvelle and the rest of the world.

Clanking of armor rang through the entrance as Empress Zollinger, the Lioness of Garvelle, stepped into the room wearing her black mail with gold filigree, the colors of the empire. Kiko left Garvelle only on rare occasions, and when she did, she never made an appearance without wearing her battle attire. Her attempted assassinations numbered in the hundreds, and at least a few of those assassins were paid for by people in this very room. The Eyes of Koth lost so many assassins over the years on Kiko alone they no longer accepted contracts on The Empress, but that didn't stop freelance assassins or fools with grudges from throwing themselves at her. The Sol War killed more people than husk ever had, and the empire bore most of the responsibility for that. It didn't matter that Kiko killed her own father to end the war. Her family's enemies were everywhere, and so she kept her armor and weapons on her always.

"Congratulations on your win, President Saunders," The Empress said. "You've come a long way from the young page I saw twenty years ago."

"Thank you, Your Majesty, and welcome back to Egal."

"Oh please, Kiko is fine in here. It's been a joy to see the city once more. Memories don't do the place justice." She looked around the room and hesitated on Bruhier for only a moment before leaning into Jessica's ear and saying, "Though, the company could be better." She lightly elbowed Jessica before chuckling and taking her place at the table. Knight Bahati stood guard over her a few feet back, looking more like a statue than a person.

Jessica clapped her hands twice. The room emptied of servants and guards, and all the doors were closed for privacy. The only people in the room now were the leaders of the five great nations. Jessica moved to her place at the table and stood in front of the Egallan flag. Everyone's attention shifted to her, even Duncan, though it took him a moment to realize no one listened to his prattling any longer. "Thank you all for coming. I know the trip was long, but you have my assurances that, no matter the outcome of this summit, you will be glad you were here."

It's happening. It's finally happening.

"I've called you all here to make a proposal. One that is more than twenty years in the making, and it becomes more and more vital to the safety of our peoples with each passing day." She paused to let the words sink in. "But first we need to establish the facts. The husk are increasing in number with each passing year, and they are doing so with an unsettling predictability. By my calculations, we have less than a decade left before our cities become islands surrounded by husk and trade all but shuts down. After that we only have an additional year or two before the sheer number of amalgamations will overrun our cities, and that will be the end of us."

"Nonsense," Duncan said. "What busybody is feeding you this information? And, even if that were true, how, *pray tell*, can you predict the amount of time we have left."

Of all the players in this game you are the worst I've seen. How, in Kohru's name, did you win an election?

Jessica turned to Duncan. "Thank you Duncan, I would love to give you the numbers. Between reports from the Guild, the Lodge, and from Garvelle, recorded husk sightings have increased every year, by nearly three percent, for as long as we've been recording. We've tried culling their numbers, but it doesn't make a dent. It doesn't even slow them. No matter how many we kill, sightings still increase every year. The number doesn't just account for husk, either. Amalgamations are up every year by three percent as well."

A look of disgust contorted his face. "I simply don't believe you," Duncan said. "In Lighton, the husk have stabilized—"

"Don't lie, Duncan," Kiko interrupted him. "Do you really think the people in this room aren't aware of the horde sitting on your northern border, knocking on the door of Nari'ko? Your farmers enjoy their peace at the whim of Nashow, Egal, and Estaba handling all the heavy lifting; transporting your goods, performing your pylon maintenance, and providing protection. I'll admit I'm impressed you managed to keep panic about the horde from spreading within your borders, but we are not as easily fooled as your citizenry, and you would do well not to deny simple truths going forward lest the protection your realm enjoys evaporates as fast as your integrity seemed to. Taking care of this threat is more important than your grain."

Kiko's low opinion of Duncan was both expected and warranted. Garvelle and Lighton couldn't be further apart geographically, and Garvelle, its entire eastern border shared with Gogallo, bore the brunt of the increase in husk numbers while Lighton enjoyed relative peace due to the sacrifices of other nations. Garvelle neither participated nor benefited from this arrangement though, and hearing denialism from a country enjoying the protection of everyone around them struck a clear nerve.

"I will not be lectured on integrity by a patricidal, regicidal—"

"Yes, and that was my father. Imagine what I'd do to a sniveling little coward from a nation that only exists due to the coddling of those around them."

Duncan rose from his seat. "I don't have to sit here and listen to threats from—"

Bruhier slapped his hand on the table. "Sit your ass back in that chair, and by the grace of the gods, shut your mouth and let Jessica get to her proposal. We've all traveled a long way for this. Your theatrics are exhausting." Bruhier dealt closely with Duncan, but Jessica hadn't expected this level of vitriol from him. The impression she had from her reports suggested someone far more level-headed. Dealing with Duncan on a routine basis could wear anyone's patience thin though, and if anyone were to shut him up, she was glad it was Bruhier. Estaba provided most of Lighton's protection from the husk, and it would take little effort to make Duncan's life difficult. He sat back in his chair, red faced in anger but quiet besides.

"As I was saying," Jessica began again, "the world as we know it is facing a threat we haven't seen since the time of Lana Danvers. We can either work to solve this problem together, or we can fall to ruin separately." Jessica pointed to the stack of papers set in front of each world leader. "Here in front of you is the data we've gathered on activities going on in Gogallo. We've long thought that whatever animates the husk resides in that blackened wasteland, but now, thanks to the hard work of Empress Zollinger's forces, combined with our scientists and engineers, we have almost definitive proof that it is true. We all know a husk can form from any corpse no matter the location, but the will behind that animation originates in Gogallo."

King Kimberly raised his hand as he spoke. "You mean for us to attack Gogallo directly. Do we know for sure that we can kill whatever is animating the husk?"

"Yes and no," Jessica said. "Scouts over the years have reported a central hub for the husk, the Heart of Gogallo. An amalgamation the size of a castle from which legions of husk and other amalgamations come forth. More recently, the production of husk from this amalgamation has coincided with our efforts to cull the hordes. Meaning the more husk we kill the more rapidly it creates them. That is the confirmed connection between the heart and the husk at large."

"Meaning we kill the heart and the husk, what? Disappear? Fall over dead?" Bruhier seemed skeptical. "And no force has breached Gogallo since Lana."

"Unfortunately, I cannot offer guarantees other than that if we do nothing, we are all doomed," Jessica said. "But I'm glad we're talking about Danvers. I will remind you all that it is this exact problem she sought to solve when she sacrificed herself all those years ago, and it is at the Heart of Gogallo where she succeeded in staunching the flow."

"But even she didn't stop them completely. All she did was stem the tide. Bought us time," Rahal said.

"She may have been the most powerful mystic ever recorded at the time, but she was still one woman. She also never sought to destroy the heart, only to seal it away using some technique she learned in Nari'ko."

"We're well aware of the history, Jessica," Kiko said. "I think it's time you tell us why we're all here."

Jessica nodded. "Very well, through great pains both personally and more generally, and with the assistance of The

Guild of Commerce we have found a way to create amalgamations that we can control."

Looks of disbelief flashed across everyone's faces save for Edward and Kiko. Edward was made aware of the project many years ago due to some necessary arrangements needed to transport supplies and test subjects, and Jessica didn't know if she could say anything that would rattle the Empress.

Bruhier spoke first, "Excuse me. You said create, right? You're *making* those monsters?"

"In a controlled environment, and more importantly, we command them. We're able to bind them to mystics who can then issue basic commands. This is the trump card I spoke of in my letters you never returned. Fighting fire with fire." *Next time return my letters and you won't be caught so flat-footed.* "Furthermore, we've developed a process for granting special capabilities depending on the amalgamation. We've found that colossi-husk combinations predispose the resulting amalgamation to certain techniques."

"Meaning?" Kiko asked

"Meaning the hoarwolf amalgamations can track for hundreds of miles, our laranees can travel in short bursts of speed akin to flickering, and we've had success in replicating an amalgamation from a werewiller that is unable to produce any sound at all. Just as a few examples."

Duncan visibly shuddered. "Since when can an amalgamation use will?"

Kiko laughed. "Always, Mr. Mitchell. I realize you couldn't be further from the Gogallo border, but husk have will just like anything else. Gather enough of it together and give it a purpose and they can use that will. I'll admit, I've never heard of a wild amalgamation performing will techniques, but there are plenty of examples of amalgamations using simple kinetics. Dreadworms use will to move through the ground."

"Dreadworms?" Duncan laughed in disbelief. "Now you *are* making things up."

The Empress continued as if he'd never spoken, "Even some animals can use will. That's where werewillers got their name after all. What I'm more curious about is how you've managed to control them. Some form of intentioned will?"

Jessica hadn't expected the Empress to know that. Most people in civilized society hadn't even heard of intentioned will. The stories told about it were nightmarish things. Propaganda spread by academics afraid of any will technique they couldn't master.

"Myself and Pulpin Rashee, The Guild's late head of research, developed a technique of imprinting onto amalgamations during their metamorphosis. Provided the imprinting takes, we can command them with a one hundred percent success rate."

"Nothing is one hundred percent," Bruhier said.

"Exactly. To say it is odd for our results to be this successful would be an understatement, but nonetheless we've found once the imprinting is done the amalgamations are controlled perfectly."

"Almost as if they were designed to be controlled in this fashion," Kiko said it with a smirk. The old woman knew something.

"How do you mean?" Jessica asked.

"Husk come from the remains of people. Not animals. Not plants. People. In Garvelle, we've long had a theory the Heart of Gogallo animates us because our bodies are accustomed to will running through them. Even the weakest among us—" Jessica noticed Kiko's eyes pause on Duncan briefly as she spoke. "—have multitudes more will than any simple animal. When we die our will leaves our body, and whatever force re-animates us takes up residence in its place. Meaning the strings have already been sewn on. You're simply wresting control of the puppet from the puppet master. The Heart has had thousands of years to perfect making a husk. That could explain the one hundred percent success rate provided you are able to take control." She smiled for the next part. "And I imagine it's impossible for you to do this to a basic husk? Yes? You realized success during metamorphosis because the force animating the husk is spread thin during the transformation. Any mystic of sufficient strength trained in intentioned will can wrest control, and—I'm speculating here—the amalgamations can withstand barriers due to the will of their new puppet masters harmonizing with our pylons."

The woman could have saved them years of research. She put together in less than five minutes what took Pulpin and Jessica twenty years to complete, and she did so as if explaining how boiling water works to a child.

"I'm not aware of a puppet master, but you are correct in that we cannot replicate this with normal husk and there is a limited window during metamorphosis in which we can imprint. And yes, they can withstand barriers," Jessica said.

"So what, we breed an army and march on Gogallo?" Bruhier sounded as if he needed more convincing.

"Obviously, there are far more logistics to go over than that, but that's the gist. It'll take a year or two for production to make enough for an army, at which point we station ourselves on the border and march on the heart."

"I assume we're to be given a demonstration of some sort?" Edward asked.

"Of course," she responded.

After all these years.

Kiko cleared her throat before saying, "The empire is behind you, Jessica. Provided this demonstration proves your claims. The longer we wait the harder this will be."

"What is your motivation for doing this? Does Egal not benefit from the increase in husk what with your monopoly on crystal trade?" Bruhier spoke frankly, which she respected.

"If you were to ask my recent opponent, yes. Paul Winnow is a creature of raw ambition, and he would watch the world burn if it made him wealthier. This plan relied heavily on winning the presidency. We still would have had the techniques to control amalgamations, but without governmental support in Egal, our only hope would have been if Garvelle stepped up to take over the plan."

Kiko gave a thin smile. "I appreciate that we have your confidence, but had Winnow won your election we'd all be having a vastly different conversation. The man would watch our nations crumble for his greed, and I would have seen his throat ripped out for it."

Jessica surmised the threat of killing a world leader might have a chilling effect on the room, but the truth is the other nations would have likely supported her and she couldn't fault them for it. Winnow would have held focus crystals hostage, and leaders like Kiko didn't negotiate with a knife to their throat. She ran her own father through for less.

"Getting back to Bruhier's question," Jessica said. "The elimination of the husk benefits us all. Yes, our crystal trade is the primary reason we enjoy the wealth our nation does, but there are countless acres of untouched land that we could have access to. People would no longer be required to huddle behind barriers. Our towns and settlements would stop disappearing. I've seen first-hand what happens to those small towns when they're overrun, and I would do anything to stop that. The sacrifice is worth it. Any sacrifice is worth it."

Edward spoke up, "Hear, hear."

Bruhier nodded his head, and for the first time his face didn't seem to hide skepticism. Bruhier and Kiko were the two votes she needed most. Jessica let out her breath. She should have the support she needed to finish her plan. They set the time for the demonstrations and closed out the meeting. Just two things left for her to take care of.

Her son, and the assassin.

***

Troy surprised her by taking her meeting. Maybe something about his trip to the seacoast helped him grow a spine, or maybe he had an ambitious plan to strike at her while they talked. Either way it didn't matter. She knew her son's capabilities, and his combat prowess wouldn't avail him against her. Tia brought him in from the hall. He sat across from her, determination writ on his face.

He waited.

She waited.

The game of determination quickly turned awkward. "How was your trip?"

Am I baiting him to see his response or am I just taking out my frustrations?

He smiled. "Refreshing! I don't get out of the city often, as you know. It was nice to visit one of my more important hubs. A lot of wildlife up north that you just don't find down here."

The glint in his eye meant he'd met her wolves. *At least I know they work.* Had they known who he travelled with they might have waited a week and sent a whole pack. Pulpin even tried talking her down from three wolves saying it would be overkill. Who could have guessed Tender Bolin and their monster of a daughter would tag along on a contract for the Guild?

She should have, but she hadn't. She'd been sloppy.

"I have a personal question," he continued, "did Pulpin know Seffin came along?"

Gods, but you are soft, aren't you?

"No, I'm not sure he would have agreed otherwise," she lied.

The truth is he would have agreed. He knew as well as she that protecting the plan took precedence over everything else. She assumed Troy asked on behalf of Pulpin's kid though, and she gained nothing from allowing the boy to think his father would throw him to actual wolves. Even if that is exactly what he would have done. The reality is that it's exactly what they both did. The chances of their children teaming up on a Guild contract for the Lodge seemed remarkably odd, though after looking over all factors at play it seemed inevitable. Of course, Troy would hide by going through the Lodge instead of using Guild escorts, of course the contract would attract the Lodge's best mercs like Tender and Kulelika Bolin, and of course Pulpin's son had befriended Tender's. They were in the same grade and took care of the laranee together after all. Predictable in hindsight. Another thing she should have caught but didn't.

Troy's determined look softened, which was her true intent. *Best he thinks I'm not completely monstrous.*

"I'm here to ask for a truce."

"A truce? What makes you think I want a truce? I could kill you here and now and have a replacement sitting in your chair by tomorrow."

He winced.

Good. He needs to know that I'm still willing to finish the job if he doesn't behave himself.

"I have assurances that if I don't walk out of this meeting, your plan is finished, and I'm sure you know that."

Obviously, you idiot, or I wouldn't be threatening. I'd be doing.

Jessica did her best to sever what little attachment she had to her son when she ordered his death, and seeing him very much alive and well annoyed her more than anything. One of the benefits of assassinating someone is not having to deal with the emotional consequences to their face. Regardless, she made the sacrifice, and fate told her no. Now, she had to see him sitting in front of her, knowing what she did to him, and she had to act what? Thankful? Humbled?

"So what do I gain from this truce?" she asked.

"The Guild will assist with your project as much as is possible. I can increase production so that you have the assets you need within a year. I may not have caught on to this game you were playing fast enough, but I am damn good at my job when I put my mind to it."

"A pity you didn't put your mind to it before."

"Enough, Mother," he said and met her eyes. "In return, no more moves without my signing off. No harm comes to the people I've been involved with. No harm comes to me."

Jessica let him sweat. Though he had her by the balls and he knew it. If he outed her, she'd be in jail, there would be a runoff, Winnow would win, and the chances of the world overcoming the husk would plummet. That snake, Tolkar, had already done all the harm he could do anyway, and she knew better than to attack the Bolins. Tender and Empress Zollinger were close friends, and right about now, Tender would be telling Kiko everything they knew. She knew Kiko would still do what needed to be done, but if she went after Tender directly there would be dire consequences for Jessica, personally.

"There is still the matter of the assassin." He knew she'd agree to his terms. No reason to give him the satisfaction of voicing it.

"Yes, well that is a problem."

He knows something.

"I would encourage you to be forthcoming with any information you have."

"The truth is that I have limited information because you sought to test me instead of bringing me in. You could have mentored me, but you didn't."

"I maneuvered you into the second most powerful position in the world, and you're trying to tell me I didn't do *enough* for you?"

"You say that like power is the only thing I needed. Like simply granting me enough of it would—"

"I didn't just give you power. I told you to listen to Pulpin. I asked you for favors on the mining legislation. I even floated the research to you, hoping you would bite, and in every instance, you came back with rules and regulations stating how you couldn't help. The research was too dangerous you said. Pulpin is your employee not your mentor you said. The mining legislation is government business you said. I don't know how I could have clued you in any more clearly without exposing myself. I couldn't trust you. You rebuffed me at every corner. Is that not apparent?"

"I thought you gave me the position to excel in the job. I didn't want the appearance of favoritism—"

"Things were spelled out for you, Troy. It's not my fault you couldn't read."

"Forgive me for thinking you did something for me without strings attached."

Jessica laughed, but there was no joy in it. "You're mad that I didn't bring you to the table and now you're indignant that my gifts came with the strings required to pull you in." Jessica sighed and shook her head. "You are far too old to act this naïve."

She stood from her chair and pinched the bridge of her nose. Looking at him now, she saw the hurt on his face despite his attempts to hide it, and a little of the warmth she felt for him budded in her chest. She pushed it back down. Most children she saw in the street would kill for a fraction of the privilege Troy was afforded, and she couldn't get stuck looking back at all the decisions she made that led them here.

This would have been easier had you died.

She put on her political smile. "Anyway, thank you for your assistance with production. I will gladly accept it. If there is nothing else, I have a lot on my plate at the moment."

He stood from his chair to leave, but before he reached the door he turned around. "What about the assassin?"

"What about them? For all we know Pulpin was the final target. Unless we have more information, there is little we can do other than increase our security and hope that if they show up, you win the fight. I hope you've been practicing."

Troy looked confused. "What do you mean you hope I've been practicing? What makes you think they'll come after me?"

"I imagine because you're the president of the guild they've been targeting."

Ren

Ren had met Su Takawa before, though he never put two and two together and so the meetings never stuck out in his mind. She was just Poppy's friend. An exceptionally large, muscular, welcoming friend that just happened to have two will-blades on her at all times. Now, as an adult, the guise didn't work so well. The beige skin, countless scars, and bodyguard were a dead giveaway. Kiko Zollinger, Empress of Garvelle, sat in his living room laughing about some mischief she and Poppy got up to in their youth.

Poppy told Ren a lot of stories of the war growing up, and in their defense, they always maintained they were true. Ren didn't even doubt them so much as he just couldn't put the stories into context. Stopping a world war didn't mean much when your entire world consisted of the house you lived in and the school you went to. Now, it all seemed very real and very important. The stakes of the election, the truth behind Gull Harbor, the husk horde gathering on the border of the Nari'ko Wilds, and the plan to strike at the Heart of Gogallo all shaped his reality in profound ways. In the same ways that Poppy's reality had been shaped by events in their youth. The difference between stories and histories felt more pronounced when one of the major characters sat laughing on your sofa about spilling ice cream on a baby.

Aisha Bahati, or Asha as she went by while they were incognito, stood by the door, stock-still, with her spear in hand like some sort of angry statue. An odd pairing to Kiko's gregarious nature. Ren brought in some tea for the group and took a seat in an extra kitchen chair they'd brought in.

"...and the poor mother apologized to me!" Kiko said to uproarious laughter.

Once the laughs died away, Ka spoke up, "So, Aunt Kiko, we're curious how the meeting went."

Ka always loved it when Su... Kiko... visited. They had a bond from when she would stay with The Empress in her youth. Lodge business sometimes demanded Poppy's attention, and on several occasions, Ka went to stay with her in Garvelle City for a few months. Ren always felt a little jealous that Ka was able to travel so much when she was younger while he had to stay in Prolivgrad, and finding out that she stayed *in* the palace *with* The Empress made him even more jealous.

Finishing a sip of her tea, Kiko set her cup down. "Your new president would do absolutely anything to stop the husk, and I got the distinct impression she's done quite a lot."

"You don't know the half of it." Ren braved a comment. He felt out of his depth, but it seemed odder to sit like a fly on the wall.

"Oh? Enlighten me, young Adegast." Kiko put on a cheery smile. It felt strange hearing his real name. Good in a way, but also like it betrayed Poppy. He lived most his life as their son. As a Bolin.

"Well, there was the Iaranee incident," he said.

"Oh!" she spoke like she'd been waiting to talk about it. "I was meaning to congratulate you on that. Truly impressive bit of work. A horrible tragedy, but thank the gods you and your friend were able to stop it."

"And then Gull Harbor."

Kiko's eyes locked onto Ren's like an eagle eying a mouse from the air. "What about Gull Harbor?"

The intensity alarmed him, but he carried on anyway, "The amalgamation that attacked came from one of her experiments. That's how it got through the barrier so easily."

Ren watched for the briefest of moments while Kiko processed the information. She knew his story, and where he came from. "Unfortunate," she said before taking another brief sip of her tea, "how does that make you feel?"

Why does that matter?

They all watched him intently. "Bad," he started, "all those people, including my mom, are gone because of her. I hate her," he said, then thought for a second. "But at this point seeking revenge isn't going to do much. If her plan works at least there will be some purpose to their deaths." Kiko leaned over from the couch and put her hand on his knee.

"That's wise for someone so young." She pulled her hand back to rest on her cup of tea. "But the woman will have to be dealt with once the dust settles. I've worked with people like her before. So focused on their goal they leave their humanity behind."

"Dealt with?" Ren asked.

"Removed from office is all I meant, dear. People like that have a nasty habit of coming up with a new goal and pursuing it with the same fervor. I will say this for her: she stomped that weasel she was running against into the ground, and I'm not sure there is anyone else that could have done it so cleanly. Egal had a close call on that one."

"Would you really have gone to war with us?"

"Unequivocally," she said. "As much heartache as Jessica Saunders has inflicted upon your family, Winnow would do that and more to countless others." She sighed. "Luckily, we do not have to worry about that for now."

"The world is about to change again." Poppy sounded tired. "I'd honestly hoped the husk problem would have waited until after I was gone."

Kiko let out a loud chuckle. "This would have been a lot easier had you listened to me about running for office."

Poppy looked at Ka and Ren, one after another. "I couldn't. These games people play for power don't interest me. I'm an engineer. I like to make things."

"You could have made a better world," Kiko said. "You could have built a better country. Instead, you have a beautiful city with a rotten core and a forgotten countryside."

"My children—"

"Are not an excuse," Ka said. "Your decision is yours. Don't cheapen it by pretending you couldn't have balanced us with the demands of the job."

Ren didn't fully understand the direction the conversation took. He never really talked to them about the aftermath of the Sol War, or why they didn't take an active role in leading Egal. Poppy loved being a merc. They practically lived at the Lodge when they weren't on a contract or inventing new tools. The Lodge opened locations in every region except Nari'ko and Estaba largely because of Poppy. It's not like they sat around waiting for the world to burn.

"Of course not," Poppy said, "but opening Lodges in other countries and sitting on the board in Prolivgrad doesn't invite the same level of danger as working in high levels of government." They nodded toward Aisha standing by the door. "And, children or no, I had my fill of living on the edge during the war. I don't want to live life worried about assassins around every corner. I would rather help in my own way."

"Just so," Ka said.

"I'm sorry for bringing up a sore subject," Kiko said. "You can't fault me for wishing it was you I dealt with in that room yesterday instead of Saunders.'"

"No," Poppy said, "I come with a lot less baggage, but if I were elected, I would have been term limited by now anyway, and I wouldn't have been able to come up with the plans she has either. I don't have the stomach for those types of... sacrifices..."

"The Lodge system in Garvelle does tremendous work," Aisha said from over by the door. "You should be proud of yourself."

The Lodges had started in Garvelle during the war. When Tristan Zollinger, Kiko's father, drafted everyone that could fight, no one was left to take on roaming amalgamations, rogue wild wielders, or even common bandits for that matter. Even in the larger cities people suffered. To say nothing of the smaller towns. Poppy built them to give people a place to go for help. When the war ended, the Lodges had become so popular, they opened one in Egal. With their foot in the door to the west, the system expanded to include Nashow, Egal, and Lighton. Estaba being the only holdout. Ren found it hard to imagine life without a Lodge. Many of the public services people needed to go about their day ran through their wooden halls. Escorts to other settlements, security, courier services, and even repair services. Ren didn't think the city could run without the Lodge.

"Where is this Rashee kid I've heard so much about? The son of the man who taught Jessica how to control amalgamations," Kiko asked.

"He's at the Lodge right now. A friend of his needed help on a contract and he's awfully bad at saying no," Poppy said. They'd been keeping tabs on Seffin since they all returned from Oleksandra's Harbor. "We're going to meet with him for dinner to discuss our next contract."

"Shame. I hope to meet the man that's supposedly as strong as Lana Danvers."

"He'd like that," Ren said.

Kiko slapped her knees. "Well, the hour grows late, and I have some business to attend to before the presentation tomorrow. Time for Su and Asha to be on their way." Kiko rose to her feet and met Aisha by the door.

"Say, Kiko," Poppy said. "Do be careful. There's an assassin running loose. I doubt you'd be a target, but all the same."

"Oh, I'm aware," she said as she opened the door. "They threaten our tenuous peace with their targets. On the contrary, I should hope they come for me next. A little fun would be nice." And with that they were gone.

That last comment sent a shiver up Ren's spine. *Who wishes for an assassin to attack them?* He asked Poppy, "Did she mean that?"

Poppy nodded matter-of-factly. "She did." They stood to their feet. "It's past time we head out. Seffin will be waiting for us by now."

They made their way to the Lodge as fast as they could. Seffin sat waiting for them in the now familiar pub, Mallory's, sipping something out of a mug. The afternoon came and went during Kiko's visit, and so Ren switched from tea to ale as they took their seats next to him. Ka ordered a whiskey while Poppy ordered an ale of their own and got straight down to business introducing Sent'o's contract to the group. It felt like another lifetime ago that Ren and Poppy met with the overly affectionate Nari'ko Wilder.

"I've waited long enough on this," Poppy said as they plunked down a black-hued crystal onto the table. "This contract is directly from Shaia Tekk, The Caretaker themself, so it is of the utmost importance that any information regarding the contract stay strictly between the four of us." Everyone at the table nodded. "On the surface it's a simple delivery. We're to take this to Nari'ko ourselves and hand deliver it to Shaia."

"Why is the crystal black?" Seffin asked.

"I've done a little poking at it, and I can't find anything odd or strange other than its color and that it doesn't seem to produce a barrier of any kind. It simply takes in will."

"So you don't know?"

"No idea," Poppy said, obviously frustrated. "I can't tell where it came from, what its purpose is, how much will it can hold, or why on earth the caretaker would be interested in it. All I know is the horde outside the wilds grows with each passing day, and they want us, specifically, to deliver it."

Ka perked up at that last comment. She'd been nursing her whiskey and eyeing a tall blonde man at the bar, only half listening. "Shaia asked for us specifically?"

"Just so," they said.

"When you say us," Ren started, "you mean you and Ka, right?"

Poppy shook their head. "No, in fact they listed all four of us by name in the contract even before Seffin signed on to our team. They also listed the deadline as 'at your earliest convenience'."

What the hells does that mean?

"How?" Seffin sounded almost offended.

Poppy only shrugged their shoulders. "My experience with Shaia tells me we'll find out when we complete the task, and since Jessica is president, Kiko has all but signed off on her plan, and Troy says the Guild will be helping with the Gogallo Initiative there isn't much reason for us to linger here any longer."

Poppy had always been terribly well informed, but the more time Ren spent with them professionally he began to realize how much they shaped behind the scenes. Any other merc would care little about who the president happened to be or what the Guild did as long as their contract paid fairly. Not Poppy though. The contracts they took all had some hook or claw into this or that important figure. They didn't want to lead, but despite that, they couldn't help themselves from trying to guide events in their own way.

Ren's fingers began to itch. That had been happening more since the night in the woods practicing his forms. It used to only happen in anticipation of stealing something. Like a small voice telling him to hurry up and do it. Take what you want and run. Now it happened whenever he doubted himself or became nervous or anxious, and it happened almost constantly whenever he was around Seffin.

"The Nari'ko Wilds is a three-month trek just one way," Ka said. "If there's any business either of you need to take care of I would do it before we go." She poked Seffin in the forehead. "Talk to your mom. It's going to bother you if you don't."

"Ouch," Seffin said, though the poke clearly didn't hurt. "She disowned me. Why would she care what I'm doing?"

"It's not for her, dummy. It's for you."

Ren must have missed something between the two of them because Ka usually saved this type of aggressive advice-giving for himself.

"Well, if it's for me then let me assure you that I don't care."

Ka poked him in the forehead again. Harder this time. "Shut up. Do as I say because I'll know if you don't."

Ka had a knack for knowing when someone lied to her. Ren knew from an abundance of experience. She could spot a web of lies from a mile off, and the best a spider could do is make sure you got to cover before she smashed it.

"Ren, tell your sister to stop mothering me."

"Why are you hassling him about talking to his mom?" Ren asked.

Ka slammed the rest of her whiskey back and gingerly set her glass on the table. "I'll let Seffin tell you that." She turned to Poppy. "I'm all but packed. Just let me know when we're heading out. I'm going to go and have a bit of fun." The man she had been eyeing earlier was now eyeing her. Poppy squeezed her hand and gave her a wink; Ka kissed them on the forehead before strolling over to join the inebriated blonde at the bar.

"Save a little bit for Nari'ko! I heard they love you there!" Ren called after her. She casually flipped him off from behind her back.

Poppy turned to Seffin. "She's right you know."

Seffin nodded. A defeated look upon his face.

"Right about what?" Ren asked.

"I'll tell you later," Seffin said. "What was that comment about Nari'ko?"

"They are, uhh, open... about their affection... or something."

Why is this so hard to talk about? This shouldn't be this hard to talk about.

A mischievous grin crept across Poppy's face as they watched him struggle to articulate Nari'ko's culture of openness. The last time he spoke with Poppy about it he'd gotten far more details than he bargained for. The images the conversation conjured in his head were best left to the uncomfortable nightmares they now occupied. Still, it left him curious, but not so curious that he'd jump at the chance to visit. The amount of touching involved seemed... excessive.

"Thank you for illuminating that, I guess?" Seffin said. He turned to Poppy. "What's he talking about?"

Poppy went over the basics of Nari'ko's society. When meeting new people, it was customary to hold hands and hug. Breaking skin contact was seen as rude. Friends tended not to be *just* friends, but far more intimate than what they were used to. This is the detail that started Ren's heart racing, and by the red in his cheeks, Seffin didn't know how to process it either. Poppy reassured him they were aware their customs were strange to foreigners, and no one would "make friends" with him unless he wanted them to.

"I don't mean to warn you off. Provided we make it to Nari'ko, I think you'll find you don't want to leave. The food is amazing, their knowledge of will techniques are second to none, and the forest itself is breathtaking."

"The trip will be nice if for no other reason than Ka can teach me more about wind and earth wielding on the way," Seffin said as he attempted a small bit of air elementalism. A light gust of wind directed upward that made Ren uneasy. Seffin may be a mystic, but his learning process still always ended with far more destruction than he bargained for. His control may be better now, but he was a long way from Ka... and an even longer way from Ren.

"We still haven't talked about how to get past the horde," Ren said.

Poppy smirked. "I've got a plan for that."

"And?"

"And we'll talk about it on the road. For now, just focus on packing everything you'll need. Oh, and Seffin—"

A blast of wind blew out the candles around their table. "Yes?" Seffin said after several apologies to other patrons and some fire elementalism to reignite the light sources.

"Did you think over my offer?"

What offer?

"I've already told my landlord I'll be leaving, and I'm mostly packed. I don't have much anyway," he said.

"Can I ask what you're talking about?" Ren said

"Seffin is coming to stay with us. We'll be gone for over half a year. I figured I'd offer him a cheaper place to keep his things."

This felt like a discussion the whole family should have had together, but Ren didn't know what he would have said in the discussion anyway. Of course, he wanted to help Seffin. It just seemed that he should have had a say in it is all.

Seffin lightly elbowed him. "Something the matter?"

"No, I'm just surprised."

Poppy put a hand on both their heads and tousled their hair. "I'm taking off." They stood from their seat. "Three days should be enough time to get things in order don't you think?"

"I'll be ready," Seffin said, looking at the bottom of his ale.

"Good, see you two later."

Ka and her blonde were making out at the bar, and Ren thought about how much he'd rather be anywhere else at the moment. Seffin started to make the hand gesture for his wind practice again and Ren slapped it out of the air.

"Hey!" Seffin said.

"Can we go back to your place or something?"

Seffin looked up in thought for a moment. "Why?"

"Because watching my sister make out with someone isn't my idea of a great time."

Seffin glanced over at the bar and back at Ren. "You can be kind of a prude."

"Sure, whatever, can we go?"

Seffin dropped some money on the table, and they stood from their seats. Meandering through the crowd of patrons chattering and waiters delivering food and drink. The pub had filled to bursting while they talked, and Ren could see why. A singer and a fiddler were setting up in the corner for entertainment and now he regretted asking to leave so soon. He hadn't heard music outside of tone-deaf beggars mewling old songs for coin in over a year. Glancing back at the bar he saw Ka and her blonde trying to combine faces again and his regret evaporated. Grabbing Seffin by the shoulder, he guided them both out of the bar, out of the Lodge, and onto the street.

As if fate was mocking him, a beggar stood half a block from the entrance with a small crowd standing around her as she butchered *Where Will the Werewiller Go*, a gruesome song about a werewiller punishing naughty children by eating their parents. Seffin stopped to toss her a few coins as they passed—for what reason he couldn't fathom—before they walked on in the direction of Kent's apartment.

"What was Ka saying about your mom?"

Seffin let out a rare sigh. Less rare than it used to be, but he still only gave outward indications of his mood sparsely. "She came over to visit me."

"Ka or your mom?"

"Both, but I'm talking about my mom." Seffin kicked a pebble down the street as they walked. "She apologized, and said she understood why I left. I didn't really know what to say."

"Well, what did you say?"

"I asked her if she knew he'd almost gotten me killed on my last contract."

Ren's eyes went wide at that. "What did she say?"

"She just started crying and left."

Seffin spoke in the matter-of-fact way he always did, but Ren had spent enough time around him now to know that it bothered him.

"I say if you're not ready to forgive her then you're not ready, but we are going to be gone for a long time. Half a year at least."

The length of time hit him suddenly. They *were* going to be gone for a long time. The contract to Oleksandra's Harbor felt like an eternity, and this would be three times that or longer if they stuck around in Nari'ko for a while. The excitement came tempered with worrying over whether he'd bought enough jerky for the road. He never wanted dried fish again.

"I am ready to forgive her," he said. "I just get angry when I see her." They caught up to the pebble he kicked earlier, and he kicked it down the road again. "It's like she's a reminder of how my life was, but she also makes me think of Kent. When I lived with them, I would see him every day, and all I can think when I see her is that I want to make her hurt as much as I do."

"I think she's hurting pretty bad already." Ren put a hand on Seffin's shoulder. As much as Pulpin had been horrible to Seffin, he was still Carula's husband.

Seffin laughed. "That's exactly what Ka said."

"Yuck. Forget I said it then." Ren smiled. A moment of silence passed between the two as a stray cat up on a fence caught their eye, shifting its feet around and staring intently at a windowsill, carefully gauging the jump it was about to attempt. "Do you want to talk to her?"

"Not really."

"Then don't," he said. "Who cares what anyone thinks? Do what you think will make you happy."

The cat leapt, landing lightly on the windowsill before perching and looking back at them, its tail flicking back and forth lazily. "Thanks." He looked at Ren. "That helped."

"Oh?"

"Yeah. I think I needed to feel like it was my decision."

"And?"

He sighed again and then said somewhat reluctantly, "I'm going to talk to her."

Sharon

B urns are a funny thing. The worse they are the less you feel at first, and for a few hours after the Rashee assassination, Sharon didn't feel much of anything, though she knew the pain would come. Pulpin's will fire had done a number on the whole right side of her body. She took stock of the damage in front of a mirror in her apartment and found her skin charred even blacker than her natural skin color, bulbous blisters had started to form, red streaks cracked through her skin, weeping blood and clear liquid down her body. Her hair turned to ash, or most of it did, the strands that weren't cooked into her swollen flesh anyway. The right side of her form glistened and began to stiffen and slow. She had mere hours before the stiffness would render her unable to move. Her mouth dried out such that, despite the state of her body, she struggled to think of anything else besides water.

No. A healer. I need a healer. Fuck water. I need a healer and I need to get moving.

Sharon donned some clothes that weren't charred, threw on a cloak, grabbed her newly acquired will-blade, and limped out of the apartment building, trying to avoid eye contact along the way with varying degrees of success. A neighbor girl's mouth dropped open when she glanced under the hood of Sharon's cloak, but she said nothing, and Sharon moved past her quickly. The girl could tell whoever she liked. It's not like she planned to come back.

Any registered mystic healer would connect the dots of the fire and murders at the Rashee residence with a burn victim walking in off the street. She remembered several underground healers that could manage wounds like this, but they were all linked to the Eyes of Koth, and if they managed to figure out her identity, they were more likely to kill her than heal her. Killing Cara came with far reaching consequences and limiting her options for healers was only one of them. She stood on a cliff with nothing but burned bridges around her. Four blocks away from her apartment it hit her. Noah. The man might just be dumb enough to take her in and not ask questions. She could wait for her body to heal to the point that she could travel more, and then seek out a healer in a small town. Or at the very least she could spend some time stabilizing until she figured something else out. Troy Saunders wasn't going anywhere. She had time.

Her right side began to itch, and her limp started to pronounce itself more and more as she made her way to Noah's place. The precursor to the pain. Clothing clung to her body, and she could feel bits of her burned flesh tear away as the fabric shifted with her gait. *A dress would have been a better idea.* From what she could tell, people did their best to ignore her. Prolivgrad's size meant it inevitably housed some unique characters, and the crowds were accustomed to simply steering clear of anyone behaving strangely. For once, the callous nature of the city's people worked in her favor. An unexpected boon. *What is that smell?* As if to balance out the scales, Prolivgrad's stench turned her stomach and it heaved, threatening to vomit. Or was the stench coming from her this time?

Finally, she climbed the stairs to Noah's doorway. She knocked, hoping he'd already come home from work. The lock sounded and she let out a sigh of relief. He was home. The door opened and Noah appeared before her. Tall, with those dumb eyes she found so adorable.

She puked.

He took a step back into his apartment with disgust. "Sorry," she managed to say between the urping, "I didn't know where else to go."

Recognition materialized on his face. "What in the hells happened?"

Now, finished emptying what little contents her stomach contained onto his threshold, she stepped into the apartment and collapsed. Rolling onto her back. The itching became unbearable, and it took all her self-control not to scratch at it, removing even more skin than had already been burned away. That's when the shivering started. The tip of her nose felt like ice, and her thirst reached a level of discomfort that she'd describe as pain if the itching and needling on her right side wasn't eclipsing all her senses. Her heart raced faster than fast. Like she'd sprinted her way here instead of limping at a slow pace. Noah put both hands on top of his head and looked down at her with wide eyes. His lips moved, but she couldn't understand what he said. The beating of her heart in her ears is all she heard. The room darkened and she passed out.

***

Cullen came home late every day, and she knew why. He liked the wilderness too much. The peace and quiet helped to calm his restless nature. After all, she had met him ranging in the north, and during their courtship, he always complained whenever she forced him to sit still. Anyway, it's not like he could help with supper. The man couldn't cook to save his life, and he had the lack of taste to match. Besides, the later he stayed out in the forest the better the gift he brought by way of apology, and Sharon had long since thought the tradeoff worth it. He'd come home with fresh meat, agates and other gemstones, or toys for Ren he bought from traveling merchants. Still, the hour grew later than usual, and no one from the patrol had come back yet. Usually, a few people filtered in by now. Dusk was fast approaching, and they all had strict orders to be back inside the town's barrier by then.

She grabbed her will-blade, scooped up Ren from his babbling over some noisemaker Cullen had bought him a few weeks back and went outside. Grandpa Ren could watch him while she checked on her crew. Patrol routes and their assignments were her responsibility, and if her people were delayed for something important, she wanted to be ready to assess the situation. When she made it to the road, she could see her neighbors heading in for the evening. With Connie in his arms, Kord waved as she walked by. "Tara's late coming home. Something up?"

Sharon waved back and gave a shrug. "Not sure, I'm going to give the Rens some time together while I go and see what's keeping them."

"That'll be difficult," Kord said, "I just saw your grandpa take off a few minutes ago. Said not to worry."

Shit

Grandpa saying not to worry was all the more reason to worry. Grandma clued her into that little quirk before she passed. Sharon remembered the first time she heard him say it. When mom dropped her off on his doorstep twenty-seven years ago, Grandpa told her not to worry. The last time she'd heard him say it was when grandma lay in bed, thinner than thin, rasping breaths and vacant eyes. He'd looked at her and told her it would be fine. Don't worry.

Her hands clammed up, but she managed to mask all the other signs of fear washing over her. "Kohru take my fool of a Grandfather, would you mind watching this one while I see what's going on?" She gestured to her son.

Kord chuckled. "Sure, Connie's had a boring day anyway. Some play time would be good."

She dropped Ren in Kord's arms and started walking toward the town's entrance. Once outside, she started jogging toward today's patrol routes. It didn't take longer than five minutes before she heard the sounds of battle.

Please let everyone be ok.

A vibration ran through the ground. An unmistakable sign Grandpa was fighting. He put will in his kicks and punches, a modification of the flickering technique he taught her, but it was anything but subtle. She sprinted toward the source of the vibrations. A loud crash and a flash of light barreled through the trees.

***

Sharon opened her eyes. The dip in the ceiling of Noah's apartment seemed to have grown since she was last here. She tried to raise her head but found turning slightly to the left is all it could muster. Even then, pain bloomed outward from the burns on her neck, and the startle response it caused felt like a torrent of lancing needles all down her right side. She whimpered as tears formed in her eyes, dripping down the side of her face. The saltwater hit the burns and a new wave of agony ripped through her body.

How long had she been out? She called weakly but no response came. Noah must have left, and she hadn't the chance to give him a story on how she ended up burned this way. What would her story be, anyway? How do you explain showing up at a fling's apartment with half your body burnt beyond recognition? Why didn't she go to a healer?

Oh, gods. He's getting a healer.

She used her left arm to pat around the bed beside her. It would be stupid for him to leave the will-blade on the bed, but she had to try anyway on the off chance he'd just tossed her belongings there. Nothing. Just some clean bandages. She surveyed the room as much as she could without moving her body. The position of the sun meant it was around noon which meant it had been at least a day since she fainted, if not longer. Looking as far down as her eyes could, she spied bandages wrapped around her right side, but she was nude and uncovered otherwise. Probably to help the fever. *He's not as dumb as I thought.* A bowl of water with strips of cloth hanging over the side sat on a table not far from the foot of the bed, and a string of drying, blood-stained strips now hung in an archway leading into the small lounging area off the kitchen.

"Noah?" she called out again on the off chance he'd fallen asleep somewhere else in the apartment, but her dry mouth hadn't gone anywhere so his name came out as a croak. Her throat ached. She fell silent, listening for any sound of movement. Nothing.

Nothing.

Nothing could be worse than this. Immobile, in pain, alone, and worst of all she was bored. Being both doomed and bored was a special kind of hell. Her eyes relaxed back into neutral position, staring at the ceiling. *Has the dip in his ceiling gotten even bigger or am I going crazy?* Her mind wandered, flipping through the choices that brought her here. Choosing vengeance over motherhood, and continuing to choose it, over and over, after each kill, sinking her costs further and further.

She could change her mind. Even now. If she could manage to get out of this, she could drop everything and run back to Ren, but after all these years, how would he take it. What would she say to him that wouldn't sound monstrous? *Sorry son, I decided to dismantle a conspiracy from the bottom up instead of finding you after I survived the attack. I loved you, but I didn't love loving you more than the idea of revenge.* She pushed the thought away like she always did. That rabbit hole always led to doubt and hesitation, and she could manage doubt, but hesitation could get her killed. Better to leave it alone. She knew he was safe, and that would have to be enough for now.

A creak came from the ceiling. Some dust floated down, twinkling in the light of the open window. A crack and a groan followed after.

Fuck.

A flurry of snapping and the sound of building materials shifting came from the dip in the ceiling that Sharon now knew for certain was growing. And quickly. She tried to move out of the way, but the pain was overwhelming, and her right side simply wasn't listening to her. The only communication it offered came in the form of pain so pure it threatened to throw her back into unconsciousness. Which it turns out, would have been just fine. She closed her eyes and braced herself as the ceiling gave way. *So, this is how it ends? Naked on a bed in a run-down building. Helpless. Pathetic.* Something blunt and wooden hit her in the head accompanied by a flash of white.

***

The grim scene in the forest outside Gull Harbor felt out of place. This wasn't her life anymore. Hadn't been for over five years. Sure, the bodies peppering the ground had their limbs splayed in unnatural directions just like the battles she fought while working for The Eyes of Koth, but the characters were wrong. The faces shouldn't be her friends. They should be bodyguards for a politician or foolish zealots following some cultist mystic. Not Tara, Kord's wife. Not Blenda, Shorda's mother. Or Kyle, who just started patrols last week. Fresh out of some basic will training with Grandpa to enhance his kicks. His legs lay fifteen feet from his body now.

Shorda sat bleeding up against a tree on the edge of the battleground. She spotted Sharon and pointed across all the bodies, toward where the battle had moved. Sharon nodded and began running.

"Wild wielder!" Shorda called after.

Obviously.

The ground looked like someone had picked it up and turned it upside down, trees lay on their sides and rocks with clumps of packed dirt stuck to their surface sat on top the bodies of her friends. Clearly an elementalist, and with no sign of wet earth or scorched branches all signs pointed to a wild wielder elementalist.

When she caught up to the battle the only people left were Cullen, Grandpa Ren, and the wild wielder, a shield of rocks floating around him. Within the span of a heartbeat, he spotted her, and a rock launched in her direction. She knew this move, and by the state of the battlefield she just ran through, it was working great for him so far. He'd try to make her dodge in a specific direction and slam a boulder down on her. Instead, she brought out her blade and deflected the rock, glancing upward she confirmed four boulders floating above them in an asynchronous pattern. Whoever he was, he had massive will reserves. Grandpa and Cullen used the moment as a distraction and flanked the wielder. Clearly planning to rush in.

Fools. You should know better.

Sharon immediately started flickering. Her world turned to frosted glass as she became keenly aware of the iron smell of blood and the stench of viscera from the battlefield behind her. She could pinpoint the beads of sweat on the wielder's face even though he stood some sixty paces away, his eyes were closed and arms folded in front of him, not using them to focus. *Deep will reserves and a master wielder. This is bad.* Her husband and grandpa rushed in, though, while flickering, it still appeared as if in slow motion. As Sharon suspected, the wielder already started shifting his rock shield to counter her family. At this rate they'd be full of holes before they could comprehend what happened. Cullen hadn't fought a mystic level wild wielder before, but Grandpa had and should have known better.

She had to decide who to save. She rushed toward Grandpa. All three of them knew how to flicker, a technique the Adegast family perfected and passed down, but Grandpa would die in the attempt, his body too old to withstand a full body flicker any longer. She prayed Cullen would realize his mistake and flicker away. She tackled Grandpa and they tumbled away as a flurry of stones barely missed them. Frantically, she turned to check on Cullen. He managed to dance away from the rock volley, and she breathed a sigh of relief.

For the briefest of moments Grandpa squeezed her shoulder. She saw why, when Cullen dodged, he did so into the path of one of the wielder's floating boulders. She made to shout for him to move out of the way, but before the words left her mouth the boulder exploded into dust and pebbles. Grandpa fell out of the air and landed next to Cullen. He sacrificed himself to punch the boulder out of the sky. A cloud of dust wafted up from where he fell.

Sharon gripped her blade, with the rock shield around the wielder used up she rushed forward to end the fight. Cullen had the same idea. A wind blast along the ground knocked her feet out from under her. Cullen leapt over it, going for the wielder's neck with his will-blade. She tumbled into a recovery just in time to watch Cullen flicker past him, liberating his head from his body. As the wielder collapsed Cullen landed in two places. His torso came to a sliding halt just out of arm's reach from where Sharon knelt, but his lower half, from the belly down, fell away and collapsed next to the wielder's headless form. His blade tumbled out of view, kicking up clumps of dirt as it skipped over the ground. Trees from the direction Cullen rushed from began to crack and fall. The elementalist had bought himself enough time to form a wind-blade and launched it at Cullen just before he died.

Sharon stood up and looked down at her husband. His paling face blankly gazing off into the distance. She felt nothing. No anger, no sadness. Her mind had frozen the moment, locking it just outside her heart, because if it made it to her heart there would be nothing left of her. If she allowed herself to feel this, she would abandon everything and everyone she had left. She'd find this wielder's family and tear them apart, slowly, and then when she finished, she'd slaughter anyone they'd ever cared about. She knew this deep down. Instinctually. The thought didn't even need to surface. Better that it didn't, really. Thinking about it would give it a chance to get its hooks in her, and that *could not* happen. Ren was still with Kord. Shorda still sat up against a tree just a short distance from where she stood. Her town had no mayor now. If she left, if she did what she wanted most, it would spoil the few bits of her life that remained.

Instead, she turned away from the scene and jogged toward Shorda. Exertion caught up with her and she broke out in a sweat. A cloudless evening sky set the stage for the sun to pierce through the forest. Sunbeams radiated almost horizontally around the trees, and she squinted as one caught her in the eyes. The yellow ray turned a reddish pink as it passed through her eyelid. The thin coloration deepened and darkened, her vision turning from pink into a bloody crimson.

***

The cough didn't work but to jar her back into consciousness. Whatever dust and detritus made it into her lungs remained, making each inhalation a wheeze and each exhalation a stab. Her face felt sticky from sweat and blood. The right side of her body burned and itched worse than anything, but it saved the true pain, the good stuff, for when she tried to move.

"Sharon?"

A muffled voice floated through her perception. *Sharon? Gods, if he knows my real name I'm fucked.* She lay there for a while, hearing little besides her own shallow breaths and muffled clunks and scrapes as whoever it was, likely Noah, attempted to wrest her from the rubble. Her prison made of building materials shifted off and on as he worked, aggravating her burns, but little could be done about it. It felt like days, though probably only an hour passed, before a brick lodged in a mess of debris above her head lifted away and a pair of brown eyes, stupid and kind in equal measure, peered through the opening. They looked at each other for a moment, and she thought maybe some understanding passed between them. He knew her true name now, he knew who she was, and still he looked at her with that gentle gaze.

"You're alive," he said with relief.

She coughed in response.

"Don't speak, we'll get you out of there."

We? Of course, we. The other part of we told him my name. I wonder who we is.

After another ten minutes of grunting, clunking, and groaning the hole above her head grew to a size that her body could easily slip through, if she were able to move it, that is. Instead, Noah grabbed underneath her arms, and with her right side exploding with pain he lifted her clumsily out of the debris, bumping, squeezing, and scraping through the hole he made. He held her out in front of him like a parent lifting a baby, and in her mostly naked, bandaged form she probably resembled a baby just a bit. A bloody, burned, dusty baby.

Sharon's eyes began adjusting to the light in the room. She could see other forms, but they were hazy approximations for the moment. Noah pulled her into his body and shifted his grip so that he cradled her. The only thing missing from her infantilization was a diaper. The humiliation grew so far out of bounds with what she thought possible she couldn't even feel embarrassed. A foul odor hit her nose and a thought crossed her mind; she'd been unconscious long enough there was no doubt she was laying in her own piss and shit, and yet this man cradled her without so much as wrinkling his nose. The kindest philanderer she ever met. She hoped she wouldn't end up having to kill him.

As her eyes finished adjusting to the light, she found two other men standing in the room. One; clearly a laborer with his big shoulders, calloused hands, and poorly groomed facial hair, the other; a tall, blonde man dressed in expensive clothing, his face uncannily attractive. Her blood boiled.

Troy.

She tamped down her anger immediately. A useful emotion for much of her work, but here it would only make things worse. She shook her head and looked up at Noah. "Tattle-tale."

Troy raised his arms as if in retreat. "I'm not here to hurt you. Though I know you'd kill me given the chance."

"If we're going to have a chat, can I at least get something to cover up with first."

Troy flashed an admittedly gorgeous smile.

"I can do better than that. I have a healer lined up at my house. Very discreet, but I need assurances you won't kill me, at least until I've had a chance to explain."

Is he really so stupid?

"Of course, if you've lined up a healer, the least I can do is hear you out. Maybe afterward we can have some tea and discuss our opinions on the weather."

That disgustingly earnest smile plastered across his face again, and she had to admit it worked. Something about his face made him easy to trust. An image flashed through her mind of Ren looking up at her with innocent eyes, holding his rattle out, trying to share his toy with his mom.

Stop it. He killed everyone you loved.

She coughed, hard this time, and some grey phlegm knocked loose from her lungs, shooting out of her mouth. Breathing felt a little easier now and she turned to the laborer and asked, "And you are?"

"Clem, ma'am. President of the Miner's Union."

"The president of the Miner's Union and the president of The Guild of Commerce both here for little old me? I'm flattered." She didn't have any inclination to turn off the sarcasm. Cradled, nude and incapacitated, in the arms of a man she barely knew, in front of the man she most wanted to kill, it was the smallest bit of control she had left, and she didn't want to give it up.

Is no one going to get me something to cover up?

"Sorry about the ceiling falling on you—" Noah began to say.

Sharon used her good arm and put a finger on his lips. "Water. Healer. I don't need an explanation for why your shitty apartment was in shitty repair." The words came out angrier than she intended, and the expression of hurt on his face stirred something in her. *Guilt? Again?*

"Sorry," she offered, her voice more gravel than the calm timbre she was used to. She gestured at herself. "I'm just very uncomfortable at the moment."

Noah smiled in understanding. The two others sought out some blankets, and together, they wrapped her up. Fully swaddled, the transformation into an infant was complete.

"I have a carriage outside. We'll have you more comfortable soon," Troy said.

The wave of exhaustion hit her like a sledgehammer. She nodded at him, then laid her head against Noah's chest, allowing the beating of his heart and the warmth of his body to lull her into unconsciousness.

Jessica

The room they were in was neutral ground, set aside in the east wing of the capitol building next to the senate chamber, Jessica's old stomping grounds. Winnow sat across a table from her, looking like he was poured into his seat rather than resting in it. His posture was angled forward, and he leaned on the armrests so heavily the wood creaked. He looked ready to either pounce or fall over.

"The mining union isn't too happy with you." A smug smile sat on his face.

"Are you offering a solution or just gloating?" She was annoyed. These meetings were pointless, and wasting her morning irked her, especially on the day she was to present her amalgamations to the other nations. The only reason she kept them up was to give the appearance of extending a hand across the aisle to the National Party. "I'd say 'Let's make a deal to help the miners out', but we both know you have no interest in helping anyone but yourself and your rich friends."

An exaggerated frown slipped onto his face. "That's a nasty thing to say. I *want* to help them, but you people keep letting refugees take their jobs."

"Winnow, do you know what the word 'refugee' means? These are *our* people. They pay their taxes just like everyone else. They're citizens for gods' sakes. Just because they weren't born and raised in Prolivgrad doesn't make them any less Egallan than anyone else living here."

This was intentional. The man was stupid and impulsive, but he was great at obfuscating the issues, and that rag *The Egal Gazette* helped him spread his bullshit at every turn. They'd spun the facts so thoroughly that even members of the miners' union were starting to break away, believing this garbage about refugees.

"Send them back to the outer towns. The people here don't want them. Most of them are homeless, lazy, good-for-nothing—"

"Which is it?" She was starting to get angry.

His face blanked from the interruption. If there were wheels to turn in his head they would be turning, but Jessica knew nothing was going on behind that vacant expression, so she continued, "Which is it? Are they lazy or are they stealing jobs?"

"Does it matter? They're both bad?"

Gods, he's so stupid.

"If you introduce another bill to *banish our own fucking citizens,* I will veto it."

"Kick out the riff raff. We have the best economy in the world, and you're destroying it."

Kicking out homeless people isn't going to help the economy. Stop. Jessica. Stop wasting your thoughts on this oaf.

"I would gladly work on a bilateral bill to improve the conditions in the mines, but I'm not loosening labor laws even more based on a pinky-swear that the mining companies are going to magically decide to do the right thing when they've proven over and over again, they'd rather watch miners die than spend even a few coins on safety improvements. And, I can't believe I need to say this, I'm *not* kicking our homeless citizens out to *die in the wilds* simply for being homeless."

"No, you'd rather burn our economy to the ground on fake claims that the husk population is spiraling out of control. The citizens see you for what you really are, and they know what you're doing."

He wanted her to ask what it is the citizens see. What the citizens *know.* She wouldn't fall for the bait, and more importantly, she didn't care what his answer would be. The citizens voted, decisively, for her. Not this overblown, lumpy mass of ego and greed.

She rolled her eyes. "Refusing to believe the facts doesn't make them any less true, Winnow. And I won the election. Not you. Did you have any bills for me to consider? Any legislation for me to look at? Did you plan on doing your fucking job *at all,* or should I move on with my day. I have plenty of actual work I could be doing."

He leaned back in his seat and smiled. "We will not be silenced."

Aaaand we're back to vague threats. We're done here.

"Gods, if only I could silence you. At least then I'd know a moment's peace." She stood from her chair.

"Where are you going? We have another fifteen minutes."

"If you want to sit here for fifteen more minutes and talk to my empty chair, feel free, but I'm a busy woman. Maybe for our next meeting you could come armed with something besides vague threats and made-up grievances."

Whatever his response was it fell on deaf ears. Jessica's mind already shifted to this afternoon's meeting. It was a strange mixture of relief and excitement when she left the room. Relief to be out of Winnow's presence, and excitement for this afternoon's demonstration.

The presidential carriage was waiting outside the capitol building to take her to the outer lab, built primarily with today in mind. Hopping inside, a guard closed the door behind her, she sat down and let out an exasperated sigh.

This is it. The world lives or dies based on what happens today.

***

Setting up a dead zone within a barrier turned out to be pretty easy. It was one of Pulpin's first offerings after they started working together. Some of the engineers figured out how to configure a pylon to soak in barrier harmonics instead of project them. You could even dial in the radius you wanted. Of course, Duncan wouldn't shut up about the dangers of so many "uncontrolled" husk and amalgamations in the facility, but Jessica didn't share his worry. Between herself, the empress, and Bahati it would take far more than a few hundred loose husk, with a couple amalgamations peppered in, to prove a threat.

They all stood on a walkway looking down at a room crawling with the undead. The smell was awful, but they wouldn't have to put up with it for long. The demonstration would only take a few minutes once things got going. They just needed all the pieces in place. Jessica could feel when the staff brought in her amalgamated rafadons, shelled creatures with eight legs, a spiked tail, and massive tusks jutting upward from their lower jaws. Of the species they planned to use for the push on Gogallo, these were the least threatening. Still, they stood taller than a human like all the colossi.

An image of a world without husk flashed through her mind. The colossi would become the biggest threat in the wilds. A heartening thought since most colossi kept to themselves. Some could even be tamed. The Burgston region of Garvelle were famous for their porcine colossi mounts, and apparently, the male in the lab's laranee pen had taken a shining to the staff. Amazing how tame a creature became when their life reduced down to eating, exercise, and sex. The mothers on the other hand, despised their confinement. Stealing their cubs away shortly after birth became more and more dangerous with each litter.

A yell from Sumiko, her new head researcher, confirmed she could start the demonstration. She felt around in her mind for the unsettling sensation at the top of her spine, where neck connected to skull, and grasped onto it. Jessica had used intentioned will throughout her life, but never so much as she did lately and rarely in front of people. The two rafadons went from lumbering about in their cages to standing perfectly still. She reached out with her arms, and using kinetics, threw open the cage doors. Duncan gasped at the sudden movement.

Using her fingers as conduits for her will, she walked the rafadons forward into the pit of husk.

"Alright," she said, "make your requests. What would you have me do?"

King Edward spoke first, "Kill that big one. Over there."

He pointed to the largest of the amalgamations. A bulbous monstrosity whose legs could barely hold its heft. *Easy enough.* Jessica's fingers danced and the rafadons skittered over to the doomed brute of a husk before she had them turn around and slam it into a bloody pulp with their spiked tails. Putrid gas floated up to where they were standing, causing Duncan to wretch. *Gods, but he is annoying.* None of the other husk reacted, though a few fell onto the mound of flesh and gore left after the rafadons' violence, beginning the lengthy process of amalgamating. But they'd never finish before the demonstration ended, when the dead zone would drop, and all the normal husk would disintegrate.

"Have one stand on top of the other," Kiko said.

Odd request, but fine.

Jessica shifted her fingers and the giant spider-tortoises obeyed. One mounted the other. She even had them wiggle their tails in synchrony.

Kiko nodded. "Now show me what they can do with will."

Jessica smiled; this is what she'd been waiting for. The top rafadon dismounted her sibling. Something about the shells on the rafadons changed with amalgamation, and they turned into walking explosives. Safely far enough away from each other, Jessica activated the far rafadon's shell. A reverberation echoed around the room like a low, violent note. Then, a loud pop as every husk in a thirty-foot radius around the amalgamation fell apart. Like a will-blade wielder went berserk and carved everything into pieces.

Bruhier whistled. "Well, that's something."

"How long does it take before it can do that again?" Knight Bahati asked. A jolt of annoyance ran through Jessica. Bahati held no authority. She shouldn't be answering to a soldier.

Jessica looked to Kiko to give her response, "Two hours for a smaller blast, but a full day will recover it fully. Just like humans."

Kiko didn't even look at her.

Bahati followed up, "And each type of amalgamation can do something like this?"

Jessica bristled and continued to address Kiko though she refused to return her gaze. "Yes, as I said yesterday. The process of seizing control causes it."

"That could prove extremely useful. How many of these can a trained mystic control at once?"

That's it.

"Empress, are you in charge or is—"

Kiko spun to face Jessica. "Knight Bahati is my most trusted advisor, and her opinion on this matters far more to me than yours. You might have noticed she only speaks when something important need be said or asked. The same can't be said for *some* of the company we're in." Kiko glanced at Duncan who glared back at her—she really did loathe him. She turned to meet Jessica's eyes again. "You've played your hand President Saunders, and we accepted. Don't be a prick about it. Answer my advisor's questions. Unless of course, you can't?"

The grin on Bruhier's face seemed wicked. He'd like it if they fought. He hated the Empress and had an intense disdain for the crystal trade. If Garvelle and Egal went after each other, no matter who lost, Bruhier would win. For as long as the world stuck around, that is. *I need to stop. Even if I earned my presidency and Kiko was born royalty, this isn't the time for a contest of egos.* Pride got the better of her. She should have just answered the question, but now everyone waited to see if she would cow to the empress.

"It's entirely dependent on the skill and the will reserves of the wielder." She chose to relent. Saving the world comes before pride. "An academy trained mystic should have no problem with four to five, but someone with large will reserves and excellent control could probably get up to fifteen. You can bind to more than you can control however, and simply cage whichever amalgamations you're not using at the time. Is that a satisfactory answer, *Knight* Bahati?"

Stupid. Stop picking fights. Why am I letting something so small get under my skin?

"Yes. When can we start the binding process with the mystics in our ranks?" Bahati continued without acknowledging the barb.

"A little less than a year. Our first wave is a smaller test batch and will be bound to me exclusively, the second wave will bind to the Egallan military. The third wave will go to Garvelle, and as we ramp up production the rest will go to the other nations as needed or desired. There will be no cost other than the oath that you all will participate in the invasion."

"About that oath, Jessica." King Kimberly stepped out from behind Bahati. "I assume it will entail more than just our word, yes?"

"I'll need assurances on my end before I sign anything," Bruhier chimed in.

The contract. The thorniest bit of the whole process. Demands being made, old rivalries reigniting, and alliance requests that would put her country in a weakened position. Fate of the world or not, these people wanted their pound of flesh. It's how they gained power in the first place.

"I already have a treaty drawn up for review. If you have any qualms about the language you can let me know. Though I would remind everyone that if this fails, we all die. So keep that in mind for any changes you may have."

Empress Zollinger stepped forward. "Garvelle issues no requests for changes." She gave a threatening smile. "We do have two orders of business to take care of, though."

Jessica nodded. "Go on."

"First, a request: I would ask to have a private audience with you." Bruhier opened his mouth to protest, but the empress' hand shot up with her finger out, shushing him. "No official requests shall be made in the meeting, Bruhier. I simply have some council to give. Second, a warning: by necessity, you will all march on Garvelle territory when we attack Gogallo. If any of you are thinking of this as an opportunity, I would remind you that our nation's roots grow deep, and they have thorns. Any army that doesn't turn around and march straight back to their homeland after the dust settles on the battlefield will find their new, permanent home in a funeral pyre." The Empress' eyes hesitated on Bruhier when she said the word funeral. Bruhier was a fighter from a nation of fighters, and as a grandson of Perren Soledar, whose assassination started the Sol War, he possessed a very personal hatred for the Zollinger family in particular.

"The private audience is granted." Jessica didn't even have to think about it. She wiggled her fingers and sent the rafadons back to their cages. "If anyone else would like an audience you may request one. Otherwise, we'll meet tomorrow to start going over the treaty."

With the demonstration finished, the dead zone in the room collapsed. All the husk, save for the amalgamated colossi, fell quickly, turning to dust and bones. Jessica escorted the empress to a small meeting room within the building. Guards were stationed at the door with Knight Bahati stationed across from them. A wooden table in poor condition had several uncomfortable looking chairs resting on each side. Jessica took one before gesturing The Empress to do the same. The two most powerful women in the world sat alone in a small, dingy office meeting room.

What could this possibly be about?

Kiko started, "I'm sure you're aware of the assassin that's running around the city."

"Yes." Jessica couldn't imagine Kiko would pull her aside for that. She had to assume she already knew.

"I wanted to make the stakes for this clear. If you die, Winnow becomes president, yes?" Jessica nodded. Technically, a special election would be called, but no one in the Labor party stood half as well against him as Jessica did. He was all but guaranteed to win if something happened to her. Kiko carried on, "Keep yourself safe, Jessica. Not because of this plan of yours, we've enough information to replicate it without you at this point anyway." That sent a chill up her spine. Her life's work didn't need her anymore. "But because many lives depend on it. Winnow will ruin everything. The trade agreements for crystals we have right now are already tenuous. He would force us all to choose between bankruptcy or the death of our people, and I can tell you most of us would take a third option." She nodded. They'd go to war. It's what she warned about during the campaign, but the Nationals were in denial... or pretended to be. Their party put too much faith in Egal's military guard and exercised too little caution when dealing with international politics.

Kiko shifted in her chair. "Ending the war quickly would give us the best shot at regrouping, and the fastest way to end a war is overwhelming force. Even then it turns this plan from a long shot into an even longer shot."

With evidence planted in Cara's office the assassin shouldn't be going for anyone else. Even if they did, their next likely target would be Troy, though Jessica didn't put all her eggs in that basket. She'd hired two bodyguards on top of the president's special guard, and she kept two of her amalgamated pets in every location she spent time in. Not to mention she could more than hold her own in a fight. Short of hiding in a cave somewhere there wasn't more she could possibly do to protect herself.

"Trust me. I have a personal interest in staying alive myself. I'm sparing no expense on my protection."

"I figured as much." Kiko stood from her chair. "Bruhier is going to ask you to betray me after we're done in Gogallo."

"He'll be very disappointed in my answer."

Kiko nodded with a satisfied smile on her face before exiting the room. Jessica sat in her chair, thumbing the corner of the table as she thought. The pieces had fallen into place. With Garvelle and Nashow all but locked in on the treaty, Estaba and Lighton would follow suit. Even if they didn't, the plan would still work. Nashow's navy with Garvelle's armies would be enough to punch through to the heart once enough amalgamations were added to their militaries. All the sacrifices, the late nights, the sneaking around, the burnt bridges, the dead colleagues. It had all worked. Now she only needed to make sure production kept apace, and there would never again be another Stockton. No more children in the street crying as death came, snapping and snarling, for their friends and family. No more lost towns with refugees limping, fearful and scarred with trauma, to Prolivgrad for safety. No more husk at all.

Egal would change drastically without the crystal trade. After all, without husk the demand for focus crystals would plummet. Perhaps they could pivot to agriculture and reduce their reliance on Lighton. She relished the idea of never having to speak to Duncan again. They could finally use the land their country controlled, and with freedom of movement, different kinds of trade would open up. People could visit cities for leisure. Yes, Egal would land on its feet, crystals or no.

Without warning, Tia walked through the door with a notepad in her hands and a scowl on her face. "If you're going to take extra meetings you could at least tell me before you do it."

"When the Empress of Garvelle asks to speak with you, you take the meeting. You weren't nearby, otherwise you'd have been the first to know."

"Excuses. You could have easily told one of the guards to relay the message."

"Enough, Tia. What is it you want? I don't have anything on the schedule for another hour at least, and I'm not in the mood to argue."

Tia looked at her clipboard, her lips pursed with annoyance. "Well, Bruhier wants to meet with you now. Apparently, you told him you could squeeze him in before tomorrow?"

Jessica chuckled. "You can tell him I'm happy to meet with him, but that there will be no talk of the treaty or of betraying Garvelle after we finish with Gogallo. My guess is that he'll retract his request, if he doesn't, I'd be very interested to hear what he has to say."

Tia continued, "How was your meeting with minority leadership?"

Jessica frowned. The meetings had been fruitless. She couldn't wait until she didn't have to think about Winnow anymore. For such a simple-minded person he threatened so much.

Wait a second.

She thought of crossing a line she hadn't considered before. You don't kill political rivals. Everyone knew not to lest blood feuds sprout up and pretty soon you're in a civil war. Nosy journalists? Fine. Old contacts that had dirt on you? Have at it. But you don't kill political rivals. The unwritten rule kept the peace, but the more she thought about it the more she realized that, at least as of right this moment, it threatened the peace. One man remained the biggest threat to the world, and she could think of no reason he should be allowed to. Kiko all but told her she should do it.

"We need to kill Winnow."

The shock on Tia's face almost made her laugh. "E-Excuse me?"

"It'll be expensive, but Kiko was right. If the assassin gets to me and he's the one that picks up the mantle a lot more people die needlessly. He's a prick anyway."

"He is a prick, but he's also the face of the opposition. If he dies people will assume Labor did it." Tia looked like she realized something. "And what do you mean Kiko was right?"

Seffin

The door to the Rashee residence was painted red inside a sand-colored brick frame. Knocking on it, Seffin realized he still had his house key. In fact, having turned in Kent's keys earlier today, it was the only key he still had in his possession. He'd thought about giving it back earlier or tossing it, but giving it back would have involved seeing his parents and tossing it seemed irresponsible. Instead, it sat heavy in his pocket.

As he knocked yet again, the thought occurred to just let himself in. A few more seconds passed before he heard the clicking footsteps of his mother approaching the door. He clenched his fists, squinted his eyes, and shook his head briefly, trying to shake his nerves away. The door opened and his mother stood elegantly in a dress she always wore for work. An expression of confusion flashed across her face before it contorted into a frown accompanied by tears and wailing.

Carula grabbed him, pulling him in for an embrace he hadn't decided if he was ready for. Tears formed in his eyes despite himself, but after a few seconds he broke off the hug.

"Can we talk inside?" Her wailing brought onlookers from the street, craning their necks, and he didn't feel like putting on a show.

Nodding a little too enthusiastically, she stood aside and let him in. The foyer windows lit the entrance up beautifully as always, a welcoming façade on a broken home. They ended up sitting in the dining room, occupying the corner of the table furthest from where they would usually take their breakfasts. Carula kept trying to hold his hands, and Seffin kept trying to pull away, uncomfortable with the forced intimacy.

"How have you been?" She said it like they kept regular contact. Like they were just catching up after a slightly longer than normal parting. Like he hadn't told her she was a terrible mother the last time they spoke.

"Good," he started, "I'll be leaving the city soon."

Carula's eyebrows went up in an exaggerated expression of surprise. "Oh? Are you moving... or?"

Seffin took the opportunity to break his hands away from hers. "No, just a contract. A long one though. Won't be home for half a year at least."

Carula frowned, tears forming in her eyes she reached for his hands again.

"Stop that!" He regretted snapping immediately. She pulled away, hurt. A moment passed where he considered apologizing.

"I'm sorry," she said. "I miss you." She set one hand on the table and one in her lap, as if she didn't really know what to do with them. "I have since you left, and now with..." Her face broke into a trembling frown again. "... with Pulpin gone I—"

Seffin sighed audibly, annoyed. "I don't want to talk about father. He tossed me aside like garbage the moment he realized I couldn't be controlled. If he were still here, I wouldn't be sitting at this table, and you wouldn't have even tried to reach out to me."

"That's not true!" She looked scandalized. "I wanted to reach out. How was I supposed to know you were staying with our butler?"

Seffin slammed his fist on the table in frustration. These were the same old tricks she played when he lived with them. "His name was Kent, and he was a better parent to me in the month and a half I stayed with him than you two were my whole life." Carula's eyes got bigger, and impossibly even more tearful. "You knew full well where I was staying. Dad certainly knew. If we're going to do this, you better start being honest with me. Because I have no interest in reconciling with someone that thinks it's ok to manipulate her way into a relationship." He knew his reputation for being confrontational. Lately, he'd been trying to shy away from it, blunting his edges. The Bolins seemed to appreciate it. But here, right now, he wasn't going to save his mother's feelings. They would have an honest conversation, or they wouldn't have one at all. Simple as that.

Carula closed her eyes and shook her head. She put her hands up in a gesture of surrender. "You're right. I'm sorry."

She sighed. "I'm sorry. I'm sorry." She looked him in the eyes now. "The truth is that I do miss you, but I don't know what I'm doing. I don't know how to talk to you. When you were younger you were so easy to reassure, but now that you're older—"

"Things are different," he said. "When I was younger, I was more gullible, Mom. That's what's different."

Her mouth hung open slightly. She was doing it again. Trying to think of what the best response would be instead of just telling him how she really felt.

"We'll get farther if you think less about what you say. I'm not a trap. I'm not a maze to navigate."

"What do you want me to say? That I liked my life better before you were born? That I chose this family over my own happiness. I gave up everything, my whole life, my job that I loved, said goodbye to the world, and caged myself in this city so I could be here for you and your father, all I had was this family and now that's gone. I'm desperate, Seffin. I have nothing left."

It didn't sting. He knew she liked her life more before him. He'd braced himself for when she might confirm that fact because he thought it might hurt to hear it. But it didn't. It was a relief.

"I can't understand why you would give up everything just to please a man who only cared about his own goals, but I can understand the resentment."

"I don't *resent* you, Seffin," she said, her tone softening. "I wish I'd stuck up for us more, but I don't resent or regret you."

His chest lightened. He hadn't expected that. He'd thought he didn't care or want her approval.

"You should leave," Seffin said.

"Excuse me?"

"Leave." He met her eyes. "You said it yourself. You're stuck in this city. You liked traveling and meeting people. You liked your job from before, so go back to it."

She looked off to the side, her eyes panning over her home. She shook her head. "I can't just *leave*." She brought her arms up and gestured at the house broadly. "What'll I do with all of this?"

"Sell it," he said. "I'm not coming back here. There's too much..." He closed his eyes and took a moment to feel the brief wave of mourning run up and down his limbs, before condensing into his chest. Heavier now than a moment ago. "It's too much." His eyes were wet. "Get an apartment. Use the money to do what you want finally. You should live how you want."

She reached for his hands, and this time he let her. "I want to know that we're ok," she said.

A tear dropped down his cheek. "I think... I think we will be."

She embraced him and Seffin hugged back. He let himself relax into her arms like he used to years ago. Afterward, they talked through what it might look like to sell the Rashee home.

Letting his father's family home fall into the hands of new money felt poetic given his focus on preserving their legacy during life. Carula offered to give him some of the money from the will Pulpin wrote him out of, but he refused. The further he could get from the Rashee name the better, and he'd landed ok with the Bolins anyway. They finished up their talk, each promising to keep in touch as best they could, but Seffin couldn't help but feel a sort of finality in it. He'd be leaving for half a year, and for all they knew she could be on some job across the continent when he returned. Carula kissed him on the forehead, and they had one final hug before he left to finish his preparations for the journey to Nari'ko.

On the way back to the Bolins', Seffin stopped at a bakery he knew Ka liked. Between the elemental lessons and her advice that turned out to be spot on, he wanted to get her a gift. Also, he wanted a croissant and a coffee. The shop's window display had the cream filled pastries Ren liked, and in front of the case, serendipitously, stood Troy, paying for some sandwiches. He entered the shop and tapped him on the shoulder.

"Seffin! It's been a while!" He gave him a handshake that turned into a brief hug. A gesture Seffin always found odd. Why both? Why not just pick one?

"That's a lot of sandwiches for one person."

Troy looked at his bag and back at Seffin. His mouth hung open slightly, the same way his mother's did when she calculated her words instead of just speaking them.

"I'm entertaining a few friends at the moment." He scratched at his palms.

"Who?"

Troy's mouth dropped open more this time. "I'm not sure that's any of your business."

Seffin felt his face get hot. "Sorry, I didn't mean to pry." He thought the question pretty innocuous, but maybe he'd let his guard down after talking with his mom, failed to edit himself.

Troy frowned. "No, I'm sorry, don't feel bad. I'm just on edge with work... and my mother isn't exactly helping." He picked up his bag and they both stepped to the side of the queue. "I really shouldn't talk about it. How's Ka?"

"Good. That's what I'm here for. I wanted to get her something for helping me out with my elementalism." He left the part out about his mother. He'd talked enough about his family for one day. "Want to come over and say hi? I'm sure they'd all love to see you."

"Come over?" Troy cocked his head.

"Yeah, I moved in after..." He didn't want to say *after my friend got murdered*. Especially in the middle of a crowded café.

Troy put his hand on Seffin's shoulder in understanding. "I don't have time today, but maybe soon. If you need anything you let me know though, ok?" He began to walk out. "Give Ka my best!"

He didn't have time to tell him they'd be gone for the next half year before he walked out the door. No matter, Troy would be here when they returned. Seffin bought some pastries and smiled to himself. It'd been a while since he felt this good about his life. The worker packaged up his purchase and handed him a coffee. He thanked them, walked back out into the streets, and started his way to the Bolin residence—to his home.

***

Three weeks passed on the road and Seffin began to truly fall in love with the life he'd chosen. Days were simple, structured. Wake up, eat, walk, train, sleep, repeat. Ka said his progress in air elementalism was coming along impressively, and Ren showed him other ways to practice control. He gave him a small metal ball with an internal maze that required precise movements with kinetics to solve. Seffin got his time down to fifteen minutes. Tender could do it in forty seconds, but high levels of control were typical for engineers. They specialized in precision and control the same way mystics specialized in power. The small maze took Ka four minutes, but Ren was even faster than Poppy at twenty-three seconds. Neither of them worked at it much. Ren's will-blade practice was how he drilled control now—floating his blade up while maintaining its cutting edge—and mystic level wielders like Ka only needed a certain amount of control to be effective, just enough to make sure their kinetics or elements didn't blow up in their faces. Seffin practiced every morning before they set off. The faster and more precise he could wield, the more useful he'd be.

Their route brought them through into Nashow now, and they were coming up on the first town with a Lodge, Lanneshire, a coastal fishing hub resting on the south-western side of the Sea of Corince. Tender said they could stop for a day to resupply and rest. Seffin hoped they had provisions beyond salted fish. He could already hear Ren's whining. Sleeping in a bed again would be nice too. As much as he enjoyed the trip so far, the thought of a mattress underneath him while he slept sounded wonderful, almost decadent.

Trees grew thick along the path the group walked, making it difficult to spot Lanneshire, but Tender knew exactly where they were. Cresting the upcoming hill would put the settlement in view. Seffin didn't know how much it mattered. He'd already been to Oleksandra's Harbor. How different could it be? He recalled how much the Lodge in Prolivgrad stood out and wondered if he'd be able to tell it apart in a community made mostly of wooden structures instead of the brick and stone of Prolivgrad. Would it stand as tall as the Lodge back home, or would it sit shorter, blending in with the community around it?

As they made it over the top of the hill Seffin's musings about the Lodge evaporated. A ship in the harbor had caught fire. The faint sound of an alarm bell rang steadily as they all stood in shock.

"Well, that's something," Tender said.

"Don't they have a mystic to douse the flames?" Seffin asked.

"This isn't Prolivgrad. Mystics aren't exactly abundant out here," Ka answered,

"Come on," Tender said, "we won't be able to help that ship, but if we hurry, we might be able to stop anything else that might catch fire. They could have need of Ka's healing too."

The group started jogging down the path. Tender's limp pronounced itself more as they ran. Less a jog and more a series of leaps punctuated by stutter steps.

"I wish we had some horses," Seffin said.

Ren let out a winded chortle. "Look at Mr. Fancypants over here. Those things would set us back most of our last payout."

"You're kidding..." Seffin almost stumbled over a loose bit of gravel. Tender glanced back to make sure he hadn't fallen and then refocused on the road ahead.

"Sometimes I forget you were so sheltered." Ka didn't seem bothered by the pace at all. You could hardly even tell she jogged while she spoke. "Horses aren't easy to breed, and training them takes time, effort, and most importantly, space. Something we don't have much of." She paused her speech for a breath which somehow seemed out of place. "They're extremely expensive. Outside of militaries and farms they're pretty rare."

"I see so many in Prolivgrad though."

"She said they were expensive. Prolivgrad's got a whole lot of rich people living in it." Ren spit. Seffin couldn't tell if he just had something in his mouth or if he spat at the idea of rich people. He thought about the wealth his own family had and decided not to ask.

Even with the increased pace, it took over half an hour to make it to the gates of Lanneshire, a simple wooden archway in the middle of a wall of timber that encircled the town. The bell had stopped ringing over fifteen minutes ago. No guards. They were probably helping with the fire. Winded and dripping in sweat, Seffin didn't know how much use he'd be without a few minutes' rest. Tender broke their stride and headed straight for the docks. Ka placed her hand on Seffin's shoulder. He felt her will spread out from the touch, and he let it flow through him. His exhaustion evaporated.

"Is that why you didn't seem tired while we ran?"

Ka winked and jogged after Tender. Seffin willed the sweat from his body and looked over at Ren, whose eyes stared, fixated on the giant plume of smoke rising from the shore. Seffin gave his shoulder a light slap. "Shall we?"

Ren nodded solemnly, and they both took off toward the docks.

They closed in on the waterfront. The still-burning ship towered over them, an inferno floating on the water. Well, an inferno sinking into the water now, but that didn't come close to solving the problem. The ship's masts leaned heavily toward the docks, threatening to snap and crush anything beneath. Seffin ran up, threw both arms out, and started to calm the fires, removing fuel from the flame as best he could. Seeing him wielding, the crowd made room.

A loud explosion rang out from the far side of the ship, the force of which briefly rolled it back to a more neutral position before it began rolling the other way. By this time, the flames were mostly quenched, but if he didn't keep the fuel away the embers would just start the wood burning again. Ren worked on the fuel too, so Seffin decided to shift his focus to water elementalism, hoping Ren could keep up the maintenance on his own. Slowing the water as much as he could, he tried to freeze the ship in place. He didn't fully understand why, but it took a lot more effort than he expected. The water seemed to fight his control. It felt like the sweat freezing Ren taught him—which he still hadn't mastered—except thousands of times larger. To compensate, he burned through his will reserves to freeze the water. It worked, barely. The ship sat at an odd angle half sunk in the sea with icicles cascading down its sides.

A cracking sound shot out from the main mast as it snapped and began to fall toward a crowd of fishermen leaping out of the way. Seffin threw his arms up again and two pillars of water shot out from the sea, holding the wooden beam aloft. He was hoping to turn the pillars into ice to keep the beam elevated. The effort was too much. Freezing the water earlier took so much out of him and controlling water that in turn held up the mast took everything he had left. It felt foreign. He couldn't remember the last time his reserves were truly tapped. The last person barely made it clear before his will gave out. The mast dropped with a loud crash as the docks and boats it landed on turned to splinters.

Collapsing to his knees, he gasped for breath, frustrated. If he had more precision, more control, he could have saved his will reserves. It all took less than five minutes, but it felt like he'd just run for a half hour. After all, he *had* just run for a half hour. A long moment passed before he felt the silence around him. He looked up to see a crowd of people, wide-eyed and awestruck, staring down at him like he had two heads. Tender shoved their way through the crowd and offered a hand up. Grasping it, Seffin let them pull him to a standing position where he wobbled back and forth unsteadily.

"What happened?" Seffin asked to no one in particular.

Tender leaned in, whispering into his ear, "Rogue mystic. We need to go. Now."

Seffin's face scrunched up in confusion as he whispered back, "Shouldn't we be helping them then?"

"We don't know who is on what side. That ship burned without anyone trying to save it the entire time, and I can't find any of the Lodge leadership anywhere."

Caught on the backfoot again, Seffin learned to just do as his team said in these situations. He nodded and went with Tender as the crowd watched, not saying a word. Ka and Ren came jogging up next to them and exchanged a knowing look with Tender. A woman in the crowd mouthed the words "thank you" before Seffin turned to leave. At least one person showed appreciation.

They made their way out of town, passing by buildings with broken windows they hadn't noticed. A few bodies lay in odd positions in alleyways, in yards, and one hanging out of a broken second story window. How had they missed that? Then he realized they hadn't missed it. *He* had missed it. Ren hadn't been staring at the smoke from the ship earlier, he was looking at all the bodies.

They passed through the wooden archway of the town entrance and immediately broke from the path. Ka covered their tracks with earth elementalism, and they spent well over an hour searching for a good hiding spot.

"Well, this sucks." Tender sat hunkered over their pack, taking stock of their supplies.

"I don't understand..." Seffin said. "How did freezing that water burn me out of will so fast?"

"Salt water," Ka said. "I'll add it to the list of things to teach you about in our elementalism lessons. You can adjust and freeze it almost as efficiently as normal water, but without taking the salt into account you would have burned through a lot of will just to manipulate it. The academy system has a lot of blind spots."

The more time he spent with the Bolins' the truer that statement seemed, so much of his education didn't prepare him for the outside world.

Ren lay down with his will-blade extended up toward the sky, pulsing will into it so the semi-translucent edges extended out and back in rhythmically. "This is supposed to be my specialty."

"Yeah well, you've never killed one before, so it's not your specialty yet." Ka shifted the earth beneath her with elementalism, digging a hole.

"It's not the same as a husk," Tender added.

"Don't you think I know that?"

Ren's flash of anger subsided quickly. Seffin knew he was just frustrated and scared, but he still didn't like him holding his will-blade aloft with his emotions so high.

"Who would do that to the village?" Seffin asked

Tender turned to Seffin, and for the first time since he'd met them, he could sense just a hint of annoyance in their voice. "Rogue mystics are formally trained wielders that dropped their registrations. Nothing wrong with that, but every once in a while, one pops up and tries to act like a little dictator. It's strange to go after a town the size of Lanneshire, but who's to say what their motivation is. Could be revenge, could be power, could be they're just a murderous prick. Mystics have a lot of power. When one goes bad, I don't usually worry too much about the motivation. Just kill them as fast as possible. Most of the population can barely lift a bowl with their will, let alone out here where anyone with high enough reserves moves to the cities for formal training. If they got to the Lodge leaders, I doubt there's anyone in Lanneshire even willing to stand up to them."

Ka, pre-empting Seffin's next question, shouted from her rapidly deepening hole, "We know it's a rogue mystic and not a wild wielder because they specialize in fire and water. Ship was on fire. Scorch marks on the bodies—"

"Water and puncture marks next to some of them too," Ren finished her thought, "and I'm the natural enemy of every wielder. A will-blade's edge cuts through their defenses without needing to get too close, and it usually only takes one strike. *If* I can get the drop on them, it should be easy." Ren pulled the will out of his blade and dropped it to his side, staring up at the canopy of the forest.

"It's never easy taking a life, Ren." Tender cinched up their pack, and walked over to Ka's hole. "How long?"

"Less than ten, more than five." Ka's voice sounded muffled now with her head beneath the ground's surface.

Tender sighed. "I'm afraid I can't use any more grenades. We'll need the rest for the horde outside Nari'ko."

"You two have killed rogue mystics before though, right?" Seffin spoke toward the hole Tender stood above.

"The last time I fought one I got this limp." They lightly smacked their bad leg. "Ka's taken down two—"

"Three!" She corrected them from the hole.

Tender waved it off. "They're rare, and *usually* there are casualties. Think about how many people you could kill if you just decided to one day."

Seffin thought about it for only a second. It seemed monstrous just imagining it. "I couldn't."

"Have we thought about just bypassing Lanneshire? We're not exactly getting paid for it." Ren sat up, some grass and twigs stuck to his back.

Tender frowned at him. Ren just looked back down at his blade. He grabbed it, stood up, walked over to the hole, and jumped in. Finally letting curiosity get the better of him, Seffin went over to see the hole for himself. It was massive. He stuck his head down and found a room the size of a small apartment, lit by a few candles. "We're staying in here tonight?"

"Our traveling crystal won't keep a mystic away, so we'll hide. Ka'll punch some holes for air and close the entrance, so it doesn't look like anything besides forest floor." Tender jumped in.

Seffin followed suit.

The dirt had been packed down to make it easy to walk on. It smelled like damp earth and iron and the room seemed to eat sound. As soon as he landed, Ka began closing the entrance. He walked over to sit next to Ren and leaned up against him. The body heat served as a bit of comfort after seeing all those dead people. He thought about this morning and how he reveled in the simplicity of his new life. He felt foolish for thinking that now.

Ren

Ren's fingers itched something fierce. He squeezed the hilt of his blade and twisted the grip in his hand to scratch them, but the moment he let the sword rest the niggling sensation returned. In the hole Ka made for them he hadn't the room to do his nightly practice or his morning exercises, and nothing felt right because of it. Sitting in some brush outside Lanneshire's walls now, they couldn't hear anything. It was getting to noon, and the crashing of the waves and squawking of the gulls were all that broke the silence. Where were the townsfolk? Hiding?

Nothing felt right.

Poppy sat next to him, two eyes flitting around the perimeter beneath a set of bushy, white brows. This morning, they'd told him the town's pylon barrier collapsed overnight, but they'd also said the mystic might have left already, simply causing some havoc and moving on. Poppy didn't seem to think so though, and they hunted for any signs of movement to prove their theory. A pair of glasses sat on their face; lenses made of some translucent, viscous liquid. A miniature telescope.

Poppy used will to dial in how far they wanted to see. The amount of will it took to use was small enough for anyone to use, the only downside is the precise control it required. Few people with will reserves that low ever trained enough to gain the control it would take to use them.

"We can't just sit here all day," Ren said.

A look of annoyance flashed across Poppy's face. "That mystic is still in there, mark my words."

"How can you be so sure?"

"The people," they said. "They were scared to talk to us. The question I have is where the hells were they when we started helping with the ship?"

"Pooping?" Seffin offered. He knelt behind them with a bored look on his face. His attempts at humor were getting better with each day, but they still tended toward the adolescent.

Poppy stifled some laughter. "Probably not. They either left already or they were busy. Given how scared everyone was and how the pylon stopped working overnight, I doubt they left."

The ground next to Poppy began to shift and turn. Like water boiling, but with dirt. Ka's head popped up, throwing clods of dirt on Ren's combat boots. "Everyone's inside their homes. I found the Lodge leaders. One's dead. The other I spotted tied up through a second story window at the Lodge."

Earth slipping. Ka moved through the earth almost as easily as anyone else could swim through water, but she only did it for herself. Adding even one more person made the task exponentially more difficult for reasons Ren hadn't bothered to put to memory. He didn't understand why earth slipping took such little effort while making a hole for them to sleep in took a full fifteen minutes and a huge chunk of her reserves either.

Annoyed, he brushed the dirt off his boots. "Did you find the mystic?"

"I'm assuming they're in the Lodge, but I didn't spot anyone wielding."

Poppy grunted and stood to their feet. "Ideas?"

"Set the Lodge on fire," Seffin said.

How am I so attracted to a crazy person.

"I dunno, the Lodge leader is in there, and we don't know if it's only one mystic or if there's other wielders," Ka spoke calmly like his idea hadn't been nuts.

"Right. Just make an earth pillar to get to the window. Break it, grab him, then Ren and I will deal with whoever comes out the front."

Poppy and Ka both nodded.

They can't be serious.

"You can't be serious," Ren said. "How are we going to tell who the mystic is? What if they kill the hostage the second the fire breaks out? What if there's more than one?"

"What if they've trained to curse? What if sitting here is giving them all the time they need to unleash it on us when we confront them? What if they get bored and kill the Lodge leader anyway?" Seffin countered.

Oh gods, curses. What if he's right? Ren hated the idea of being injured for the rest of his life, or having bad luck, or losing his voice. Why couldn't they come up with a plan that surprised the mystic instead of confronting them head on?

"This isn't a plan. It's just running in," Ren said.

"Running in can be a plan," Ka said. She elevated up a few more feet from the ground so her arm could get free. "Besides, between you and Seffin, that mystic would have to be a monster to stand a chance."

That's true, the mystic *wouldn't* stand a chance. The mystic they'd have to kill. Ren didn't want to do this. It's not that he didn't think whoever this was deserved to die. He saw the bodies of their victims, the agony on their grey faces, this mystic deserved what they were planning to do to them. Ren killed plenty of husk and amalgamations before, but they were already dead. Dead things don't laugh or cry. They don't have fear. He didn't even know if they experienced pain. People though? They wept and screamed and struggled to survive. Connie had. His mother had. Gull Harbor flooded his mind, except he was the werewiller. He was the monster that killed Shorda before she knew what was happening. It was his foot that pushed Connie's small body into the gravel, bones cracking with an unheard scream frozen on her face.

Ren shook the thoughts from his head. "I'll make it quick."

Don't think. Don't hesitate.

Ka nodded. "I'll get in position. Should only take thirty seconds for me to do my part. I'll go when you start lighting the place up." She dropped back into the ground.

"I'll handle anybody else that comes out. You two focus on the mystic." Poppy started hobbling toward the town's main entrance.

"Once we know who it is," Seffin said.

It took a few minutes to make it to the Lodge. On their way Ren noted all the bodies were gone. They should have turned husk, and either been put down or wandering around. *Strange.* Ren could see people peering through their windows, probably curious if the mercenaries would win the day or end up broken and cold on the ground like their friends and family.

Poppy took up a post off to the side of the main entrance, and Seffin wasted no time in putting the Lodge to flame. He lit up the side entrance first, and in mere moments the eastern face turned into a wall of fire. The smell of smoke tinged with... something else, almost as stifling as the heat. The sound of the upstairs window shattering was barely heard over the roaring inferno of Seffin's will fire, a faint tinkling amid a hurricane of heat and embers.

Ka had the Lodge leader in her arms and hopped off the roof, the ground came up to meet her halfway and cushioned her fall. She untied his gag. "Amalgamations!" he shouted, panic in his wide eyes. "He turned them into amalgamations."

The door to the Lodge blew open, throwing fiery splinters everywhere. Poppy leapt out of the way in time to dodge most of it. Three bloated, fetid monstrosities lumbered out. Limbs sticking out of odd places, mouths peppered their bodies like age spots on the elderly with dozens of blinking eyes darting around. Behind them the figure of a man shrouded in flames, arms outstretched. A grim puppet master.

Ren turned to Seffin. "I thought your father was the only one that knew how to do that to amalgamations."

With practiced efficiency, Ka pinned one with a rock spike she brought up from the ground, and Poppy, almost as big as the amalgamation themself, took out its upper half with their will hammer. Rancid gore and coagulated blood painted the side of the building.

Seffin shrugged at Ren before turning another one into an inferno with his flames. Ren rushed forward and cut the third one in half before pushing into the Lodge with the mystic. The smell of rot invaded his nose and lungs, the taste of a bog on his tongue. He threw a fireball at Ren. Snatching it out of the air with his will, he slammed it onto the floor behind the rogue who fell forward onto his face. Ka had been right. It wouldn't be much of a fight. The man got to his knees and bowed his head. He seemed so small up close, unassuming.

"Spare me. Please," he said.

Ren wasn't ready for this. In all the stories Poppy told, the rogue mystics and wild wielders were crazed monsters that fought to the bitter end, not sad, defeated little men begging for their life on their knees. The rot smell became overwhelming, and Ren braved a momentary glance around the room to see where it came from.

He tasted acid in his throat and rage put his hairs on end.

Children. Tied to posts around the main entrance and turned husk. Dried blood beneath each of them. Ropes around their heads and gags in their mouths to hold them still. They jerked and struggled against their bonds with a ferocity unconcerned with pain. Nothing left of them but the little monsters they'd become.

Ren swallowed the acid in his throat back down and turned to the rogue mystic. When he spoke, his voice came out tight, like an overwound spring threatening to release. "I should thank you for making this easy."

The mystic looked up, fear in his eyes.

Ren put will into his blade and spun it twice, whip quick, removing both of the rogue's hands. His mouth opened, probably to scream, but Ren didn't hear him. The roaring of the flames and a buzzing in his head is all that broke through. He booted the rogue's face hard enough to throw him onto his back, making thin cuts in the hips and knees, then the elbows. *That's where Ka said tendons connected, right?* Ren set his sword in the flames and fed them fuel with his will as he waited until it turned a dull red, then a bright orange, and finally a brilliant yellow. All the while the man writhed on his back, his mouth moving fast.

What's he saying?

Ren put his boot on his chest, and held his blade aloft, hilt up and tip down. Slowly, he brought it down on the mystic's mouth, his head shaking back and forth wildly, trying to avoid the inevitable. His lips finally broke their silence, not with words or screams, but with hissing and popping as he tried and failed to keep the blade from entering his mouth, bubbling until they were black as ash. The teeth creaked like an old hinge before cracking and snapping away. The man's... the monster's eyes were pools of bloody water, boiling next to the heat of the blade. Not until the bone in his neck did Ren feel any resistance at all. With a little muscle the blade broke through the man's neck and jaw.

There. I killed him. Done.

Ren turned to face the entrance of the Lodge. Poppy handled the children—the husk. Seffin and Ka stood in the doorway, Seffin frowning and Ka's hand over her mouth. Suddenly very tired, he plodded over to the pair, dropped his blade, and collapsed into Seffin's arms with the full weight of his body. A guttural wail erupted from him. Ka wrapped her arms around them both as Poppy came up and rested a hand on his head.

***

Marin, the Lodge leader Ka had freed, explained what happened. The rogue mystic's name was Sorca, and he came from Prolivgrad a year back to pick up merc work. He'd been taking jobs and renting a room. It's not unusual for mercs to move on from a Lodge, but all the higher-ranking members of Lanneshire's Lodge started to leave at once, which felt like a pattern. The other leader, Tandy, found their bodies hidden in the woods, their wounds bearing the telltale signs of a mystic's handiwork. The remaining mercs confronted him a week ago with terrible results. Tandy died along with the other mercenaries, and in response to the attack, Sorca threatened to hunt down anyone in the town who tried to get away. After a while, some of the townsfolk tried to stand up to him again. That was the day Ren's group arrived. Sorca killed them all, set the ship aflame in the harbor, and took the children as hostages in response. That's where he had been while they put the flames out on the ship.

Whatever his motivation was, no one could say. The strangest thing of all was how he could control amalgamations. Outside of Pulpin's experiments, Ren had never even heard of that technique.

They had stayed two additional days so Poppy could help Marin prepare a report, fix the pylon, and send a runner off to request assistance from Prolivgrad's Lodge, but Ren had had enough. Two days was two days too long. Nothing about this experience felt right from the beginning, and by the time they were back on the road he felt like running from the place. Lanneshire rested behind them now though, growing ever smaller as they walked the path that would eventually lead them through the country of Lighton, and into the horde surrounding Nari'ko. Ren's whole body still vibrated with anger and disgust. Seffin did his best to console him, but he hadn't quite figured out how to manage it. Reassuring that "he deserved it" or "it's not your fault" or "people are awful" didn't calm him, it only brought the memories back stronger. He had killed someone. He'd become the monster.

Ka and Poppy seemed to take the event in stride, but he didn't have the stomach to ask how. Ka expressed more interest in his well-being than anything else, like she hadn't seen the same thing.

What have they been through that this doesn't affect them?

And it wasn't about how much Sorca deserved it. Ren shoved his heated blade down a man's throat, slowly and agonizingly. How does someone come back from that? He had to live with the knowledge he could do that to a person. He could blame Sorca for making him do it, but the truth is that no one *made* him do it. He *enjoyed* doing it. He could have simply done it quick like he planned, but no. No. He delivered justice, and while he watched a man's eyes boil inside his head a little part of him jumped up and down with glee. Glee that the ghoul got what he deserved. Glee that the pain Sorca inflicted fell back on him. Glee that he got to be the one to do it. It became a part of him, and it made him sick. He'd let that small, evil little man inside his head, and all he wanted in the world right now was to get him out. Forget this ever happened. Cut the memory out and carry on like it never happened.

Ka, because of course it was Ka, set her hand on his shoulder while they walked. "Stop," she said.

The word hung there for a moment, wedged into his world, and then slowly expanded as it took up space in his mind.

"Stop what?" he asked.

"Stop thinking about it." She moved her hand down to his back, in the space between his shoulder blades and massaged the muscle. The way she'd done the day he showed up on the Bolins' doorstep. It relaxed him in a way he hadn't been able to since before Lanneshire. "It's too big right now," she said, gazing off into the distance.

"I can't just *stop* thinking about it."

"Think about something else then," she said. "Like Poppy's plan for the horde."

Poppy's plan? Poppy's plan made no sense. Mathematically they should be able to make it through. At least by Poppy's math, but Poppy only ever understood Poppy's math. His guardian had never let him down before but putting faith in a plan he didn't fully understand left an uneasy feeling. An uneasy feeling made worse by the guilt and shame and horror of recent events. A pall of dread settled on him, and something on his face must have tipped Ka off.

She sighed. "What is it?"

They both knew the question was rhetorical, but Ren answered anyway, "What are we even doing this for?"

Ka's face scrunched up in confusion. "The contract?"

"No," Ren started, "well... yeah. That too I guess."

Ka arched her eyebrow. "Is this all it took to ruin your dream? You've been dying to be a merc since Tolkar left you with us in Prolivgrad. What did you think we did?"

"I thought you killed husk. Monsters. I mean, I knew about rogue mystics and mad wild wielders. I knew about all that, but when I dreamed about the job, I guess I just didn't think—"

"Listen, Ren, I'll admit this was a particularly bad couple of days even for me, but sometimes the job is like that. Helping people is hard. But asking what it's all for is stupid, even for you." She smirked, trying to lighten the conversation. It didn't work. "I mean it, though. Do you not understand you helped those people back there?"

"Well... yeah."

"So what you're saying is that's not enough for you."

"No!" Defensiveness crept into his voice despite himself. "That's not what I mean."

She turned on him. "Then what do you mean? You saved lives, Ren, and the Lodge is going to pay you out for doing it. You killed a man, yes, but did you really expect everything you do as a merc to *feel* good?"

"No!" His anger flashed. "We were there! We were less than a hundred feet from where they were... where they were..." he couldn't say it. "We could have saved them, but we ran."

He felt Poppy and Seffin's attention turn toward their conversation.

"What? Did you think you'd always win?

"Yes." That was a lie. "No." Also a lie. "I didn't think about it, ok?" The truth, finally. "Screw me, I guess. I didn't consider it. Call me naïve. Call me what you want—"

"You're naïve, then. Less today than yesterday, and hopefully less tomorrow than today. It's not a crime, but stop wallowing in it, and by gods don't use it as an excuse to languish in regret over every choice you've made. That's life, little brother. You do what you can with the knowledge and understanding you have at the time. Sometimes you're right. Sometimes you're wrong. Unfortunately for those children, we were wrong, but I'll tell you what," she said, looking him dead in the eyes. "I wouldn't change a damn thing."

"How in the hells can you say that?"

"Because we retreated to protect ourselves." She grabbed him by the shoulders. "To protect you!" She shook him to emphasize the point. "And I would watch Lanneshire burn to the ground before I would put you in danger. You can't save anyone if you're dead, Ren."

"But I would have been fine! Any one of us would have been!"

"What if it was someone like me in there?" Seffin said it quietly, like he still hadn't fully considered the thought yet. "What if the mystic wasn't a pushover?"

"What if the sky were green instead of blue? What's your point?" Ren knew he'd feel bad later for lashing out, but right now he didn't care.

"My point is that you're acting like we should have taken action then with what we know now. I understand why you feel bad, but—"

"*You* understand how *I* feel?" Indignation mixed in with the anger. "That's real rich coming from someone that hasn't even shed a tear over what happened. Are you *sure* you care?"

Poppy's voice rang out. "Kulelika stop—"

Ren's vision went white, and his ears started ringing. The dull pain in his nose almost an afterthought. He tried to bring his hands up over his face when the second hit landed in the same spot with a crunching noise. This time the pain took center stage. Knees buckling, he fell to the ground, gripping his broken nose.

"You self-centered little shit! Have you ever *once* considered someone else's feelings before your own? Do you remember when you were asking us to *leave* the town to die?"

The blood from his nose flooded over into his mouth, and he spit it out onto the gravel beneath him.

She continued, "Since you seem to think you have the monopoly on *caring* I'll let you find some other healer to fix that for you."

He heard her walk away in a huff, the crunching sound of the gravel beneath her feet not unlike the sound his nose made when she broke it. Another set of footsteps came closer to him and stopped. Wiping the involuntary tears of pain from his eyes he looked up to see Seffin standing above him.

"What? You come to hit me too?"

For a few moments Seffin only looked down on him, his face unreadable.

"What?" he said again.

"You can be a real asshole, you know that?"

Seffin

Two months had passed since Lanneshire, and the Bolin band now walked through northern Lighton. Acres of waving grass and farms dotted the landscape. Pylons were everywhere, protecting the farmland and its workers from husk. Guards both from Estaba and Lighton patrolled the highway. More often than not, they walked under the cover of a barrier, which was well and good since they could focus on charging Poppy's grenades with will in the evening—part of their plan to deal with the horde outside Nari'ko—instead of recharging their traveling crystal.

Many of the travelers they encountered didn't seem to know there even was a horde to the north. Some of the patrols knew though, and while they were reluctant to part with the information, they said it kept spitting out amalgamations, threatening the safety of anyone living on the border. The looks on their faces when Poppy explained the group was headed in that direction spoke volumes. Nothing good awaited them up there.

Ren spent all his time walking through Nashow and into Lighton mouth breathing or wheezing out his broken nose. Ka stuck to her word. Tender tried to talk her into fixing it, but she remained adamant. The broken nose would need to be fixed by someone else. Initially, Seffin agreed with her. The accusation that he didn't care about the victims had stung, and Ren finally facing a real, long-term consequence for his words felt fair. Especially once she told him how often Ren weaseled his way out of any sort of punishment growing up. Maybe this would shake him out of his thoughtless, selfish behavior. Now though, with the day they would pass through the horde fast approaching, even Seffin thought it might be a good idea to relent. Ren would need to hold off the horde while they moved through it, and the broken nose could prove a distraction.

They looked for a healer in every small town they stopped through, and every time they came up short, Ren became more and more surly and resentful. Seffin worried the more irritable Ren became, the less likely Ka would take pity on him. Ren had apologized the day after, but nothing he said convinced her to change her mind. Ka joined in the search for a healer the last couple towns they passed, though why she would only help in that way instead of just fixing it herself, Seffin couldn't say.

According to Poppy, Miller's Town was just over the next hill. It would be the last stop before they exited the network of pylon barriers, and three days march to the horde if the last set of patrolmen were to be believed.

As they walked, Ren followed separate from the group. Even with two months of time, Seffin still felt awkward around him after what he said. They all seemed to. It didn't help that his voice sounded like he had a cold and his face looked, well, still attractive, but definitely tarnished. For better or worse, it served as a constant reminder of how callous he could be.

Ren's nose whistled as he idly kicked a small rock off the road. "What are the chances we find anyone here?"

"Low," Poppy said. "Unless a traveling wild wielder happens to be running through town, and even then, they'd have to have trained in healing."

Ren kicked another pebble.

Ka turned around from leading the group in the front. "Well, we'll ask around anyway."

"What if we don't find anyone?" Seffin asked

She shrugged her shoulders. "If we don't find anyone I'll help, but Ren's not going to like it."

"How could I like it any less than this?" His voice sounded nasally when he said it, and when he got frustrated, the whistling came through in his speech, like an annoying bird interrupting his words.

"Well, let's just say whether we find another healer or no, you better hope they have a pub. Because you're going to want a few drinks before it gets fixed."

Seffin thought about her words for a second before it clicked in his mind. The nose would have healed wrong on its own by now. This was part of the punishment. She knew the likelihood of finding another healer on this trip had been low, she and Poppy had been this way before, so she intentionally let it sit long enough to heal crooked. Ka would have to break his nose again to set it correctly.

"Gods, that is mean," Seffin said.

Ka shot Seffin a knowing smile. "Figure it out?"

"Figure what out?" Ren looked at Seffin with desperation in his eyes.

"She's going to have to break your nose again to correct it."

"What?" Ren's voice pitched up and his nose whistled with a piercing shrill. "Why?"

Ka stopped in the road to say, "Because Ren, you need to understand that when you hurt people it lasts longer than the apology. Say you're sorry all you want. We'll forgive you, but it doesn't cure everything. You'll always be the guy that stole money from us to buy shoes, you'll always be the guy that set Seffin up to take the fall for you when you stole those boots in Oleksandra's Harbor, you'll always be the guy that takes his anger out on us when your emotions get to be too much. The apology is nice, but I'm sick of hearing how sorry you are. The truth is that you're not sorry. You're only sorry that you have consequences."

"It was a little harsh, Ka," Poppy said, walking past her.

"And I *am* sorry," Ren said, "truly."

"Yeah, well your apologies haven't stopped you from repeating the same damn mistakes over and over. Instead of being sorry, how about you stop? When push comes to shove, you choose yourself. Your feelings come first. Your wants. Every time."

That didn't seem true. When Kent died, Ren visited Seffin daily. He made him food, bought him boots, and helped him grieve. Part of him knew that Ren did those things because he had a crush on him, but Seffin had a crush on Ren too. And he wanted to believe he'd have done those things for him regardless of their flirtation.

"Fine," Ren said, "just fix my nose."

He looked down and kicked a rock off the path. Seffin met his stride and walked with him for a while.

"I really am sorry," Ren said.

Seffin put his hand on his back as they walked. "Let's just focus on getting you good and drunk for the procedure." He smiled, trying to lighten the mood.

Ren stopped and turned to him. "I feel like ever since I got to know you, all I've been doing is apologizing for how stupid I've been." His plugged nose made him sound like a child with a cold.

Seffin chuckled. "Have you tried not being stupid."

Ren smacked himself on the forehead. "Why didn't I think of that?"

"Because you're stupid."

"Oh, right."

They walked on over the hill, and Miller's Town came into view. It couldn't be more than fifteen homes and a pub with a well nestled in the middle. A pylon sat next to the pub, idly spinning with its satellite crystals orbiting around it on metal hoops. In Lighton, the network of barrier coverage dictated where pylons were constructed, so seeing one in the middle of a community counted as a novelty. Pylons served as more a marker of distance than a sign of civilization here. Farmland stretched out in large squares fanning out around the homes.

Squinting in the sunlight, Seffin spotted what had to be the whole town out working the land. Horses pulling equipment, small children pulling weeds, older children tending to the livestock, and the adults harvesting. It seemed like a wonderfully simple life. All the barrier coverage of Prolivgrad without the crime and smell of a big city. Nobody out here had to worry about walking home late at night. Seffin imagined whatever Lodges happened to be in Lighton would be calm compared to Prolivgrad.

As they came closer to the town a woman walked out of the small inn and started closing the distance between them. Tall, brown, and broad shouldered, she ambled her way to the entrance, leaned on a fence post, and waited for them. Clar was her name, and she seemed to have a smile for every occasion. Poppy greeted her and her smile said, *'Who in the hells would come to a town this far out of the way?'* After some brief explanation, her smile said, *'Well I'm not going to turn away good money now, am I?'* And after a look at Ren's nose her smile said, *'We don't need any trouble.'*

Before long they secured two rooms, meals, and a place to bathe. Three weeks had passed since they stopped to take a proper bath, and the stink coming off Ren, in particular, reminded him of warmed-over trash. Seffin's little baths he gave himself with water pulled from the air had reached the end of their usefulness too. Nothing proved a good replacement for a soak in a warm tub and a bar of soap.

They all shuffled into the inn and made themselves at home in their rooms. Seffin roomed with Ren, and they were the first to go searching for the baths. For such a small town their inn had an exceptionally large tub, a pool really, elevated above the ground with a fire underneath. The room was a luxury the town clearly took pride in. It sat empty though, and Clar made it clear the townsfolk wouldn't help with filling and heating it until this evening. Harvesting took precedence over strangers' baths, but that didn't stop Ren and Seffin. They used elementalism to pull in water and filled the tub within an hour. A little kinetics and the water steamed at the perfect temperature. Clar smiled at them while they worked. A smile that said, '*I don't care that you did it yourself I'm still charging you full price.*'

"Do you want to go first?" Ren said, looking down at the steaming pool with longing.

"What do you mean?" Seffin said as he removed his shirt.

"Oh, you mean you want to go in together?"

Seffin cocked his head. "It's a bath, Ren. Just get in."

He shucked his bottoms and hopped into the pool. The heat felt like millions of tiny, pleasant needles poking at his skin. The muscles in his back, calves, and feet shed months of tension in moments. He looked up at Ren standing next to the water.

"You do realize there's nothing I haven't seen before." He decided to mock him a little. Ren seemed to drop his inhibitions more when he had something to prove.

It worked.

Ren glared good-naturedly at the challenge before stripping and hopping into the water with a splash.

"It's hot!"

"It's nice," Seffin said as he leaned his head on the side of the pool. Closing his eyes and letting the heat and the weightlessness relax him.

Minutes passed before either of them spoke.

"Can I ask you something?" Ren said.

Seffin opened his eyes and shifted to look at him directly. "Sure."

"I like you."

"That's not a question."

"Ok, fine. Do you like me?"

Seffin smiled. "See, that's a question."

He closed his eyes again and laid back against the edge of the bath, a smirk on his lips, he used his head to stabilize himself as his body floated up off the base of the pool.

Ren splashed him in the face with some water.

"Don't be a dick! Do you like me?"

Wiping the water from his eyes he looked at him. The black waves of his hair framed his sad, brown eyes. A toothy smile with big dimples above a strong chin. A strong neck with broad, muscular shoulders. The dimples were what killed him, though. They were always there, but when he smiled the gods could strike him dead and he'd die happy.

"I think so." He smiled, coy.

"Well, what the hells does that mean?"

Seffin glanced at Ren's nose. A reminder of how awful he could be. "It means just that. I think so." Seffin brought himself upright in the water. "You don't exactly make it easy."

Ren looked down, a slight frown on his face.

Seffin swam over next to him. Using his pointer finger he pushed Ren's chin up to match his gaze. Setting his jaw, he spoke with sincerity, "I can like you all I want, but I've dropped my guard around you twice now and both times it bit me in the ass." Ren opened his mouth to speak, but Seffin put his finger in front of his lips, shushing him. "Stop. No excuses. No apologies. No more broken promises."

A look of recognition flashed across Ren's broken face.

Seffin thought about what he wanted to say for months now. He'd mulled it over in his head and waited for the time. Because he wanted to give this a real shot. He wanted to give it the chance it deserved. "If it weren't for you, I'd probably be slaving away at the Guild trying to live up to my father's legacy right now. You helped me realize what I wanted out of life. You will *always* be important to me, but this really is your last chance to be with me." He moved his body closer, their faces nearly touching. He could feel the small water currents wafting off Ren's body, pushing against his own.

He kissed him.

Not a peck. A kiss. Seffin put his lips against Ren's and felt them part as they shared more of each other. Ren closed the gap between their bodies and let their limbs entangle as they squeezed, trying to come together. Trying to destroy the space between them. Seffin brought his hands up around Ren's face and cradled it, gently pushing it away. "I mean it. This is your last chance."

It felt a little silly giving him an ultimatum with his body—all of his body—up against him, but he wanted to make sure Ren understood. As good as this felt, he'd throw it away if he needed to. He'd cut this part of him out just like he did with his parents.

Ren pulled away. "I can't promise I'll never hurt you again."

Seffin waited, he had more to say.

"But I can promise that I'll never hurt you the way I've done before, and I can promise that I'll always do everything I can to make it up to you."

Seffin shrugged. "Fuck it." He brought his face close to Ren's again. "Good enough."

Their mouths connected, and then their tongues, and then Seffin wrapped his arms around Ren's neck and his legs around Ren's hips. Fumbling to hold onto him. They each took huge breaths between kisses, the panting muffled by the steam and the water.

Slowly, a rhythm developed. The beat of Seffin's heart kept the time, heavy breaths formed the foundation, and the gentle splashes of water echoing around the room formed the melody. They crescendoed and everything was pushed from his mind, nothing mattered besides the song they were making.

And then it was over. Ren collapsed forward, draping his head over Seffin's shoulder, and kissing his neck in between panting breaths. He couldn't tell who started laughing first, or why. Nothing was funny, at all, but they both started giggling, which turned into a chuckle, and then graduated into laughter so intense he thought he'd cry. Something in his chest was light and feathery, dancing around inside his ribs. It was happiness.

Joy, in its purest form.

***

As the sun set on Miller's Town their group met in the dining area. All of them drunk on the heat of the baths they'd taken.

"Let's get this done," Ren said. He grabbed his sister's hands. "Please."

Ka raised her eyebrows. "Are you sure?"

"Yes."

"No drinks first?"

"Just do it."

Without hesitation Ka slammed her fist into Ren's face. Seffin could tell she angled it to break where she needed. Ren yelped and gripped the edge of the table. Clar, who stood behind the bar, gave a threatening smile that said, '*I thought you understood that I didn't want trouble.*' Blood flooded down Ren's face. Ka put her palm over his nose, and they all watched as it pivoted into its original position. Within moments the flow of blood stopped, and Ren's face returned to normal. Ka pulled her hand away and made a flourish with her fingers. Ren took a deep breath through his nose, and for the first time in a great while, no whistle sounded. He spoke and the annoying, nasally sound was gone.

"You could have done this the whole time!" He wiped tears of pain from his eyes.

Ka flashed a smug smile. "I think you mispronounced thank you."

"Thank you!" he said and hugged her.

Clar walked up with a platter of food and drinks. "Can I ask what in the hells just happened."

"I can breathe again!" Ren said.

"Honey, you could breathe when you got here. It just sounded like you were calling birds."

Poppy spoke up, "Well his bird-calling days are over. Thank you for the drinks"

Clar set everything down on the table and flashed a smile that said, '*okay crazy people.*'

Ka took a large swig of her ale and sighed. "How long do we have to linger here?"

"Well, I have bad news," Poppy said. "The horde has grown. It's only a two-day march from here."

Ka's face went as pale as it could, given her warm complexion. "You're saying we have a full extra day of travel *within* the horde."

Poppy took a sip of their tea. "Yes, well, a full day meaning at least another eight hours. The grenades aren't going to last the whole time, and the traveling crystal will give out before we make it too."

"What are we going to do?" Seffin asked.

"We're going to sleep on it," Poppy said, "and no matter what we do, you three are going to have a lot harder time of it than we planned."

"I can handle it," Ren said. The confidence he gained from simply fixing his nose seemed overmuch, but Seffin found it attractive, so he said nothing.

Seffin lowered his voice. "What if we took a pylon?"

Ren looked over at him, shock on his face. "What is it with you and crazy ideas?"

Poppy smiled. "I knew I liked you."

Sharon

The healer Troy set up for Sharon came from the Guild. Better than nothing, but not exactly what she would call quality. Mystics came from the academy system, and the academy system's reticence to use wind and earth elementalism meant their healers couldn't compete with a quality wild wielding healer.

Charles, the dolt of a healer Troy found, may have knitted her wounds back together, but he came up short with scar prevention. She couldn't care less about her looks or the pain, but extensive scarring limited movement. Movement she'd need to complete her mission. Chuck or Chad, or whatever his stupid name was, had prescribed exercises to help her stretch the scars out so she could start walking around and eating on her own, but the flexibility and fluidity she needed to fight, to flicker, he all but said those days were behind her.

The hells they are.

She did his stupid exercises, but she pushed herself much further than Chester recommended. The first time her skin snapped open from overstretching it felt like someone gripped her upper and lower thigh and ripped the flesh apart. Channing didn't like that. He ordered bed rest for a day after his healing and warned against going too far too fast. The brat had no idea who he was talking to.

The second time her skin snapped she passed out. When she awoke, Chip apologized profusely. She soon found out why. He'd already knitted the scar tissue back together from her flank ripping open, but it was tighter than a cinched girdle. Standing up straight was impossible. She turned around, standing lopsided, and looked him straight in the eyes before jolting upright. The movement was so rapid the scar tissue burst, spraying him with what Sharon would call a small amount of blood, but Chance didn't seem to agree.

That was the last time she saw Churchill. He knitted her side up again, this time with her body arched in a way that the resultant scar tissue wouldn't restrict her movement as drastically and told Troy he was done. Apparently, his silence could be bought, but no amount of money could help him overcome his crippling inadequacy.

"Good riddance," Sharon said as the door closed behind Chesney on his way out.

"You might have tried working *with* him." Troy gave a look of disappointment, and she found herself feeling guilty. Something always gave her an impulse to please him. In the months of recovering in his home she'd pinpointed what it was.

Troy was hot.

Stop it, you horny old woman. He's half your age, and the fool can't even find a half decent healer to fix these burns.

"The right side of my body feels like it's made of rubber and moves like I'm stuck in syrup," she said.

"And because of your impatience it'll remain that way. Few healers set up shop in Prolivgrad, and you just alienated the only one I had any way of keeping quiet."

How did this incompetent get to be the head of the Guild? Oh yeah, nepotism by way of his evil bitch of a mother.

Sharon couldn't bring herself to hate Troy anymore, not after he told her the full story of what happened in Gull Harbor. Pulpin and his mother, Jessica, the President of Egal, were the reason the Guild team had been recalled. Aggravatingly, he had the evidence to prove his innocence, so her target shifted from son to mother which meant she had one more mission left before she could retire. Still, his lack of resourcefulness annoyed her.

Months had passed while she healed and recovered—if anyone could call this recovered. She took stock of herself in the mirror, half her body looked like someone poured cake batter on her. From scalp to toe her skin had ridges and folds that would probably feel weird if she had any surface feeling. Other than when the skin ripped open it just felt numb or achy at times. Chaney didn't know how to help with that either.

"Did you even *try* looking in the outer villages?" she asked.

"You're the most wanted person in the country right now, and the most prominent feature people know about you is that you're burned. I can't exactly inquire about burn specialists without showing my hand."

She clenched her fist in anger. *Pulpin. You whoreson. I'd kill you again if I could.* There had to be someone that could help her with this. Even if all they did is soften the skin so she could move. She'd take it. How could she help with Jessica if half her body had a built-in lag time?

Troy sighed. "I'll keep looking. It's not like we're in a rush."

"I'm not waiting much longer. Chaz wasted enough of my time already."

"You mean Charles?"

"Sure, whatever."

Troy shook his head. "Whether she's behind bars tomorrow or behind bars in a few more weeks it's the same result."

Almost. She almost rolled her eyes at that. His naivete exhausted her. He actually thought she would stay her hand from the heart of the beast just because he helped her. Jessica had tried killing him too after all. That's why he needed her in the first place, because if he tried to bring Jessica down himself, she'd slice him into tiny pieces with wind blades. That was a bit of intel Sharon had been thankful for. Jessica had kept her wild wielding under wraps, a deadly oversight if she'd gone after her alone.

How did such a callous, calculating woman raise such an optimistic buffoon? Gods, I hope Ren isn't this stupid.

During her recovery, Troy subjected Sharon to his full plan. He'd out his mother publicly and stand in as her replacement in the subsequent election. Somehow, he thought revealing her whole plot would create enough trust in his character that he could get the votes to win the presidency. Every household knew the Saunders name already, and he sat in a position of authority as president of the Guild. With the laranee incident, the husk growing out of bounds, and the other nations all but promising war if Winnow took the seat the people would vote out of fear, and when you're fearful you go for what's familiar.

Or so he claimed.

With so many variables, Sharon doubted its feasibility. She'd played in politics in a past life, and she knew something this complicated couldn't hold the attention of the public. The minute you start explaining yourself, you've already lost, and a conspiracy that reaches back over ten years required a lot of explanation. Besides, Jessica would have to accept their terms, and from what Sharon knew of her, that would never happen.

As if fate brought him into the room to argue on her behalf, Clem popped in through the door, clearly excited and breathing heavily. "We did it! She'll meet with us next Tuesday."

Troy looked surprised. "That seems a little—"

"Perfect," Sharon said, "I'll make it work. I've taken down plenty of wild wielders before. Between the two of us we'll be fine."

"It's not just my mother I'm worried about. It's the amalgamations she has tethered to her, the bodyguards she hired, and the president's special guard. And, if you recall, the goal is to *not* kill her."

"*You* don't have to worry about that, *I* do." She used her mayor voice to project authority. It failed last time she tried it over ten years ago, but threatening and condescension weren't great options either. "I just need to find an avenue of ingress into the meeting room."

"No bodies," warned Troy.

Sharon waved her hand dismissively. "I'm not stupid. I don't want a fight before we make contact with your mother. We just need to find out where the meeting is at. I'll stake out my options for meeting you there on my own."

"How are you going to stake out anything looking like that?"

Right. The scars. She could cover most of them, but anyone that got a look at her face would know immediately. The security around the capital building would be on the lookout for her too.

"I need pants, a smock, some boots in poor repair, and a worn cloak."

"For?"

"Just tell me which room I'm trying to get into and get me those clothes." She tried walking out of the room with as even a gait as she could, given her right thigh kept trying to snap back to neutral position.

She ambled through the hallway to the room Troy set aside for her. Larger than her entire apartment. If she and Noah combined both their apartments this room would still be larger. The musty, sickly smell of dressings drying permeated the air, but other than the odor, she kept the room in impeccable order. Her crisply made bed sat between two windows taller than they had any right to be, lines hung between the bed posts and the windows for drying out the bandages draped there, an oak dresser with a mirror sat along the wall with a straight razor and emptied wash basin resting on its surface. She always kept her hair short anyway, so shaving to match the burned side of her head mattered little, though it did require more frequent upkeep, which she hated.

The rest of the room sat empty intentionally to perform exercises. Despite its size and openness, the room felt claustrophobic. Her world shrank down to sleep, eat, heal, and exercise; liberation from the monotony couldn't come soon enough. Though, what came after the mission still brought on waves of nausea. Ren was fully grown now, and she missed all of it for what? For this.

Stop it. Think about it later.

Looking around, she admitted to herself how gracious a host Troy had been. Sharon held no delusions he only did what he did to further his own agenda and to make up for his own past mistakes. During her time here though, she had softened on him. He smiled earnestly and treated her without preconceptions. A hard task when taking your own would-be murderer into your care, but he made it look easy. If roles were reversed and she had found him lying naked, burned, and under rubble she would have simply lit fire to the apartment and walked away. He took a chance on her. The fool. He would make a horrible president. Far too sentimental, far too forgiving, and far too willing to stick his throat out for people to cut. A wonder no one had yet.

Standing in the open area of the room, Sharon began her stretches. Staring at the wall, she rotated her arm, bending and extending it as she did, getting back into the familiar rhythm of her daily routine. She thought about the sequence of events that landed Troy in Noah's apartment of all places. It all hinged on Clem. Noah went to his union president for help when his lover turned up burned and half dead, Clem being the enterprising asshole he is saw an angle and called on Troy, who in turn came up with the plan to unseat his mother. Noah saves his lover, Troy puts his mother behind bars, and Clem gets his mining legislation passed.

She finished her final stretches on her back, pulling a rope wrapped around her foot to flex her thigh until the skin looked so taut it could snap again. A knock sounded at the door, but Noah entered without waiting for an answer. He carried the clothing she requested, a frown of worry tainting the otherwise simple serenity he usually exuded. "You going out?"

"Unless you have the layout of the capital handy, complete with guard patrol routes, then yes. I'm afraid I have to."

He waved a piece of paper in the air. "Troy said you'll need this to find the meeting room."

He would offer to scout for her, and she would decline. Not because she didn't want to accept, on the contrary, she hated this part of her work, but Noah's job in the crystal mine shafts didn't exactly make him a reliable scout. If she needed a wall broken down or some large objects moved, she might call on him, but barring that, she relegated him to gopher and stress-reliever. His attraction to her remained even with the scarring, and she took advantage of his services whenever possible. Like now, for instance.

He opened his mouth to say exactly what she thought he would say, but she shushed him and beckoned him to the bed. The argument could wait until after they both finished, or she could slip out once he fell asleep like he always did. He looked her in the eyes as he removed her blouse. Despite his calloused hands he handled her gently, deftly even. Kissing her, he cupped a breast and thumbed her nipple with one hand and untied her bottoms with the other. She bucked her hips up so he could slip them off, then sat up, slid her hands down his pants, and squeezed.

"Take these off."

She playfully shoved him backward and he shucked his pants before diving back on top of her. The weight of him felt amazing as their mouths and bodies reconnected. His heart beating against hers. They laid like that for a while, sharing each other's warmth and kissing, until she removed her mouth from his and cradled his face, looking him directly in the eyes. The signal that she wanted him.

An hour passed and Sharon found herself at the wash basin, wiping off sweat and cleaning up the mess of two lovers pretending not to acknowledge that whatever this is would prob-ably end soon.

Wherever Troy found the clothing for this disguise, he'd done a good job. The stains would help her look homeless, and after the last hour the sweat stink coming off her would encourage people to keep their distance. The boots however, appeared new. She made a mental note to step in some garbage on the way to the capital. Stealing a last look at Noah before leaving the room, she popped outside before he awoke from his postcoital snooze.

The air outside was cool compared to the lover's den she left behind, but she welcomed it. The busy streets of Prolivgrad offered a different kind of stink, and her anonymity offered a different kind of safety. One she hadn't felt since knocking on Noah's door months ago. The hour-and-some-change walk she signed up for turned into a two-hour-and-a-lot-of-change walk with her leg refusing to bend properly, but she made it to the capital building all the same.

My oh my, something must have happened.

The street swarmed with people, and the guards, of which there were many, couldn't control the mob. Whatever had happened, this presented an opportunity, and Sharon would not let it pass her by.

Most of the mob wore a splash of red on their clothing: scarves, hats, bandannas, and the like. A symbol of the National Party. She passed through the crowd, pickpocketing what she could get her hands on given that she still resembled a homeless beggar and people wanted nothing to do with her. With a bandana and a scarf, she fashioned a crude turban that would cover one side of her face. A bizarre accessory for this part of the world. On any other day the disguise would stand out terribly, but everyone seemed to be wearing odd outfits. A man with a horned helmet and two red scarves waving in the air smiled at her and winked. *Gross.*

Maybe the wink meant more than a poor attempt at coming on to her because he raised his hands in the air and shouted something about justice for Winnow and the crowd surged past all the guards.

Where do they think they're going?

Sharon allowed herself to get swept up in the torrent of people rushing into the capitol building. *Are they really just going to stand down?* The answer turned out to be yes. She spotted a few mystics among the guards, but who knows how many stood among the mob. The situation felt fraught and dangerous. All that need happen for hundreds of people to die is one mystic to decide on violence. She needed to separate herself from this pack as fast as possible, but stuck in the middle of the mob, little could be done with any sort of expediency. Before she knew it, they crossed the threshold into the capitol, and her prayers were answered as everyone split up, running around, tearing down or vandalizing everything they could.

Sharon made for the upper-level, east side, the president's wing. A throng of people ahead of her kept the attention of the guards, and she slipped into the room printed on the slip of paper from Troy. A large, highly polished, circular wooden table sat in the middle, and behind it two large windows overlooking the city. Looking down through the windows Sharon saw a sea of people with splashes of red.

Why?

It didn't matter. Refocusing on the task at hand, Sharon surveyed the room. A servant's door structured to look like a continuation of the wall seemed promising. She limped over to the door; this is the most walking she'd done since the Rashee assassination, and her skin began a dull aching. She almost preferred it to the numbness. Pushing on the door it gave way into a hallway that led down to a servant's area. Putting some will into her hand, she busted the lock. It still had the appearance of working normally, but it would turn with or without a key in it. That alone wouldn't make much of a difference, but the goal was to eliminate as many obstacles as possible. She hobbled to a window and gave it the same treatment, then the doorway at the end of the hall, and the door leading to a stairwell, and another door leading out the back of the building.

That's one option.

Climbing, miserably, back up the stairs she came to the roof access and snapped the lock. The roof had several ladders resting along the edges. Emergency exit options in case of a fire. Grabbing one she used it to climb down, took it, and then hid it in some bushes.

That's a second option.

That would have to do. If maintenance at the capital worked night and day, they may notice all the broken locks, but she doubted they'd have the time to actually fix them by Tuesday, and they'd assume the mob did it. Pulling the red cloth from her head she yanked her cloak over her face again and began limping back to Troy's.

Twilight arrived at the same time Sharon did. The foyer had a stool to sit on, and she thanked all the gods she didn't believe in for that. Troy came in with a worried expression as she sat shivering after coming in from the cold, winter air.

"I was afraid something happened," he said.

"Oh, something happened alright."

Troy gave a slight nod. "The riots."

Sharon nodded back. She practically crawled here, of course the news traveled faster than that.

"What was all that about?"

"Apparently, my mother tried to have Paul Winnow assassinated."

The burst of laughter that came out of Sharon's mouth echoed through the house, and she couldn't stop.

Troy continued, "Winnow lived."

She doubled over and fell onto the ground. Out of breath, wheezing for air, and crying from both the laughter and the pain of rolling around on her bad side.

Troy raised an eyebrow. "What in Kohru's name is so funny?"

"Your mother—" Sharon couldn't get the words out

"What about her?"

Sharon did some deep breaths, calming herself down. "I only made it into the capitol *because* of the riot."

She fought off another laughing fit.

"And?" Troy began to sound annoyed

"And... don't you find it a little poetic that trying to assassinate Winnow is what puts her in the path of the assassin she's been worried about the whole time?"

Troy grimaced, he didn't seem to share the same sense of humor.

Ren

Poppy hobbled ahead of them as Ka, Seffin, and Ren shared the load of the pylon, carrying it with kinetics. Something in the carefree way Poppy meandered down the road annoyed him. *A master with their servants trailing behind.* That thought didn't make much sense though, Poppy had little in the way of will reserves, certainly not enough to carry the pylon, but the contrast in exerted effort still made him envious. Probably because both Ka and Seffin appeared unphased while he struggled to pull his weight. Ren asked when the next break would be, but Poppy only chuckled and told him he could take a break whenever he thought it necessary. *Clever.* They knew he wouldn't demand a break until he well and truly tapped himself out. That would be holding the others back, and after all the drama of the past months he had a lot to prove.

"I could go for a breather," Seffin suddenly said.

Finally.

Ka turned her head to look at Seffin with a grin. "Oh? *You're* tired are you?"

Seffin returned her gaze with a mischievous look on his face. Suddenly, the pylon became extraordinarily heavy. Ka and Ren both stopped in their tracks. They couldn't hold it, the pylon slowly started floating down to the ground. Ka's brow furrowed in concentration, and she threw both arms out in front of her with palms facing the pylon, trying to increase her focus. As the crystalline structure gently reached the earth Ka and Ren both fell to their knees, gasping for breath.

"What was that for?" Ka said

Seffin fished in his pack for some jerky, smiling. "You look like you could go for a breather too."

Ren couldn't believe it. He did believe it, but he *couldn't* believe it. His own will reserves impressed most other mystics. Dunreedy himself told him that. But Seffin's will seemed to eclipse even Ka's, and Ka could do things Ren didn't have words to describe. Every time he thought he had his head wrapped around how strong Seffin truly was he would do something like this, proving he stood in a class all his own without even trying. The worst part is, he didn't even think Seffin had meant to brag.

"How much of that were you carrying by yourself?" he asked.

"Most of it," Poppy said, turning around to face them.

Poppy could sense barrier harmonics, but they could also feel out general will usage too. All engineers could. It's part of what made them so useful. High levels of control coupled with training as an engineer came with a lot of perks, and Ren suspected Poppy could do a lot more with their small reserves than they let on.

Poppy continued, "In fact Ren, you probably don't need to help so much. Ka and Seffin could be doing a lot more than they are."

He liked the sound of that. Will reserves could take a full day to come back, and with their journey through the horde starting tomorrow, Ren wanted to save as much as possible. He fished in his pack for his own slice of jerky and tore off a piece with his teeth before beginning to chew. *So much better than salted fish.*

The pylon sat in front of them, on top of its metal base, slowly spinning in a clockwise direction as harmonic crystals spun counterclockwise around it. Procuring it took little effort. They simply found one on the edge of the barrier network and grabbed it. Lighton kept extra pylons on the edges as a buffer anyway, so no farmland or small towns would be in danger. A patrol could find it as soon as today, but by the time they figured out where they were headed it would be too late. Poppy said the pylon barrier's size and longevity increased with vibrations from the harmonic satellite crystals fused to metal braces, and the vibrations from the crystals harmonizing with each other caused the perpetual motion. The takeaway, Ren learned, was not to touch the braces. Denting or altering them in any way could throw off the harmonics and cut the pylons effectiveness by, well, Poppy didn't say a number, but they implied that it could ruin the whole mission.

In this case, ruining the mission meant they all died.

"Break over, we need to get to the edge of the horde before nightfall so you all can fully recover by morning." Poppy clapped their hands to punctuate the command like a primary school teacher rallying their students.

Ren assisted with the pylon again, using far less will this time, and neither Ka nor Seffin seemed to notice the difference. At one point he pulled out all his will, just to see if they would notice at all, which prompted a glare from Seffin, so he resumed helping as they made their way to the edge of the horde.

They noticed the smell first. Sunbaked, rotting meat with some sickly sweetness mixed in. Once the horde came into view, it practically took up their entire field of vision. Ka hallowed out a hole in the side of a hill overlooking the sea of husk before them. They nestled the pylon in the back of the hole, so if the horde noticed them, they'd bottleneck and reduce how much pylon energy they used up.

Seffin and Ren went out to survey the mass of husk stretching out before them, as far as the eye could see laid a carpet of shambling corpses. Ren used Poppy's looking glasses, and just at the edge of its magnification range, he could see the forest. A perfectly straight line of densely packed trees barred the husk from entering. Some type of barrier must keep them from pushing through the forest line, but Ren couldn't find anything resembling a pylon. Something about Nari'ko kept them out of the forest.

Amalgamations stood out from the horde like flies in a soup of decay. The true danger of the horde. Husk gathering didn't present much of a problem for anyone trained in wielding until they started combining, and when an amalgamation combined with other amalgamations the result was a lumpy mass of limbs, hair, eyes, and teeth unable to hold itself up, clawing its way across the ground. If left alone long enough the carpet of husk would turn into a literal carpet of husk. A deadly welcome mat at the door of Nari'ko.

As Ren surveyed with the looking glasses, Seffin transcribed the information to make a rough map of the route they'd need to take in order to avoid the largest of the amalgamations. They would likely move a bit before tomorrow, but that, too, would give them information on how best to avoid them. Night fell on them as they worked. When they packed up to leave, Seffin suddenly grabbed Ren and kissed him.

"What was that for?"

Seffin shrugged. "I just wanted to get one in before tomorrow."

Ren looked in Seffin's eyes and noticed something there behind the tenderness... *he's worried*.

"We're going to be fine," Ren said.

Seffin's smile hid some doubt, but Ren knew nothing he could say would help. Instead, he wrapped his arms around him tightly, and bear hugged him. Lifting him off the ground for a few seconds, Seffin groaned and laughed.

"Let's get back," he said.

Poppy gathered some wood and built a fire while they were away, and Ka sat by it, grilling some unfortunate critters she'd found for supper. Ren and Seffin joined them, handing over the map they prepared. As the meat finished cooking, Ka passed around skewers. "I kinda hate this," she said, handing the last one to Poppy.

"Well, it *is* one of the more dangerous things we've ever done."

"What's your best guess at why the caretaker needs this crystal?" Seffin asked as he took a bite out of his... rabbit? No, squirrel.

Poppy sighed. "I genuinely can't guess. I imagine they'll use it to address *this*," they said and gestured to the horde in the distance, "but as for *how* it will help I haven't a clue."

"What makes you say that?" Seffin spoke with his mouth full.

"You'll learn when you meet them. The caretaker never does anything without a good reason." They chewed for a second before adding, "That is to say, they rarely do anything at all, but when they do, it's for a good reason."

"Well, at least if I die, I'll know it was for a good reason." Seffin chuckled afterward. He meant it as a joke, but he obviously believed it.

Enough of this.

Ren stood up. "I know I haven't been the most dependable member of our team, so it probably doesn't mean much when I say this... but lean on me tomorrow. You all have a lot on your plate guiding us, keeping the pylon charged and carrying it. I'll do everything I can to keep the amalgamations off you."

"What do you mean you haven't been dependable?" Poppy said

"I just mean that... well, when we've gotten into fights I haven't exactly done much. Seffin practically killed the laranee on his own."

"I did not." Seffin seemed offended. "I'd have died if you weren't there. Dunreedy too."

Ren was taken aback. Whenever he thought about the incident in the academy, he only pictured Seffin piercing it with his fire elementalism. "Well, I didn't do much in the fight with the hoarwolves."

"It was night and we had no vision. They attacked who they attacked," Poppy said. "It was just dumb luck they didn't go for you."

Ren shook his head. No. He could have helped more. He could have got to the one that had Seffin in its mouth, or he could have stopped the one that attacked Troy. His reaction to everything had been slow, lacking.

"Next, you're gonna say the mystic in Lanneshire didn't count?" Ka stood up, matching Ren's intensity. "That he was a pushover, so really you've been useless the whole time?"

"My point is that I want you to lean on me because I know I can handle—"

Ka spoke over him, "We *know* you can handle it."

She seemed frustrated and angry, which worried him. The last thing he wanted was another fight the day before they dove into a horde the size of a small city.

"Godsdamnit, Poppy was right," she said. "I went too hard on you." She threw her empty skewer aside, putting one hand on her hips, she wagged her finger at him with the other, emphasizing her words as she said, "That mystic wasn't a pushover. He took down an entire Lodge on his own, do you know how hard that is? Or do you think Lodges outside Prolivgrad have nothing but weaklings running them?"

"I don't—"

"He was a pushover *for you,* Ren. Most other mystics couldn't grab that fireball and throw it back, why do you think he surrendered so fast? You're just as important to this team as anyone else. Family or not, you wouldn't be here if you weren't. We'd have left you in Prolivgrad, where it's safe." She took a deep breath and let it out slowly. "Sorry, I don't mean to get mad at you again, but it's frustrating hearing you tell us to rely on you when *we've been doing it the whole time.* That's *why* it's so annoying when you fuck up, but the only reason we're attempting this plan tomorrow is because we *know* you have our backs. I, for one, couldn't be happier you'll be with us to-morrow, bro." When she said the last word her face scrunched up in disgust.

Poppy chortled, and Seffin stifled a laugh.

"Excuse me, what?" Ren said, "Bro?"

"I knew the moment I said it. Can we forget that part?"

"No problem, sis."

Ka closed her eyes tight and pinched the bridge of her nose. "I will murder you."

"Let's not escalate things too far, daughter." Poppy could barely get the words out.

"Wow, I guess I'll have to kill all of you then."

"What did I do?" Seffin protested.

That got everyone laughing, and for a while, the ominous thoughts of tomorrow's task faded into the background. After a while, Ka came over and apologized to Ren directly, which she didn't need to do. Things worked out ok in the end, and he'd said what he said. It's not like he hadn't deserved it. Insisting on the apology, she elbowed him good-naturedly and retreated into the hole to sleep, unofficially signaling the end of the evening.

A realization caught Ren for a moment. *This is it. It's happening tomorrow.* He liked to think himself prepared for moments like these. With merc work you never know which day will be your last. All it takes is a bit of kinetics or a blade to cut in the wrong spot to kill you, or someone close to you. But he realized now, with increasing clarity, no preparation would be enough. This is the job. It's not cutting down husk, running errands, escorting people through the wilds or even saving a village from a rogue wielder. It *is* that, but that's not the hard part. This, leveraging your life against your own skill or power or both, this was the hard part. That's why Ka wouldn't heal him. That's the lesson. You are just as fragile as the people you're trying to help, and failing to respect that fragility, failing to protect yourself first, doesn't just hurt you, it hurts everyone.

You can't save anyone if you're dead.

They watched the fire eat away at the remaining sticks in silence, throwing chaotic shadows on the grassy hill behind them. Poppy slipped off to bed and left the fire for the two laggards to handle. They always stayed up longer, sitting together, listening to the crackle of the fire as it slowly died. Finishing out the night, and without so much as a look at one another, Seffin robbed the fire of fuel while Ren iced the embers. A simple thing, wordless communication born out of the familiarity from traveling together, from sharing in the comfortable monotony of a routine. A simple thing, but precious.

With the fire out they headed off to bed, uncertain of tomorrow, but resolved to see it through.

***

Day broke harshly into their hole. The sun's rays beamed in with ferocity, stirring them all to wakefulness despite the impulse to turn over and snooze for just another five minutes. Poppy, already up and prepping for the marathon they were about to run, tossed some jerky and freshly filled water skins at them as they sat up, bleary eyed and cursing the world for inflicting consciousness on them yet again. After snatching the looking glasses out of their pack, and with a stern warning that everyone better be up and ready when they returned, they hobbled off to cross check the map Ren and Seffin made the day prior.

Ren collapsed back into his bed roll and began gnawing on his jerky while Seffin dutifully rose and began packing his things. Turning to see Ka's pack already organized and resting against the side of the hole, Ren gave in to his better impulses and stood to join his boyfriend in cleaning up. *Boyfriend.* The thought still tickled him.

Before long, Poppy returned with a smile on their face. "The amalgamation movements were all within expected parameters."

"I'm glad they're behaving themselves," Seffin deadpanned, topping the charge off on the pylon and swallowing the last bit of jerky he'd been working on.

Ren startled as Ka popped up from the earth like a fish leaping out of water. He hated it, but she hadn't stopped the first fifty times he asked her to, so he did his best to pretend it didn't bother him anymore.

They all stowed their packs on the pylon's base and made their way to the edge of the horde, carrying the spinning crystalline structure as they went. The edge being a relative term in this instance since the pylon's barrier kept the edge quite far away from them regardless of where they stopped. Poppy adjusted the pylon to keep a much smaller, more concentrated barrier rather than the giant umbrella its original engineer intended, but it still formed a safe zone of a hundred feet give or take a few for harmonic fluctuations while they carried it.

They passed into the mass of husk, and a shiver went through Ren's spine at the point the horde fully encircled them. *No going back now.* He pulled out his will-blade and cut down the husk in front of them to preserve the pylon's charge. The less husk it had to disintegrate meant it used less energy meant Ka and Seffin had to put less into charging it meant the less precarious their situation. Also, it was kind of fun. Like cutting down swaths of wheat, but smellier.

Poppy guided up front, on the lookout for avoidable amalgamations while Ren made short work of those that weren't. Two hours in, they hit their first hiccup. One of the larger amalgamations must have caught wind of their living will and decided on a snack. More limbs than anything else, Ren cut it down without much issue, though one of its many claws clipped his calf. They stopped for a few minutes so Ka could tend to the wound, but the horde took the opportunity to surge. It amounted to little as the barrier handled all the husk throwing themselves at it easily, but still, they decided on no more stops unless absolutely necessary. Twenty hours was long enough already without adding to the time and danger of the situation.

At hour twelve, everyone began to feel the exhaustion. Poppy's eyes turned squinty and red from constantly scanning the horde, Ka and Seffin trudged along over the plains with bags under their eyes, and Ren's sword arm had turned to jelly.

Will-blades take remarkably little effort to cut through objects, but they still had weight and any continuous, repetitious motion became tiring after twelve hours.

"Ya know," Ren said as he carved through husk in front of them, "if we had only gotten here a few months ago we'd already be through to the forest by now."

Poppy pulled their looking glasses off and glared at him, bleary eyed. "I love you, but have you thought about shutting the hells up sometimes?"

Seffin chuckled, which is all Ren really wanted.

Poppy turned to continue watching the horde.

"Shit," they said.

Like an arrow through armor, an amalgamated sunback burst through the barrier, striking for Seffin first. Ka must have noticed it because the earth around Seffin shot up, and the colossal snake's bite missed Seffin entirely, hitting the tip of the pylon instead with a metallic ring. Ren darted for its head as it started coiling around Ka and Seffin, it whipped its tail and hit Poppy, throwing them outside the barrier into the middle of the horde. Ren closed the gap just as the snake went into a striking pose and decapitated it with one swing, the massive head fell from its body and onto the pylon, destroying the satellite rings. The barrier shrunk down to the fifteen-foot diameter safe zone the travel crystal and the charged grenades in Poppy's pack produced.

Ka disappeared into the earth with stern instructions to stay put. The seconds felt like minutes while they waited. Her arm suddenly popped out of the ground next to them, physically pulling her and Poppy from the earth. Ren and Seffin rushed to pull them up. She'd used earth slipping to save them, but Ren knew the will cost of bringing anyone along on an earth slip to be enormous. Still half in the ground, she began to heal Poppy's more egregious wounds. A bite in the neck and a puncture wound in the abdomen. They coughed up something red and mucilaginous, swearing in the same breath. A good sign. Ka pulled her will out of Poppy and collapsed, sucking in air.

Poppy must have missed the snake amalgamation. Colossi are normally easy to spot for obvious reasons, but a serpent sliding around on its belly in the middle of a horde would be difficult to see from ground level for anyone, even with Poppy's height. To make matters worse, dusk crept closer every minute and the looking glasses had been lost in the scuffle. With Ka's will reserves tapped, Poppy's injury, and no way to see approaching amalgamations, their chances of survival dropped significantly. The rest would be up to Ren and Seffin.

Poppy scrambled to their feet. "We can't rest. We have to keep going, especially now."

Ren pulled Ka to her feet while Seffin grabbed their packs and handed them out. The traveling crystal and grenades were already consolidated into Poppy's pack, so they treated their disheveled, limping guardian like the new pylon. Ren started carving through the husk in front of them, heading toward the tree line while Seffin kept his eyes peeled for anything large enough to withstand the small barrier they now had to make do with.

Eight more hours, at least. Their vulnerability at the forefront of his mind, the familiar itch returned to Ren's fingers. Nothing he couldn't handle, but godsdamnit could it be more annoying? He focused on his task: *cut down the husk in front, keep the forward momentum, be ready. Don't stop. Don't rest.*

Poppy's voice came from behind him, "Stop."

I'm not supposed to stop.

A grenade sailed past Ren's head and landed fifty or so paces in front of them. He covered his ears too late, and the explosion left them ringing. *Gods, this again.* The air glittered in the low light of the evening with crystal dust left over from the blast. The husk didn't like it, and ambled away from wherever the coruscating particles floated, but while his ears didn't appreciate the blast, his tiring sword arm didn't mind the respite. The group appeared as ragged as he felt. Dripping in sweat and caked in dirt, eyes baggy and red. They all needed a rest.

When only two hours remained on their journey Poppy threw their last grenade. They would have to rely solely on the traveling crystal for protection now. That, and the skill and stamina of their two mystics. Walking through the cloud of crystal dust, they could see the tree line against the starry sky growing closer with each passing minute. That's when they felt a tremor. At first Ren thought it was just his knees shaking from all the walking, but the husk seemed to struggle to keep balance too.

"What the hells was that?" he asked no one in particular.

"We need to hurry." Poppy gave him a non-answer. He didn't need a real answer anyway, few things could produce a shake like that, none of them good. They picked up their pace. Ren stopped cutting through the horde. His arms felt ready to fall off, and barring any incidents, Poppy said the traveling crystal would hold.

Another hour later, possibly more, time was difficult to keep track of now, the feeling in his finger flipped from an itch into more of a burn. He preferred that. The itch tempted him to scratch at it constantly, at least with burning it didn't feel like he could do something about it. He just had to get comfortable with being uncomfortable. He could do that.

Another tremor rippled through the ground.

They started jogging now, the tremors started coming more frequently, and to keep the pace up, Ren resumed his new hobby of cutting down groups of former people, helping them into their second graves. The barrier may be able to get rid of the husk, but it couldn't manage it with the speed Ren could.

The tree line towered over them, cutting the night sky in half with its height. *Almost there. Fifteen more minutes? Ten?* The ground began to quake continuously. Off to the west they could finally see the source. A gargantuan amorphous amalgamation, flopping at them. He had no other way to describe it. Like a giant fish out of water, the mass of what must be thousands of husk wiggled, wriggled, and flopped in their direction.

"Run!" Poppy yelled, but they had all already started running.

Ren put more will into his sword and extended the edge out even further, swinging relentlessly back and forth as he tried to keep his balance and pace against the shaking of the ground. The burning in his fingers began to trickle into his hands and arms. The giant... thing was almost on top of them now, and they wouldn't make it to the forest in time.

Don't do this. This is stupid.

Ren stopped and turned to Seffin. "I have an idea. Get them to the tree line. I'll meet you there."

He shook his head. "I won't."

"Fuck you Ren, keep going!" Ka screamed at him.

"I wasn't asking. I was telling."

He didn't want the look of hurt and betrayal on Seffin's face to be the last he saw of him. He would have preferred his laugh, or the cute, puzzled look he seemed to make so many times in a day.

"I'm sorry."

He didn't wait for a response. Ren sprinted straight for the giant amalgamation, a huge blob of gnashing teeth and soft, spongy skin with limbs and bones and hair pressed together into a nightmarish, menacing pit of hunger. Cutting his way through the horde he began to dance into his forms as best he could with the ground shaking beneath him. *Please work. Please work.* He pushed himself to his limit, and when he felt he had nothing left, before the horror looming in front of him, he fell into the form his mother taught him so many years ago. The burning sensation that trickled into his arms lanced through his body, and the world changed into something almost unrecognizable.

As if suddenly behind frosted glass, everything blurred and refocused into far more than his eyes could tell him. He could taste the putrid air and hear the gentle thuds of his family's footfalls as they sprinted toward the forest. The smell of the trees mixing with the stench of the dead. Every sense revealing far more about the world around him. The air seemed thinner, and his movements came easier. Like he'd been wading through water his whole life, and now, without the resistance, he was finally able to move freely. The ground ceased its shaking, and instead seemed to gently sway as the giant dead thing before him continued a slower version of its odd, flopping movements.

He bolted toward the giant amalgamation and, throwing as much will into his blade as he could to extend it, began the grisly work of chopping it to pieces. Slicing off chunks the size of houses and plunging the blade in as far as he could stretch the edge. He leapt into the air in an upward swing with all his strength, and found himself twenty feet off the ground, looking down at the fused mass of undead. His skin began to burn and flake away as he fell, he couldn't keep this up for long. He landed on top of it, and its skin gave way to whatever force compelled him as he plunged into the bony, sharp insides of it, slashing wildly the whole time.

Not so much landing as ceasing to fall, he came to a stop suspended inside, hanging from stringy, wet tendons, slick offal pressing up against his stinging, burning body. Even now, hanging in the guts of a giant, he could separate the smell of the trees from the stench of death, and he put everything he had into making it to those trees. To the living. Kicking and slicing and burning and so much pain and anger and kicking and burning, he burst out the side of it, kicking off what had to be some bones, through the air, sailing over the horde, and into the tree line, he slammed into the forest floor, tumbling over rocks and logs, coming to a stop against an old birch tree.

He rolled over onto his hands and knees. He could sense them. They made it, and they were coming. Not fast enough, though. He couldn't catch his breath. The burning became unbearable, he didn't know how to stop it. The skin on his body boiled and flaked off, he shut his eyes, the smell of burnt skin and dead leaves, and then nothing.

Jessica

Bad didn't even begin to describe the shitstorm Jessica found herself in. Winnow survived the assassination attempt and blamed it on the Labor Party. Without a substantive meeting to address miner safety, Clem had threatened another strike. Rioters destroyed entire sections of the capitol building before the army could quell the mob. And Tia, her assistant's usual scowl plastered on her face, stood in front of her, turning in her resignation.

"Are you fucking kidding me?"

Tia refused to make eye contact. "I told you not to send that assassin. Winnow's a rat, but he's a survivor. Even if you had killed him, it was a bad move."

"It was the only move to ensure the plan goes forward if something happened to me."

Tia dropped the resignation on the desk next to her and met her eyes. "Let me know how that works out for you."

She walked out the door. Twelve years working together and she left like it meant nothing. Like quitting a job at an inn or a pub. Loyalty meant little in politics. Everyone endlessly chasing greener pastures. Tia had been different though, she stuck by her through everything, holding onto secrets, unafraid to give tough advice. All of that gone now. A new, reliable assistant would be hard to come by, especially with her name muddied.

How did he know it was me. Did the assassin sell me out? Did Winnow buy them off?

Jessica sighed, but it didn't calm her. The next meeting was a tough one. Clem and Troy, an odd pairing. She had a sinking feeling this meeting had nothing to do with miner mortality rates, the Guild and the Miner's Union should be natural enemies, to team up there must be something else going on. Yet another fire to put out.

Fucking Tia. Fucking Troy. Fucking Clem. I made them what they are. Godsdamned ingrates.

The thought to slam a fist onto the table crossed her mind, but it would feel too much like throwing a tantrum. Instead, she stood and crossed the room. She filled a glass to the brim with whiskey and slammed it back. There. That felt, not better, but different at least, and different would have to do for now. She busied herself writing up a response to the Nationals' claims against her before heading off to the blue room for the meeting.

Standing next to the window, looking down at the city she tried to save, the same city that wanted her head, time ticked by. A knock at the door brought forth her one o' clock. Clem entered and stood next to the door, a scared puppy, but Troy came through with a determined look on his face, walking up to shake her hand. *He's confident. This is bad.* They all took their seats around the table.

"What's this about?"

Clem started, "Seventeen dead in the last three weeks—"

"Shut the fuck up, Clem. Troy, tell me or I'll have the special guard escort you out."

Maintain control.

They looked at each other with concern.

"We want you to resign—"

"Oh, fuck all the way off you little—"

"You'll be removed from office regardless, and you know it."

She fumed. Clem's face flushed, sweat beading on his brow, sitting next to Troy with his blue eyes piercing into her own. The two had conspired against her, but Troy wasn't wrong. Winnow did something to that assassin to make them squawk, the claims he made were too specific, too close to reality for him to be guessing. Setting aside her ego she considered the facts. If she tried to keep her position, Winnow would petition the senate to remove her. A few seconds of mental math proved the obvious, she wouldn't have the votes. Especially after the Nationals little show of dominance in raiding the capital. At least if she resigned, she could... *that's it!* Something like pride filled her breast. Pride or relief or grace she couldn't tell, but for once, the stupid boy would prove useful. No, better than that, he would save her. Save everything.

Something on her face must have clued him in because he softened. "We'll keep your work going, but you can't be the one to take it over the finish line. That ship sailed."

She scoffed. "I feel like it's closer to everyone jumping ship, but I take your meaning." She walked over to the whiskey decanter and poured two glasses, one for her and one for her son. "So what, I play the villain now? You save Egal from one corrupt politician, and act as a shield against another corrupt politician. You think that will work?"

He accepted the glass of whiskey from her as she went back to her seat. "It'll have to. It's the only option we have at this point. I can repeal the mining legislation to rally Labor's base, and I'll have to leverage approval from the other world leaders to try and grab some moderate votes."

Well, his naivete isn't completely gone.

"That won't work. Moderates in Prolivgrad are still hawkish with international policy. Better to make it seem like you're pulling the strings with The Garvelle Empire than flaunting their approval." She sipped her whiskey and thought for a moment. "No chance for a pardon once this is all over?"

He pretended to consider it. Which is honestly more than she could ask for. The tears in his eyes came off as genuine, though. *Still too soft.*

"I'm sorry, but no," he said. "Even if everything works out the way we want it to, there's little chance—"

A thud came from behind the servant's door stealing everyone's attention. The latch clicked, and something more demon than woman, dripping in blood and appearing half melted, stepped through.

Troy jumped to his feet. "We agreed on no bodies!" He'd never sounded so angry. The woman had a will-blade in her hand. Tall for a woman, dark skin.

No fucking way.

"Yeah well 'excuse me' didn't seem to work."

"You promised me." A bit of whininess overtook his tone.

Jessica stood from her chair. "How are you alive?"

The woman gave a crooked smile, probably because half her face didn't seem to work. "I don't die easy."

"Neither do I." She reached for the hoarwolves in her mind, and something went wrong. They were there when she got to work, what happened?

The woman, Sharon Adegast, Flicker of the Eyes of Koth, seemed to fight back laughter as she said, "Your pets are dead. Found them on the way in."

Clem bolted for the door, but almost faster than Jessica could comprehend, Flicker sprinted in front of him, skewering him with a sword. Not a will-blade though, a dueling blade.

Troy's sword.

Clem collapsed to the ground dead with Troy's sword still thrust into his body. The puzzle pieces clicked in place. She would likely die here. Flicker's list of kills included countless wielders and mystics. Whatever plan they concocted to corner her into resigning had been usurped by Flicker in order to kill

Jessica and blame it on Troy. She was injured and emotional though, maybe she could use that.

Troy rushed between them, pulled his sword from Clem's body, and leveled it against the bloody witch. "Sharon. Please, I'm begging you to stop. She agreed to the terms."

She tried to sidestep him, but he shifted his body to continue acting as a barrier. The demon made a flourish with her blade so casual it seemed purposeless, but the tip of her blade struck Troy's with a piercing clang so loud it hurt Jessica's ears. His arm swung upward violently from the force of the strike, losing his balance. While he struggled to regain his footing, she hopped forward and struck him in the face with the hilt of her blade. In response, he brought his sword down on her, but despite her injured appearance, she moved like liquid around his strike. A frantic slash on an upswing was met with a calm, almost lazy parry using the lower end of her will-blade, near the hilt, to catch and guide the tip of his sword safely away from her body. Jessica searched for an opening to strike, but they were so close to each other, and Troy was so big, it was hard to keep track of Flicker behind all the muscle and broad shoulders.

Her voice sounded more annoyed than angry. "Stop it. I have a will-blade. I could have ended this immediately. Move, Troy, or you'll be joining your friend over there."

"Over my dead body." Jessica couldn't believe the words left her lips. *Where did that come from?* How many months had she wanted him dead, and now, because he tried to save her work, she suddenly wanted him to live more than anything else she'd ever wanted in her entire life?

Flicker's head peaked around Troy's shoulder, and she raised her one good eyebrow. "Oh? Now you care about him? Didn't you just get done trying to kill him?"

Troy lunged and Sharon parried his sword to the side gently but firmly, like she was guiding a naughty child to a time-out chair, and then followed up with an elbow to his face.

Jessica wouldn't be lectured by an assassin on parenthood. "Rich, coming from someone who hasn't seen their kid in over ten years. How is Ren, Troy? I heard he and his friends helped you out near Oleksandra's Harbor."

"You know Ren?" Flicker seemed taken aback.

Now.

As surreptitiously as she could, Jessica threw two wind blades hissing around Troy and into Flicker's position. Before they even landed, she began pulling chunks of rock from the walls to act as a barrier. Flicker's greatest strength was closing the gap between herself and her target in an instant, but she couldn't get through a rock barrier without punching herself full of holes, and reports said her will-blade couldn't extend beyond six feet.

A yelp rang out. At least one of the wind blades had hit its mark. Flicker must have done something, because Troy crumpled to the ground, groaning. *At least he's alive.* Rolling onto his side he looked up at her, his piercing blue eyes wide with shock.

What are you looking at?

A thin, red, vertical line cut through the middle of her vision. *Oh.* Looking down, a slick, sharp edge extended out her abdomen. *That's it then.* She gazed over at Troy on the ground, his face said everything her body hadn't told her yet. *I'm sorry.* Her legs felt soft and sharp at the same time. The blade shrank out of her vision in an instant, and she collapsed to the floor, unable to see her son. She coughed up... something. She couldn't tell. This was wrong. So much went wrong.

Troy. She thought. *I'm a fool.*

Sharon

They say revenge feels empty. It eats away at you on the path, and when you reach the terminus, all that's left is a string of bodies and a loss of purpose. Sharon didn't feel any of that. Only a profound sense of relief looking down at the woman who stole her life away.

Jessica gave the order to pull back the mystic sent for Gull Harbor, letting everyone die, and then instead of taking responsibility, she hid like the snake she was. Now she lay in a heap on the floor, her forked tongue silenced forever. Sharon exhaled, trying to force her body's post-kill jitters to match her mind's serenity. Troy's groaning and crying fucked with the moment, but she promised herself she'd spare him. She walked over to his crumpled form, streams of blood falling down her right side. Flickering with these scars caused a lot of them to break open, but luckily, the wounds were small. Favoring her left side while she flickered slowed her down a bit in the moment, but either that or turn the murder into a murder-suicide.

Rolling him over with her bloody boot she saw him cradling his arm, severed below the wrist. Jessica's wind blades had hit their mark, though they veered too close to Troy, clipping his hand. Noticing Jessica's shoulder movements, Sharon had flickered behind her immediately. After facing off against so many wild wielders she took no chances. Cut them down before their rock shield comes up or the fight would turn into a drawn-out affair, and a protracted fight wasn't an option in this case.

It surprised her that Jessica hadn't noticed her presence, though. A full half a second had gone by while she raised her shield with Sharon standing right behind her. The woman's reaction times and skill had proved far less impressive than she'd been led to believe.

Sharon went to kneel next to Troy, but with her scars already tearing open she decided against that and nudged his face with her boot until he opened his eyes instead. Tears kept streaming down his face.

"You did this," she said and gestured to the room.

"You betrayed me." His lips quivered, and spit flew out of his mouth in pain and anger when he spoke.

Gods, maybe I should have kept Clem alive instead.

She kicked his head, not as hard as she wanted, but hard enough. "*You* did this. Do you need me to spell it out for you any more than that?"

"They'll kill me," he said. "What's the difference if you do it or if I'm executed for killing the president."

"You're a smart boy, I'm sure you'll figure something out." She meant it. Troy wasn't stupid; he was naïve. Maybe this would be what he needed to develop the instincts he lacked up to this point, or maybe he'd die as he said. Either way. Not her problem.

Guards would be popping in at any moment now. She left him moaning on the floor and exited out the servant's door she came through. Two guards in four pieces lay next to an adjacent door in the hallway, guarding the room Jessica stored the hoarwolves in.

Sharon shook her head. Soon she'd be away from all of this. No more hiding behind fake names, no more manipulation, and no more constant death. A brief wave of guilt shivered through her body at the thought of killing both Clem and the guards. She hadn't had much choice though; the guards had signed up to protect the president and they failed. Clem, well, that was just unfortunate. The feeling lingered longer than she liked, a sign she made the right decision. Better to finish the game hard than languish long enough you become too soft to finish it at all.

She hopped out the window she came through and slid down the ladder. Landing too fast, the pain in her right side spiked and she fell to the ground. She stood and threw her cloak around her shoulders as she started to make her way out of the capital, into the streets of Prolivgrad, and toward Noah's new apartment. Walking in the best approximation of a normal gait she could muster, she noticed the people of the city felt different. For one, she hadn't seen a child since she left the capital building. For two, the usually busy streets felt far emptier. Like everyone got a memo to stay inside that she missed. Splashes of red on many of the people walking around gave it away. The Nationals were up to something.

Maybe Noah would know what's going on.

His new apartment was in a nicer part of the city. Glittering in the sunlight the way almost every building did in Prolivgrad, it stood four stories tall and sat half a block from the Lodge, on the ground floor it had a little café with a delightful menu and the best coffee she'd ever tasted. She could get comfortable here. She wouldn't, but she could.

Noah expected her. Clean bandages and clean water waited, ready for her wounds, also he bought some rum. *This man is too good for me.* Dutifully, he wrapped her legs, torso, and arms as she started buzzing on the rum. When he bent over to check on her foot, she could see the top of his ass coming out of his pants. A seat with a view. Using her good foot, she stuck her toe in the crack, teasing him. Yelping, he swatted it away and laughed.

He paused for a second, the laughter on his face faded. "So, how'd it go?"

"Like I thought it would."

He finished up the last bandage, securing it with a pin, and then put back a shot of rum. "So Clem's..."

"Dead," she said. "It couldn't have gone another way."

She trusted him with much of her real plan days ago. Not just because she needed a place to stay immediately after the job, but also because he'd proven he could be trusted. He saved her and then watched over her while she lay helpless in Troy's home. It helped that he didn't care overmuch for Clem, though he did say he didn't wish him dead.

"So, she wouldn't go along with Troy's plan?"

"She couldn't."

Not a complete lie, but also not anywhere close to truth. He'd buy it though, because he wanted to believe her more than he wanted the truth, the man's loneliness blinded him.

"Without a healer, these are going to take a few weeks to heal."

A sly grin crept across her face. "Whatever will we do with the time?"

In answer, he slid his hand up her uninjured thigh and squeezed. She sighed and bit her lip. Not because she wanted sex, she wasn't in the mood at all right now really, the wounds were too fresh and the pain too sharp, but because she wanted him to want her, because *that* felt good. He came up and leaned in for a deep kiss. Now, this she wanted. The high after a successful mission was wearing off, her skin craved touch and her heart ached for connection. Hungry for life after dealing in death. Bringing her good hand up to his chest, she rubbed her knuckles up against a nipple, lightly pinching it with her thumb and forefinger until it hardened. She broke the kiss off and nuzzled into his chest.

Reading her cues, he picked her up and set her on the bed, lying next to her with his arm over her chest, breathing into her neck, he fell asleep. Exactly what she wanted; the oaf had become excellent at knowing what she wanted. She clutched his arm, large and muscled but also warm and soft and comforting. Weighing her down. Anchoring her next to him as he breathed, in and out.

She wept.

Not loudly. No sobs, or quick breaths, keeping her shoulders perfectly still to not wake him. She wept for her freedom. For the weight lifted off her, and who was she kidding, for the fear of what she had to do next. Meeting her son again.

Ten years.

He's a man now. He probably worked with Poppy as a merc. Such a precocious child wouldn't settle for a desk job or some dead-end Guild position. Her tears dried while she thought what he might be up to right now. Probably escorting some nobleman or taking down an amalgamation threatening a small town. She'd find out soon enough. For now, she had to focus on recovering. She leaned her forehead against Noah's lying next to her, the oil on their skin smoothing out the coarseness that age gifted them, and sleep took her.

***

Two weeks.

That's all the time it took for Prolivgrad to go from The Glittering City to a suffocating hellscape of martial law. The Nationals *had* been up to something. A coup. They were lucky she'd done their job for them, Jessica's wielding was a well-guarded secret, and she would have butchered them easily, robbing Nationals of much of their leadership. The looks on their faces when they found their target dead would have been something to see.

Anyway, Sharon had other worries at the moment. Noah started working eighteen-hour, mandatory shifts at the mine. With the union president dead nothing stopped management from demanding overtime, and no one in government had the backbone to fight production demands, not with The Nationals so willing to inflict violence on anyone who disagreed with them. Winnow gutted union rights as his first order of business anyway, and since the jobless vastly outnumbered jobs, it meant they could just throw bodies at the mines to keep their quotas. Miners died daily.

Sharon worried for Noah, not just because she actually cared for him now, but because she needed him. Leaving the apartment always meant taking a risk looking this way. The wounds had healed, mostly, but the scarring would never go away, not unless she found a wild healer, even then she may never find one capable of fixing her.

As the night dragged on, her worries proved founded. Something must have happened to him. Either dead or at a healer. A pit formed in her stomach. *Why am I so godsdamned hung up on this guy?* She knew the reason but hated herself for it. Without the mission to focus her, she'd already started to go soft. A piece of paper slid underneath the apartment door.

Ominous.

She scanned the writing on the paper and her heart jumped despite herself. He'd commissioned a merc to drop the letter off, an accident happened in the mines, a healer was taking care of him. He'd be back in the morning. The relief she felt was profound, and that right there was the problem. She'd let herself get too close. Besides, her presence alone put him in more danger. If Troy decided to out her, several organizations would come looking, not the least of which were The Eyes of Koth, and they wouldn't leave witnesses. Her walking looked mostly normal now, and the cloak she used did a good enough job at hiding her face, the time had come to rip the scab off.

She left.

She grabbed her belongings which consisted of: a will-blade, the clothes she currently wore... end of list. When she emerged from the building, the first thing she noticed was all the red. People wearing red, buildings with red flags, and red graffiti everywhere. The sole structure without any red stood four stories high made of nothing but timber.

The Lodge.

She ambled up to it. Far fewer people shuffled in and out than before. Lodges were built to be a sort of connective tissue between the different countries, among their other purposes, but Nationals had always hated them. They loved freedom, but not *that* kind of freedom. Not the kind of freedom that brought people together, but the kind of freedom that gave them the right to inflict their will on another, the kind of freedom Garvelle had during the Sol War. The kind of freedom rogue mystics loved. Freedom to kill, not freedom from being killed. Their freedom was a synonym for power.

Sharon felt a pang of regret. If she'd let Troy enact his plan, this might not have happened. A possibility for Jessica behind bars and Troy helming the Gogallo Initiative existed, and she spat in the face of that optimism. After ten years spent on a singular purpose, she operated solely on cynicism. She knew better than that. The mayor of Gull Harbor would have anyway. Was this worth it? How many people died in the coup? How many imprisoned or killed since?

An explosion blew the top off the front edge of the Lodge, followed by several more explosions throughout its structure. One of which came close to knocking Sharon over. It didn't take long before the entire thing turned into an inferno. People ran frantically from the building; some injured, some unscathed, some clearly too far gone to save. The heat became overwhelming, and she had to move back. A few mystics tried to quiet the flames, but another set of mystics, prominently wearing red, skewered them with ice lances as they tried. They hung limp against the pillars of ice going through them, a warning to anyone trying to stop the inferno. Sharon was a little girl during the end of the Sol War, but she remembered the stories, they reminded her of this hell, and it would only get worse.

The flames of the burning Lodge monopolized all her senses. The smoke left her nose stinging, the flames aggravated her scars, the ash on her tongue and skin, the smell of bodies cooking. A small fire caught her eye off to the left. A man, already dead, blanketed in flames, seemed to shrink away as she watched him burn.

I did this.

Seffin

It took four days of waiting before it happened, but now that it was happening, Seffin didn't know what to do with himself. Shaia Tekk, The Caretaker of Nari'ko, said to have a direct connection to the will of the planet, had summoned them for a meeting. The enormity of it was getting to him. His worried pacing annoyed both Tender and Ka who kept telling him to stop, but once he stopped pacing his foot started tapping involuntarily, the nervous energy had to go somewhere.

"Seffin!" Ka and Tender said in unison.

He apologized, though he couldn't say he was really sorry. Their lackadaisical attitude to a summons from the closest thing to a god the world had made him even more nervous. What did they know that he didn't? They knew Shaia Tekk from their last visit here, but they refused to comment on them. All they said was "don't worry", or "calm down". The ominous feeling in his chest wouldn't stop though, even his body knew something big was coming.

Seffin turned his back on the massive wooden door leading into the caretaker's chamber and gazed out on Nari'ko. Maybe taking in the sights would calm him. The city sat nestled in a forest so massive that even at his current elevation, at least forty stories high, he couldn't see the forest's edge, and he knew from conversations with locals that the forest went on for a long, long ways past that in all directions. Depending on which direction he marched he'd find himself in wholly different situations. North would pop him out in a frozen tundra blasted by an endless blizzard that only the people of Kori'ko could navigate. East or west would drop him off a high, sheer cliff face into the ocean, and south, where they came from, sat the horde and the entrance to the continent of Sol.

Unsurprisingly, the city itself was made of trees. Wild wielders here possessed a way to grow them with planned out hollows the exact shape of whatever home they wanted. Complete with reading nooks, kitchen counters, shelves, beds, tables, chairs, washbasins... everything.

Light was managed differently here too. At night, leaves on every branch cast a pale green luminescence, lighting rope bridges, forest floor walkways, spiral staircases, and all those funny little decorative, spirally vines that grew in eye catching patterns and bloomed with pale pinks and creams and yellows. Inside homes and businesses, more traditional fire light was used, the yellow of it spilling out of windows and doors, turning the view of the city into a work of art.

The massive door behind him creaked and groaned as it opened, starting Seffin's heart beating fast again. A tall, beautiful man, because everyone here seemed like they were sculpted instead of born, came out and told them the caretaker would see them now. The longer Seffin stayed in Nari'ko, the beauty of the people seemed less physical and more like an aura of calm they emanated, as if they'd never known a single hardship in their lives. But that couldn't be, Nari'ko warriors were known around the world as peerless fighters, and you didn't gain a reputation like that without hardship. Regardless, the smiles and gentle looks they all gave intimidated him more than anything, but despite his nerves he'd come here for a purpose.

They entered the chamber.

Inside the giant tree they walked into a hollow that had no ceiling, or rather, a ceiling too high to see. Lit by a combination of luminescent leaves and torches, the room held a large, circular wooden table in a pit with chairs all around, and more rows of chairs cascaded outward. In one of the chairs sat a black-haired boy and adjacent to him sat a tall, alabaster skinned... person? Hard to tell from this distance, but they possessed features Seffin hadn't seen before. Pure white hair that flowed back into a ponytail, high cheek bones, and eyes that, from this distance, seemed completely blue. A pure, deep blue that, next to the monochromatic whiteness of the rest of their body, came off as shocking. They both wore matching robes of white, and the blue-eyed one hopped up and started waving with a childlike jubilance.

"Hi hi!" they said, as if it were one word.

Ka smiled. "Hey, Shaia, long time no see."

"I see you brought the voiceless one like I asked."

Tender and Ka turned to look at him with a quizzical look.

"What are they talking about?" Tender asked.

His palms started sweating. "I'm not sure."

"It's rude to stand and talk amongst yourselves. Get over here," they said it with a smile, but their tone suggested they were serious.

They all walked down to greet Shaia, who gave each a hug and a kiss on the forehead. The immediate affection continued to feel strange to him.

"Welcome! Ka, Tender, Seffin, this is Polk." Shaia gestured to the boy sitting next to them. He hadn't so much as made eye contact until this moment when he heard his name. "Polk will be going with you when you leave."

"Excuse me?" Seffin asked.

Tender, handing over the black-hued crystal they were charged with delivering, appeared unamused as well. "I'm dying to know how you'll convince us of that."

"No, you're not," Polk said in a voice too high pitched, even for a little boy. "You seem to be in good health, save for the—" Polk said and looked down at Tender's bad leg, "dent."

Tender's flat look turned into a frown.

"It's an expression, Polk," Shaia said and waved it off. "Polk here is going to be the next vessel for Koth. Lana's longevity is coming to an end, obviously," they said and snickered when they said the word obviously, "and Polk volunteered to take her place. I mean, he *was* made for that purpose, but it's still his decision either way." Shaia beamed at the boy. "I couldn't be prouder of him."

Seffin couldn't help himself. "What do you mean a vessel for Koth?"

"Oh, right. These two probably haven't told you yet, which is good. Following orders and all." They winked at Ka and Tender. "Lana is the vessel for Koth similar to how I am a vessel for Kohru."

Seffin almost asked what the hells that meant, but Shaia shushed him before the air in his throat even began to produce the sounds required to make the inquiry.

"Just listen," they said and gestured to the seats around the table. Everyone sat except The Caretaker, who continued standing to facilitate the grand movements they made while they spoke, "A long time ago this planet was nothing but a giant rock. Kohru, fleeing her siblings, chose this rock for her home." They held their hand in a balled fist, and like a bird diving down at prey, brought the pointer finger of their other hand and smashed it into their balled fist. "They grew the world you know of today. Water, plants, trees, people, animals. None of these would have happened on this world without Kohru." They took both hands and fanned their fingers out like a flower blooming. "There are worlds which existed without this kind of help, but this is not one of them."

"Other worlds?" Seffin asked.

"Shush, voiceless one," Shaia said. "Anyway, Koth followed his sister, and was able to implant himself before Kohru's will filled this world's Sea of Intention. Now, they fight for dominance over this planet's sea. Koth's influence is a fraction of Kohru's, but it's enough to fill the bodies of dead humans, implanting them with a single goal: to consume the will of the living and feed it to Koth such that he can usurp Kohru's control, drive her out, and kill her. When a husk is killed, the will it accumulated is added to Koth's. They are a direct representation of his ever-growing power."

Seffin's head spun. Outside of his mother, he knew very few people that even acknowledged Kohru or Koth as anything but old myths. Dead religions from a bygone era. Sure, some of the churches had a lot of patrons, but the churches were few. If Koth and Kohru are real, did that mean the others were as well?

"Yes," Shaia said, "they are real. Koth, Kohru, Coruscare, Gaku, Svoboda, and Torthuil are all siblings—born unto their godhood together. Several of their number would see our world sucked dry of its will, if they could find us that is. A number of cycles ago, we tried to teach everyone the real story of both the gods and our world in an attempt to unite the people against Koth, but the knowledge was warped and mangled and used as pretext for humans to kill one another, accelerating Koth's grasp on this planet's sea. That sent us into a spiral of worse and worse cycles until Lana Danvers' sacrifice."

Ka and Tender looked at each other with annoyance, and turned to Shaia. "We can't tell what Seffin is thinking, remember?"

Shaia sighed. "Sorry, he was wondering if all the old religions are real." They turned to Seffin. "Before you ask yet another question, as a vessel for Kohru I can interpret the intentions of others. You have no inner voice, which means your thoughts veer closer to raw intention than your friends. Because of this you are easily read."

They smiled pleasantly as if what they said made any sense at all.

"Please, stop." Shaia put both hands on their temples. "You think loudly, and your anxiety adds an unpleasant thorniness."

"Sorry," Seffin said.

"Unpleasant, but not unexpected. Anyway, onto the real reason I brought you here. Stopping Koth." They held the black-hued crystal aloft. "We need you to escort Polk to The Heart of Gogallo. There, the crystal will allow him to take over as the vessel for Koth. Also, Kelsig and Karm have made pacts to aid at the end of a cycle, I'll ask that you meet with them to ensure their participation. You'll need as much help as you can get to infiltrate The Heart."

"And this will solve the problem with the husk?" Tender asked.

"Nope," Polk said, his voice like a canary, "it delays it. It'll reduce the husk dramatically, but it'll only last about a thousand more years."

Shaia continued, "Killing Koth outright is the only way to stop him for good, but that would cost us the crystal, there is no guarantee of success, and the chances are lower now that you've lost a champion." Shaia looked at the three of them, suddenly very tired. Like someone sucked out all their energy. "It would also mean Kohru's siblings could find us." They put their hand up to stop Seffin from asking another question. "That story is something Tender and Ka can tell you." They turned to look at the two them. "You have my blessing to share everything with them."

They stepped back from the table. "Polk, escort our guests out for now. I need a rest."

Back outside, Seffin couldn't believe what he'd heard. He had so many questions, so very, *very* many questions. He turned to Polk. "What's a champion? Why did Shaia get so tired all of a sudden? Does our will go back to Kohru when we die? What are Kohru's siblings like? How does the crystal help you become a—"

"Seffin," Ka said and touched his shoulder, "there will be time for all of that later. Let's get back. I'm sure Ren is curious how all this went."

He nodded; Ren would want a full breakdown. Pulled behind them on a makeshift litter for a week, and in bed for another four days. For someone that liked to move about as much as Ren did his current predicament bordered on torture. They should get back as soon as they could.

Polk looked up at him expectantly.

"Yes?" Seffin asked.

"A champion is anyone with strong enough intentions to stop Koth that The Caretaker can sense them in the Sea of

Intention. Vessels need to meditate near their respective focal points for the majority of a day, Shaia simply needed to go back to meditating. Yes, your will returns to the Sea when you die, unless you are killed by a husk. Kohru's siblings range from benevolent to what you would consider evil, but we're hidden from them. However, killing Koth outright would cause a large enough shift in the Sea that they would sense it and certainly find us. The crystal houses Koth so the new vessel can bind him."

A million follow-up questions popped into Seffin's head, but Tender interjected, "Let's be on our way."

As they stepped onto the gently swaying rope bridge that would lead them back to the inn, Polk waved at them with the consistent lack of emotion he'd shown on his face since they were introduced. The boy was a puzzle he could figure out later. The walk back to the inn they left Ren at would take more than an hour alone, and anytime Tender and Ka went out they'd run into old friends that insisted on bending their ears overlong.

The hour-long walk ended up taking almost two.

They shuffled into the inn to find Ren sitting at a table in the main room, hunched over a plate of venison and a flagon of what Seffin hoped wasn't ale. He should be recovering, not getting drunk. When they found him in the forest, Ka healed his body, but she said something had happened to his will with which she couldn't help.

Apparently, Ren did something called flickering to save them all. A rare technique that required extensive training to perform properly and took a toll on the user's body. Untrained, Ren was lucky to be alive. Even as late as yesterday, he could barely walk, but his energy seemed to be returning to him slowly.

They all sat down next to him, ordered their own plates of food, and recounted what they learned from Shaia. Seffin ordered one of the inn's specialty dishes made of vegetable mash balled up with seasonings, breaded, and fried in oil. He ordered an ale to wash it down. Ren idly laid his head against Seffin's shoulder while they talked

"Gogallo?" Ren yawned while he spoke, responding to Tender's recounting of the mission they were asked to complete.

Tender frowned as they stabbed at some of their own venison. "We don't have to take the job."

"They seemed confident we would." Seffin popped one of his fried, vegetable balls into his mouth and immediately regretted it. Burning his tongue and the roof of his mouth, he spat it back out onto the plate, sad that he partially ruined his meal with his impatience.

"That's because we will," Ka said. "Shaia knows the type of people we are, and they know we'll accept. If they thought we'd refuse, they would have tried harder to convince us, or chosen someone else."

"It still feels like someone is making the decision for us, and I hate it."

Seffin hadn't known Tender to ever grumble about anything, let alone about doing something that would amount to so much good. "Why does that bother you?"

"I refused leadership after the war. I took in Ren. I raised Ka while setting up Lodges around the world." They took a bite and continued to talk while chewing. "My life is mine to control, and I hate when someone tells me what to do."

Ka giggled. "They're not telling you what to do. They just know that you'll accept."

"Well, they could pretend to ask at the very least." They swallowed their food. "Shaia just gets under my skin. If I'm going to risk my life for something I want to be the one to make that decision, and this feels like conscription."

"So, refuse," Ren said, his eyes barely open.

"No!" Tender barked, like a child being told they needed to go to bed. They set their fork down and took a sip of their lavan, a floral wine popular in Nari'ko, and sighed. "I'll do it. I don't know how in the hells we're going to get through Orphan's Cry and into The Heart of Gogallo without a lot of help." They sighed. "For now, let's just enjoy a well-earned break while Ren recovers."

"What about Polk?" Seffin asked.

Tender cocked their head. "What about him?"

"Well, won't he die when we take him there? I don't really know how I feel about that."

"We could kill Koth instead." Ren's eyes were fully closed at this point, nestling into Seffin's shoulder. A grin crept onto his face, joking then.

Tender sighed again, and answered him as if he'd been serious. "Pretending for a moment that we even could, that would change everything. Drastically."

"But the husk would go away," Seffin said. "Plus, Polk doesn't need to die then."

"He wouldn't die," Ka said. "He'd become a vessel for Koth. It's much worse than dying."

Seffin only looked at her. They'd been around each other enough at this point that she should know exactly what he wanted without saying anything.

"The vessel houses Koth's essence within their own will reserves, preventing him from directly controlling the husk or signaling his siblings. It's a constant battle they maintain for hundreds to thousands of years until Koth becomes too large for them to hold back, at which point Shaia sends someone with even larger reserves to take over, allowing the old vessel to die. That's the cycle they kept referring to."

"Yeah, I don't want to do that," Seffin said. A bit of Ren's drool started to seep onto his shoulder. He let it happen. Ren needed the sleep anyway.

Ka shrugged. "Well Shaia said we lost our best chance at killing him, so I don't know that we have much of a choice."

"There's always a choice," Tender said, grumbling into their food, "but we don't have to make it today."

Seffin shouldered Ren to wake him up enough to walk back to their room. He'd pushed himself too far. Seffin put one of Ren's arms around his shoulder and excused himself as he helped to walk him from the table. Halfway to the room, he perked up. "So, do we know what we're doing?"

"Not a clue."

Epilogue

The dungeon now set aside political prisoners, The Pit, was only a twenty minute walk from the capital, but it might as well have been a different world. Dug deep into the mountain, the descent alone took a half hour. Spiral stairwell after spiral stairwell, no windows and no way to see other than whatever torches the guards remembered to light. Complete silence save for the echoing footsteps of prisoner and guard trudging to whatever cell they were assigned. The room they dropped him off in consisted of three walls with a fourth wall made of bars, and two piles of straw, one for sleeping and one for pissing and shitting. Something like food was placed at the door three times a day, served with dirty water in a small cup.

The cold, damp air chilled Troy to the bone. He sat in the corner of his cell, knees tucked up under his chin to conserve warmth, his left arm stump aching furiously, cursing the name Sharon Adegast with every spare moment of thought he had.

A month went by give or take. Hard to keep track of days without a window, but by counting the meals they served him he had a pretty good idea. Ninety meals divided by three meant thirty days. Thirty days since he watched his mother die in front of him. Thirty days since the betrayal. Thirty days shitting in the corner of his cell.

What are they waiting for?

They believed he killed the president, why wait so long to execute him? Was this some type of torture? Isolate him until he goes insane and then chop his head off anyway? Maybe they would treat it as an event. A public execution of the traitor to Egal would bring out quite the crowd, or maybe they forgot about him completely. That seemed fitting. He fought for acknowledgment his whole life, why would he get it now?

Footsteps echoed down the hall, though mealtime wasn't for another hour at least. He wrote it off as a guard on his way to someone else's prison cell, except the footsteps kept coming closer and closer. The quality of the steps sounded different too, less of a clang from a guard's armor and more of a scuff from someone wearing leather or cloth. The light from the visitor's torch licked at the walls and steadily grew brighter until a man stood before him.

Is it finally time?

Troy felt embarrassed for not recognizing him at first. He struck a unique silhouette with his thinning hair and his oddly proportioned body, his gut protruded outward at a harsh angle. Paul Winnow stood in front of him with that shit-eating grin he always wore. Troy felt a spark of hope flash in his chest.

"Hello, boy." Condescension dripped off the word boy.

"Hello, sir," he said, trying to sound as meek as possible. It came hard, acting like this. Pretending he was someone he wasn't. But he wouldn't spoil his only chance by returning the animosity. He wanted to appear as non-threatening as possible.

Winnow chuckled. "How would you like your old job back?"

The hells?

"I-I... would like that very much," Troy stammered, not looking a gift weasel in the mouth.

"Good." Winnow fumbled in one of his pockets and produced a key. "I want information on how your bitch of a mother was controlling amalgamations. If you can do that, you're free, but the Guild will answer to me and only me. Crystal trade is solely at the discretion of the new National Government. One mistake and I'll see you're thrown back in here and forgotten about."

"I can do that," he lied. He had no idea how his mother and Pulpin achieved control over those amalgamations, but getting out of this cell would be a step in the right direction.

The key clinked into the lock, but he didn't turn it.

"First, I want to know the truth. Did you do it?"

Troy didn't know the answer he was looking for. If Winnow believed he killed his own mother, would that make him happy? Or would that only prove him untrustworthy? If he told him he didn't kill her and it got back to Sharon, she'd kill him, but if that's what Winnow needed to hear then he didn't have a choice.

"Yes, I did." Winnow would walk over anyone to get what he wants. Troy banked on that.

An oily grin slithered onto his face. The key turned and the door opened. "Welcome back to the game."

Cradling his aching arm, he stumbled out of the cage, letting Winnow lead him up and back out onto the streets of Prolivgrad. Into a world unrecognizable from the one he left.

Thank you for reading!

Did you like this story? Please consider leaving a review. They are more vital to a new author's success than most people realize, and golly, I sure would appreciate it.

Want more from the world of Kohru? A free short story will be released in conjunction with each of my first three novels. The Eye is already available if you subscribe to my newsletter at mjlindemann.com. Make sure to whitelist me so you can keep up to date on new releases, as well as pictures of the cutest dogs you've ever seen in your entire life. Not that I'm biased or anything...

You may enjoy my other works set in the world of Kohru, both are due out in 2024:

An Eager God

The Lies of the Heavens